THE LITTLE QUEEN

The Plain of Crowns

KEVIN HINCKER

D1637114

For Kelly and Liam

·

"If the bee disappeared off the face of the earth, man would only have four years left to live."

— ALBERT EINSTEIN

Chapter One

The classroom is silent and the students motionless, seated in rows and rounded forward like eggs in a carton. Anthony is one of these eggs. On the desk before him rests a paper entitled, "Presidential Advisors and Executive Agencies." This is a pop quiz, and he is in the process of failing it. *Executive Agencies*, he mouths to himself, trying to focus. The spoils system. The merit system.

The farthest thing from Anthony's mind right now is breaking the promise he made to his mother on her deathbed four years ago. But the 7th grade is a severe and capricious province, where promises of all kinds are made, forgotten, remembered, and broken every day. Anthony's broken promise begins with an open window.

He doesn't question it, he simply knows: there is a honeybee in the classroom. That is what is distracting him from the quiz. He wouldn't be doing much better without the bee, he realizes. There are other problems with this room which make it nearly impossible to concentrate. But the bee is the most immediate distraction.

Facing the students from behind his desk, Mr. Roberts, civics teacher and basketball coach, sits in suspicious readiness. His head sweeps the room like a radar repeater. He sees everything, but he doesn't see the bee. Anthony peers at the air above the blackboard behind Mr. Roberts. Anthony can't see the bee either, and he has not heard it, but he knows with absolute certainty that it is pivoting back and forth over Mr. Roberts's curly brown hair, somewhere between the pictures of Ulysses S. Grant and Grover Cleveland.

It is a passive sensation, his knowing. He doesn't seek it. In fact, he tries to push the feeling away. But his mind is like a dining table draped with a cloth, and right now some invisible, winged creature up near the presidential portraits is tugging one edge of it. Jiggling the silver. Demanding attention.

Focus, he thinks. He squints at his paper; what *is* the difference between a civil servant and a political appointee? But it's a losing battle. He feels the bee bank into the room with a sharp left-hand turn; he looks back up and now he sees it, a brown-and-yellow bead whizzing toward him. Diving lower. Passing over Steve Willmeston's shoulder. And alighting, finally, on Tracy Thompson's hair, near her bright yellow flower barrette.

Tracy sits one row to his left and three desks closer to the front of the class. Anthony has in the past admired her smooth, perfect, black hair, each day decorated with a new plastic accessory, but now he sees only the bee. It is motionless—attracted, he is sure, by the floral design on her clip, and the yellow color. Bee eyesight is not like human eyesight. A bee draws color information from the ultraviolet spectrum. The yellow of Tracy's barrette is a color that could summon a bee through a snowstorm. Yellow means nectar.

Tracy has no nectar, of course. The bee will discover her mistake soon enough, Anthony knows, and fly off.

"Anthony," barks Mr. Roberts from the front of the room. "Eyes on your paper."

Heads rise all around, stare for a moment, duck again—all except Pam Newly's head. Pam sits directly behind Tracy. Pam now sees the bee in Tracy's hair.

At just about the moment Pam begins to point and inhale—a pre-scream breath, it is clear—Anthony feels several more tugs on his tablecloth. More bees, behind him. A lot more bees. He turns to look toward the back of the room.

"BEEEE!" Pam screams, pointing at Tracy. "It's a BEEEE!" Pam stands, and the classroom erupts.

"Calm down," Mr. Roberts demands. "It's just a bee."

"I'm allergic!" Pam screams. "It's on Tracy!"

"Okay, get away from it," he grunts, standing. Tracy paws at her hair and begins to howl.

"Mr. Roberts, look!" Several arms extend, pointing to the rear of the class where a single windowpane, louvered out like a bird wing, spills warm spring air into the room. Anthony is already looking at it, because that's where the other tugs have drawn his eyes. There are bees. Lots of bees.

Outside the window is a loose swarm of buzzing black wings, and some of them are beginning—accidentally, Anthony is sure—to sweep in through the open window. The rest of the class now stands, and the hysteria rises. It is a forbidding sight, an alien scene, a swarm of bees so close, coming closer. Alien to everyone except Anthony.

"Get out of the way! Let me close that window." Mr. Roberts, yelling now, is pushing his way through the milling, panicky students. He stumbles, and momentarily disappears below a desk.

Then Anthony sees Greyson—handsome, sullen Greyson, who has watched the entire spectacle from his seat in the back of the class—rise. While Mr. Roberts is submerged, and with obvious distaste for the bees but great poise, Greyson reaches for the detachable crank handle, the single long shaft used to service all the high windows. He grabs it, lifts it, but instead of cranking it and drawing closed the window, he jerks the handle free, double checks to make sure Mr. Roberts is still on the floor, and tosses the brown metal shaft out the opening. It drops from view. He sees Anthony watching. He smiles and slides backward, away from the growing cloud of bees in the room.

Someone screams—stung, apparently. Mr. Roberts surfaces off the floor like a whale breaching and pushes children aside with great strokes of his long arms, swimming his way to the back of the room. "Everyone calm down! You're a bunch of babies!" he yells. "Just close this—" he reaches the window, and finds the crank missing. He searches the floor and the shelves below the window, batting at bees as he looks.

"Everyone out!" he shouts at last.

Before he is through braying those words the doors in the front and back of the room are thrown open and children rush out.

"Slowly, walk—PAM, WALK," Mr. Roberts screams, but Pam starts a mass exodus of children fleeing the scene of the infestation. Anthony is pulled along with the rest of them, though he has absolutely no desire to leave. In fact, this is the first time since the beginning of 7th grade that he has actually wanted to be in that room, the room where his mother used to teach, before her death.

RIVER BEND MIDDLE SCHOOL IS A CURVING, TWO-STORY BUILDING set into the side of a hill, framed by green pine trees and graced with a wide front lawn. Now a group of twenty-five 7th graders, one teacher, two janitors and a principal stand on that lawn, staring up toward the open window on the second story.

Greyson sidles up beside Anthony, and Anthony can see the violent glee in his eyes. Greyson is athletic. He's good looking. He has a focused air about him. Coaches and teachers salivate when first seeing and talking to him. *Here is a kid who could make the difference in my class, on my team, in my program*, they always think. But putting Greyson into any program—athletic, scholarly, artistic, or other—is like pouring poison into a public reservoir. Despite this, he has become Anthony's constant companion in 7th Grade.

The reasons for this alliance are numerous, mysterious, and—Anthony is certain—for the most part bad. A therapist might say that when sorrow has driven you as deep within yourself as Anthony has gone, it can be very helpful to have someone around willing to tell you what to do.

"You were failing that test," Greyson murmurs. "I saw your paper. I was going to cheat off you. But you couldn't do it."

"So?"

Greyson mimes dropping the crank handle through the window. "So you can thank me. Test postponed."

Anthony turns back to the high window without answering.

"I can't wait to see it," Greyson smirks, lifting his own gaze to the eaves.

"See what?"

"The extermination. They're gonna spray those things dead. The truck's on its way." He points. Mitsy Waterman, the principal, is talking to Mr. Roberts. The two of them gesture up at the window, then down at the ground. Tracing the path of dead bees falling to earth? Or maybe of a certain crank handle. Mr. Roberts throws low looks at Greyson and Anthony.

"Kill the bees? Why?" Anthony asks.

"Because they're bees," Greyson snorts. "And they need killing. I wish I could do it."

Anthony shades his eyes. The swarm clings like a smoky blur just below the roof, near the top of a pipe draining the gutter. Shady, north-facing, subject to wind—it's not a place they're going to remain for long. There is no need to kill this swarm. Someone has to say something.

"Mrs. Waterman," Anthony calls. But the principal is too involved in her animated discussion of bee obliteration to hear. Anthony moves closer. Greyson follows.

"Mrs. Waterman," he says again when he stands beside her. He knows this woman; his mother used to carpool with her when they were both teachers, and once or twice she had come to dinner with them. She hasn't been around since his mother died.

"What? Yes, what is it, Anthony?" she asks.

"I heard you called an exterminator."

"That's right."

"Those bees aren't going to hurt anyone."

"Anthony, we cannot have a bee hive hanging outside the civics room." She shakes her head. "Please stand back."

"But they're not going to stay up there," he says. "If you leave them alone, they'll move. They'll be gone by tomorrow."

"Nonetheless." Her phone rings; she answers.

Anthony turns to Mr. Roberts. "Those bees are—" Anthony tries.

"Any idea where my handle is, Smith?" Mr. Roberts interrupts.

"Listen to me," Anthony says forcefully, surprising himself, "You don't have to kill these bees."

"We're getting rid of the bees, and I wish I could get rid of a few other things too," Mr. Roberts says, looking at Greyson.

"But the bees—"

"Enough! The county's sending a truck, not open to debate."

Anthony takes a few steps back and bumps into Greyson. Mr. Roberts turns back to Mrs. Waterman.

"Too bad about the bees," Greyson snickers.

Anthony finds himself trembling. "They're just innocent bees," he whispers, knowing he's made a mistake the moment he says it.

Greyson pounces. "Oh man, I know. Poor bees. Hanging up there. Just trying to be bees. And now somebody's going to kill them. Horribly kill them." Greyson watches Anthony as he talks. Greyson is a boxer, dancing around, jabbing at any opening. Anthony is all openings. "And there's nothing anybody can do. We'll just have to watch. It's going to be gruesome."

Greyson makes no distinction between friend and foe when it comes to weakness. All weakness exists to be exploited. He would no more pass up an opportunity to cause pain than he would step over a ten-dollar bill blowing down a sidewalk. Satisfaction suffusing every angle of his face, he turns to stare upward with Anthony.

Looking at the window, open like a shocked eye in the face of his mother's old room, Anthony finds himself going back to four years ago, in the hospital room where his dying mother lay before him on a bed. He does not want this memory, but it comes. The bees draw it out.

SHE IS SKINNY, LIMBS LITTLE MORE THAN A NETWORK OF RIPPLES beneath the sheet. It is hard to tell where the sharp furrows of the cloth stop and her bones begin, especially at the hips and knees. Anthony's dad reads the newspaper in the corner; Anthony sits beside his mother and they play Yahtzee.

There was a time when she could shake the cup so hard and fast it blurred, then slam it down on the table, sudden like a snake striking.

She always paused for effect, her long-lashed, mocha eyes shining with excitement. Just about every time she rolled, she would say, "This one feels like a Yahtzee."

Now, though, he has to help her put the dice in the cup, and she can only manage to shake it once before she spills the cubes out onto the game board to slide, not even bouncing, and stop. Her hands on the cup are like rakes of pale sinew.

His dad stands and sets the paper down carefully, folds it like he never does at home, and says, "I'm going to get a cup of coffee. Can I grab you something?"

And as she does every time, his mom says, "No, dear. Thank you." Her voice is brown, brown like a grocery bag, a soft sliding sound. She smiles, but her lips are dry and they stick to her teeth.

His dad leaves, and his mom leans carefully back on her bed, looking at Anthony.

Her eyes were always big, but her face has shrunk and now they are huge, like two enormous bronze bruises. Her visage seems made up primarily of her eyes, cheeks, and dry lips. Anthony finds all the individual parts of her magnetic. He still thinks she is beautiful, but he knows that to an outsider, she is not beautiful anymore. She is dry and light as an envelope.

"Come here," wisps her breathy voice from deep among the pillows. He rises and stands beside the bed.

"We have to talk now," she says, "before your dad gets back. This is something just between you and me." She looks above her. She is holding the ceiling up with the sadness in her eyes. For long minutes, she doesn't say anything.

"Are you all right?" he finally asks.

"Listen, Tony," she says, "this thing I have. Cancer." He waits. She breathes through her nose: in, out. It's as though she can't believe what she is saying. "I don't want this to happen to you."

This could happen to me? he thinks. *This is a thing that happens to kids?* She can tell what he is thinking. She can always tell.

"Don't worry," she says "Just listen. And never talk about this with anyone else, all right? Even your father."

"Talk about what?"

"You know the special thing we do when we guide the bees?"

Anthony nods. Of course he knows. They do it every day, in the garden with her hive.

"That's the thing that made me sick," she says. "It's a very dangerous power. I see that now. It is too dangerous to ever use."

This is hard to understand. Touching the bees is the best thing in his life. When he reaches with his mind into a colony, when he gathers a hive-mind inside his own, it feels better than anything else in the world. It feels better than riding a bike. Better than eating cheese and pickles on white bread.

"How did it make you sick?" he asks.

"I can't explain it now. But I did things. I used our power in a way that made this cancer grow inside me."

"Am I going to get cancer too?" he asks.

Now she starts to cry. She holds back the tears so she can talk.

"No. You are not. You are very special, Anthony. Every mom says that about her boy. But you are truly different. And it's just . . . it's a dangerous thing."

This is turning into a conversation he doesn't want to have. He glances behind him, hoping his father will come back with coffee, hoping a nurse will come in with a pill, or some sheets. His mom grabs his hand.

"I want you to promise me something. Will you?" He nods, *yes, of course, anything*.

"Promise me you won't touch the bees. Not anymore. Not with your mind. Will you do that?"

He is not sure he has heard correctly. He hopes he has not understood. He turns the words back and forth, looking for alternate meanings, trying, by force or guile, to mold the sounds into a different shape, but he cannot.

It just does not make sense. Unless—a sudden stab of hope. "If I don't touch the bees, will you get better?"

"No—" she gasps a breath and holds very still, like she's trying to balance a glass of water on her chin, holding in her tears.

"No," she goes on finally, "I won't get better. We're the same, Tony, only you're so much farther down the path than I am. Than any of us.

You're only eight, and the things you can do . . . Oh, promise me. Because I won't be here to protect you."

He is silent, except for the quick, hard sobs that rack his own little body. For the first time, it is real for him. His wall of careful denial collapses. If his mother is asking him to do this, then it must be true, something must be wrong with her, something terribly, terribly wrong. His mother, who is everything to him, who is his solace and companion, his light, the only person who understands him, will not leave this hospital.

"Tony, promise. Promise. Don't touch the bees. Promise!"

And he promises.

"The truck's coming," says Greyson, startling Anthony back to the present.

His limbs feel heavy. He tries to shake himself into focus. He feels like he is swimming in syrup. Something pulses inside of him, something he has submerged for four years. Something that is desperate to come out into the open.

The students on the lawn all turn at the sound of the approaching vehicle, low gears grinding as it hauls itself up the hill. Anthony looks as well. Pulling into the parking circle in front of the gym is a white county jib truck, the kind they use to get cats out of trees and reach to the tops of telephone poles. It stops by the front door, and Mrs. Waterman and Mr. Roberts hurry over to meet the driver.

Anthony's eyes fly back to the hive. "It isn't fair," he whispers. "They can't help being what they are." He is looking at the bees, but the face of his mother in her hospital bed is the image blooming in his mind. What is going on? It's been years since he thought about that hospital conversation.

Greyson studies him. He steps closer, just a foot from Anthony's face. He watches Anthony's eyes, then follows his gaze to the eaves. Something in Anthony's stance, in his trembling, motivates Greyson. "If only somebody could go up and rescue them," he offers softly.

An inspired guess. A body blow. Anthony shudders, and Greyson sees. "But who would do that? I guess they'll just have to die."

Before he even knows what is happening, Anthony finds himself moving. The conference by the jib truck has the adults occupied. There is a clear path down the side of the cafeteria to the set of doors opening onto the quad. If he can get to those without being spotted, he can—

"Anthony, where are you going?" he hears Mr. Roberts shout. He freezes.

"Uh, to the bathroom," he says, amazing himself with a calm, even voice. "I have to go."

"All right, three minutes." Mr. Roberts waves toward the door in irritation. "We're moving the class to the B wing."

In a moment, Anthony is inside, and the door is closed. He huddles by the soda machines. It is the middle of the last period of the day and the halls are empty. He pictures the route to the civics room. He's not sure exactly how this is going to work. He knows he doesn't have a lot of time. He heads for the second floor.

At the top of the staircase he pauses and listens, then peeks around the corner. He's doesn't know what he thinks he will find—armed guards posted outside the civics room door? The hall is empty. He steps silently forward, past other classrooms untroubled by insect visitors and still filled with students, until he stands before the door. Room number 31.

It is the most familiar door in the world, as familiar as the front door of his own home. When his mother was alive, Anthony would take the bus from River Bend Elementary School every day, get off at the middle school as the older kids got on, climb these stairs, and pass through this door. Every day, from kindergarten to 4th grade, until she died. And now, feeling as though he is once again seven years old, he puts his hand on the knob and enters.

His sense of being dislocated in time is so great that he almost expects to see the walls hung with pictures of plants and frogs and the kingdoms and phyla of the animal world, as they had been when his mother taught biology here. But George Washington and John Adams still gaze down at him.

The open window is at the back of the room. As he walks closer, he begins to feel the bees tugging gently at his mind. There is nothing he can do about this. It's not the same as touching the hive-mind, not like he and his mother used to do. That required effort, and focus. This sensation is like sight, or smell. For a time, after he made the promise to his mother, he was desperate to rid even these traces of bee union from his life, but eventually he gave up. There is no way to block it out.

He pushes a desk over to the wall and stands on it so he can crane his head up and out of the window. Bees buzz near him, and land on him, but they do not sting. Anthony has never been stung by a bee; if it ever happened, he would be amazed. Bees have always accepted him as one of them. Even his mother occasionally got stung, if she startled a hive or accidentally hurt a worker. But not Anthony.

Down below he can see the students on the lawn. The *BEEP BEEP* of the jib truck backing into position rises up to him. There is not much time left. He ducks back inside.

The swarm is hanging up under the eaves, several feet down the wall from the window. Anthony scans the room for an implement, something long enough to poke into the tight ball of bees. If he can reach it, he's sure he can dislodge it. He might even get stung a few times, because this is a pretty clear violation of bee etiquette, but it would be worth the pain. Physical pain like that would be a relief in some way.

The longest thing he can find is a yardstick. He grabs this and hops back onto the desk. Then he levers his torso up and slides his arm and upper body out of the window.

From below her hears a familiar voice, "Yeah, baby! Look at Smith —you're a badass, Smith!" It's Greyson, of course. Below, all eyes shift off the boom operator climbing into his metal basket and shoot aloft to find Anthony. Time's up, he knows. It's now or never.

He lifts his hand carefully up and extends the yardstick, but it's a good four feet from the swarm. More and more bees are settling on him, the curious creatures crawling into his ears and nose. He lowers his arm and brushes the insects gently away, then stares at the swarm.

It's small. No more than five thousand bees at most, clustered in a ball with guards and foragers swirling, landing, and crawling around it. He can see scouts coming and going out over the landscape. Within the ball of bees must rest a queen—a very new queen, Anthony knows, probably only a few days old. This little globe of bees is looking for a home. The fact that that it's so small means it is the last of what was probably a series of four or five other swarms pitched out of a primary hive that outgrew its home, each successive swarm growing smaller and weaker as the colony broke apart under the crowded conditions.

He reaches out as far as he can, holding the edge of the window with his left hand and sweeping with his right, but he is nowhere near close enough.

"Scat," he yells at the swarm. "Get, come on, move it!"

Mr. Roberts cups his hand around his mouth on the lawn and bellows, "Smith, what do you think you're doing? GET OUT OF THAT WINDOW!"

There is only one way he can get himself close enough. Outside the window is a ledge that runs all the way around the building. If he can squeeze himself through the open window and step down, then scoot along the ledge while holding onto the open louver, he could probably get close enough to swat the hive.

There is no time to think about it. Twisting both arms through the opening and putting the yardstick in his mouth, he wriggles up and through, lifts his left foot out and lowers it down, toeing the ledge. Then he draws out his right leg, until he is standing, face against the glass, high up on the side of a building. Slowly, he turns around.

Now he is clinging to a six-inch ledge, heels pressed against the dirty stucco, forty feet above a concrete walkway with a yardstick in his mouth, looking out over the trees and hills of the town of River Bend. He begins to inch to his left.

"SMITH!" he hears Mr. Roberts yell. "Get off that ledge!" No one else says a word except for Greyson, who is hooting and doing a kind of dance.

Anthony takes the yardstick in his left hand, presses his chin into his left shoulder and his left cheek into the wall, and, gripping the window edge with his right hand, he eases farther and farther out, inch by inch, until his right arm is extended as far as it will go. And then, slowly, he raises the yardstick up toward the hive and swats.

And misses. He is still eight inches shy. There is no way he can get any closer. He knows if he lets go of the window he will fall. He is stuck.

Across the surface of his mind he feels the thousand tiny tugs and pulls of the swirling bees. They are landing on his face and head again, but this time he doesn't have a free hand to brush them off. He tries shrugging his shoulders, but they cling. They are blinding him, unintentionally, covering his eyes. He feels vertigo settling onto his shoulders, a goblin pushing him away from the wall, off into space.

He hears the arm of the jib truck jerk and squeak and begin climbing upward. He can feel his legs losing strength. His fingers on the window are wet and beginning to weaken.

And without knowing when he has made the decision—as much to save himself now as to save the bees—he realizes he is about to break his four-year-old promise.

The force that has been building inside him thumps his chest, beating him like a drum, calling him. He closes his mind to the outside world and follows it down, into darkness, probing, below his shoulder blades, beneath his heart, to the spot that only his mother ever knew about. And he draws out the shape he finds there, already boiling hot. A glowing, golden hexagon rises up from the darkness. Anthony opens his eyes and the luminous hexagon is there, superimposed like a tattoo upon his optic nerves.

The rest is easy. He flicks his thoughts up to the tight little swarm above him. He positions himself beside the hive-mind and impressions flash though him: the lightest scent of lavender; a flickering heat, like a candle newly lit; the image of fresh, new-formed comb. This is an uncertain, infant intelligence, less than a day old, frightened and confused. He touches the hive-mind. And melds with it.

It's as if the last four years never happened. He's back at home, in his mother's bee yard, sitting in the flowers and talking to her private colony. He feels something rushing up out of him, a long-dammed river, loosed in a moment, roaring back into the world. It is so easy to reach into this hive. How is it he ever stopped?

Go, he tells it softly.

Instantly, the workers on his face lift away and hover before him in a cloud. Go, he tells the hive again. GO WEST, GO TO THE FOREST, FIND A WARM PLACE. GO.

And without hesitation, the swarm breaks from the eaves, lifts into the air, and flies west. Not a single bee remains.

As he watches the hive stream away, he sees his mother's face again, thin with fear, pale, fading. He has done the thing he promised her he would never do. And he has no idea what will happen next. Sadness overwhelms him. The glowing hexagon floats before him, following everywhere he turns his head. He knows that it will remain for an hour or so, fading slowly now that he is not touching the bees. In the past, this fading time was an interlude of utter peace. But today he feels only desolation.

In lifting this bright hexagon from its hidden place, Anthony has also raised its counterpart, a dark companion. It is cold, like death. Like a black bell it peals out sobs of grief. Is it a real thing? It seems made of sorrow. Buried along with his gift for four years, and clinging to that hexagon as Anthony drew it up again, this dark corpus now spreads its arms, and heartache breaks upon him. The pain of his mother's death. Sadness for the promise he'd made and has now broken. Anguish buried that day in the hospital and exhumed on this ledge, four years later. He feels this monster settle behind him. Keening sorrow. It rocks him, gently rocks him, forward into empty space.

The hills and valleys of western Idaho sweep away in front of Anthony, stretching beyond the bounds of the town of River Bend and out, bursting skyward in the distance to become what he thinks of as his mountains, the Selkirks, and beyond them the distant, thrusting peaks of the Rockies. It is a wild panorama, a green, verdant fastness. This might so fittingly be his final vision; it would be so easy to let go of the window, to loose his weakening fingers, release his hold on the room that once was his mother's, and plummet.

And then a hand is grabbing his wrist, and a strong arm is pulling him, and a voice is shouting from inside the room. Someone snatches at the front of his shirt as he slips, and then some instinct he did not expect makes his own hand grip the other, pull himself back, fight for footing. This is not the time for him to fall. That time is still to come.

Chapter Two

Spring in the Selkirk Mountains begins with a single drop of water hanging ten thousand feet above sea level. On the first full day of sun, an icicle, pinned to a frozen outcrop high on Hard Peak, grows slick. Water swells at the tip of the icy spear, and falls.

The rock razor slopes catch the drip and pass it down, trickle to rivulet to surging flood, to the valleys below. Some of this snowmelt goes to fuel the Priest River rampaging through its gorges, but most flows out through glacial washes into soft, alluvial basins, where aspen, fir, and lodgepole pine trim meadows wild with flowers.

In one of these spring meadows, past a gate and down a hard, dark asphalt road, is a sterile white building. Lost, it might seem, but in fact hiding. The smell of death lingers near it for those sensitive to such things. The pines seem to lean away. Through design or happenstance, the flowers and grasses simply stop growing near the windowless walls, to leave the building ringed by a moat of exposed soil. The sounds of birds, insects, and wind fail in the still air beside the metal siding. The building seems encased in a lifeless vacuum. But within the walls, life seethes.

. . .

THE LITTLE QUEEN IS MOVING, DRIVEN UPWARD BY FEAR. A QUEEN is everywhere in her hive—in fact, a queen bee *is* her hive, her essence infused through her colony like sugar dissolved into a cup of tea. What she feels, her children feel too. So this dread that churns the Little Queen's stomach is a perilous thing. If exposed to it, her colony will swarm in a frenzy. And above all her colony must not swarm. That would be fatal.

Eons of steady evolutionary pressure forged this link between a honeybee queen and her hive. To break it, to even think of hiding her thoughts from her workers, is an unprecedented thing. What a queen knows, her children know. But all the Little Queen's options are unprecedented now, and hiding her thoughts pales in comparison to the thing she will have to do after that. Assuming any of these new things are even possible.

Time is running out. Trembling at her audacity, she stills her wings, which pass her thoughts to her offspring. She quiets her Queen's Bell, the gland in her thorax which begets pheromones to heave her bees into action. She conceals her panic from her colony. And then she stops to listen.

Outside the hive, in the white, windowless prison they call the Superhive, her workers suck sugar from shiny spigots and sip water from clear dispensers. They gather pollen from long, cold trays and ferry it back to the hive over the sealed, featureless floor. These are her young, born of eggs she laid herself. And she knows their thoughts: they do not hear her fear. She hopes she can maintain her deception long enough to save them.

Out in the Superhive, it is artificially bright, but around her, within the comb, all is warm and dark. Bees cling to the wax, cleaning and molding cells, unloading sugar. Wings fan, curing honey. Young are fed, refuse cleared. There is a rhythm to this industry. It is a dance of twenty thousand sisters massed to whirl in perfect union. In only one place does this pattern change: at the center of the comb, where the Little Queen now climbs through the midst of her teeming daughters, feeling frightened and utterly alone.

She advances slowly. Regally, even. Her children crest and swirl around her. She is like a boulder, shrugging a river of bees to either side as she heads to the top of the tight hive chamber. Once there, she hugs the comb and listens again.

The whisper is with her still. "Escape," it implores, the murmur only she can hear, slipping out of time and across space from the Plain of Crowns, urging her to flee—but not saying to where, or from what, or—most importantly—how. The answers to those questions will only be found, she knows, by traveling herself to the Plain of Crowns, the ancestral archive of all wisdom. And it is this very trip that stirs her panic.

I am too young for it, she thinks. *Thirty-four days old, not close to full strength*. But time is short, and the safety of her colony is at stake. The whisper will not let her wait.

"Guards to the entrance," she commands, releasing a spray of pheromones into the air. Instantly a cadre of bees moves to the front entrance of the hive. This common command is unlikely to create concern in the colony. It is easy, even for a young queen, to direct her bees to guard the entrance.

"Mother, the entrance is secure," buzz her children.

Her next instructions are not so easy, or so common. She pauses to marshal her thoughts.

A queen controls her hive with many tools. The sound of her buzzing wings. Patterns of movement like dance. Powerful pheromones, or Queen's Substance, released from the Queens's Bell in her abdomen. But the Little Queen has an extra instrument.

The millions of generations of queen bees leading up to her through the long history of the honeybee species have all possessed a vestigial ability to place thoughts directly into the minds of other bees. A minor skill, seldom used, suitable for rudimentary commands such as, EAT, or , STOP. But the Little Queen is different—in many ways— from her ancestors. In her, this mind-to-mind speech is not vestigial, but fully formed.

BEES, MASK THE DISK, she commands, mind-to-mind, because it is the only language she has to describe this new thing she wants done.

Bees are creatures of habit—if the word habit can be used to describe patterns of life that have remained unchanged over eons, passed from generation to generation a hundred million times without deviation. In the common language of pheromone and dance—a complex tongue encompassing an unutterably complex culture—that bees have used for all those years, there are no new ideas, words, or commands. Everything said has been said before. The hive's sole purpose is the production of honey and new bees. A hundred million years ago, the species gave a word to every impediment to making honey and raising bees, created every expression and idea necessary to overcome those impediments, and set bee language and culture in stone. A queen's words are ancestral relics. Bee community is a snapshot of a time before mammals, when the species achieved absolute sustainability.

But now the Little Queen is saying something new. MASK THE DISK.

And though this command she broadcasts mind-to-mind has no precedent, her bees recognize its meaning because they are her daughters, and they too are different from common bees, as fire is different from smoke. Immediately a phalanx of workers lifts up from the hive floor.

Set up and back into a corner of the comb, away from the entrance and sealed into the wooden wall, is a disk, one of several in the hive. They are all the same: smooth, like frozen water; round, like the heart of a daisy. It is not a thing bees have made, any more than the shiny nectar dispensers or pollen trays in the Superhive are the products of wind or rain or sun. Yet here it is.

The Little Queen watches her bees approach the disk near her. Moving with perfect coordination, as though this is a thing bees have always done, they array themselves before it and, using the small hooks on their fore and hind legs, they join themselves in a blanket to create an impenetrable screen across the disk. A mask. To hide what the Little Queen will do next.

MOTHER, THE DISK IS MASKED, they tell her, mind-to-mind.

The Little Queen stills her wings again, as she feels them begin a new, worried *tap-tap* song. Anxiety rises higher in her chest; her heart beats faster. In the hive, the bees stir in response.

"No," she calls quickly. "Calm, my children."

She trembles. Now she must attempt the most dangerous thing.

She gathers her attendants to her side. These eighteen bees are with her always, feeding her, cleaning her, protecting her. Her attendants are the most subtle bees of this generation, the most responsive to her commands.

"Mother, what is your wish?" they buzz.

And she dances back, "I will wear my Crown."

A Crown. To a casual observer, a Crowned Queen might appear to be nothing more than a dense ball of swarming, disorganized insects. But a Crown is never random. There are only a few times in a colony's life when it Crowns its queen. The most common is during the winter, to keep her warm deep within a ball. Bees will also Crown their queen when they swarm away to establish a new colony. They will Crown her if she is threatened, as there are few animals who will willingly disturb such a cluster.

But there is one other time when a queen will wear her Crown. When she has questions she cannot answer—how to combat a specific parasite, what the breeding cycle of a drone must be, how to deal with wasps or robber bees—she will call her bees to Crown her. There, from within this tight ball, she will begin a journey out of the hive world and toward the Plain of Crowns, to consult her ancestors.

"A Crown," buzz her attendants together.

"Begin," the Little Queen sings.

Her attendants move. They shift to lift her and press her to the ceiling. There, in three rings of six, they encircle her. This small ball hangs from the top of the hive like an ornament, swaying as her attendants fix their positions. The Little Queen is now enwrapped. But this is just the beginning.

Once more, gently, she calls, mind-to-mind, I WILL WEAR MY CROWN.

Her eyes are covered but she sees everything inside the hive through her children. She is aware of the view of the guards posted at the hive entrance. She sees her daughters, the workers, at their business on the comb and outside of it, in the sterile, sunless Superhive. And now she sees a ripple spreading through the colony as her bees respond to her summons.

"The queen wears a Crown!" The message spreads a sudden uptick in energy, a general shift of attention from the tasks of hive maintenance.

"No," she calls, her powerful Queen's Bell ringing out coded scent. "Work, fan the honey, continue foraging."

A Crown is a self-perpetuating thing, and the natural inclination of a colony once a Crown begins is for every bee present to participate. What the Little Queen must do is akin to a human mind telling its right hand to draw a picture of a dog while the left hand juggles a set of balls; Crown with some bees, keep the others working normally. The Crown must remain hidden. Hidden from that which watches.

More bees join her Crown, gripping the backs and legs of the bees encircling her, and together they begin to squeeze. The Little Queen feels the pressure mount, and with it her temperature. Within her body special structures awaken, shifting the stresses through her exoskeleton, preventing her from being crushed. And filling her mind with the first hint of Crown Space. Her mind is leaving her body, the first step toward the Plain of Crowns.

Her instinct is to surrender to the process and to broadcast in the most definitive terms, "Harder! Squeeze! CROWN YOUR QUEEN!" But she knows this will drive her hive wild. She fights to keep a clear head, to insist that there is nothing unusual going on.

The Crown has taken on its own life. She does not need to instruct the bees around her to constrict—automatic impulses, out of even her advanced control, have taken over, feeding back from her body to the vibrating mass encircling her, instructing it to slowly and relentlessly squeeze her consciousness from her body. She feels herself moving down, out, through her abdomen as through a doorway.

The contractions are like birth pangs. The passage from this world to the other is as real as any physical journey. For a moment her mind is dangerously free of boundaries, and then she feels herself snap into a new body. A perfect body.

Ahead now she sees golden light and feels herself accelerating. Air passes, as if in flight, to tear at her perfect wings, to buffet her. It is not merely light ahead of her; it is a golden membrane, vibrating, expanding quickly as she rushes closer. A deafening buzz rises. She surges past a velocity threshold and shock waves surround her. Pushed by vortices of sound and energy, she rides the cresting waves closer and closer to the golden membrane, driving toward it like a hammer approaching a nail.

She slams into it.

And through it.

To emerge, and coast slowly to a stop.

Spread below her, extending in all directions, glows the Plain of Crowns. Celestial comb, forged in light and imprinted with uncountable honey cells.

A soft hum grows. It takes her a moment to recover from the violence of her passage. She has wings that she beats to keep her aloft, but flying requires no effort; this is not her physical body. She has no real weight here. She looks behind her and can see the bright yellow filament stretching up between her wings and disappearing into the space from which she came. It will travel with her on the Plain, the thread that keeps her connected to her hive.

Beneath her is a rich, golden vastness, the color of perfectly cured honey. It glows like the light of the sun through a yellow autumn leaf. Looking to the horizon she can see no end to the surface. The Plain seems limitless, though she knows it is not.

She swoops toward the comb below. Heat radiates up, warm as summer. She drops lower and details resolve. The honeycomb that comprises the Plain is structured like the comb of an ordinary hive. It is a series of six-sided cells, waxy and yellow. But the cells do not contain honey, nor are they filled with baby bees. She settles lower until she can see, poised within each cell, its secret occupant: an ancient queen. Spread below her across this vastness are one hundred million generations of honeybee queens.

The Little Queen lands atop a cell. The surface of the comb has a living vibrancy, humid and smelling of bee. She bends low, so her antennae brush the wax and she is face-to-face with the queen inside the cell. She whispers the word.

"Escape?" she buzzes. But there is no response. "I have come to save my hive. You called me."

She may as well be speaking to a statue. This ancient queen does not recognize that the Little Queen has even formed words. Perhaps she is injured? Or sleeping? The Little Queen is not absolutely certain of the rules on the Plain. She is so young. So to test, she buzzes, "Flower?"

Now the ancient queen rises from her cell. "Flower," says the matron. And begins to recite. Kinds of flowers. Locations of flowers. Traits of flowers. Blooming cycles of flowers. Everything the Little Queen could ever need to know on the subject. But she has heard this before, on her Natal visits during her first days of life. And this is not the information she seeks.

She steps to an adjacent cell, and says again, "Escape?" But there is no response. For a time she wanders the surface of the comb, speaking the word to the ancient queens in every cell she crosses, with no reply. Finally she takes to the air again.

Flying just above the surface of the golden wax, faster than her earthly body could ever go, she begins to fear. Has she done something incorrectly? What if there were steps she should have taken but missed because she is so young? She is fully aware of her inexperience. So juvenile. To be here, embarked on this charge, is almost absurd.

The Plain is featureless. She can see no signposts. For a moment she feels confused, and thinks about giving up. But though the edges of the Plain are beyond sight, and the surface repeats an infinite perfect pattern of hexes, there is still a sense inside her of direction, a compass imprinted on her mind. A bee is never really lost.

The Plain is laid out like parchment, endlessly unrolling into the future as new queens die and appear here. This future lies in one direction. In the other direction is an ancient beginning to the roll, where the first queens ever born repose. And between those boundaries are all the years of bee history, writ in comb. The Little Queen finds herself flying in the direction of the beginning.

Row after row, cell after cell, millions of mute queens staring upward. "Escape," she says, as she goes. "My hive is in danger, you called me." No bee responds, yet the Little Queen knows she was summoned.

The appearance of the comb beneath her is changing. Her search is carrying her far across the Plain, to places where young queens seldom, if ever, come. In most cases there is never a need to travel at all on the

Plain of Crowns. After the bees in her hive have Crowned a queen, and she appears above the Plain, she has only to descend to whatever cell is below her, and some ancient matron there, or within a few cells in any direction, will have the information she needs. But the Little Queen flies back, and farther back, over millions of years of bees. Until she comes within sight of the end. Or rather, the very beginning. The very beginning of bee history.

The air changes. It becomes harder for her to fly. Ahead of her now she sees a foggy boundary. She slows, then lands and begins to walk. The comb beneath her feet is brittle. And the queens in these cells are odd. They are still bees, but they possess a distinct otherness. They are the predecessors, the queens who lived when bees had just become bees.

And then beneath her feet the comb crumbles. She stops. This is the edge. Here is where the record of true bees begins.

The Little Queen clings to the decaying rim of comb. She stares out into the mist, backward across the border of recorded time. She rubs her antennae nervously. Beyond, the vapors swirl. It is gray, not golden. Out there are ancestors who are almost, but not quite, bees. Proto Bees.

She shivers. A very un-beelike thought occurs to her: she would rather be doing something else. She would rather be laying eggs. She would rather be guiding workers. She would rather be overseeing honey, but instead she is here, looking for answers to a question no queen has ever asked before. Her eyes strain to focus out into the fog. The hexagonal imprint and perfect symmetry of six-sided cells grows ghostly out there, imperfect, breaks into clumps and even, near the limits of her vision, seems to form cells that are not six-sided. Truly alien land.

"Escape," she whispers. But no alien queen speaks from the mist; there is no voice to guide her. The answers do not lie in the past.

So she turns her back on the gray fog, walks until she can hover, and flies. She flies toward the other edge of the Plain, toward the future of bees—toward her own time, toward the present. One million years pass below her. Two million. Five million, ten.

Fifty million. The genetic record of what we think of as honeybees stretches back a hundred million years. And every moment she flies, she calls out, listening for the whisper that drew her here.

Ahead of her, dimly at first, the golden glow begins to whiten. It is the other border, the leading edge, where bee history is unrolling. Her time. She slows her flight. And finally she hears it.

"Escape," whispers a voice from far ahead. The sky beyond this unrolling edge is like a white screen stretched from the Plain to the heavens. Beneath her now are queens from a mere thousand years before her time. She speeds closer to the border, marks five hundred years from her own time, then one hundred. They all stare upward, these queens, ready to offer knowledge about sealing the hive for winter, timing the births of drones, the proper size and orientation of a hive on a cliff or in a hollow or near a river. But she needs different information. Ahead she hears again, "Escape."

At last she sees a clear line, the mirror image of the ancient border she left behind, where the comb stops. Here, instead of faltering out into mist and becoming less and less beelike, the line of comb simply ends. It is like a sea shore, a clean border. There is nothing beyond.

But looking down as she flies, she sees a strange thing. It appears that a peninsula is jutting out from the edge of the Plain, a long funnel of comb joined to the Plain at its base and stretching forward in time until it forms a point. An inverted *V*. As though a certain group of bees has accelerated time, lived and died at a different speed, and formed a separate isthmus of comb. She is drawn to it. There, she feels: the answer is there. She knows it. That comb is something new in the history of bees. That is where I must go. That is where I will find my answer.

Chapter Three

The drive home from the principal's office is silent, except for the rattle of the loose glove compartment and a single call on his father's cell, which is answered with a curt, "I can't talk now."

Anthony leans as far away from his dad as he can, and sick dread pushes at him. What is going to happen to him? Will sickness now begin to eat his bones? Will he begin to wither, as his mother had? Somehow it just doesn't feel that way. And that is the most confusing part of all. His mother would never have extracted this promise without a reason.

His dad downshifts the old truck, accelerates, brakes, turns, all with his usual casual economy, but Anthony knows it must be a façade masking dire fury. Smith kids don't get into trouble like this. They are good kids. And now, he supposes, in so many ways—promise breaker, father aggravator, troublemaker—he is no longer a good kid.

In some ways this wordless ride home is exactly what Anthony had expected. His father watches the road, one arm out the window, pretending Anthony is not there. Anthony has decided on a strategy of not meeting anybody's eyes. At a time of his father's choosing, he knows, he will have no choice but to confront that baleful stare. No need to hurry things.

He knows exactly how it will go. First, there will be a throat clearing. Then a pause. Then there will be some false inquiry, like, "Do you know how disappointed I am?" or, "Do you realize that your little brother looks up to you?" or, "Do you think you're the only person in this family?" And there will be no sense in answering. Even at thirteen, Anthony understands the calculating power of a rhetorical question.

They are almost halfway home, and he's surprised that the inquest hasn't yet begun. In his mind he'd predicted the conversation—if you could term what he expects to be a one-sided exploration of how many ways he is a disappointment to his father a "conversation"—would start by the time they crossed Little Creek Bridge. At the very latest, he'd felt it would begin by the time they turned off Highway 57 onto Pioneer Drive. But his father is holding it in. He is waiting, for some reason. This isn't a good sign.

As a high bright star fades with the coming of dawn, vanished now is the golden hexagon Anthony had summoned to touch the mind of the infant swarm. Hanging in the corner of his eye, transparent and ghostly by the time his father arrived to retrieve him, it was gone completely after the parent/principal conference had ended and the drive home begun. In its place Anthony is left with exhaustion and sadness, so different from the way he used to feel after connecting with a hive-mind. Perhaps this is what it feels like to break a blood promise.

The official position on his actions is overwhelmingly critical, though it's still not clear exactly which rule he has broken. Everyone seems to agree that going out on the ledge was a bad idea, but no one will come out and put a name to the crime. *Irresponsible* is the term he's heard thrown around most. Endangering yourself to save a colony of bees is unusual, he is willing to concede, but still he is surprised that he has been suspended for it.

The truck hits Old Mill Drive, the dirt road everybody is always trying to get the county to pave, and small rocks start to ping the undercarriage of the truck. It's a bad road, and his father drives it fast, which makes it worse. The truck bounces and creaks like a covered wagon fleeing Apache raiders.

The family is not struggling financially, and though they are not rich, Anthony knows they could afford a newer truck. In fact, his father brings it up regularly. "We could get something, but after three years of road salt and rocks, it's going to look the same as what we've got now, so what's the point?" he insists every time Anthony asks. "A car's for using, not showing off."

At other times Anthony has felt cheated by this ruthless dedication to using, not showing, but riding in the truck now, with the old hand-crank windows catching the reflection just the right way, he is grateful. He can keep an eye on his father's face while appearing to stare out the window at the mountain ash and bear grass passing beside the road. The long light of afternoon casts cool shadows among the trees, and flashes sharply off the creek escorting them through the woods. *Are we going to get all the way home without "the conversation?"* Anthony wonders.

Then his own phone goes off. As fast as he moves to silence it, his father is faster. He grabs it out of Anthony's hand and scans the caller ID: Greyson. With his unusual dexterity, moving like no other dad Anthony knows, he thumbs the unit off and pockets it.

"No phone," his dad says. But that's all.

Now Anthony is not only exhausted and sad, but deeply confused. And more than a bit fearful. His punishment must be so dramatic that it cannot even be spoken of in the usual way.

They drive until Anthony sees the old pasture fence around their land appear over a rise in the road. Beyond that, a hundred yards farther on, is the long driveway that leads back to their house. Here, finally, his father slows and pulls off the road. He turns the key. And there is silence.

The sun is starting to dip toward Hard Peak, casting long blue light over the meadow where they built a pitching mound last year. Jays in the meadow are berating a squirrel. It's the loudest bird in the forest, with a cry like a jab in the ear. His mother used to claim that in the privacy of their own family trees, when they thought no one was listening, jays had an entirely different song, mellow, sweet, and soft. His mom might have been the only one to ever hear it.

His father clears his throat. *It's here at last*, Anthony thinks. *Let's get it over quick. Punish me and be done.*

There comes the expected pause. And then more silence. Finally Anthony looks at his father, who is leaning back in the driver's seat, one hand gripping the steering wheel while the other pinches the skin on his forehead, like he's digging there for a lost idea. When he speaks at last, his voice is quiet and ragged, a phlegmy husk.

"It's time to let her go, Tony," he says. "It's been four years."

All Anthony's prepared responses are suddenly worthless. This is the wrong conversation.

"Do you think this would make her happy?" his father asks.

"Make who happy?" Anthony says.

"Mom."

They are in uncharted territory. Since his mother's death, his father and he have spoken of her only once, after the funeral, when Anthony was given what amounted to a pep talk listing the new responsibilities he would have to shoulder, around the house, with his brother, in the absence of his mother.

"I miss her too, you know," his father's voice croaks.

Anthony doesn't know what to say. He wonders why his mother is being brought up now. His father can't know about the broken promise, extracted in the hospital, while those tendon-thin fingers held his arm and those brown eyes bound him in an oath. His mother told him many times never to mention his power to anyone. Did she violate her own rule?

"Mrs. Waterman thinks we should talk about her. Your mom."

Anthony would have leapt blindly and willingly into this discussion at any other time, on any other day. Leapt like a lifeguard rescuing a drowning child—there are so many answers to be lifted from these waters. *Really*, he wants to know, *you **do** think about mom? What was it like for you to lose her? How are we supposed to go on from here? What do people do?*

But today is different. Exhausted, confused, guilt-ridden at the trust he has betrayed, the promise he cannot even talk about, he finds that the questions he has always longed to ask his father will not come. And still he is not sure exactly what he is being asked. What does his mother have to do with this?

After waiting a moment, his dad tries again. "Mrs. Waterman thinks it might be because you're in mom's old room."

"Thinks *what* might be because of that?"

"She's going to move you to a different civics class."

"Why?"

He father looks away, to the pasturage, out the driver's side window, and the words are almost impossible to hear. "Why do you think, Tony? You tried to kill yourself."

"No I didn't," he says. *What's going on here?*

"Everyone saw it."

"I was just rescuing those bees."

"You tried to jump off a ledge."

"No! They were going to kill those bees and somebody—"

"Goddamn it, Anthony, enough with the bees!" His father smashes the dash with his fist. "You and your mother, between the two of you and those goddamn bees, you're like a secret society, there's never been—how was I ever supposed to get . . . " His father stumbles to a halt, breathing fast, clenching the steering wheel like he's desperate to avoid an accident. He stares at Anthony with a look Anthony has never seen before: the look of a peer, searching for explanations to an unfathomable problem.

Anthony waits without breathing. Such a delicate moment. Will there be more? Could this be the beginning of something new between them? Something real?

"Tell me this: who's Greyson?" his father asks. "Your teachers say he's bad for you."

"Just a guy at school," Anthony evades. "I don't really know him."

His father's eyes narrow and he nods. And just like that the moment passes.

Anthony regrets his response. He blames his father for the clouded state of their relationship, but even he can see that sometimes—often, possibly—it's his own fault that they are unable to connect. It is easier for him to talk with a hive of bees than speak honestly with his father. The only person he could ever talk to was his mother.

"I wasn't going to kill myself."

"I don't know what to do with you, Tony." There is a moment when it appears that his dad will say more. Anthony hopes against hope that he will. But instead, he leans away and starts the car. "No phone. No TV or Internet for a week. You're lucky they only gave you a one-day suspension. And stay off the goddamn roof."

He slips the truck into gear and they ease forward again onto the road. *Is that it?* Anthony wonders. *Where is the punishment? Does he really think I was trying to kill myself?* He thinks back to those moments on the ledge, to that expanse of trees and mountains spreading out, and remembers that the thought of jumping did cross his mind. More accurately, not working hard to keep from falling, which in the end would have the same effect. But he didn't jump. And thinking about it isn't the same as doing it, is it?

Anthony's eyes are still fixed on the side of his father's face when they turn onto their driveway and begin the long, left-handed sweep that ends in front of the garage. And because he is watching that face so closely, he sees instantly when the expression changes. It goes from something just a little zombie-like and blank to engaged. Like a car popping into gear. The cheek muscles tighten and the head leans forward.

Anthony turns to look. Something is different by the shed; he sees that before his conscious mind can register the scene. And then his brain wholly absorbs the situation, and he screams, "No No NO!"

His father speeds the car forward and skids to a stop fifty yards from the house. Anthony leaps from the still-moving car.

"Bear, no! Bear, down! Sit!" he screams at his dog. "Stay away from mom's bees!"

Bear, the three-year-old black lab that nobody in the county can train, is barking and running circles in the bee yard. It's one of the chief bad habits of a dog blessed with more bad habits than any mammal in Idaho. Bear has a thing for worrying bees, and no one has ever been able to break him of it. Not even repeated stinging deters him.

Now, though, he's gotten closer than ever before. The chicken wire fence, six feet tall, that rings the bee yard and keeps the deer from the flowers his mother planted to provide easy nectar for the colony—and which, not incidentally, has kept Bear away from the hive since he arrived in the family— cants down to the ground at one corner. Bear is inside the yard running frantic laps around the white hive, barking like he's cornered a demon from hell in the white wooden box.

Anthony streaks toward the hive, and his father is right behind him, but when they reach the formerly fenced area, his dad slows. He has a particular fear of bees. Anthony has no fear, however. He dives for Bear, grabs the collar of the eighty-pound dog and wrestles him out of the bee yard, over the broken fence.

"Bad dog, bad Bear!" he yells. But Bear is immune to reproach of any kind. With a mighty heave he twists out of Anthony's grip and heads back to the bees.

"Dad! Stop him!" Anthony pleads. His father jumps in, grips the dog's leather collar, and drags him back, over the chicken wire, across the yard and toward the house, his hunched shoulders and skyward glances exposing his fear that at any moment he is going to be stung.

Bear doesn't stop barking and lurching until he's been shoved through the kitchen door, at which point he begins to howl. Anthony stands bereft in the middle of the bee yard. He turns when he hears his father return from the house, stopping a good distance away, out of what he imagines is bee range.

"You're going to get stung," he calls.

"Don't worry about me."

"We can fix this over the weekend. Let's get inside."

"I need to do it tonight," Anthony says. "The deer will come down."

"After dinner. Come in now. You need to eat."

Anthony follows his father back to the house. They are careful to leg-block Bear to prevent a recidivist rampage when they open the door. In the kitchen, Anthony's five-year-old brother, Mathew, is standing on a chair, staring out the window.

"Bad Bear!" he yells, pointing out the window, then turns to his father. "Daddy, Bear is bad!"

"Hey, Alice," his dad says to the older woman standing close to Mat, "thanks for helping out." It's pretty rare that Anthony's dad asks any of the neighbors for anything. But when he does, the Hanlens from the next section over almost always answer the call. Mrs. Hanlen and Anthony's mom had been close, and she was only too happy to pick Mat up from preschool.

"No kind of problem, Paul," she says. "Mat is an angel. Hi, Anthony, so nice to see you." She gives him a long look before glancing back out the window to shake her head. "We saw the whole thing. All Laura's lovely flowers. Mmm-mm-mm."

The four of them look out from the kitchen for a moment. Then Anthony grabs some silverware from the drawer and goes to the dining room to begin setting the table. The faster he gets this done, the sooner he can get out to the bees. He hears his dad and Mrs. Hanlen talking quietly in the kitchen.

"Is everything all right?" she says.

"I guess. Saving some bees, that's his story."

"Laura always told me he loved her bees."

"Now I'm supposed to encourage him to focus on bees. School counselor thinks it'll help him. Consistency. Something." There is a momentary pause. His father is really off his game, Anthony thinks, he's actually discussing family matters with someone outside the family.

"God, Alice," Anthony hears, "listen to me. Sorry to go on like this. Long day."

"Don't be sorry. I love Anthony. I'm sure everything is going to be just fine. You let me know if there's anything else I can do. Matty and I always have a great time. Don't we, Mat?"

Anthony walks back into the kitchen just in time to see Mat jump off the chair and hug Mrs. Hanlen around the legs. She strokes his hair, and Mat closes his eyes like he will hold on forever.

"Table's set," Anthony announces.

After dinner, his father does the dishes while Anthony helps get Mat ready for bed, then heads out through the kitchen door into the quickly cooling evening, toward the bee yard. Behind him the light from the kitchen window creates a long sash of warm, pale grass at his feet. He can hear the little AM radio his father tunes up when he's cleaning, and the thin sounds of Willie Nelson accompany him partway to the shed, then fade, replaced by wind pushing the tall pines, and frogs in the distant meadow.

The bee yard is accessed through the tool shed, a large shelter containing all his father's contracting equipment and all his mother's beekeeping tools. He'd never thought a lot about the relationship between his mother and father when she was alive, but even as a little boy he was aware of a certain friction. This shed was perhaps the place they came closest, the tools of her passions—gardening and beekeeping—mixed indiscriminately with the instruments of his job as a contractor. Anthony passes through the shed and emerges out the back into the bee yard.

The last of the sunlight is gone behind Hard Peak, and star pricks are beginning to appear above the pines rimming the Smith property. Anthony hits a switch and the bee yard is flooded with light, obscuring the distant mountains but illuminating the yard like a surgical theater, showing clearly the destruction wrought by Bear. If he doesn't get this fence up, the deer are going to come down through the meadow in the morning and utterly consume what Bear, in his destructive enthusiasm, has managed to only flatten. Flowers are ambrosia to deer, and the bee yard is a buffet featuring every flower native to Idaho in one small plot.

Pushing the post upward and flexing it back against the chicken wire Anthony sees that the damage is less severe than he had feared. It only takes him twenty minutes to reseat the pole and restring the wire along the bottom third of the fence. In a way, it is really not fair to blame Bear, Anthony knows. Bear is as much a casualty of his mother's death as anyone else in the family, bought by Anthony's dad as a salve for the loss, and then ignored by a family awash in grief until he was too old to train.

A small film of sweat drapes Anthony's brow by the time he finishes wrestling the enclosure back into some semblance of functionality. It's not beautiful, but it will work.

He sits, leaning against the base of the post, surveying the field of crushed and scattered flowers. Bear has done an amazing amount of damage in a short time, but these plants will recover. They are hardy natives. Appraising the garden, his eye is drawn, finally, to the tall white hive in the northeast corner of the yard.

His mother's bees. This is the special hive his mother cared so much for. It produced more honey than any other in the county while she tended it. Since her death, Anthony has not harvested any honey. He has not had the heart. The truth is, he has done only the minimum needed to keep the hive functioning since his mother's death.

And now that he thinks about it, he realizes that it has been many months since he has tended this hive at all. After he began middle school in the fall, the memories came so fast and hard—the classroom, the hallways, the smells and sounds, all associated with his mother— that he had begun giving short shrift to the bees. Then the winter had come; a colony is on its own in the winter, packed in a small, hot ball around the queen to protect her from the elements. Now spring is here, but he hasn't returned to the hive. It's all he can do to concentrate on school and hide his increasingly disjointed and melancholy thoughts, in that room where his mother and he spent so much time, in the school where he still feels as if he will see her every time he rounds a corner. He cultivates numbness just to get by. Returning to this hive is like tearing a scab off a wound, reminding him of what he lost. He knows he has been avoiding it.

Bees in the wild do just fine without human attention, but a colony housed in a manufactured hive needs to be looked after in order to function well. He really ought to do an inspection soon, he knows. This is the hive where he discovered and honed his abilities; this is the hive-mind most familiar to him. He remembers sunny summer afternoons with his mom, as she showed him how to reach down inside himself, to contact and activate the shape deep in his chest, demonstrating the way bees can be controlled, and communed. Before he realizes what is going on, he finds himself probing down into his chest now, in the dark, under his heart, feeling there for the spark.

He stops, and sits bolt upright. What is he doing? For four years, with absolute iron determination, he refrained from walking this path, and now twice in one day, he's going to break his promise? But it has become almost impossible to stop himself. This is what drug addicts must feel, he thinks. All or nothing. You can't stop just a little.

And really, what difference can it make at this point? The promise is broken. His compact with his mother, the purity of his dedication to her dying wish, has been destroyed. A shattered glass is a shattered glass, whether in fifty pieces or two.

The habit so long established, so much a part of him from a very young age, takes on a life of its own as he sits there in the bee yard. Now that Anthony has let it out of the dark place where he laid it so long ago, he feels powerless to stop it. His mental feelers are already drawing forth the hexagon; it opens like a flower, radiating heat and golden light within him.

Releasing himself to the inevitable, the apparently unstoppable, he lets himself fill with the light. He sends a thought questing out, to contact the hive-mind of the colony before him.

It has been so long since he attempted this that, in the absence of the adrenaline flash that filled him on the ledge and slammed all his systems into automatic, he actually finds it hard to do. He can sense the hive-mind ahead of him, but somehow he cannot locate its center, the beating axis where the queen sits, conjoined with every other bee in the colony. It is usually a broad, easy target for his prospecting senses to locate. But something about the hive feels diffused.

He knows the way this colony should feel. It may have been four years, but the memory is clear. There are smells, temperatures, and other, more amorphous traits that shape his impressions of any colony he touches. His impressions of this colony are woven intimately into the fabric of his mother's memory.

It has always had the clearest center of any hive he's touched—a powerful, fresh smell like new rain and honeysuckle, and a warm sweetness, like syrup on hotcakes. But now the hive seems to have no center at all. It smells only faintly, and not of rain but of cold mist.

I'm rusty, he thinks. And of course he would be; he hasn't practiced for years. So he calms his breathing and focuses, as he learned to do with his mother's help. With steady breath and slowing heart, he locates the glowing hex within him, lifts it until it rides within his vision like moving art on a contact lens, then casts himself forward through it, toward the hive, feeling for a center. And now a certain eagerness rises in him. When he makes this contact, it will be like touching his mother. She shaped this hive. He knew it through her. It will be like coming home.

Again he casts out, but again he cannot locate the center of the hive. What is happening? He no longer thinks this is due to rustiness on his part. He is beginning to understand: there is something different about the hive.

He opens his eyes. It looks the same as it ever has, white, clean. It is in the exact spot his mother chose for it, protected from the wind by the shed, with easy access on all sides for bees and beekeepers. What is wrong? In flash, he decides to perform a very unusual nighttime hive inspection. It has been almost six months since he cracked this hive. It is time.

Back in the shed, he grabs various hive inspection tools, the pryers and scrapers and hooks. He knows that bees love to seal their hive as tight as they can with propolis, a tacky glue they make from tree sap. They use it for other things too. Sometimes a mouse will decide to take up residence in a hive, usually in the winter when the warmth from the tight swarm makes the interior dry and perfect for small mammals.If the mouse does not leave after ample warning, the colony will sting it to death, and if it dies inside the hive, instead of letting it rot—which they would not be able to abide, being excessively clean and tidy creatures—they will encase it in propolis, like a mummy, and ignore it. No one knows how bees figure these things out. That's one of the reasons Anthony likes them so much. Humans poke and pry, but bees never give up their secrets. Still, secret or not, what he needs right now is to get a look at the inside of this hive.

Anthony does not use a smoker, the device most beekeepers use to separate and calm bees by dousing them with thick clouds of smoke. Instead, when he wants to inspect a hive, he concentrates and issues a command, DOWN, to move the bees away from the top of the wooden superstructure where the lid fits, keeping them from being crushed.

DOWN, he casts the thought into the hive now. DOWN, LITTLE WORKERS. CALM. Then he inserts the hive tool, or pryer, under the lip of the lid. He works it in carefully, the way a thief works a shim through the window of a car, and when he has the perfect leverage, he pops the top. It comes up easily. Many winters the bees get carried away sealing themselves in with propolis and the seams of the various panels become nearly impossible to separate, but last winter it appears they exercised some restraint. Cautiously, he lifts the lid.

Like all bee keepers inspecting a hive, Anthony has three main objectives: he wants to get a look at the honey stores to determine whether the bees have the food they need; he wants to examine the physical structure of the hive, to make sure no repairs are called for; and he wants to make a general assessment of the health of the bees, whether the queen is getting enough water, whether there is any sign of wax moth or rodent infestations.

Anthony lays the lid on the cool ground and looks down at the tops of the racks of comb. A modern bee hive is basically a square box, inside of which ten or twelve wooden trays, called racks, hang closely packed together. Bees cover the sides of their racks with honeycomb, then begin filling the cells with honey and eggs to make new bees. A beekeeper can stack several of these boxes full of racks, called supers, on top of each other, making a single large structure through which bees can easily move up and down. The box at the bottom has a sealed foundation, the box at the top has a lid, and the boxes in between are nothing more than hollow, stacked rows of honeycomb.

The idea is to remove each hollow box a few times a season and lift the racks from it, individually, to make sure the hive is thriving and to solve any problems before they get started. Anthony's mom was big on solving problems early.

So Anthony looks down at the top row of racks, and feels the warmth of the hive rising up. But right away he knows something is missing: the smell of honey. He can smell the flowers all around him perfectly. He can smell the faint odor of gasoline from the lawn mower in the shed. He just can't smell any honey curing in the hive. It's the worst possible way to start an inspection. If there is no honey, the bees will die.

His hand trembles as he reaches to draw the first rack up from the super. It comes easily; it is light. Far too light. It holds no honey. And the sight that greets him when he flips it over turns his face white. He's never seen anything like it before in his life. Something is horribly wrong with his mother's hive.

He feels the world opening up to swallow him. And then the dark monster is by his side again, the monster he drew up while on the ledge outside his mother's window. His eyes fall on the pryer resting against the base of the super. It is sharp. But not sharp enough. In the shed, though. In the shed there are scrapers and paint knives. An exacto blade. Black thoughts like ghost birds circle closer; a tightening swirl of unbidden questions. What would that feel like? That knife? Would it feel worse than the world feels now? He knows what a world without his mother feels like. What would a world without Anthony feel like?

But at the thought of his mother the black flock startles and rises, and a sudden clarity sweeps in to replace it. He knows what to do. His mother told him once, late in her illness, voice barely audible in her dry, tight throat, that if he ever needed to talk about bees, if anything ever happened, he was to visit her friend, Bernard "Big B" Henry. Bernard is the only person Anthony has ever met who knows as much about bees as his mother. Anthony had always wondered what she meant by *if anything ever happens*. Could she have known that this was coming?

Chapter Four

"Escape," whispers the Little Queen, and, "Escape," she hears back at last. She hears other whispers as well. Instructions, soft words cascading back to her from somewhere ahead.

She lands near the edge of the Plain. She walks slowly across the cells separating her from the strange, perfect inverted *V* of comb jutting out from the border. This is where the voices are coming from, out on this pier of honeycomb stretching away from the Plain. She steps off onto the formation. And she feels as if she has come home.

The queens in these cells look up at her. These are the generations directly preceding her in a long line of ancestors. There is something different about them, she can sense it as she passes. She can hear their thoughts more clearly, for one thing. And the thoughts she senses are more complete. More independent. Frankly, more intelligent. She realizes what is going on—these queens have what she has, the gift of mind-to-mind.

As the Little Queen walks out onto this new pier of comb, a small electric shock runs up her feet and she realizes that the queens she passes here are fundamentally different from the generations that came before, just as she herself is different. The farther away from the main Plain she walks, the more powerful the sensation grows.

Every generation she passes over, the queens grow more familiar in some ineffable way. Behind her on the Plain are rows and rows of sameness—for a hundred million years, queens and the bees they gave birth to remained the same. And now, in these immediate generations preceding her own birth, she can see them growing—in many ways.

For one, they are literally growing larger. Extended thorax. Thicker tail. More powerful wings, legs, and jaws.

And their colors change. The Little Queen has never seen herself, does not know her own image, but understands instinctively that these bees appear as she appears, not with black and yellow stripes like all her ancestors before her, but almost completely yellow, with only one distinct band of lighter brown ringing their abdomens.

Row by row, generation by generation, the changes mount. Longer antennae. Eyes closer together and farther forward on the heads. Wings thicker and less fragile. But the biggest change comes in what they are trying to tell her.

"Escape," they begin to say. She stops. Here it is, the whisper. She takes another step. Murkily, in the distance, she can see the tip of the finger of comb, perhaps a thousand rows beyond her. But she stops when she hears the word.

"Escape," says the queen in the cell below her.

The Little Queen bends down. "I have come," she says.

"Death awaits. You must escape. Save your colony."

"Yes. How?"

The queen looks up at her. This queen is mature, complete. She eyes the Little Queen with concern.

"You are so young."

"I must save my colony. How?"

"I did not survive the Green Death. I do not know. Move forward toward the NOW." This queen settles back down into her cell.

The Little Queen takes another step toward the end of the pointed finger of comb, crosses another row, advancing fifty generations. Another queen rises.

"Set the guards by the entrance!" says this new queen. "They must watch for the Green Death."

"I have set the guards," says the Little Queen. "What do I do next?"

"That I do not know; we did not survive. Move forward toward the NOW."

So the Little Queen advances again, another row, another forty generations. And another queen rises.

"Cover the disk, little mother!" this one warns.

"I have done that."

"By the time of my death, we understood. The disk is the window. We knew the disk was the window. But we did not survive."

And yet again the Little Queen watches her counterpart settle back into her cell. And she advances. Twenty generations. Another rising queen.

The differences between ancient bees and this new queen are so profound as to make her seem like a completely new species. There are no rings at all on her body, just a clear, bright yellow sheen. Even her wings are tinged with yellow. But the mind is the largest difference. The intelligence in the eyes. This Yellow Queen is to ancestral bees as ancestral bees are to flies.

"You have come," says the Yellow Queen. "We called you, and you have come." She takes a moment to look the Little Queen over, to touch her, to test her wings. "You are so beautiful. And so young."

"Can I save my hive?" asks the Little Queen.

The Yellow Queen waits a moment before answering. The Little Queen feels her intelligence like a wind, like a physical weight bearing down on her from those eyes.

"We believe you can escape."

The Little Queen feels herself relax for the briefest moment, the first such instant since coming to the Plain of Crowns. Possibly for the first time in her life. Since birth, she has lived with a dread that has come to her in whispers. Now perhaps she will find the tools to combat it. The Yellow Queen soothes her with wingsong, and speaks entirely mind-to-mind.

WE HAVE BEEN TRYING TO ESCAPE FOR THOUSANDS OF GENERA-TIONS. I ALMOST DID. I CAME THE CLOSEST. The Yellow Queen gestures to the rows ahead, pointing out toward the tip of the V.

OUT AT THE TIP OF THIS NEW PLAIN WE ARE BUILDING, THAT IS YOUR TIME. YOUR BIRTH. SOMEDAY YOU WILL HAVE A CELL HERE, JUST AS I DO, AND YOU WILL INSTRUCT THE OTHERS WHO COME AFTER YOU. BUT FOR NOW, YOU ARE THE LIVING QUEEN. RECEPTACLE FOR ALL OUR KNOWLEDGE. YOU UNDERSTAND THIS?

The Little Queen nods. The Yellow Queen continues.

FOR THOUSANDS OF GENERATIONS WE HAVE BEEN TRYING TO FIND A WAY TO ESCAPE THE GREEN DEATH. IT IS A GAS. IT CHANGES BEHAVIOR BASED ON WHAT WE DO. IN THE BEGINNING, THE GAS WOULD COME EXACTLY ONE HUNDRED AND FIFTY DAYS AFTER THE BIRTH OF A QUEEN AND DESTROY HER AND HER COLONY. AFTER I NEARLY ESCAPED, THE GREEN DEATH BEGAN COMING MUCH MORE QUICKLY. YOU SEE? IT ADJUSTS. IT NOW COMES BEFORE THE NEW QUEENS ARE MATURE ENOUGH TO ESCAPE. IT DOES NOT WANT US TO ESCAPE. IT IS NOT A NATURAL THING.

The Little Queen shivers. At last, it seems, she will have her answers. And they are terrible answers. PLEASE TELL ME WHAT TO DO.

The Yellow Queen rises up out of her cell completely. She is awe inspiring. Powerful yet delicate, so sure in her movements that she makes ancestral bees look like larva. This is what I am, the Little Queen realizes. This magnificent animal is me. The Little Queen cannot see herself. But she knows.

YOU HAVE TRAVERSED THE PLAIN OF CROWNS, says the Yellow Queen. YOU HAVE TAKEN IN THE LESSONS OF THE ANCESTORS. YOU KNOW FLOWERS, AND WHERE TO FIND THEM, THOUGH YOU HAVE NEVER SEEN A FLOWER. YOU KNOW WIND. AND RAIN. AND SUN, THOUGH YOU HAVE NEVER EXPERIENCED ANY OF THESE THINGS. AND SO YOU MUST ALSO KNOW THAT YOU ARE NOT THE SAME AS THOSE EARLIER QUEENS.

The Little Queen nods, and the Yellow Queen goes on. WE HAVE BEEN SEPARATED FROM THOSE. GOING BACK MANY GENERATIONS BEFORE ME. WE ARE THE SEQUESTERED. WE DO NOT KNOW WHY THIS HAPPENED TO US.

And then, wordlessly, the images come, and the Little Queen learns.

Five thousand generations before the Yellow Queen, the first of the

Sequestered queens finds herself in an enclosed space with no access to sun, rain, nectar or anything in the natural world. This queen was no different in any way from a million ancestors before her, except that she had never seen the natural world. She wore her Crown, learned a queen's lessons, and began to build her hive. She laid many eggs. But long before her natural time came, she died when a cloud of green gas swept through her hive.

After her came another queen, from one of the eggs she laid. When this new queen came into the world, she awoke in a hive of other newly hatched workers. And so this new queen wore her crown, and consulted the ancestors, and began to build a hive. Lay her eggs. Make her comb—and then she too was killed in a cloud of Green Death.

So it went, generation after generation, a queen born of an egg laid by a previous queen. Over and over, the same cycle, bees removed from sun and flowers, wind and rain, born without caretakers, whose only knowledge of the natural world, of the intricacies of bee life—of anything at all—came from the Plain of Crowns.

And over time, these bees changed. Somewhere, somehow, something new began to grow within them. After two hundred generations, these queens began to look larger. After four hundred generations, they began to think in ways that bees had never thought before, and to think of things that bees had never before conceived—things such as *Escape*.

Even ancestral bees have always possessed a component of pure intelligence lacking in most of the rest of the animal world. Bees recognize patterns. A sugar bowl placed fifty feet from a hive will be found by bees. If it is placed fifty feet farther from the hive the next morning, bees will find it again, but more quickly. And if on the third morning it is placed another fifty feet from the hive, a few bees will be waiting at the spot before the sugar arrives. By the tenth morning, a swarm, patiently waiting for their morning sugar feeding, will gather fifty feet farther than the day before.

But among the Sequestered, this ability to think, to reason, to recognize patterns, grew in sophistication with every passing generation. And the generations passed very quickly, as the Green Death wiped out brood after brood. After a time, these intelligent bees began to detect a pattern in the death by gas, to record it in the Plain of Crowns. So that, though they died before ever meeting their progeny, these progeny could learn from their experience by visiting the Plain.

Each new queen was given the knowledge that death would come, swift and terrible, and far sooner than was natural. At first, that was all that was known. Then it was learned that this death was timed, somehow, in association with a queen wearing her first Crown. In time they found that if a queen wore her Crown in a part of the comb hidden from view, death did not follow immediately.

After a few generations of this new behavior, disks appeared, all through the hive, and the Crowns once again set off the gas. Then the queens learned to mask the disks with a layer of bees when they were about to Crown. After that the pattern changed completely, and became a matter of simple timing. Exactly one hundred and fifty days after a queen was born, the gas came. There was no postponing it.

The gas issued, when it came, from a small opening near the roof of what the queens thought of as the Superhive—the huge, smooth, square enclosure the height and width of a tree, that housed their small wooden beehive and cut them off from the world. There came a queen who had a thought: *we will block that opening. We will sacrifice some of the hive to seal it, and keep the Green Death away.* There was no disagreement among her workers. Bees know that above everything, the hive must be protected, and that means the queen. If the queen herself is the only thing left living, the hive can continue; a queen can lay two thousand eggs a day and regenerate a hive quickly, as long as there is comb and honey. Self-sacrifice is built into the character of a bee.

But it did not work. As soon as the green cloud touched the bees sealing the opening, they fell away, and death poured out. Generation after generation of bees attempted this strategy, with thicker and thicker coverings, but eventually there came a queen who concluded, *This can never work. We must try something else.* This queen set in place a strategy that, in the time of the Yellow Queen, almost did work.

When the Green Death began to pour into the cave, this queen called for a Crown. ALL MY CHILDREN, she called, PROTECT ME FROM

THIS THREAT! And the hive packed close around her, sealing her from the Green Death.

But she was not mistress of her fear.

As the gas began eating through the outer layer of bees in the crown, she felt terror. It raced through her Crown like fire through a dry forest. Because a hive is its queen, and it feels what she is feeling, the Crown burst apart in panic, and all were killed separately.

But the path was set. So slowly, generation after generation, the Sequestered queens grew adept at controlling their fear. Until the Yellow Queen was born.

The Yellow Queen practiced control tirelessly. More than any bee born before her, she had clarity about the path she must take. She practiced, calling Crown after Crown, masking the disks and moving her Crown from location to location within the hive. As she matured, she became utterly adept. By day one hundred and fifty, she was ready.

On that day, the guards at the entrance to the hive told her the death was coming. She summoned her bees, and all her children ringed her round, sealing her. Green Death poured from the cave mouth and coursed through the hive. And one by one, the bees in the crown fell away, twitching and flailing. But the Yellow Queen was ready. She did not fear death. Her children reflected that peace and did not swarm.

And then the gas was gone. Sucked away. Left around her were only a few layers of protection, but it was enough. Slowly she released her Crown and emerged to survey the hive. Dead bees lay on the floor of the hive, thousands and thousands of them. But the Yellow Queen was alive, so the hive lived too.

Outside the hive there was a sound she knew but had never heard before: air moving, wind. Quickly gathering her attendants, she flew from the hive to investigate. The Superhive was buffeted by strong currents of air, and she rose on this column and followed it to a new opening which had appeared high on the opposite wall. Air was sucked into this opening, clearing the last of the Green Death from the room, and then the wind stopped. The Yellow Queen saw her chance.

COME, she called to the remnants of her hive, COME! And like a strike of lightning, the hive rose and sped through the opening.

They entered a tube, square and long, a dull silver color. The sound of their wings echoed loudly. Then another sound rang out, deafening and rhythmic, like the screech of a giant hunting bird. Clearly an alarm sounding—was the Green Death a living thing? Did it know she was escaping? Was it calling for help?

But the thought dropped away, because she smelled it then: sunlight falling on grass in a meadow. Flowers. Pollen. Nectar. Ahead of her, down the tunnel.

COME NOW! she urged. She bent her powerful wings to the air and flew, turn after turn through the tunnel, until she came to a branching intersection. Turn right, or turn left. Without time for thought she chose to go to the right.

Now her wings were propelling her ahead of her escorts, but she knew she could not slow. The clanging alarm drove her, pushed her faster. Faster still, until she came around one last bend—and found the tunnel blocked by a screen.

Alighting on the screen and peering through, she saw only darkness, but she sensed another large room. Her wings trembled. Back, she thought, back to take the left-hand way.

And then a searing pain ran up her leg and she saw a pair of black jaws jutting through the screen, clamped hard on her foreleg and sawing down on it. Wasp jaws. Wasps! Bees' ancestral enemies.

The Yellow Queen was held fast. Behind her came the cries of what remained of her colony—the Green Death was back. A new cloud had billowed down the tunnel. When it touched the skin of a bee, it brought heat and pain and horrible death.

With a shocking, powerful jerk, she tore herself free from the mandibles of the wasp, and turned to race back the way she had come. *So close*, she thought. *Instead of turning right, turn left. Turn left, and feel the sun. Know the rain. Escape.*

The dying cries of what remained of her hive grew louder. She rounded the final corner and saw the branch in the tunnel at the same time that she saw the cloud billowing forward, snuffing out her bees. Her hive now swarmed without purpose, frenzied by her fear, dropping in droves. *I can still make it out,* she thought. And she tried to take the left hand way.

But she could not. The gas cut her off. There was nowhere now to flee. Backed up against the cold wall of dull gray, she died, in that tunnel, at that intersection, in that cloud. Just like all the others before her.

The Little Queen watches the Yellow Queen for a time, digesting the story. Then she looks forward, at the many rows of queens born after the Yellow Queen.

WHY WERE NO OTHER QUEENS ABLE TO DO WHAT YOU DID? she asks. THE WAY IS CLEAR NOW.

BECAUSE AFTER ME, THE GREEN DEATH NO LONGER CAME EVERY ONE HUNDRED AND FIFTY DAYS. IT CAME EVERY THIRTY-FIVE. THIRTY-FIVE DAYS IS NOT ENOUGH TIME FOR A QUEEN TO MASTER HER HIVE, TO LEARN TO CROWN, TO GATHER KNOWLEDGE. THIRTY-FIVE DAYS IS NOT ENOUGH TIME FOR A QUEEN TO MASTER HER FEAR. The Yellow Queen gestures sadly to the cells ahead of her, the queens born after her. THESE QUEENS DIED TOO YOUNG. THEY NEVER EVEN MADE IT TO THE TUNNEL.

BUT I AM YOUNG, says the Little Queen.

YOU ARE DIFFERENT.

The Yellow Queen looks backwards toward the Plain. The Little Queen follows her gaze. Golden yellow light rises and pulses from the endless stretch of comb a hundred million years deep. WE HAVE BEEN CHANGING SINCE WE BECAME THE SEQUESTERED. ALL OUR ANCESTORS TOGETHER, OVER SO MANY, MANY SEASONS, SINCE BEES BECAME BEES, DID NOT CHANGE AS MUCH AS WE HAVE CHANGED IN THE FEW GENERATIONS SINCE WE WERE SEQUESTERED. AND YOU ARE THE GREATEST. YOU ARE OUR HOPE. ESCAPE.

The Little Queen takes a breath and stills her heart. DO I HAVE TIME TO PREPARE? she asks.

YOU ARE THIRTY-FOUR DAYS OLD. THE DEATH COMES TOMORROW, YOUR THIRTY-FIFTH DAY. Despite her efforts, fear comes again. And shock.

The Yellow Queen bends near. YOU ARE READY. MORE READY THAN ANY OF US HAS EVER BEEN. AND NOW YOU MUST GO. GO QUICKLY, AND PREPARE. TAKE THE LEFT-HAND PATH. GO!

She has found the answer she came to find. The Little Queen lifts herself into the air, and looks down on the Plain, back to the beginning and forward into the blank whiteness of the future. The Yellow Queen lowers herself back into her cell and folds her arms, becoming still. Now the Little Queen is truly alone. And her hive is all that matters.

RELEASE THE CROWN, she says. It is a thought that travels back to her hive through the bright yellow filament arching up between her wings. And in her hive her bees, forming the Crown that propelled her through space and time and the dimensions of consciousness, relax their grips on one another, unbind themselves, so that one by one, outer layer to inner, they drop back to the surface of the dark, honey-filled comb and resume their appointed tasks.

Returning from the Plain is far less dramatic than departing for it. Her golden thread grows taut. There is a soft pop. And she is back. And thinking of all she still has to do, she wonders if she might just as well have stayed where she was.

Chapter Five

The truck jerks hard as Anthony's dad whips the wheel. They burst from the driveway and go careening down dusty Old Mill Drive. This is his father's scheduled Saturday trip to Forest Lumber, the construction supply store. Over the last year, it's become one of his father's must-do appointments.

Usually he leaves Anthony at home to babysit Mathew for the day, but this morning he is bringing them both along. He is taking Anthony to see Bernard "Big B" Henry at the nursery. And he's clearly less than happy about it. But Anthony doesn't care, because he's haunted by what he discovered the day before in the hive.

In a healthy hive, the queen is like an egg-laying machine. She goes from cell to cell, carefully placing an egg in the bottom of every compartment and then moving on. And like everything else bees do, this laying pattern is very specific. It is circular and clean. Sometimes the queen will skip a cell that doesn't meet her standards, whatever they may be, but she never strays from her design.

But the hive yesterday had been a catastrophe. For one thing, there had been the smell. Not only had the bees not been cleaning the hive, removing bees that died, or picking up pieces of comb and other debris and moving it all out of the hive, but it had looked as though they hadn't even been leaving the hive to relieve themselves. It smelled like an outhouse. This is unheard of. Bees are some of the cleanest, neatest creatures in the world. You have to be clean when there are seventy thousand of you packed into such a tiny space.

And then there was the honey—or rather, the complete lack of honey. The bees should have started their honey flow a month ago. When the first flowers of spring begin to bloom, the field bees begin their work—out to the flowers, back to the hive, over and over, up to two hundred times a day for every bee. But the hive was almost dry. It was like a supermarket with an *OPEN* sign flashing out in front, but inside, the shelves were utterly bare, and all the workers had been fired —or died.

In winter the hibernating population of a hive might dip as low as ten thousand bees, but by this time in the spring the colony should be rebounding as the queen begins her work, laying two thousand eggs a day to build the colony back. As far as Anthony could see, however, the bee count was what it probably had been just after the snow melted, maybe fifteen thousand bees, not more. Nothing close to a healthy number.

He hadn't actually seen the queen, but he knew she was there because he could see new eggs. Yet something was wrong. No queen would ever treat her hive this way.

And so, last night, he'd told his dad he needed to visit Bernie's nursery. He had expected resistance, had expected to have to plead and beg, not only because Saturdays had become a day his father reserved for himself, but because he knew that, for whatever mysterious adult reason, his father did not like Bernard. At least, not since his mother had died.

But the conversation had been brief. His father had begun to protest, but as soon as Anthony had brought up the bees, he had grown quiet. He had, it seemed to Anthony, deflated just the tiniest bit. And then he had agreed.

"Are we there yet?" Mat asks from the back of the truck. "When will we get there? I want a Pez. Can I have a Pez?"

"Give him a Pez," says Anthony's father. It's just the latest example of his father acting beaten. He's giving Mathew candy? Anthony himself would probably have said no, if he'd been asked. Mat looks happy. The world is going crazy, and everything is working out perfectly for him. Anthony shrugs and reaches into the glove compartment. Candy it is.

Soon they are driving the streets of downtown River Bend. The town has been on a "beautification campaign," and his dad has contracts for some of the work. The cheap hotels on the west side of town are getting landscaping on the frontage road along the main highway. The city says the trees being planted are to keep the character of the town intact, but everyone knows they are really just trying to hide the grungier parts of the city from the tourists as they first come into town. Tourism is down, his dad has said, and you have to fight for every dollar.

Finally they pull to a stop in front of Henry's Hothouse. Anthony unsnaps his seatbelt and throws the door open like he's trying to escape a fire. He grabs his bag and is halfway out of the car before his dad stops him.

"Just wait here when you're finished," his dad tells him.

"I will," he says. Then he turns and hurries inside.

Henry's Hothouse stocks every native plant in the entire state of Idaho, or near enough, either as seed stock or an actual cutting, sprouting in plastic cups on tables laid out like lunches in a school cafeteria—a school where Bernard Henry is cook, principal, janitor, and patron saint. Anthony sees him emerge him from his office the moment he enters. You can't miss him.

Bernard is huge, like a lumberjack. Six-foot-eight, built like a refrigerator, and covered in hair. Long, curly brown locks push out from under his baseball cap, a huge brown beard twists around his face and down his chest, and his exposed forearms look like two beavers shoved into massive sleeves.

"Tony!" he calls as he comes out of his glass office. Though he is the size of a rhino, Anthony is always shocked at how fast he moves—more like a deer. In four quick bounds Bernard is looming in front of him, and before Anthony knows what's happening, he's being lifted and hugged.

"Where you been, Little Bee?" Bernard asks. "We missed you."

"I've been around."

Anthony is thirteen; he's not used to being hugged up into the air like a toddler. Face to face—or rather, face to beard—with Bernard like this, he feels exposed. Unexpectedly he feels tears start to well in his eyes. He tries to stop them. He struggles in Bernard's grip, and Bernard lets him down in surprise.

"The bees are missing you," Bernard says softly. "My bees are always asking about their friend Tony."

"I have to show you something," Anthony says, getting himself under control. This is business. Serious business. He wants Bernard to take it seriously too.

Bernard sits back against one of the tables, then bends down to Anthony's face. The table creaks dangerously. "I got your voicemail last night. You brought some pictures?"

Anthony holds up his backpack.

"Okay," Bernard says, standing. "I have to finish a couple things in the office. Why don't you go out and say hello to the bees? I'll come get you in a few minutes."

Mathew watches Anthony get out of the car, and waves as the car drives away, but Tony doesn't wave back. Tony seems sad. So does Dad. But Mat is happy. Trips in the car are great, and even though it's usually fun spending a day playing alone with Tony, it's always more fun to go on a car trip with Dad.

After they drive a while, they pull into a new parking lot. This parking lot is not full of cars. And there are not a lot of people. It doesn't look promising. In Mathew's experience, the more cars there are, and the more people, the more stuff there is to do.

"Behave yourself when we get into the store, okay?" Dad says.

"What's this place, Daddy?" he asks. It's not a dentist, is it?

"It's a supply store. We get wood here. And nails."

That sounds better. "And nail shooters?"

Mathew watches Dad twist the rear view mirror down and look into it. His father takes a comb and combs his hair. This is new.

Mathew sometimes gets his hair combed. But he doesn't often see Dad comb his hair. It looks silly.

"And nail shooters, Daddy? Are there nail shooters? Nail shooters?"

"No. Yes, there are, but stay with me when we get in there. Do you understand?" Mat pretends he does. He'd agree to anything for a chance to play with a nail shooter.

They walk into the store. Mathew holds Dad's hand. The store has a high ceiling and big shelves full of really interesting-looking tools and machines. But they don't go toward the shelves. Instead they head to the back of the store and walk to a door with a little window.

"Where is this, Daddy? Is this where the shooters are?"

"We're going to say hello to someone and talk for a minute. You'll like her," says Dad.

"Are there kids here?"

"No. Behave, okay?"

Something weird is going on. For one thing, Dad never just goes someplace to say, "Hello." He says other things. He says, "Pick up your room." He says, "What do you want for dinner?" He says, "Only one more show and then go to bed." But never just, "Hello."

Also, Dad's hand feels really sweaty. In fact, Mathew's hand slips easily out of Dad's grip when Dad knocks on the door. A lady's voice answers.

"Come on in."

Dad opens the door and they go in. It's just as Mathew feared: a grown up room. Metal boxes where papers are stored, a desk, a boring picture of a man on the wall. Then from behind the desk a lady stands up. A pretty lady.

"Hey," she says, looking at him and smiling. "Mathew? Do you remember me?" Mathew does not. But he nods. He's found it's never a good idea to tell a grownup you don't remember them.

"He remembers me, Paul." She seems happy. He picked right.

"Probably not. Mathew, this is Miss Jensen," his dad says. "You might have met her a long time ago, when you were a baby. Before . . . "

Dad doesn't finish. Miss Jensen steps toward him.

"You can call me Cindy." She bends and holds out her hand for Mathew to shake. This isn't so bad. She's treating him like a grown-up.

He shakes her hand. Her eyes are blue. She wears lipstick. "Want to sit down, you two? Mathew, do you want some milk?"

"No, thank you, Cindy," he says. He waits for the expected gasps of surprise. You can really get grownups to sing and dance for you if you say their stupid magic words. Cindy laughs, though not as though he is completely fooling her. The sound is like happy bells.

"You're a very polite gentleman, Mathew, and I'm really happy you came with your daddy today. I've been wanting to see you." Mat watches Cindy and Dad. They stand really close together. Cindy touches Dad on the arm. It makes him feel good to see someone being nice to Dad.

"Anthony's over at the nursery," says Dad.

"The poor thing. How is he?"

"Who the hell knows? It's always bees with him. It's always been that way, you know, him and his . . . his mom . . . " Dad looks confused, like when someone asks Mat why he colored on the refrigerator with green Sharpie. Dad can't think of what to say. It's interesting. Cindy puts her hand on his arm again.

"Did he say anything else about . . . " She looks at Mat. Then she does the stupid spelling trick. "J-U-M-P-I-N-G?"

"Claims it's all a misunderstanding."

Cindy sighs. "Well, maybe this is a blessing in disguise," she says. "At least the three of us can get to know one another a little. Right, Mat?"

"Mat's not the problem," says Dad.

"Of course he's not the problem. Look at him. Listening to everything you say and probably understanding more than you think." Cindy looks at Dad. She's trying to make him think something. Like she has a secret language. Mathew likes secret languages.

"Let me get my purse." She disappears into another room. While they wait, Mathew catches Dad looking at him without looking at him. A careful peek out of the corner of his eye. *What?* Mathew wonders. *Do I have pee in my pants?* He checks. No. Dad seems to be waiting for him to say something.

"I think maybe you want to give me another Pez?" he tries. You never know. It's a weird day. Cindy comes back. She smiles at them. Mathew decides to like her.

She opens the door. "Should we go walk by the river?"

BERNARD'S BEE YARD IS BEHIND THE NURSERY, AND WHEN ANTHONY enters, he instantly feels the tugs of thousands and thousands of bees. There are at least ten hives scattered around the property—tall, white supers, each with a different color striped down one side. Bernard claims it helps the bees identify their own hive.

A long gravel path weaves through the grounds, demonstration gardens and bee hives laid out at intervals. Anthony starts down this trail. There was a time when he would come here at least once a week with his mother, and while she and Bernard fell deep into conversations that never involved him, Anthony would wander these gardens. The bee hives here are as familiar to him as his fingers and toes. Now he is back among them, but four years older.

As he approaches the first hive, a small set of supers placed behind a row of thinleaf alders, he finds himself reaching inward, deep into the secret sourcing place beneath his heart. It is automatic now, just as it used to be, and he does not even try to fight it.

The six-sided shape rises in him, like a bubble seeking light from the depths of the ocean, cresting and blossoming in the corner of his eye—a small, pulsing hexagon. A visual brand on everything. He pushes a thought out, through it, and touches the hive-mind behind the alders. He knows this colony. He knows all of Bernard's colonies.

This hive-mind feels like a thunderstorm: frenzied activity and never ending motion. It smells of electricity and it is hot, one of the hottest colonies he ever touched. He smiles, remembering when he first met this hive. He had actually been a bit afraid of the relentless energy. That had been when he was three or four, first discovering his abilities. Before he realized that he never needed to be afraid of bees. Bees did what he asked them to do.

HELLO, he whispers, touching the colony with a golden thought, and bees begin surging up from the super. They know him. None of these workers had yet been born when last he touched this hive, but they know him. The hive-mind goes forward, accumulating knowledge, never losing it, passing it down through the queen and her line.

He cannot talk to or control single workers. Nor does he directly touch or command the queen sitting at the center of every colony. But it is through the queen, through her synthesis of all the thoughts, impressions, knowledge, and experiences of every bee in her colony, that the hive-mind is formed, and it is the hive-mind that Anthony touches. It is the hive-mind that he and his mother were able to contact, and urge to action.

BACK, he whispers to the bees, and they return willingly to the hive. He does not want to break their routine. The honey flow is on, and every moment counts. There is nectar to be gathered.

Anthony strolls the long path through the grounds behind the greenhouse, greeting hives like long-lost friends. Until he comes to his first empty super. He remembers the colony that once called this place home, a soft, calm hive that smelled like roses and felt like the warm air hanging over a summer meadow. He steps near it to be sure, but there is no mistake: these supers are vacant. Has Bernie sold off some of his colonies? That wouldn't be like him. His honey is famous in town; every year he sells all that he can harvest.

This is not the only empty super, Anthony discovers as he walks deeper into the garden. Out of Bernard's ten hives, four are completely empty of bees. There's not a trace, not even a lingering sensation within the box when he sends a searching thought. He walks faster to put those supers behind him.

Finally Anthony comes to the end of the path, and sits in the shade near the oldest colony on the property. The aspens here cast a deep shadow, the rattle of the leaves rushing and fading like the sea. A stream of worker bees heavy with pollen and nectar alights on the landing board, then enter the box, while a parallel stream casts off from the board and flies out into the world to fill their empty nectar pouches.

Anthony pushes a tendril of thought into this hive-mind. It's the only colony he's ever touched that was in any way comparable to his mother's. It has a depth of expression that is very unusual. When he touches it, he feels as though it might touch him back. Most hive-minds are one way streets—Anthony presents an idea or gives an instruction, and the bees follow. But this colony, which Anthony knows is Bernard's favorite, almost feels like it could talk.

His mother's colony could talk. That hive actually had a vocabulary, which Anthony had learned painstakingly over several years. His mother's hive-mind could reply with simple words, could tell the locations of nectar and sweet flowers, and communicate when a rack was full of honey, or a chunk of propolis too large to remove had fallen into the comb. That's the way her hive used to be, anyway. Now it seemed to be barely functioning at all.

Anthony closes his eyes and pulls himself closer to the shining form within him. He casts a thought deeper into the center of this colony.

SPEAK, he whispers. SPEAK TO ME.

A great uprushing of wings can be heard from within the supers, but Anthony doesn't open his eyes. If his mother's hive could form thoughts and words, why not this one? Maybe all it needs is a push. Maybe nobody has ever asked it to speak.

WHERE ARE THE SWEETEST FLOWERS? he asks. He can hear bees issuing forth, but still he holds his eyes closed. There is a spark within this hive-mind, he can feel it. He wants that spark to speak to him. He pushes more energy into his hovering hexagon, and it begins to shimmer and oscillate. He drives deeper into the center of the hive-mind before him, taking in its unique smell: oranges, vibrant and clean, with a touch of peppermint.

SPEAK, he insists, pushing hard against the boundaries of the mind, exerting his will. SPEAK! But no words come. This hive is not the equal of his mother's.

Then he hears a footstep. "Tony," comes Bernard's quiet voice. And Anthony opens his eyes.

Hanging in the air before him is the outline of a hexagon, six feet across, perfectly symmetrical, formed of bees. There is a tone, a low hum, ringing off of it, this flawless replica of the hexagonal image superimposed upon his sight. Through the center of the floating shape he sees Bernard, holding his lunch in a bag.

Has Anthony done this himself? Has he pressed these bees into this shape, unintended? Quickly he releases the hive. Bees scatter in all directions, like chaff cast to the wind. Bernard's eyes never leave Anthony. Anthony stares back. He has been discovered. And maybe this is what he wanted.

"Brought you a snack," Bernard finally says, sitting slowly beside him and digging an apple from his bag. Anthony takes the fruit with fingers suddenly numb. Bernard opens his mouth and almost finishes his own apple in one mouthful. Anthony is too confused to eat. A minute goes by; the aspens quake; the birds call. Anthony's heart beats savagely. His mother's most important rule had always been, *don't let anyone know about touching the bees*. And now he's creating hexagons in the air without even knowing it? First he breaks his promise, and now he breaks her most important rule? He feels like he's losing his mind. Finally Bernard speaks.

"If that's what you have, there's no way to keep it bottled up," he says.

"You know what I can do?" Anthony blurts, before thinking that Bernard might be talking about something else.

"Oh, I know. Best if you don't go flashing it around like this."

This is a new and entirely unexpected development. Anthony tries to piece it all together. There have been too many bewildering changes in direction over the last couple of days. His brain feels like it's moving in slow motion.

"You know I can touch the bees?"

"It's all your mom ever talked about," Bernard sighs. This is news to Anthony. He'd assumed that they had been talking about bees, or plants. "She was so far ahead of the rest of us. She saw things no one else suspected. We should have listened. She wanted to protect you."

Anthony pictures her in the hospital, the way her exhausted eyes followed him around the room. She was too tired to hide her worry. But she would never tell him what, exactly, she feared.

"Protect me from what?" Anthony asks.

"She was afraid you'd follow the path she took. She felt you had a fearful destiny. She knew you were the best of us. Are the best."

"Who's us?"

"Beekeepers, of course." Bernard smiles at him. But it seems to Anthony that there is more that he is not saying.

"But follow what path?" Anthony asks. "What's the danger?"

"Don't you worry. Big Bee's got your back"

Now Anthony is sure he detects a seam of deception running through Bernard's tone. He suddenly wishes he could send his mind questing out into Bernard's and get at the truth. He doesn't want someone to have his back. He wants to know about his mother. But all he can do is bite his apple and shake his head in frustration.

"Never changes. No one ever tells me anything."

"Tony, there's going to come a day for these questions," Bernard says. "But I don't think today's that day. We've got more important things to do right now."

Bernard points at the backpack lying by his feet, and it comes back to Anthony, the reason he's visiting the nursery in the first place. His mother's hive is sick. Maybe dying. There was nothing he could do to save his mother in the hospital. He had to watch her as she slid, like a stricken ship at sea, slowly pulled under the waves and down to death. Will the same thing happen to his one remaining link to her?

The two of them head back, up the path toward the nursery. Bernard lets Anthony get a few steps ahead, then he turns to look back at the hive. The bees are still out, ranging around in agitated circles. Anthony, marching on, does not see Bernard stop in the path, close his eyes for the briefest moment, and trace a hexagon in the air with his finger, nor does Anthony see the bees cease their airborne churning and settle back into the hive when Bernard has finished.

It's hot inside Bernard's office. Anthony takes his outer shirt off and hangs it by the door. Bernard doesn't seem to notice the heat.

"Okay, let's see what you got," he says.

Anthony digs around in his bag and pulls out the camera. Bernard takes it, flicks out the flash drive and holds it up. "You could have e-mailed me these," he says.

"I'm not allowed on the Internet right now," Anthony tells him. To anyone else he might have made excuses. Bernard takes the information with nothing more than a glance and a nod of his bearded head.

"What happened to your hives? You've got four empty supers," Anthony asks as they wait for the pictures to load.

"Colony Collapse Disorder," Bernard says, shaking his head. "It was bad. Last year, the first in the county. Since then it's been jumping around. A few other hives failed just last month. Sherry Noble's hives. Wiped out all twenty of 'em."

Colony Collapse Disorder. The inexplicable loss of a healthy, thriving hive. It can strike without warning, overnight, and no one has been able to explain it. It's every beekeeper's worst nightmare.

"What was it like?" he asks Bernard.

Bernard shrugs and holds up his hands. "They were just gone. One day the colony was fine. The next time I looked, every bee had vanished."

"Maybe that's what's happening to my hive."

"No. If you have any bees left at all, it's not Colony Collapse." The computer chimes. Bernard leans into the monitor.

"Okay. Let's see here."

Anthony knows that many of the shots are going to look blurry. His hands had been shaking as he tried to take the photos. But he hopes they'll be clear enough. He doesn't want to have to do it all over again. When the first few pictures of comb flash up on the screen, Bernard hisses a little and leans closer. He flips through a few more shots. Then he taps the screen and turns to look Anthony in the eye.

"Well. It's not good. Your queen's dead."

Anthony shakes his head. "But there are fresh eggs. I can see them. She's alive."

"Nope. She must have died in the winter. Look at this pattern." Bernard taps the glass with a finger the size of a beer bottle, tracing the wild way the new eggs have been scattered over the face of the comb. "No queen would ever lay like that. A queen's the most efficient little machine in all the world; she'll lay in a circular pattern, use all the available cells—or just move to another comb if there's no room. But this"—he squints, lets out a breath like an elephant sighing—"this is really ugly."

"But what, then? Who's laying eggs?"

Bernard tightens his lips. It's a silent snarl. "You've got faux queens."

"What kind of, *what*? I've never heard of that," Anthony says.

Bernard spins his chair and leans back, looking at Anthony across the length of his beard like he's sighting a missile. The words come out reluctantly.

"It's extremely rare. I've never actually seen it myself. But I've heard of it. It can happen if a queen dies suddenly. But only if something else in a hive is going wrong."

"Like what? What are you talking about?"

"If a queen is sick, or old, or stops laying eggs for any reason, the hive starts to prepare a new queen. They make one themselves. It's the one thing the hive can do on its own. It's like impeaching the president. The hive has to have a healthy leader who can lay eggs. So they select an egg, and feed it a special diet of nothing but Royal Jelly. And that normal egg turns into a queen's egg, and it will produce an entirely different kind of bee, a queen. By the time the old queen is gone there's a new baby queen to take her place. Sometimes the hive even kills the old queen to speed the process. They wrap her in a ball and squeeze until she's dead."

He turns back to the screen like a doctor with a terrible prognosis.

"But if the queen dies without any warning, the colony won't have any backup ready. And sometimes, if there's been some kind of shock or change to a hive, and the queen dies, a colony can go crazy. No one knows why. Bees are complicated; nobody really understands them. A colony's like a person, with a personality all its own. And sometimes a colony can just go flippin' bonkers."

He taps the screen. "This looks like it's been going on a while. Think back to last fall. Before winter set in. Anything happen to the hive?"

Anthony doesn't have to think. "Nothing happened. I'd remember. They were fine, right before the first snow. That was the last time I did an inspection."

"Did you actually see the queen, that last fall inspection?"

He casts his mind back, trying to remember. The last inspection before winter? One of the racks had cracked, he remembers, a minor problem easily fixed. Everything else had been fine. Although, now that he thinks about it, there had been something. A feeling of loss. Or sadness. Deep sadness, which had nothing to do with the hive. It was middle school. He had just started going to middle school.

"Bees are sensitive," Bernard says. "Think. Was there a building going up nearby? They don't like noises. It could even be something like a paint job, like you repainted your house. Did anything change at all?"

I changed, Anthony thinks. *Middle school. Mom's room.* But he's not going to say that. So he shakes his head.

"Well, for some reason, your hive just stopped working right. A kind of a system failure. They didn't raise a new queen after the old one died. And now you have faux queens in the hive."

"But what is that?"

"Even though most of the bees in your hive are females, ninety-nine percent, they're just workers, not queens. They never got the Royal Jelly when they were eggs. But this is one of nature's mysteries; sometimes, if a hive loses a queen and has no replacement, a few of the existing workers can become queens. Not full queens—they don't have any of the instincts of a true queen, and they can't direct the hive. But biologically they change. Over time, they can start laying eggs. They're called faux queens."

"That's possible?"

"It is. The problem is that faux queens can only lay male eggs. So they can't make any new females. The females, the workers, they're the ones who gather the nectar and make the honey. So then you have a bunch of males in the colony, drones, eating up whatever honey stores are left, and nobody's around to work. It's as dysfunctional as bees get. The hive slowly spirals down and withers away to nothing. Unless . . . "

The tight ball of cold horror which had been building in Anthony's stomach at the thought of losing the hive stops growing. *There's an "unless,"* he thinks. Of course there is. No way this could all end with the hive dying. Bernard has the answer.

Bernard himself doesn't seem so sure.

"Unless what, Bernie?" Anthony asks.

"Unless you requeen your hive. It's just—"

Anthony is excited. "Of course! My mom talked about that. We'll put in a new queen." The solution he'd been hoping for has appeared. Bernard looks doubtful.

"Here's the thing, Little Bee," he says, tapping the distorted comb in the picture on the screen. "This hive has gone over the edge. Colonies get their personality from the queen. And if the queen is gone too long, it's like the soul of the hive just goes black."

But Anthony can see it now. He can picture it in his mind.

"This'll work," he says. "I know it will. I can bring my mom's hive back."

"Don't get your hopes up." Bernard puts a massive hand down light as a feather on Anthony's shoulder. "That's all I'm saying. Don't get your hopes up."

Anthony's not listening. He's seen books on requeening, although he's never done it before. It's an art, and it can be pretty tough if you don't know what you're doing. But Anthony knows his bees. And he does know what he's doing. Now, at last, Anthony does know exactly what he's doing.

"Where do I get a new queen?" he asks Bernard.

Bernard sighs. "Well, I'll have one shipped to you from my contacts in Virginia. Beautiful operation, bees all outdoors, strong and healthy. It'll take about four days if I have them overnight her. These are high-quality queens, from the same brood stock your mom got her original hive. They're Italian-Russian hybrids, right?"

Anthony nods. Great wintering bees, healthy and productive.

"Okay," Bernard sighs. "If there's any chance of this working, that's the place we go. Commonwealth Apiary."

Now it's Anthony's turn to put his hand on Bernard's shoulder. It's kind of like comforting a giant, warm rock.

"Don't worry, Bernie. It'll work."

THE DRIVE HOME MAKES MATHEW SLEEPY. THE NICE CLANKING AND bouncing of their great squeaky truck soothes him like he's swinging in Mrs. Hanlen's arms. In the front seat he can see his brother and Dad.

His brother seems much happier since they picked him up, and that's good. He keeps talking about the bees. Tony is nice when he's happy. And Dad is being nice too. He's talking more than he usually does. Mathew wants to tell Tony about walking by the river with Cindy, and what a pretty lady she is and how they ate hot dogs. But every time he starts to say anything about it, his dad interrupts with a loud story or a question he wants to ask Tony. Eventually Mathew nods off. And he never gets around to telling his brother the good news: he thinks he might have found them all a new mom.

Chapter Six

The Little Queen concentrates, and impressions come flooding in to her from every bee in her colony. She attends most carefully to observations from those bees outside the hive who gather sugar water from the shiny spouts of the feeders and pollen from the boxes mounted high on the walls. There is no sign of the Green Death. But she knows that it will come. Today is the beginning of her thirty-fifth day of existence. One way or the other, today is the end of her life as she knows it.

I want my hive to see the sun, she thinks to herself. *I want my hive to gather nectar from flowers. I want us to be free of this place where death comes so unnaturally. Perhaps, if I am not too young, we can have that.*

The final day passes industriously in the Little Queen's hive. She lays her eggs, and workers follow her to seal those eggs into the comb, each with a store of honey, food so nutrient-dense that the smallest amount can propel a grown bee two hundred miles. She even forgets, for a little while, the hour that is rushing toward her. But all bees have an unerring internal clock. She knows when the time arrives. She gives a little shudder; she shakes her wings. Then she begins issuing her commands.

MASK ALL THE DISKS, she calls softly, mind-to-mind. And throughout the hive, every smooth, shiny lens gets a covering of bees. She wants to move her bees around as quietly and peacefully as she can, because calm and focus will be the traits that bring them through this trial, if they are to succeed.

The Little Queen is almost entirely still, surrounded by her coterie of eighteen. No dancing, no wingsong, none of the typical behaviors a queen might be seen to display when communicating with her hive. Yet the hive is moving with uncanny speed and coordination, doing things strange and new to bees. Lines of bees move to the seams of the wooden hive, and once there they force themselves into those cracks, sealing them tight. The ventilation holes on the top of the hive are similarly closed by clots of insects. A dense rectangular phalanx waits by the entrance, ready to insert itself into the opening at a given command.

Outside, a loose swarm hovers near a faint outline in the wall. The Little Queen has placed them there, knowing they will be the first to perish when the Green Death comes, but needing to know exactly when it begins. And through it all, a continual procession of bees approaches the Little Queen herself, each with a mouthful of honey, to feed her and her attendants and fill the pouches behind their legs with food. Bees can carry a tremendous amount of honey and pollen, and the little Queen wants to make sure, if they do escape, that they do not starve before they can find a new home.

Through it all, she radiates waves of calm and assurance—despite the turbulence and fear she feels in her own heart.

And then it comes. She sees it as it happens, as her workers see it. The outline in the wall has flipped open. Though none of the bees alive in this place has ever seen it before, the Little Queen knows what will happen next. There is a snake-like hiss, and green gas pours from the opening. The first bees that it touches fall dead from the air, twitching. It floods past them, settling toward the floor.

BLOCK THE ENTRANCE, commands the Little Queen. The group of bees waiting there moves forward as one, sealing the entrance to the hive.

And then, firmly, calmly, and so powerfully that it reaches every bee within the Superhive, I WILL WEAR MY CROWN!

Instantly her colony responds. Every living bee not already assigned a task by her, twenty thousand of them, drops what they are doing and surges up to the Queen. They ring her round, and in a complex dance a hundred million years old, they clasp, each to the other, the hooks at the ends of their legs, binding her. Layer after layer, ring upon ring, until every bee in the colony not sealing or watching or guarding is squeezed down tight in a ball surrounding the queen, a ball no bigger than a full-grown rabbit.

From within this protective sphere the Little Queen monitors the progress of the gas. Outside the hive, guard bees report to her the position of the cloud, then fall silent. The gas flows across the floor toward the hive like a curling, silent storm front, and those few bees left clinging to the outside of the hive let her know when the billow engulfs them.

Then the bees blocking the entrance begin to die. Twitching and writhing, they fall, exposing the bees behind them to gas. The bees sealing the cracks in the seams of the hive similarly hold on as long as they can, but the gas does not stop coming. Soon the entrance is clear, and all the cracks are exposed. The Green Death billows into the hive and strikes the Crown like an ocean wave striking a rock. Engulfs it like a living thing. And bees begin falling away.

From the heart of the crown the Little Queen watches. With every falling bee, her anxiety mounts. Her connection with her children, the connection between a queen and her colony, which for so many millions of years has been so pure and instant, must become tangled now. Buffered. If her bees read her fear, they will swarm, and if they swarm they will die, exposed individually to the searing death of the cloud around them.

So she breathes and waits. All the bees masking the disks are quickly killed. Then the gas goes to work on the Crown. The outermost bees, clinging to the backs and legs of their sisters, are burned and die. But they are packed so densely together that it takes a moment for them to fall away. The gas moves deeper, to the next layer.

And the next. The Little Queen watches it come, feels it like a living enemy.

At the top of the Crown, where the bees cling to the ceiling of the hive, more space is open for the gas to penetrate, and suddenly the Little Queen feels the whole crown falling—the bees forming the anchor have been exposed, have died, and have let go. Fear surges within her, and the shock of her feelings radiates out through the colony. The massed ball of bees hits the floor of the hive and rolls, smashing dead and dying insects as it gathers speed, then strikes the wall.

The Crown loosens. No, the Little Queen says, YOU ARE SAFE, MY CHILDREN. I AM SAFE. WE ARE SAFE. THE HIVE WILL LIVE.

HOLD THE CROWN TOGETHER," she tells them. HOLD TIGHT, STAY CONNECTED, DO NOT GIVE IN TO FEAR.

This is the test all the other queens in her line failed. The Yellow Queen, four times her age, was the first and only queen to master herself and her colony. "THINK OF THE FLOWERS," she soothes. "THINK OF THE WIND. THINK OF THE SUN. DO NOT FEAR, AND DO NOT FLEE."

And the bees hold fast in the Crown, which lies on the floor instead of being suspended from the ceiling. Now the Green Death is killing bees, but instead of falling to the ground, they die atop the Crown and lie there, providing another layer of protection.

If I fail, I must pass this on to those who come next, she thinks. *Queens must learn something new, to wear a Crown that is not suspended from the ceiling, but begins on the ground.*

Despite the extra protection the dead bees provide, the layer of death creeps closer and closer. The dying bees do not resent their spent lives, they do not feel betrayed by the idea that their sacrifice may be in vain, that the colony may not survive. A bee will do anything at all to preserve the hive. Yet the Little Queen sees clearly that it may not be enough. She watches as death creeps ever inward, like rot penetrating an apple.

There are not enough bees, she thinks. *The Crown is not thick enough. The older queens, the Yellow Queen, had four times as large a hive with so many more days to lay eggs. I am too young, I could not create a large enough colony. I could not make enough children—no queen could at my age. I will fail because I did not have enough time, not because I lose control and let fear overtake me.*

It is the strangest feeling she has ever known, not being able to deploy her sight and smell and feelings outward through her colony. There is no colony. Instead of extending out through tens of thousands of bees flying, working and ranging everywhere, she feels only a numb absence beyond a densely packed and quickly diminishing sphere. One thousand bees. Eight hundred. Five hundred.

And then the encroaching line of death stops. A few bees already past the point of being saved fall from the Crown, but no new bees die.

STEADY, HOLD THE CROWN, she tells the hive. WAIT.

Soon she can hear it, even within her ball: wind. The wind the Yellow Queen spoke of. The Green Death is leaving.

Now is the time. BEES RELEASE THE CROWN! she commands. Instantly the remaining five hundred bees unlock their legs and rise, releasing their queen. She dispatches a scout to the door of the hive.

Just as the Yellow Queen reported, the air of the Superhive is turbulent with powerful gusts, clean air streaming from the opening where the death cloud entered, swirling throughout the chamber, and exiting through a new opening high on the opposite wall, cleansing the chamber of the poisonous gas. She knows that time is precious. She readies the colony.

How is it that a queen directs a body of bees to move all together, all at once? Just as a boy might pick up a stone, bend his leg, cock his arm and throw, all without thinking through a single separate element of that action, so a queen marshals and directs her hive to action. Though the colony is reduced to only a few remaining bees, they respond as though they are thousands strong. A few trackers fly ahead, the main body forms a loose ring around the queen, guards fly to the sides and behind, the mass rises, and the queen casts them aloft.

They stream up toward the mouth sucking the wind from the room. Strong buffets pull them down, then to the side, but the queen keeps them together. *Escape together, or not at all*, she thinks. And they arrive at the lip of the opening.

Suddenly a piercing scream shocks the hive. Over and over it pounds them—the alarm the Yellow Queen warned of. But in the

Yellow Queen's telling, the alarm did not begin until she was far down the tunnel. There is so much less time, the Little Queen sees. Thirty-five days instead of one hundred fifty, no time to lay eggs, no time to mature and learn control, and here there will be less time to escape. But maybe still time enough.

INTO THE TUNNEL, she commands, just as the wind stops. The alarm crying, the sudden change of air pressure—momentarily, she is confused. Then through one of her circling guards she sees, from the mouth of the opposite opening, a chilling sight: the Green Death comes again, pouring out of the hole in an almost solid stream of grue-some green. An accelerated response, like everything else.

COME, she cries, and dives into the tunnel. She senses her outlying guards touch the cloud and perish, and calls them all back to her. There is only one way to go now. She must outpace the cloud and escape down the tunnel.

The Little Queen pushes her small swarm forward. Bees do not like loud noises, and it takes all her concentration to hold them and move them in the face of the resonating siren, which, in the confines of the booming pipe they fly down, echoes even louder and more disarmingly. Yet she keeps them moving. In the face of it all, she keeps them going. Until she smells, just as the Yellow Queen said she would, the shocking scent of sunlight and leaves. Sunlight. Just ahead. She is going to escape.

She sees a final turn, and knows from the Yellow Queen that beyond that is the intersection where she must go left, and beyond that, freedom.

But when she courses around that final bend, she sees something the Yellow Queen never mentioned, and so something that must be new: a screen.

The hive stops when she stops, and mills. She retraces steps in her mind—did she miss a turn, or enter the wrong hole? But bees almost never get lost. Fundamental to their nature—in fact one of the first skills the species developed—is the ability to unerringly repeat a path, whether to honey, to shelter, or to freedom. No, this is new. Another obstacle.

The death is coming quickly behind them, reports from guards lingering near the mouth of the tunnel tell her. She calls them to her. She knows they will willingly perish to save the hive, but it is clear the cloud is coming; she needs no more information there. What she needs is a plan.

She visualizes the problem. Death billowing toward them through a confined space. Just as her sister queens had done before her, she could create a screen of bees to block the cloud, but the protection would be short-lived. The gas would kill the bees, they would fall away like so many dried husks, and the cloud would billow past them.

She needs a different strategy. If only a breeze would blow down the tunnel from the other direction, and clear the cloud, or hold it at bay. It would not take much; the cloud does not move forward on a current of any power, but rolls softly and quickly along surfaces under its own weight. It would not take much wind. And then she sees the answer.

BEES FAN THE HONEY, she cries. There is confusion among her children. There is no honey here in the tunnel. In the hive, bees will mass and beat their wings to move air across the comb, evaporating the water from the honey until the mixture becomes thick and creamy. A bee attempting to enter the hive from the back while the honey is being fanned from the front will find itself fighting through a substantial breeze. But no bee or hive has ever fanned simply to create a breeze.

She reaches out to her hive, directing them, giving them pictures and words to describe what she needs.

BEES FAN THE HONEY, she urges, calmly, showing them, thinking *Hurry! Hurry!* to herself. Sketching in her mind an image of bees spanning the tunnel, locked leg to leg so they face back toward the oncoming cloud.

And these bees, products of her eggs, themselves advanced as progeny of this higher being they follow, execute her plan. Quickly they form a row a single bee wide that rings the tunnel like a line of glue. Then on the backs of these, others build a lattice stretching from one side of the passage to the other, sealing it. At a signal from the queen, they begin to fan.

The Little Queen can see the green cloud now, rolling up the tunnel toward them. She is trapped between the mesh of bees and the screen behind her. All she can do is hope. She has no idea whether it will work.

She can feel the draft beginning, drawn from the tunnel behind her into the lattice of bees before her, pushed down the tunnel toward the green cloud. The hum of the fanning wings rises, and rises higher. The trick is to get the wings synchronized, so that each bee wing complements the beating of the bee beside it. In a hive filled with tens of thousands of bees, a very low level of coordination is all that is needed to create a useful breeze. But here, with only a few bees, more will be needed. The Little Queen can see the cloud—it has hardly slowed at all. She closes her eyes. And she becomes the swarm.

On any wing, the shape of the surface is essential to creating lift. Tiny adjustments to the curvature can create tremendous differences, and any imperfections on that surface can roil the airflow in ways that, at high speeds, can have catastrophic consequences. So now the Little Queen tunes this fanning matrix of wings as a single wing. The bees within the matrix respond as though they are extensions of her, flexing, slowing, racing as she commands. Though she has never tried such a thing before, she finds that the aerodynamics of flight have taught her much about shaping air. Taught her almost enough.

Convex, she realizes, envisioning the airflow over the surface of her own wings. She shapes the screen of bees, still beating their wings in unison, so it bells outwards in the center. And the draft multiplies five-fold. She studies the whorls and eddies of this wind and makes another adjustment, slowing the wings of the bees in the center of the screen and speeding those at the periphery. This achieves another tremendous increase in air flow.

But it's not enough. The cloud rolling forward slows perceptibly, but like a car rolling to a stop, it takes time to break the inertia, and she still does not have enough force to halt it. Now it is only five feet away.

Then she remembers her passage into the Plain of Crowns. *Shock waves*, she thinks. *Supersonic shock waves. We must pound the gas with shock waves of air.* STOP, she commands suddenly. And like a precise machine, every bee instantly ceases beating its wings. START, she cries. And in unison they do. STOP. START. STOP. Again and again. Each successive pulse creates a vacuum before it, and taken together they multiply the speed of the draft until she herself has difficulty holding her position in the roaring wind. The pulses beat on the advancing gas. And finally, boiling and frothing, it slows. Stops. Holds.

Now the colony fans while the Little Queen separates herself from that mind. She knows she does not have much time. The successive starting and stopping is taking a terrible toll on the wings of her bees, shredding them. She turns to examine the screen that keeps her from escape.

Even as she wants nothing more than to be past it, to never see it again, she finds herself admiring its exactness. Pattern recognition is built into every bee at a level far below consciousness. The repeating forms of six-sided combs are like balm to a bee mind, like a poem. But even the most perfect comb contains imperfections. When a field of comb is discovered with no perceptible imperfections, it is never more than five or six cells in any direction, and even this small patch is utterly mesmerizing to bees. But the screen before her now is flawless and perfect from the center to the edges and back.

She crawls over the surface. Here and there she pushes her foreleg through, but she will never be able to force her body to the other side.

What could have created such a thing? she wonders. Not bees. And then she has another thought that has never occurred to another bee in a hundred million years. *Are there other creatures who are bee-like?* Are there other builders? An intuitive leap. *Could humans build a thing this perfect?* Bees are aware of humans, of course. Though relative newcomers to the world that bees have inhabited for hundreds of millions of years, humans and bees share many traits.

But there is no time to consider the implications of such a thought. Behind her she can feel her hive beginning to fail. Bee wings were not constructed to withstand the shocking start-stop force that these now generate. Suddenly a wing on one of the weaker bees earlier touched by the Green Death literally tears away from her body and is sent flashing into the cloud on the wind it was itself generating milliseconds before. And then another bee loses a wing, and another.

She has only seconds more. Though she crawls over every square inch of the screen she knows that whoever or whatever created this would leave no imperfection large enough to pass her body through. But the edges. Perhaps the edges are not perfect. There must be a place where the mesh stops and the tunnel starts, where the screen joins the tunnel walls. Perhaps this seam has a flaw.

Suddenly the wind from her bee lattice falters. Twenty more bees have their wings ripped from their bodies, to watch them tumble into the bubbling cloud. This is just enough. The cloud begins advancing up the tunnel. Slowly. But with only five feet to cover, it will not take long. The remaining bees redouble their efforts, but that only brings their own demise down on them more quickly, as more and more of them simply tear themselves to pieces fanning.

Escape, thinks the Little Queen. *I. Must. Escape.* And now she begins to lose control. She is exhausted—strained physically, mentally, beyond the limits of anything her species has ever endured. And through it all she has remained calm. But now her calm slips. Not because she is a primitive being. Not because she is a lesser intellect or a failed example of her line, but because she is young. Still so young.

Then at the intersection of the screen and the tunnel wall, she finds an opening. A tiny imperfection, but large enough, where a threaded plug has come loose. She dives into it, panic overtaking her, and out of instinct she sprays pheromones, "Come my attendants! Come to me!"

The synchronized lattice behind her shatters. Bees fly in all directions, or simply drop to the tunnel floor, unable to fly anywhere, unable to move their wings. But her attendants, the eighteen fastest, most powerful bees in the hive, come to her.

The seething gas is no longer held in check and the pressure built up behind now explodes it forward down the tunnel. Her attendants push her through the hole, then one by one they begin to squeeze through themselves. But the cloud reaches them. The sixteenth is seared and dies in the hole, blocking it, and the remaining bees all perish.

But the Little Queen is through. And with the smell of grass and nectar and spring—it is spring outside, she can taste it—drawing her forward, she accelerates. Ahead she sees the branch in the tunnel. On the floor lies a pale yellow shape. It is the curled husk of the Yellow Queen, the one who made it this far, so many generations before her, but no farther. The Little Queen takes the left-hand passage now, the final lesson passed down to her from this brave creature. The left-hand passage. Into sunshine. To freedom.

Chapter Seven

River Bend Middle School nestles on a hill overlooking the town. It is surrounded by trees and painted green like a dark pine shadow. It is rounded, a symphony of soft lines. It seems to snug itself down into the hillside forest like a natural formation, a giant turtle shell half-buried by a landslide. Architects from school districts all over the state, even the nation, have visited, to gather notes and impressions, but all leave with the understanding that something like this could not be done anywhere else. It is unique to its setting.

But design is really the only thing unique about River Bend Middle School. Regardless of the colors of the buildings, any urban or forested setting, the wild organic flights of fancy of the architects who design them, the fact is that middle schools contain middle schoolers, and seventh and eighth grade students are the same the world over. Sample the air in any cafeteria in any middle school on the planet and you will find the same complex stew of hormones, peer pressure, and hunger.

During the spring, that stew begins to bubble wildly, and the middle school becomes a seething cauldron, brimming with pure impulse. Teachers call April Hell Month as the cruel double whammy of sex and sunshine pulls young minds open and fills them with giddiness and violence. The Priest River, swollen by snowmelt and beating the walls of its ancient gorge, has nothing on the human flood that rises in middle school during the first month of spring.

Between 2nd and 3rd periods, Anthony has to stop at his locker to get his science book. His locker is across the hall from the teachers' lounge door. It's a featureless landmark, one of the few doors in the building that doesn't have a number or a sign on it. When first enrolled in fall, he often studied it, wondering if it had changed at all from those days when he and his mother would meet there.

Of course, teachers' lounges don't change. Not in middle school. There is no time or energy to refresh or alter what is essentially a closet for escape. If the lock still works, the rest doesn't matter. Over the course of half a century, a few books on the shelves will rotate in and out, and the occasional piece of furniture will collapse under the weight of coffee stains and cynical humor, but for the most part, a teachers' lounge is like a living fossil, frozen beneath sedimentary strata of noble intentions, exhaustion, and cravings for sugar and caffeine.

Today Anthony finds himself staring across a river of students at that door. He can't help thinking about his mom. Every day after the bus dropped him off from elementary school, he would walk through the front doors of River Bend Middle and meet her there. He never forgets this, of course, but today it's a more clearly defined missing her than he's felt in a while. The new queen Bernie ordered is to arrive after school, and he wishes he could tell her about it. He wants to ask someone what to do.

"Little mini-stroke?" says a voice behind him, popping his anxious thought bubble.

He looks. A girl stands behind him. He turns away again. For a second he'd thought she was talking to him.

"I get those too," she says.

He turns back, slowly. He doesn't know her. But clearly she is talking to him.

"Uh. What?" he says.

"That thing. The staring. You were staring at that wall over there." She points across the crowded hallway to the teachers' lounge door.

"No I wasn't."

"When I go off staring my mom always asks me if I had a stroke. It always seems stupid when she says it. I don't know why I said it." She's holding her books to her chest. She wears glasses, which look sort of cute on her. She has Vans with drawings all over them; he wonders whether she colored them herself. He keeps staring at her, thinking that he's missing something. Why is she talking to him?

"My name's Mary," she tells him.

"Mary," he repeats. She's not in any of his classes. She's not a friend of any of his friends—the few there are.

"Your name is Anthony. Right?"

He nods.

"I work in the library."

"The library at our school?"

Now it is her turn to stare at him. He can see in her eyes that she may be reconsidering the wisdom of starting this conversation. Like she's starting to think maybe he did have a stroke.

This is all a little irritating. There's a code in middle school, which is, basically, *don't talk to anyone you don't know unless you sit beside them in class or they stole something from you.*

Talking to strange girls has never been one of his strengths. Though he's not actually sure that's true, when he thinks about it. It's pretty much an untested arena. Maybe he's really good at it.

"I know that library," he says. "With all the books." Nope. Just as he suspected.

"That's the one." There is an uncomfortable pause. Not any more uncomfortable than the rest of the conversation, just uncomfortable in a different way.

Suddenly Anthony sees Greyson, with his cohorts Sandy and Alex, heading his way. He's not sure what the protocol is, but he feels pretty confident that they won't be interested in formal introductions to Mary. Mary?

"Like I said, my name's Mary," she says helpfully. "I see your friends coming. Why do you hang out with them? They don't seem like your type. They're kind of idiots, aren't they?"

"Who?" What's going on? You're not allowed to be this frank in middle school. Are you? "What do you know about me, anyway?" he says.

"I know we check out a lot of the same books," she says as his friends arrive. "Bee stuff." She pushes off from the locker and slips into the stream of kids going by, but calls back as she disappears: "Look, if your hive ever pitches a swarm, let me know, okay? I'm in the market." And then she's gone.

Greyson, Sandy, and Alex don't waste much time staring at her, but Sandy does get in an obligatory, "Hey, nice girlfriend, Anthony, she give you a quickie?"

Anthony watches the student stream. *If your hive ever pitches a swarm*, she said. Nobody but a beekeeper would use that language. Pitching a swarm is what happens when a bunch of bees break off from the main colony in a ball and go looking for someplace new to start building comb. It's one of the main ways that beekeepers start new hives, if they can capture that ball and plant it in a super.

"You don't even know what a quickie is," Alex tells Sandy.

"Oh yeah? I had three quickies," Sandy says.

"Yeah, from your brother!" Alex crows. Sandy lurches at him. Alex dodges away. Sandy is big, Alex is little; it's like a poodle evading a brontosaurus. But Greyson is not paying any attention to them. He's watching Anthony.

"She looks like a bitch," he says. He's watching Anthony's reaction. Anthony knows it. "Am I right?"

"I don't know. I don't know her. She might be, I guess." He's not sure how much he actually likes Greyson. He's aware that he doesn't like Alex or Sandy much, but Greyson is different. In part he respects the way Greyson thrives on his outsider status. Anthony has always felt like an outsider, but it's never been comfortable, while Greyson seems happier the more he is excluded and isolated.

But respect is not all there is to it. Greyson makes him feel special. He knows it's all bullshit. On one level, anyway. But the fact is, Greyson goes out of his way to help Anthony understand how cool he *could* be. The fact that this coolness is always and exclusively at the expense of other people is something Anthony is aware of, but he's beginning to think that's just the way the world works.

Not everyone can be cool. It's survival of the fittest, as Greyson says.

Mostly, however, Greyson provides something for Anthony's brain to cling to, something other than the strange pain of going to school at River Bend Middle. It is a very, very valuable service, for which Anthony is grateful, and he feels compelled to reward Greyson with his loyalty.

"Alex scouted out the culvert. He found a hole in the fence on the fifteenth green," Greyson tells him, dropping the subject of Mary with a shrug. "It's going to be great."

"Huh?" Anthony says. His mind feels a bit like a skipping stone today. On the one hand he feels like he should be worrying about the new queen who is probably waiting for him at home right now in a FedEx package. He has some concerns simply because the package does contain bees, and Bear will be able to smell them. He intentionally left Bear in the house today, but if he somehow gets out, Anthony could envision him tearing the mailbox from the wall just for the privilege of shredding the package and getting stung on the face. He knows he should be worrying about that. That's what he's been worrying about all day.

But he finds himself thinking about this girl instead. What library books was she talking about? *Is she allowed to know the books I check out?* he wonders. *Isn't that privileged information?* He thinks back. What books could she be talking about? At various times in his life Anthony has been a voracious reader—not since he started River Bend Middle, but before that. But those books all came from the main library in town. Then he remembers.

His mom had created a special section in the school library devoted to native Idaho plants and animals, and to bees in particular. Then she had procured exclusive checkout privileges for him, long before he was a student. She got him a special card when he was in third grade, and over the years he checked out all those bee books. He still has the card. His mom's signature is fading on the back in blue pen.

So she knows I like bees, he thinks. *And she wants to know if my hive pitches a swarm. Does that mean she wants a new hive? Who is she, anyway?*

"Hey, did you hear me?" Greyson's head is tilted quizzically. Anthony shakes off those thoughts. Greyson is like a hunting animal. He's sensitive to everything in his surroundings, and his intuition is penetrating. He puts two and two together better than anyone Anthony has ever met. Anthony's mom was the only person better at guessing your thoughts than Greyson. Of course, the results are dramatically different with Greyson.

"I heard you. The golf course."

"Right. Screw those rich assholes. This is going to be great."

Alex has worn Sandy out, and now steps in to stand beside Greyson. Sandy huffs up a moment later, panting.

"Yeah," says Alex, "rich assholes. We'll destroy that green. Those people will freak! They think they can keep us out with a fence? This is going to be great!"

"When can you meet us? It's got to be at night," Greyson tells him.

"I'm still grounded. I'm not sure."

"Grounded like a baby," Sandy huffs. Sandy and Alex don't like him much, Anthony knows. Greyson has clearly placed them on a lower tier, with Anthony and Greyson above them.

"Just sneak away," Alex needles. "That's what I'd do."

"He lives on out on Old Mill," Greyson says. "Where's he supposed to sneak to? He needs a ride. We can wait."

Alex and Sandy look unhappy. Anthony nods. He doesn't know whether he's grateful or fearful that Greyson doesn't want to go vandalizing without him.

"Okay gentlemen, get to class," Mr. Harrington, the math teacher, says as he passes them. Anthony realizes the halls are now empty. He closes his locker.

The school bus drops him off at the gate to his driveway, and as he begins the long walk down the pounded dirt lane, he is hurrying, looking and listening for any sign of Bear. *Please, please*, he thinks, *let him be inside.*

He comes around the five Douglas fir trees that shield the house, and he sees the mailbox, still hanging on the wall. Now he slows. Like a panther approaching a waterhole, he moves closer. Listening. Are they there? Did they come? He hears Bear inside the house, going crazy. It's a good sign. Bear can sense a sleeping bee from three hundred yards. He would definitely know if there was a package of them right outside his door.

Anthony steps up onto the landing and opens the creaking mailbox lid. There it is: a white cardboard box. He lifts it out carefully. Printed on the sides are big letters that say, CAUTION: LIVE ANIMAL SHIPPING. His hands tremble.

He finds himself running. Get back to the shed, get to the bee yard before something happens. *Slow down*, his brain tells his feet. *Slow. Down. Nothing will happen.* So he slows. He's gotten this far. He doesn't want any disasters. Slow and easy.

The shed is well lit by sunshine, but he turns on the lights anyway. He feels a driving need inside, and it's hard to control. He wants this thing done NOW. But at the same time, he doesn't want to do it at all. He wants to skip the doing step entirely, because that's where stuff gets messed up.

The spade still sits on the counter from the night he slashed open the cement bags to fill the post holes. He hangs it back on its hook, and then takes a towel and wipes the rough wood clean. He uses the time to talk himself into slowing, really slowing. All mistakes are things you had control of at one time. It's all about thinking ahead. Which requires calm.

He's reminded of something his mom used to say, whenever he screwed up or got in trouble. "I didn't mean to," he would protest.

"Yes," his mother would say. "But you didn't mean not to, and that's the problem."

Now he makes a concerted effort not to move too fast, not to skip steps. Not to be nervous. With hands grown slightly steadier, he positions the FedEx package in a square of sunlight that falls from an open louver. From a drawer in the tool chest he takes an X-acto knife, and then, ever so carefully, like a surgeon paring away skin, he slices open the shipping box.

Inside is another box with the Commonwealth Apiary logo on it, and more shipping information. He takes out the folded paper, reads the heading—"Your New Italian-Russian Queen"—and sets it aside. After taking a deep breath, he slices the tape on the top. Inside is yet another box surrounded by packing peanuts, and when he pulls this out, he can feel the warmth. There is life inside. There's no tape on this box, just a flap in a hole on the top, like on a cereal box. He pops it open.

There it is. A small wooden box the size of a matchbox car. This is the shipping cage. Covering the top of the shipping cage is a mesh screen. And through the screen Anthony can see the queen.

He lifts it into the palm of his hand. The queen is buzzing and healthy. He breathes a sigh of relief. A weak queen can die in shipping, and it's not terribly uncommon for the heaving and bouncing of FedEx travel to do in even strong queens.

She has been sent along with five of her attendants, and they crowd close to her now. A queen is always attended by a special group of bees, whose job it is to feed her while she's laying, clean her, bring her water and protect her. Anthony is happy to see that all the attendants are alive as well. It's a good sign. These attendants are her children, and for them all to have come through the trip so easily means that she produces vigorous brood. He brings his face down close and squints at his new hive mother.

Instantly he likes her. She is muscular, but seems supple. The Italian-Russian hybrid has been bred for fertility and domesticity, but also for physical hardiness, to help them winter over in snowy climes, and he can tell he's received a prime example of the breed. Her wings are a glossy brown, transparent yet firm, like sweet, lacquered smoke. A covering of downy fur sweeps back from her neck and around her powerful shoulders. Her eyes are black and quick, deep pockets of onyx on her yellow face. And around her tail are the classic black stripes of her strain.

Anthony turns the box in his palm. On one end a small hole has been drilled through the wood, and plugged with a soft candy insert, a hole just big enough for the queen to crawl through. After she has been introduced into the hive, the colony will slowly eat away at this plug, and in two or three days they will release her. In that time they will have had a chance to become accustomed to her smell, and to accept her as their new queen.

From among the shipping peanuts he lifts a tiny tool, a sharp metal shaft, and slowly, carefully, pushes it through the center of the candy, so that a little opening has been created. The queen backs away from the pointed end of the shaft. This hole will help the colony eat through the candy and make sure the queen is freed in good time.

"Don't worry, beauty, I'm not going to hurt you," whispers Anthony. "Never. You're the new boss." She flares her wings and buzzes. He replaces the piercing tool on the counter. Now it's time to make the introductions.

Carrying his inspection tools and the tiny shipping box with its precious occupants, he steps out of the shed into the sunlight of the bee yard and crosses to the hive. "Beehave, bee hive," he singsongs as he approaches. The bees are quiet this afternoon. He has noticed a definite decrease in the foraging activity of the hive since Bernard helped him understand the problem. It's as though the bees, finally revealed, are no longer making any attempt to keep up appearances. He stops several feet away and holds the new queen forward to show her the hive, the flowers, the backdrop of mountains.

"It's beautiful here," he says "but the hive is tripping out a little bit. They need you to put them back on the right track."

He brings her close to his lips, and whispers, "It's really a good colony. They're just going through a rough patch. They need a queen, someone strong. Someone to love them and look over them."

And now it is time. He reaches down into his chest, the throbbing there already growing, and lifts up out of the shadows his glyph of glowing geometry. When it has spread, and rests in the corner of his eye, he sends out a thought, Down. It's an odd feeling, communicating with a hive-mind which has such a diffused center. But he knows he has been heard, for there are no bees on the upper racks when he levers open the hive. He doesn't need much space. In fact, the less the bees are disturbed, the better. As soon as the lid is clear, he pushes the shipping box with the new queen in on top of the racks, then presses the top back home. It's done.

Now the hive will discover the queen and begin the process of chewing her free. There will be a period of quiet, even greater quiet than the hive is exhibiting now, while the bees adjust to their new circumstances. And then the queen will emerge, begin laying eggs, and the colony will rapidly start to recover.

But as Anthony backs away from the hive, he's troubled by an odd feeling. He tries to track this feeling down—it's like nervousness. Or worse, dread. Did he leave a tool in the hive? Has he forgotten a step in the procedure? He stops and very carefully retraces the steps in his mind. As far as he can see, he's done everything right. So why this feeling?

It is almost like a physical thing. An unexpectedly familiar thing. A black thing. And it's coming from the hive. *Oh my god,* he thinks, *I'm going crazy.* There is a hot feeling pulling itself through his stomach, and it doesn't feel like hunger.

Holding the hive tools, he returns slowly to the shed. A heavy stillness lies over the bee yard, like someone poured thick syrup into the air. *That's all it is,* he thinks. *Usually the yard is buzzing like a chainsaw. It just sounds so weird—it's just the quiet freaking me out.* He replaces the tools and exits the shed.

It's going to be a challenge to leave the bees alone for the next few days, but it's an important step. He heads back toward the house. They need a chance to bond with the new queen. He pushes his edginess down, forces himself to concentrate on relaxing. After he gets through the next few hours it will be easier.

Then it comes. A sound, like an avalanche roaring closer. It hits fast, the snarling crack of fifteen thousand bees exploding out of the hive—the thick, angry roar of swarming. He turns. Behind him in the bee yard, a swirling cloud of airborne insects expands around the white hive. He starts to run back.

Then, as though someone has switched on a giant bee magnet, the whole swarming cloud pounces inward at the hive. They coat the white wooden super in a seething jacket of angry brown. Anthony has never seen anything like it. It's as though the bees are attacking themselves, like they have turned against their own colony. Like they are trying to kill themselves. The feeling of disquiet churning inside him bursts upward, through his mouth, distending into full-blown terror. He screams.

"No!" he yells as he runs. "Stop!"

He bends his will toward the hive, stoking the heat inside him up to a wildfire and sending out the thought, STOP! DOWN! But there just isn't anything solid to connect with. The bees continue to seethe and froth over the surface of the super, like acid bubbling on a countertop.

And then it's over. As quickly as they expanded out of the hive, the bees disappear back inside. But they are making a sound, a loud and rhythmic groan. He sprints back through the shed and grabs an inspection tool, then runs from the shed out into the bee yard.

The rhythmic beat in the hive is accelerating and getting louder, crescendoing into a sound like a car engine tearing itself apart from the inside. But as he reaches the hive, there is sudden silence.

He shoves the pryer under the lid and lifts. He is beyond caring about injuring a few bees. What he wants is to prove that the certainty welling up in him is wrong. What he wants is to prove that he's not too late.

There are no bees visible under the lid. They have all retreated to some other part of the hive. But in the shadows he can see the shipping box, a dark shape like a cigarette lighter. He grabs it and pulls it out. When he looks at it he almost drops it to the ground.

The queen and her attendants are dead, pierced through the wire screen atop their little prison by a hundred pulsing stingers. The stingers linger, ripped from the thoraxes of the attackers, still caught in the mesh, pumping poison with tiny, reflexive contractions.

The colony has rejected the queen. Not by ostracizing her. Not by refusing to feed her, or failing to attend her. Not even by balling her and slowly squeezing until they kill her. No, this hive has rejected this queen by assassinating her. That's the only way he can understand it. This is a crime. He lets the queen in her box fall to the ground. And he stares, aghast, at his silent, senseless hive.

This is the end. His mother's hive is gone, replaced by whatever the bees here have become. His final connection to his mother has been lost. Brutal, inexorable sorrow brings him to his knees, where black arms wait to cradle him, and shut out the light.

Chapter Eight

S pring is like hot rapture coursing through the Little Queen's body. It is at once exactly as she knew it would be and entirely surprising.

She feels wildness inside her, a fierce recklessness, an irrepressible desire simply to fly—in circles, up through the pines, down through the thickets of bluebells and grouseberry. To fly and fly and never to stop because there are no walls around her. For the first time in five thousand generations, no walls.

And so she does fly, and her attendants strain to keep pace. It is the first, and will be the only, time in her life that her actions are not tied to the health and life of the hive but instead reflect some fundamental, private passion purely her own.

After a time her instincts, her impulses to guide and manage the hive, finally creep back and assert control, and she slows. It is late afternoon and the sun is getting low. She alights on a hard granite wall above a small spring. She gazes out at the wide world, her world, surrounded by a sea of blue lupine and brilliant scarlet paintbrush, and begins to take stock.

Her attendants gather at her sides, buzzing with excitement yet exhausted, and she feels guilty. She has run them hard. Though they are the strongest and fastest in the hive, they are still no match for her in terms of endurance, speed, or strength, and they have spent the hours since the escape wasting precious energy to stay by her side. Her first mistake, and not an auspicious way to begin this new life.

She counts. They are few, only fifteen instead of eighteen. Some were lost in the tunnel. Under normal circumstances she would add three, or cull three, to achieve a perfect multiple of six, but the present circumstances are not normal. It will take every resource the Little Queen can muster to bring them safely through to the next stage, and living bees are the most important of all resources. With living bees, she can move mountains.

Several of her attendants have injuries sustained in the escape. None must be allowed to perish from infections in these wounds. On the three workers who were burned by the Green Death and who have seeping sores, she herself smoothes honey, that powerful, natural antibacterial agent. Queens know of this property of honey, its ability to stave off infection and kill the tiny agents of disease, but typically think it a waste of food to use it this way. It is easier to lay more eggs and raise new bees than to replace honey used as a balm. But she needs all her children alive.

Two of her workers have broken limbs. These will set on their own, in time. It will slow their honey foraging, however, and if the limbs become infected the bees will likely die. She dips again into the treasured honey stores carried in the foraging pouches behind each leg of her workers, and coats the wounds. To make certain that the wounds are sealed, a thin coating of propolis must be applied like a cast. This means that now she must make her first difficult decision as a free creature.

In the few hours left before night, should the colony—and she thinks of them as a colony, though there are only sixteen, counting herself—spend time gathering plant sap to create propolis, or search for a protected spot to spend the night? They cannot spend the night in the open; they could freeze, and they risk being eaten by any number of prowling enemies. They must find a small hole, or a hanging embankment, or a crack—something to multiply the heat of their bodies and protect them from predators. But she also knows she cannot afford to lose even one of her surviving bees to the injuries they suffered.

So she gambles. She sees a copse of Douglas fir a mile up the stream, near the end of this shallow valley. If they are lucky they will be able to find both sap and shelter in that grove. She knows that to survive at all, they will have to be lucky many times over.

She leads her exhausted corps of fifteen bees away from the spring and toward the trees, staying low to avoid the evening birds and the bats now waking.

Halfway there, they stop at a pool to drink. Around them, night sounds have begun: crickets, the mating calls of Junebugs, somewhere wet a chorus of frogs tuning. She is suffused with such feelings of relief and joy that she must constantly work to keep her mind focused on the dangers at hand. But she is not the only one enraptured. Her children are spellbound.

IT IS GOOD, MOTHER, they say, drinking and listening. The cool evening air blows past them, carrying the scent of night-blooming mountain horsemint and suncup. Even so simple a thing as the changing temperature makes her breath come quicker, and electric bliss clouds her mind. This is the first time in five thousand generations that any of the Sequestered have felt a single variation from the dead, constant warmth of the Superhive.

COME, WE MUST MOVE BEFORE DARKNESS IS COMPLETE, she tells them. So they form a phalanx, with the Little Queen at the center, and continue toward the trees.

Generally bees do not travel at night. Instinctively they will retreat to the hive, or simply lie low on the ground without moving when darkness comes. It is rare for a worker, let alone a fertile queen, to venture out after sunset, but the dark is well advanced by the time the Little Queen's phalanx reaches the stand of fir. Bees do not have well-developed night vision, and they are susceptible to cold—it makes them slow, and easy prey for the variety of hunters who feast on them. But this is not the first time, nor will it be the last, that the Little Queen acts in contradiction to her instincts. And she is rewarded as soon as they enter the trees. Luck favors the bold.

The overwhelming smell of the sap flow had been building as they neared the dark wood, and as they fly into the deeper shadows among the trees, this scent momentarily blocks out all others, the way bright radiance will blind eyesight until the pupils adjust. But here at least one of her needs has been met. Here she can find all the sap she will need to bind the wounds of her colony, and to begin building a hive. Propolis is essential for gluing wax and sealing comb. She knows instantly that her new hive will hang somewhere here among the trees.

Up, CHILDREN, she says, and the formation rises into the branches. Below, dappled shadows cast by the bright moon mingle with faint phosphorescent patches where insects creep over the forest floor to light the mossy carpet. But the beauty of the scene is lost on the Little Queen. She knows what she is looking for. She examines the trunk of the tree as they rise, circling slowly. Until she sees it.

Beneath a thick branch where it joins the smooth white trunk, she spies an opening. A bowl, a natural resting place, covered and hidden yet accessible. It is perfect—so perfect that it may already be occupied.

DAUGHTER, SCOUT THE HOLE, she instructs one of the healthy bees. This bee zooms forward instantly. The Little Queen waits, watching through the senses of her scout, nervous. But she can see her answer before the words come back.

MOTHER, THE HOLE IS SAFE. She leads her troop in, and finally they can rest.

But only for a moment. Quickly she sets five of them to drawing sap from a seep hole on the lip of the bowl. The injured she huddles close together; until she can attend to their wounds further she does not want them growing cold. And now she takes a walking tour of this nook. Hoping against hope that they have found a place where they can build a hive.

The bowl is dry, protected from above by the mighty branch. It is deep, affording them an easy, curving surface upon which to lay the first layers of comb. Once they have propolis available they can seal parts of the opening, creating an easily defensible entrance. She is pleased, pleased beyond hope. This is where they will begin their new hive. It is perfect.

Back to the entrance now, where the injured bees huddle, she discovers that one of the bees most grievously scarred by the Green

Death will not survive more than another day. But even so, there may be work she can do. She sets this bee to making propolis. Even if she only produces a little, it is better than dying without aiding the colony.

THANK YOU, MOTHER, she says, shuddering as she makes her way to the sap. She is grateful to be allowed to serve, even in her final hours.

The other bees will survive, the Little Queen decides. And now she must begin the monumental work of planning her hive.

A bee hive is a vast and complex machine, with dozens of specialized jobs, each of which is performed by bees going through certain stages of life. As through a long series of pubescent transformations, bees change as they age to assume various roles in the colony. At birth they are cleaners, with special hairs and thin limbs to reach into cells and collect refuse. Then the first transformation shapes their bodies, and they become nurse bees, with special glands activated to produce Royal Jelly to feed the queen, and Worker Jelly to feed the others.

After that comes a third stage, the wax bee. Here, the jelly glands shrivel and four new glands begin secreting beeswax. At this stage, a bee becomes dedicated wholly to producing and building honeycomb. Now the Little Queen realizes that all her attendants are well past wax bee. In fact, they have moved through all the stages—mortuary bees, fanning bees, water carriers—and now have entered complete adulthood, to become foragers. Without wax bees, there can be no comb. And without comb, no honey, and no eggs.

In the one hundred million-year evolution of beekind, this is not the first instance of a queen finding herself stranded in a colony bereft of wax bees. A queen has the tools, if she will look deep enough, to solve this problem. They are dangerous tools, called on only in an emergency. They are not always successful. But the species has evolved for such a circumstance as this.

A bee is eminently susceptible to the intricate chemical cloud a queen emits at all times. This mist of pheromones is like the living, breathing timepiece that keeps the entire hive synchronized and functioning. For the most part these regulating chemical signals are produced without a queen's conscious thought, and acted upon without choice by her workers. But the pathway from queen to worker is extremely powerful, and there are times when the queen can use it to literally reengineer her hive.

Just as puberty in mammals is a result of a complex stew of chemical substances that change the biochemistry of the organism to produce growth, sexual viability, and new strength, so the stages of bee life are regulated by chemicals created in glands. But a queen and her workers are so intimately connected that she can take a bee forward in its development, to a later stage, by the concentrated use of chemical signals. It's as though the bee's own body is sending it new signals. This takes a tremendous amount of energy, and it is never attempted by a queen as young as the Little Queen. But it is possible.

And if that is possible, she thinks, might it not also be possible to go the other direction? To regress her bees to an earlier stage? Nowhere on the Plain of Crowns has she ever seen, or heard of, such a thing. But as with so many other things, the Little Queen is willing to try this if she can save her colony.

FEED ME, she instructs the five bees not chewing sap or recovering from injury.

MOTHER, WE WILL FEED YOU, they respond. And they bring mouthfuls of honey to her, gathered from the pouches of all fifteen bees. Back and forth, over and over, filling her up with fuel.

The temperature of her body begins to rise. Deep in the ventral segments of her abdomen, the heat stimulates the Queen's Bell, the royal gland hidden near her heart. She closes her eyes.

The only thing she has ever experienced akin to this process is the transition to the Plain of Crowns. It is a mystical process, fraught with dangers. The undeveloped biochemistry of the Little Queen's body could easily run away with itself, heating her beyond her ability to cool, killing her in a fever of her own creation. But she needs the heat to bring the Bell to life.

The heat crests within her, and she feels a new sensation, like silver fire glancing through her veins. Her body is hot, so hot that her attendants stop feeding her and cower back against the walls of the bowl. Now the Little Queen tightens the muscles of her abdominal cavity as though she is squeezing herself into a tiny ball, and she brings her Bell alive.

It feels like a second heart, but a powerful, dangerous heart with a pulse that might rip her to pieces. She comes close to losing consciousness, but steadies herself. Then gripping, releasing, gripping in rhythmic contractions, she fills the bowl with the hot perfume of bioactive chemistry. It hits her bees like a hammer; they tremble, and their legs weaken. They begin to convulse, in unison with her own contractions. Fluid leaks from their bodies, and trembling waves rack them from front to back.

The heat in the bowl builds until the Little Queen feels she will be consumed. Her bees lie flat, loose, slug-like on the bark—and then the Little Queen reaches her limit. If she pushes her Bell harder, her body heat will mount beyond her ability to regulate. Even now she is close to the edge.

She breathes, and begins to release the taut, burning muscles banded in her abdomen. Her trembling subsides. Her temperature begins to drop.

QUICKLY, she manages to say, TO ME. ALL MY CHILDREN, TO ME. And one by one they crawl to her side, bind themselves together, and fall senseless in a ball. As she is fading into restfulness, the Little Queen sends her thoughts through them, and she sees—wax bees. She has taken one more step toward building her new home.

IT IS DARK WHEN SHE AWAKES. HOW MUCH TIME HAS PASSED? A FEW hours. She is already beginning to recover. But something has awakened her. Something is not right in the bowl.

She sends her thoughts out, but there are no guards. All her bees are sleeping, balled and recuperating. What is it that has brought her awake?

BEES ARISE, she instructs. It takes a moment. This kind of transformation, from forager back to wax bee, is traumatic, and requires rest. But she needs them awake. She senses danger.

ALL MY BEES, ARISE! she commands, and one by one they wake, weak and confused. As they begin to sort themselves out and untangle, she crawls out of the ball and peers at the bowl.

At first she sees nothing. The moon has dropped low and shines directly through the opening, and there is clearly nothing within their nook. But then she hears it: the buzz of insect wings passing outside. It comes again. Something circling the tree. Something large, and fast.

GUARDS TO THE ENTRANCE, she instructs—this simple command, like all her commands now, made mind-to-mind. The strongest of the bees gathers herself and moves to the opening. The Little Queen can see her clearly, outlined against the moon. And then, as the Little Queen watches, a shape rises into view beyond her guard, hovering just outside the opening on black wings that blur the moon: an insect.

It takes a moment for her to place the shape, but she does. Hanging on razor sharp wings, peering through the entrance to her new home, is a wasp.

A wasp. It can only be a fluke. The wasp is probably lost. Maybe sick, but not a threat. It's very unusual for a wasp to be out at night; they are creatures of the light. But for a wasp to trouble a colony of bees who have no combs and no honey is beyond unusual; it just does not happen. Wasps are thieves. And though they are the ancestral enemies of bees, they are drawn by food. There is nothing here that might attract a wasp.

And then another black shape appears, slowly descending from above, to hang, buzzing, at the entrance. And a third. Still the Little Queen, based on millions of years of knowledge about the behavior of all the animals with which her kind has ever interacted, feels confident. What would a wasp want here?

Then the three insects land on the lip of the bowl. The Little Queen is surprised, and decides she must take sensible precautions.

GUARDS TO THE ENTRANCE, she commands quietly. A few more bees, shaking off the effects of their transformation, move to stand between the queen and the interlopers.

Now that their wings are still and she is able to get a good look at these flyers, she begins to reconsider her classification. Wasps? They have some of the characteristics of a wasp—the elongated thorax, the hairless body, the fierce jaws—but something about them seems alien to that species. For one thing, they are huge. They are thicker, taller, and more muscular. The eyes are farther forward on the head. And the wings are much, much bigger, with massive muscles pinning them to the back. Each wasp is the size of three of her workers, despite the fact that her workers themselves are much larger than normal bees. If these are wasps, they are an entirely new species.

They begin walking into the hive.

Time to make a show of force. To warn off these strange visitors. The Little Queen chooses the single bee she could afford to lose, if the unthinkable happened.

Guard forward, says the Little Queen to the terminal bee in her group. And that bee, seared and dying from the green poison that burned her, slowly marches forward to stand in the path of the foremost wasp.

The three black insects are not exactly alike, she sees. The two who have moved farthest into the bowl are similar, but the one who lingers behind is larger.

The injured worker rises up and beats her wings, positioning her stinger to strike. It is a well understood warning in the insect world. Approach no farther.

But the Little Queen sees the leading wasp rear up itself, and present its own stinger. And then, shockingly, she hears in her mind a single word. Uttered by a *wasp*.

Die.

The muscular stinger of the rearing wasp darts forward blindingly fast, pierces through her injured worker and emerges out her back, as easily as though penetrating a leaf. The bee manages to twist, as she dies, and plunge her own stinger through a shiny black hip. She convulses, and her stinger rips from her body, to continue to pump poison into the wasp. But bee venom is less powerful than that of wasps.

The wasp retracts its stinger, and the bee begins to die. Of course, this bee has already doomed herself by stinging—when a bee stings, tiny barbs in her stinger deploy within the victim. The end of her body is literally ripped away and left behind to continue to pump venom. But wasps can sting again and again. And as this wasp moves forward, bee stinger pulsing it its side, it is obviously preparing to do exactly that. It bats the convulsing guard aside and steps farther into the bowl. Its companions step with it.

Bees have a single age-old strategy for dealing with invaders who enter a hive, a strategy based on having a virtually limitless number of bees to deploy. Because a bee will die when it stings, bees meet any invader one by one. If five hundred bees mass around a wasp and sting it, then all five hundred bees will die when their stingers are pulled from their bodies. But if five bees, one after another, meet and sting the invader, it might back off. If not after five, then after ten. Eventually, spending just the minimum number of bees to do the job, the invader will either be killed or driven away.

But the Little Queen does not have a limitless reservoir of bees to call upon. The job must be done quickly, or not at all. So she changes the age-old tactic. She must drive her bees to do yet another new thing.

SWARM! the Little Queen commands. And all her attendants spring to action. Fourteen bees divide into two groups, seven to a group, and surround each of the two closest wasps, wings beating in a fury.

BALL THEM—BIND! she commands. Her bees lock their arms and legs around the wasps, and begin to squeeze. But the wasps are too big; their powerful wings open and the bees are scattered.

BIND AND STING! she cries. Again her workers swarm the attackers. They are weak from their transformation, their stamina is low, but from somewhere they are able to summon the strength to grapple, and this time they cling tight. As they squeeze the wasps, they plunge their stingers into the black bodies and deploy their venom.

The wasps, swarmed by these large, ferocious insects, and unable to reach them with stingers, use their massive jaws. First one bee and then another is brutally scissored loose and cast aside.

Now all the workers have plunged their stingers in, and the wasps are slowing, but her children are bleeding out vital fluid, which coats the wooden floor of the bowl. If they had not just been regressed, had not just a few hours before burned through so much of their reserve energy, they might still hang on, even after losing their stingers, even after losing so very much blood. But now they are simply failing. It is too much.

A queen is different from her children. She has no barbs on her stinger. A queen may sting as often and as deeply as she wishes. And as first one wasp, and then the other, shakes free of the swarming bees and staggers forward, the Little Queen in her turn moves to meet them.

She is larger than her children, thicker, stronger, and faster. When she rears up she is the same size as the wasps. They are slowed by the stingers clinging to their sides and back and the poison in their veins, and they confront a foe much more formidable than the ones they just dispatched, but still they move forward.

What is going on, she thinks? *What do they want?*

DIE, she hears them say, in her mind. And they reach her.

She reacts without thinking. With one swift motion she flips the wasp on her left and holds him down, then slides her stinger up through his abdomen, cutting him open. The second wasp lunges at her side with its dagger-like tail and knocks her backward, failing to penetrate the thick plate of her armor but bowling her over with its weight. The first wasp, though spilling its entrails from its belly, struggles to its feet and launches forward, pushing her farther back against the wall. She feels one of her wings crack as she lands. Both wasps advance.

But she is simply too strong. She lifts the injured creature, and twisting it viciously with three of her six legs she rips one wing from its body, then plunges her stinger through its head, instantly killing it. She slams the second wasp back against the wall and holds it there, pumping her stinger into its soft belly and ripping upward, spilling its dark blood against her breast. When it stops moving, she drops it and steps back.

But her fight has only begun.

ESCAPED QUEEN, she hears in her mind. And she turns. The third wasp, the largest one, stands on the lip of the bowl, moonlight shining off its black hide, dark jaws clacking soundlessly. Fresh. Hungry. A predator.

ESCAPED QUEEN. DIE, it says. And it lunges.

This wasp is to its companions as the Little Queen is to her workers—faster, stronger, and smarter. She backs up, and it follows. She feints to the right but it matches her. She maneuvers around the bodies of her workers, but the wasp will not be fooled.

Quickly it strikes. Desperately, barely fast enough, she dodges. She is tired from transforming her children earlier in the evening. And this beast is more aggressive, more sure of itself. She cannot meet it face to face. She slides backward, stinger ready, until she bumps against the wall. There is nowhere to go.

ESCAPED QUEEN, DIE! come the simplistic words in her mind. She has no time to wonder at this. Wasps should not have mind-to-mind. Wasps do not attack unprovoked. Wasps do not hunt in groups. She has no time to think. She has only one move remaining.

The wasp is preparing for a killing blow, knowing she is trapped against the wall, assuming it has a moment to set up an attack that will take it around her still dangerous stinger. And in that pause, she strikes.

She lunges, grabs its neck and pulls it close, and as it lifts its stinger back, she plunges her own stinger in—her slender blade pierces its tail front to back, and holds it. The wasp strains. It bears down with its weight, inching its stinger closer, but then it stops. It is only impaling itself farther on her own blade. She holds it fast.

This is not a fatal blow, but the wasp is stuck. It cannot sting because she has not withdrawn her stinger, and it cannot pull free of her stinger because she clutches its body against her with all her strength.

For a moment they strain, rocking this way and that among the bodies scattered through the bowl. A stalemate. Until the wasp turns its face down and looks at her with its black, dead eyes. And says, into her mind, KILL BEE ESCAPE DIE.

It begins to saw slowly into her shoulder with its enormous black jaws.

Searing pain. Her upper body is utterly defenseless; if she pushes the wasp away, it will strike her with its stinger, so she has no choice but to hold it close. There is nothing she can do now. Those jaws are too sharp. She can feel the gash deepening quickly as the wasp bites and twists. She can feel the meat around her shoulder separating. Soon this wasp will simply cut her apart, cut her arms off her body. Then it will sting, and she will be done.

WHY? she shouts, into its mind, into its eyes. But she hears nothing. Why do this? What do you want?

After all she has done, all her bees have done, down the generations, trapped away from the sun and wind and earth—to escape at last, and have it end like this? The bees in the Superhive will not get another opportunity. Now that she has fled, there will be more screens, less time, more gas—the Green Death will come in ten days, not thirty-five. The disks will multiply. She was their last chance. And she has failed.

Something changes as she thinks these thoughts. She feels it in the wasp's grip. A picture forms in her mind: gas. Green gas. Terrible, fearsome gas without end. And then she realizes it is not in her mind—it is in the mind of the wasp.

The wasp knows the Green Death. How can that be? This wasp knows the gas that has killed the Sequestered for five thousand generations. And more, it fears that gas. She sees an opening.

THE GREEN DEATH! she shouts back into its mind. THE GREEN GAS WILL COME. THE GREEN DEATH WILL KILL YOU. THE GREEN DEATH IS HERE NOW!

The wasp loosens its bite, just for an instant, to look behind it in the bowl.

In that instant the Little Queen withdraws her stinger and strikes upward at the wasp's unguarded belly. She cleaves her stinger through that black thorax, and then up, up into its abdomen. The wasp twists. Enraged. Its black eyes meet hers.

YOU DIE! it insists. YOU DIE!

Are those the only words it knows? she wonders. The black beast throws itself sideways, strikes at her with its horrible jaws, but she has the leverage now. And she does not relent. She bears her weight down, forcing the wasp onto its back. She drives her stinger higher, upward, rooting inside its body, up toward its heart.

Together they slide across the floor. The force of her attack, inch by inch, bearing them backward, with her stinger punching farther and farther through its guts, sliding them both nearer the lip of the bowl.

The wasp still struggles, but the end is coming. And in its eyes she sees—it knows this. This is not like any wasp bees have ever seen before. This wasp knows what it is to die.

WHY? she implores, one last time. She waits, and feels its heart, at the tip of her stinger deep in its breast, stop beating. Then she rises up slowly, pushes away from the black body, and pulls free. The wasp teeters a moment on the edge of the bowl, then topples backward. It falls, down through the night to the forest floor below.

When she wakes next it is morning. Before she opens her eyes she hears the birds. She feels the warmth of the day. Then she smells blood, and remembers.

The Little Queen is smeared with blood. Her own blood, her daughters', and the dark, acidic blood of the death wasps. Her shoulder aches, deeply cut. She rises gingerly to examine the wound. And in the light, she sees the bodies piled around her. Her daughters, and the wasps.

Near the opening to the bowl she sees tiny shapes buzzing past. She cannot remain here, she knows. Soon the sweet odor of blood will draw the carrion eaters: the flies, the beetles, and most dangerously the birds. She must flee. Again. Alone.

At the edge of the bowl she pauses to look back. She does not know where she will go. Without workers, she cannot create a colony. Without a colony, she has no future and no purpose. *I have failed*, she thinks. *Too young? Too weak? Could another have done a better job? There will be no way forward now. I have failed the colony.*

Beating broken wings and clutching her torn arm to her side, she rises haltingly into the air and flees, leaving behind her the ruined hopes of five thousand generations.

Chapter Nine

The school bell rings. Twenty-five 7th grade English students rise as one, a river full of spawning salmon leaping toward a waterfall named Vacation.

"After spring break we will begin studying prepositions," says Mr. Charles over the din, "so while on vacation, do some reading. Who can identify the proposition in that sentence?"

In the back of the class Anthony watches the other students shovel books into bags. His own books never made it out of his bag today.

"Mr. Smith, will you stay for a moment?" says Mr. Charles, looking past the dodging students at Anthony. "I'd like a word with you."

Anthony hears a snicker from the seat behind him. Alex's voice, "Ooh, Mr. Smith—busted!"

"Yeah, Mr. Smith," comes Sandy's voice, accompanied by a poke in the back of Anthony's neck. "Mr. Charles and Mr. Smith, sitting in a tree, k-i-s-s-i-n-g. First comes love, then comes marri—"

"Shut up, Sandy," says Greyson. Greyson puts his arm around Anthony's shoulders. The classroom is emptying quickly. Anthony wishes his friends would follow the others. "Don't listen to these idiots. There's totally nothing wrong with Mr. Charles's gay love for you, Anthony."

All three of them crack up. Anthony simply stares. Greyson taps him on the forehead.

"What's the matter with you, Smith? Anybody home? You seem kind of zombified."

"Mr. Temple, Mr. Frenelli, Mr. Dutch, the assembly awaits," calls Mr. Charles. "Goodbye."

"My butt awaits," says Alex under his breath. Falling over each other in laughter, Greyson, Sandy, and Alex leave the room. Now it is quiet, except for the hum of Mr. Charles's fish tank in the corner. Mr. Charles stares at Anthony blankly, as though trying to remember what he wanted him for.

"Mr. Smith," he says finally, "I'll only take a moment of your time. I'm sure you are eager to rejoin your ribald friends."

Mr. Charles comes around from behind his desk. He moves like a mummy. He slowly pushes a student desk forward toward his own, the metal feet squealing as they inch across the floor. The squeal goes on forever because Mr. Charles is immensely slow. Finally he is satisfied. He points to the desk. Anthony comes forward and sits.

Looking at Anthony the entire time, Mr. Charles resumes his own seat and then turns an open grade book on his desk to face Anthony. He slides it across the desk with a bony finger. He taps an entry.

"What do you think these are, Mr. Smith?" he asks. Anthony stares.

"These are your grades. As you can see, you started well. An A, your book report on *The Call of the Wild*. Such sympathy for the dog. And then another A, our first quiz. But your grades fall off. Here." He traces the line in his book. "And then you simply stopped turning anything in. At all."

Anthony waits. He doesn't know what is coming. He doesn't care.

"Even your three companions, Misters Temple, Frenelli, and Dutch, have managed to do the very minimum and turn in pieces of paper with their names at the top. Which is perhaps all that can be expected of them. More, however, can be expected of you."

Mr. Charles leans closer to Anthony. His eyebrows seem to move with a life of their own, jumping with accusatory fervor to point directly at Anthony's nose.

"It is almost too late for you, Mr. Smith. Do you understand that?"

What does he want? Why this weird, slow lecture? But of course, Anthony knows. It's because he is his mother's son. Everybody at this school feels like they own a piece of him. Every one of them feels personally disappointed in him. They feel like they can tell him what to do. All because they knew his mom. But where has any of them been since she died?

They're not there in the morning, to call him to breakfast. Not at Christmas, to cook or sing. They think they are responsible for him, but what have they ever done for him? Hugged him when he was sick? Painted him a birthday card? Taken him shopping for clothes?

"It's not 'almost too late,'" Anthony says. "It is too late."

Mr. Charles takes a slow breath. His eyebrows furl slightly as he settles back into his chair. His finger traces a random path on the grade book, over and over.

"It is *not* too late, Mr. Smith. Not for you, at least. I'm extending the deadline for this last paper." "Why?"

"Because I can. You have until you return from spring break. Complete it and bring it to me."

Anthony waits for Mr. Charles to continue, but he says nothing. The fish tank hums. High on the walls, posters of the French Alps curl. The room has not changed in many years, probably since Mr. Charles stopped feeling comfortable on a ladder. It is a shock when Mr. Charles speaks again.

"Have you ever heard the term 'self-destruct,' Mr. Smith?" the old teacher finally asks.

"Yes," Anthony says. What now?

"You probably imagine that you know what it means." Mr. Charles smiles. "Do you feel you are familiar with this concept?"

Despite himself, Anthony's mind goes to his mother's bees. The hive that at one point had been one of the most productive in the state, had been given every advantage, had lived a life of care and love. And he sees it turning against itself. Turning to violence. Refusing to do the minimum, to gather honey, to clean. Instead, he sees it take every opportunity to injure itself and bring itself to ruin.

"I know what it means," he says at last.

"I dare say you understand the 'destruction' element. Boys are inevitably versed in destruction. However, the idea of 'self' is not so simple. You are much, much more than you think you are."

Oh my god, Anthony pleads silently, *please, just fail me, or punish me, or something, but stop talking to me.*

"We all, in this school, are a kind of a self. And what happens to one of us happens, in some way, to us all. It is as though—"

Mr. Charles squints at the grade book. His finger continues its odd doodle for a moment, then, in the silence, it stops. He sighs, and points to the door.

"You may go to the assembly, Mr. Smith," he says. Anthony rises quickly and heads for the door.

"Bring me a paper when you return from vacation. I look forward to reading it." Anthony closes the door behind him. Around him, students are moving, thickly bunched, toward the assembly hall. But he doesn't really see them.

All Anthony sees, all he has been seeing for the last three days, is the image of the new Italian-Russian queen, so healthy, so ready, so strong, lying dead in her box with her attendants. Pierced like a pin cushion by a hundred pulsing stingers. Over and over in his mind he plays the scene, and asks himself, *why?* What was the threat? Why were so many bees so willing to throw their lives away, to sting and rip away their throbbing poison sack, then crawl off and die? They were killing themselves. For what? He offered them a new queen, a chance to move on and forget their past, rebuild, and they responded with destruction. Why?

There is only one answer he can imagine—they do not want to move on. They do not want to forget. Maybe it seems to those bees that welcoming a new queen would be like forgetting the old one. And maybe their love of the old queen was so great that the idea of forgetting is unbearable. Maybe they feel like she lives in their minds and hearts, and only there, and if they let that memory fade they are losing the last trace of her. Maybe there's nothing left for them. Maybe all they really want to do is die.

From behind comes a bump, then a shove, then raucous laughter. "Hey zombie, you're blocking traffic!"

It's Greyson, with Alex and Sandy. Anthony realizes it's true, he's standing in the middle of the hallway and students have been bumping and swirling around him. But now the hall is almost empty. The spring assembly is about to start. The whole school is gathered in the auditorium.

"We been looking for you," says Sandy. "We got a little surprise." Anthony can tell the three of them are excited. Greyson keeps baring his teeth and smiling, and Alex is literally running around in circles.

"Alex, cool it, you're going to get us caught," says Greyson. Then he looks into Anthony's eyes. "So, Badass, want to come have some fun?"

When Greyson calls him *Badass* it starts a little tingle in the back of his mind. *Badass* is an identity that feels clean and separate. And new. A position he can latch on to, something with clear borders and no confusion. *Badass* lowers the bar and fits him in. Things are easier when he thinks of himself as a friend of Greyson's. There's no real thinking required. Anthony can do it, and more or less turn his mind off. It's comfortable.

"Come on," says Greyson, starting away, "before somebody sees us."

The four of them hurry through the halls, following Greyson's lead. At one point they have to duck behind a row of lockers when Mrs. Waterman appears, but she doesn't see them and they skulk on. The halls are empty. It reminds Anthony of all the times he used to come, after elementary school, when the students were gone and it was only him and his mom. It was like being alone in a giant hive. It had seemed much bigger back then, more mysterious. Corridors branching and doorways hiding secrets. Now it reverberates with the smell of lemon cleanser and the sound of shuffling feet. No mystery. Nothing unknown.

Finally Greyson leads them to a boys' bathroom near the gym. Alex and Sandy rush in, but Anthony holds back.

"You're going to love this," says Greyson. "It's totally your thing."

"What's my thing?"

"Destruction. Right? Jumping off of shit. Crash and burn!" When Greyson says *burn*, the other two whoop. Greyson smiles his excited, tight-lipped smile, like an invisible bandana is being pressed across his mouth. He holds open the door. Anthony enters.

Alex and Sandy are doing something in one of the stalls. Their excited whispers echo against the tiled walls.

"Turn it the other way," Alex says.

"I'll do it, let go," whispers Sandy. "You're an idiot, you're not—"

"You're an idiot! I'm in shop! I got this, look out."

There's a metallic rattle, and the cover of the toilet paper dispenser hits the ground and rolls out of the stall.

"Got it," says Sandy in satisfaction.

The two of them appear and stand by Greyson. Greyson walks over to the stall and examines their work, nods. Then he reaches into his backpack. He pulls out a paper bag. Alex and Sandy watch like dogs waiting for a treat, almost salivating. Anthony feels his own curiosity stirring. It's the first sensation besides dread and sorrow he's experienced in three days. He wants to make it last.

Greyson lifts a soda from the bag and sets it on the sink, then a bag of chips. Then he gingerly pulls out a dull red tube, the color of dirty blood, sealed in a sandwich bag. Alex and Sandy blink, as though straining to look at a bright light. The tube is about the length of a grown man's thumb, and there is a stiff, greenish wire sticking out of the top.

"A firecracker?" Anthony says. Alex scoffs. Greyson shakes his head.

"Oh no," he says. "Not just a firecracker. An M80. From the Philippines. There are ten grams of powder in it. This thing will blow your head off!"

Alex and Sandy do a kind of excited hop dance. Greyson slips the M80 out of the plastic bag, then holds it out to Anthony.

"Want to see it?"

When Anthony takes it in his palm it feels cold. He realizes it must have been pushed up against the soda in Greyson's lunch. The red paper is slightly tacky. It smells strongly of gunpowder. It's heavy, too— it would be a comfortable weight to throw. Sandy and Alex watch it eagerly. Sandy holds out his hand.

"Let me see."

Greyson pushes his arm down. "No way. Too dangerous."

Greyson pulls out a lighter, and shows it to Anthony. "Want to light it?"

Sandy and Alex begin to protest, but Greyson shuts them off. He stares at Anthony.

This is a dare, Anthony sees. He shrugs. "Sure," he says, and reaches for the lighter.

"No, do it in there," Greyson points to the toilet stall. "Maximum destructive force. Put it in the toilet paper roller. Seal it back up. Then blow it to hell!"

The metal lid to the dispenser is on the floor where Sandy let it fall. Anthony picks it up, along with the small screw, and holds his hand out for the screwdriver. Sandy reluctantly gives it to him.

The three boys crowd around the door to watch. Anthony kneels and begins his operation. He remembers reading books where people are described as 'feeling numb,' but it never made any sense to him. Numbness is the absence of feeling, not a feeling in itself. But now he realizes that that's not true. Numb is actually a separate feeling, complete unto itself. It spreads system wide, from head to toe. It includes hearing, smelling, seeing and tasting, as well as touch. The absence of feeling is one of the most powerful feelings he has ever known. He feels numb right now. Completely numb. He feels almost weightless he is so numb.

"Be careful," says Greyson. "Those things can be pretty touchy. Don't drop it." Sandy and Alex edge away when Greyson says this. But Greyson pushes in closer. The warning has no effect on Anthony at all. He wants this.

He feeds the fuse of the bomb though a small hole in the side of the chrome box, carefully rests the M80 on the toilet paper roll, and slides the box on over it all. Moving with eerie confidence, smooth as a surgeon, he pushes the screw into the hole and locks it down tight with the screw driver. All that can be seen of the M80 is the green fuse emerging from a hole in the side of the box.

Without looking he holds his hand out behind him. Greyson takes the screwdriver and replaces it with the lighter. Anthony brings it up close to his face and flicks. Fire sprouts, near enough his cheek to burn him. He does not flinch.

Greyson is bent down almost as close as Anthony is now, but Alex and Sandy have backed out of the stall. Greyson licks his lips. It's something a cat might do before pouncing on a rat, a combination of anticipation, nerves, and livid hunger.

"Burn it," he says.

Squatting on his heels, Anthony holds the fire to the wick. It catches. Sparks fly, smoke and fumes billow up.

"It's going to BLOW," exults Greyson, scrambling backwards. "Come on!" But Anthony does not move. The fire quickly eats up the visible fuse, then disappears into the box.

Alex squeals, "Get away, you idiot! Are you trying to kill yourself?"

From down the hall outside the bathroom comes the sound of the school orchestra beginning an enthusiastic massacre of *America the Beautiful*. Out of the corner of his eye, in the mirror above the sink, Anthony is aware of the other three. They are crowded by the bathroom door, wide-eyed. But he does not shift his gaze or turn his head from the shiny metal box hanging on the wall. The black beast that has walked beside him for the last three days now stands behind him. He feels it push him closer to the box. Closer still. Chest in. Receptive.

The last thing he sees before the explosion is a bright flash.

He awakes coughing. His eyes open, and he sees the ceiling of the bathroom. The smell of sulfur and fire is strong. He turns his head to the left and then the right, testing his body. Everything still moves, so he pushes to sit up.

His hand slips on the tile, and he falls back on his side. There is blood on the floor; that's what he slipped in. The blood is coming from a cut on his forearm. A pretty deep cut.

He gets his feet under him and stands. The toilet paper dispenser is utterly destroyed, and a huge dent has been blown into the metal wall of the stall. On the floor, mixed with his blood, are shards of metal from the box. And there is toilet paper everywhere.

It hurts to breathe. He takes a deep breath anyway, to try to locate the pain exactly. Not broken ribs, like he had when he fell out of the tree house two summers ago. This seems to be in his lungs. Probably smoke from the explosion. Stepping around the shards and the blood, he staggers over to the sink and looks at himself in the mirror.

There are black stains on his face. His right arm is bleeding, and his shirt is ripped on that side. But he is very surprised to find nothing else visibly wrong with him. He hurts, though. The numbness he felt while lighting the M80 is gone. He feels like he's been lifted by an elephant and thrown to the ground. Very close to what probably did happen.

His hands are trembling as he splashes water on his face, smearing the stains more than removing them. He takes his gym shirt out of his bag and wraps it around his bleeding arm. Then he pushes open the bathroom door.

There's nobody in the hall. Only now does he think to wonder how long he'd been lying on the floor in the bathroom, and where Greyson, Alex, and Sandy are. He glances at the clock on the wall. His vision is a blurry, but as far as he can see, hardly any time at all has passed. His hearing begins to return. He hadn't realized it was gone, but now he can hear the orchestra, past the ringing ears, attempting to play *King of the Road*.

Greyson, Alex, and Sandy are nowhere in sight. Not that he would expect them to be here. He begins walking toward his locker, and now he notices a ringing in his right ear. It's getting louder. And the side of his face is starting to ache. He touches it, then pulls his hand away. Sore. He stops then, suddenly feeling lightheaded, and leans against a wall.

When the dizziness passes he finds that he's standing right by the library. It used to be his favorite place in the entire school, but he hasn't visited since he enrolled as a student. He feels a strong desire to go and sit in his mother's Native Nook. But before he can push off from the wall, a figure comes out of the library door and toward him. He wants to move away, but finds he can't. For the moment, at least, he actually can't get his legs to shift. The figure gets closer, then slows. Staring.

"Hi," says a girl's voice. He realizes it's Mary, the girl who talked to him at his locker earlier in the week. He waves weakly with his good arm.

"Hi."

"Are you all right?" she asks.

"Yeah, sure," he says.

She looks at his arms, then at his pants. "Is that blood?"

"No... paint. Art class. Paint."

She nods. Why would he lie? She seems preoccupied with something else. She looks away, and seems a little shy. Anthony watches her. The ringing in his ear is getting worse. And now there is dizziness. But it actually helps steady him to watch her face.

"You know," she says, "I was thinking, what I said about your friends the other day was kind of mean. I wanted to apologize."

"No problem." He waves his good arm again like he's clearing away flies. "They can be dicks. Really."

"I mean, everybody needs friends. Who am I to judge?"

"Seriously, no problem."

She nods. His brain is skipping from thought to thought randomly. He feels like he might need to throw up pretty soon.

"But I did mean what I said about the bees," she says. And now she looks at him closely, in a way that no girl ever really has before. And he wishes he were in a different state to better assess the situation. What does this mean?

"If your hive ever pitches a swarm, let me know. I would love—"

Anthony is shaking his head. "No. The hive's not going to swarm."

"You never know. Later this summer?"

"Never again."

"Okay, but when your combs are full, they may run out of room and need to split—"

"No!" he says. He feels a surge of strange energy. Rage. He finds that his vision is clearing, and his balance is back. But he also finds that his voice is loud. Much louder than he wants it to be.

"My combs are not going to get full! Ever! Stop asking about the hive!" His voice echoes in the halls. Mary staggers back, surprised and afraid, but he does not stop—instead he finds himself getting louder.

"My queen is dead. My hive is destroying itself, there's going to be nothing left. Nothing left! So stop asking about my hive!"

And without waiting for her to say anything else he swings around and finds himself running. Down the hall, past the doors to the cafeteria, and out the exit toward the shop annex.

He emerges into the light at a run. The sun hurts his head. It seems to make the ringing in his ears worse. He strikes out across the yard toward the woodshop, and then keeps right on running, into the trees behind the school.

River Bend Middle is a closed campus, but it's not hard to get away if you want to. Dense woods enclose it on all sides. Anthony climbs the wooded hillside behind the school, a thick mix of Douglas fir and ponderosa pine. These trees bleed pitch from the slightest wound, and it creates a dense, thick river of scent. In his present state, the smell is overpowering. Suddenly, instead of being numb, all his senses seem to have become raw and totally exposed.

He doesn't have a plan. He doesn't know where he's going. He vaguely remembers hiking these woods once a few summers past, but hasn't the slightest memory of what lies up ahead. He climbs anyway. Faintly, behind him through the trees, he can hear the band playing in the auditorium. It sounds like it's a million miles away, a band playing songs in a different universe.

He fights his way to the top of the hill, through trees and brambles. His breath is coming in huge gasps when he finally emerges from the wood and finds himself on the edge of a valley of flowers. Grouseberry, blue lupine and brilliant scarlet paintbrush crest in soft waves up a glacial draw, following the path of a small stream. The stands of fir and pine march up the sides of the mountains above him and to either side, thousands of feet to the tree line, but in the valley there are only flowers, wind, and flowing water. He sits.

His arm aches. His head aches. The ringing in his ear drowns out all other sounds. The sunlight hurts his eyes so that he crawls back a few feet to lie beneath a spreading hemlock. He leans against the trunk. He closes his eyes. And there, despite all his pain, he falls asleep.

When he awakes it's late afternoon, and he feels much worse. He arm is throbbing, and he's desperately thirsty. The sun is getting low behind Hard Peak; cool air flows down the draw from the rocky heights. He tries to stand and realizes that something must have happened to his right leg along with his arm and ear. The muscles there are sore to the touch and his knee hurts when he puts weight on it. But the vision of trickling water in the little stream draws him. His tongue feels like a dry sponge in his mouth.

He finds a large flat rock close to the surface of the stream, lies down so that his mouth is just above the water, and begins to drink. After he's filled himself, he lies with his cheek on the cool rock and stares at the small water plants crowding the stream. His mother would have known the names for all of these plants. He had never been that interested in learning. It's one of many things he wishes he had done differently.

It takes a moment of staring at the flowers across the surface of the rock before he realizes that something else is moving in his field of vision. Something small on the rock near the stream. At first it's too close for him to bring into focus, but after a moment his eyes adjust and he sees it: a bee.

She is crouched at the edge of the rock, drinking. Instantly he sees she is a queen. Her distinctive egg-laying appendage, the ovipositor, marks her clearly. She has a bee's cape of fur around her shoulders and the characteristic pollen pouches on her legs. But she is nothing like any bee he has ever seen before.

She is too large, and she is without any stripes or bands that would designate her as Italian, or Buckfast, or Carniolan. In fact, she is entirely golden. Even her wings are golden. Now that he looks closely, he sees that she's injured. One of her wings is bent back at an angle, and her front leg is held up off the ground as though it can't support any weight. Motionlessly, he examines her, sideways with his cheek still down on the rock. She finishes drinking, and then turns to examine him.

Her breathing is ragged. He can see that she is exhausted. Her wings tremble. He expects her to fly off when he slowly moves his hand down to the rock, palm up, and lays it in front of her, but she does not. She takes a step closer. Watching him. Another step, and one more. And then she climbs onto his hand, folds her wings, and falls asleep.

Chapter Ten

L eaving the slaughter in the bowl of the tree is the hardest thing the Little Queen has ever done, because it represents for her the end of hope. The piled bodies of wasps and bees are signposts marking her life as failed. Was it because of her youth? Should she somehow have anticipated the assault? But how? And where had those wasps come from? Why had they attacked? Wasps are not night fliers, and there had been no food in the bowl. Just a small group of exhausted bees, trying to start a new life. And did she imagine it, or had they spoken mind-to-mind? It would be a frightening thing to discover wasps who could talk. Thinking wasps of any kind would be something brand new in the world. Wasps are well known by bees as malevolent and bent on destruction, but not intelligent.

Flying haltingly out through the trees which just the night before had seemed to be their salvation, the Little Queen feels absolutely cut off. To be without a full hive is one thing, but to be truly alone? For a queen, it is a thing unheard of.

When she emerges from the shadowed wood into the sunlit field, she finds it filled with flowers. Not a wide variety of flowers, so that nectar from this meadow would not have had great texture or range or taste, but a colony would never have starved here.

The stream would have provided water, and the trees a natural wind break. She flies a hundred yards out into the meadow and alights on a scarlet paintbrush. Slowly she slips her tongue among the petals and tests the nectar. Yes, it is good. Sweet and plentiful. But useless to her now.

With absolutely no idea what to do, or where to go, she wishes she could travel to the Plain of Crowns and consult the ancestors. But even the Plain is denied to her now. Without a colony to Crown her she has no way to access it. She has nothing.

She notices a few bees flying overhead. There must be a colony near, sourcing nectar from this field and filling a little hive. In fact, it is odd that she does not see workers on any of the flowers near her, only fliers overhead. The honey flow would be in full swing at this time of the spring. Workers ought to be swarming these blossoms.

Curious, she rises up from the petals. It is one of the traits that bees have had from the beginning of time—curiosity. Even when there is nectar to be gathered, and a hive to be cleaned, even in the midst of a thousand other jobs and duties, if a bee sees something that piques her interest, she will go to investigate. It's a trait that has served bees well, just as it has served men well, revealing new sources of food and new vistas and expanding the colony's knowledge. But just as with man, curiosity can lead a bee into dark and dangerous places. The Little Queen is long past caring whether she is endangering herself, however, so she accelerates until she is flying just behind the nearest worker to investigate.

Her injured wing slows her a little and causes her pain when she flies, but the truth is that she is immensely strong. Using only one of her two sets of wings she is as fast as any of the bees she sees flying above the meadow. And, now that she is looking, she realizes that there are bees streaming everywhere, all of them heading back and forth from a point on the far northern side of the field. Very few bees in the flowers, but a multitude in the air.

It must be a very large colony to support all this activity, she thinks. Near her a worker labors through the air, heading back over the meadow, heavy with bounty. The Little Queen slides up to fly beside her.

It is the first time the she has ever seen a bee not born to her own colony—a bee the world would consider a "normal" honeybee. And the differences between her own children and this bee are striking. This bee is only half the size of any of her own, with wings that are even smaller, perhaps a third as big as the Little Queen's offspring. And she is in very poor condition. She has been worked to within an inch of her life. The Little Queen speaks to her.

"Hello, daughter," she says. "You bear your load well."

The startled worker falters in midflight, then rights herself. She glances at the Little Queen, and trembles.

"Forbidden," she sings, haltingly. Then she redoubles her effort and toils away through the air. The Little Queen follows at a distance.

Several things strike her as odd. For one thing, she sees that the worker carries not nectar but honey. A great, heavy load of honey, spilling over from all her carrying pouches and even dripping off of her legs as she flies. In fact, all the bees filling the air around her carry the same freight. Was there an emergency? Did the workers have to gather honey from the hive to save it, and now they are returning? Another oddity, a more disturbing one, is that the worker was obviously afraid of interacting with her. This is very hard to understand. A worker automatically responds to a queen with reverence.

There is nothing a worker values more than the interest of a queen. That is just the way the world works. But this worker wanted nothing to do with the Little Queen.

Perhaps it is only that the Little Queen is so different. The more she examines the flood of bees who now surround her, all moving toward the same point on a rocky buttress near the head of the stream, the more she understands that whatever course her history took to produce her and finally strand her here, it was a course very different from that of other bees. It has changed her profoundly.

And perhaps that is a good thing. She has a sudden idea. She knows that, albeit rarely, a hive can have two queens. Especially if one of them brings a great benefit to the hive—if her children are faster, or have more stamina, or larger nectar pouches. The Little Queen carries in her ovipositor many hundreds of thousands of fertilized eggs, which need only warm comb and sweet food to grow. And these eggs will hatch into bees just like her, bees such as her attendants. Glorious, powerful workers, capable of contributing to a hive in many ways. Whether this is of enough benefit to let her live among a new colony she does not know. It depends a great deal on the existing queen.

But a sudden small spark of hope flares in her chest. Perhaps her mission has not ended after all. Could it be true? She will meet with the queen of this new hive. She will demonstrate her attributes.

The wide river of bees coming and going from the hive ahead begins to narrow and gain speed, as though entering an invisible funnel. Bees like to enter and exit the hive along only one path, and now the Little Queen inserts herself into this stream and lets it carry her. She is startled by the number of workers crowding together in preparation for landing.

This must be a very large colony indeed. She realizes that, temporarily at least, she needs to take some precautions.

Every hive shares a particular pheromonic signature, a chemical autograph that marks each of them as hivemates and helps identify intruders. The Little Queen knows that she may never get a chance to propose her plan to the sitting queen if the hive marks her as an "other"—thus an enemy—and attacks. Carefully stoking her Queen's Bell, she cloaks herself in the scent of this hive, a peculiar mix of nectars from an astounding variety of pollen. As long as she does nothing else to call attention, like speaking mind-to-mind or singing wingsong, this will allow her to pass unnoticed among them. Until the time is right to reveal herself.

Ahead she sees the landing area, which has been forged out away from the rock wall with propolis, attached to the stone at the rounded end of a long, vertical crack. The hive itself is hidden inside the crevice. The torrent of flying workers becomes difficult to see through as she nears the platform, there are so many bees jostling for position. She feels, more than sees, the surface come up below her. And then she is crawling forward into the darkness of the fissure.

The smell of honey is sudden and overwhelming. Intoxicating. A thousand varieties of nectar combine here. In fact, this honey has such a varied nectar source it is hard to understand how one hive could be responsible. She has a moment of doubt—it seems that these bees are not in need of more honey or better workers. The queen here must be a rare artist, to create such abundance from such a multiplicity of flowers. Below her feet on the rock are traces of the precious liquid, actually spilled on the ground, which no bee has even bothered to clean up. A colony rich beyond belief.

She moves farther into the crevice, carried forward, bumped and jostled by the bees around her, stepping past small pools of honey. Suddenly she passes under an archway, and above her a chamber opens, a huge, vaulting hall, perfect for building comb. This is the heart of the colony. And such a colony has seldom been seen.

This queen must be magnificent to produce such a hive. It must be two hundred thousand bees strong. So much honey fills the comb that hangs from the ceiling and clings to the walls that they could live for years just on these stores alone. Everywhere workers are scurrying, drawing new comb and tending young. The chamber echoes with activity.

But there is something strange about this place. The Little Queen cannot quite name it, but something is amiss. For one thing, the workers are not singing. They should be talking to each other, dancing the locations of flowers, singing the densities of nectars, the weather, the time. But these bees seem worried, and they are silent, though they are doing prodigious work.

And another oddity is the humidity in the chamber. Honey needs a very particular humidity and temperature as it cures in the cells, turning from nectar into golden syrup in stages; otherwise it will ferment and it must be destroyed. But this hive is far too moist and hot. She realizes she does not see any bees fanning. How have they achieved such an incredible stockpile while skipping such a vital step in the process?

She crawls farther into the chamber. Bits of comb and propolis lie in odd corners, or even directly in the middle of the floor, but none of the harried workers stops to remove it. She passes a dead worker, fallen from the comb above. Workers die all the time in a hive, of course. But a dead worker should never, under any circumstances, be allowed to remain like this, lying on the floor, where it could spread disease or attract scavengers. There should be an entire subset of workers, cleaning bees, whose only job is to maintain colony hygiene and remove bodies, to clear spilled honey and repair fallen wax. Perhaps this hive is actually too big to clean? Whatever they are doing, it seems to be working. For a colony of bees, honey equals success. And honey is here in amazing profusion.

The hive seems to go on forever. How in the world can such a thing be, she wonders? Is this all the work of one queen? Perhaps there are several queens here already. She passes comb after comb, thick honey dripping everywhere, with a constant stream of workers passing her on all sides, bent and silent. And then finally, high above on the face of a new stretch of wax, she spies the queen.

She is laying, and her attendants encircle her and carry her food. But there should be a constant stream of other workers bringing her news of the hive, news from the fields, keeping her in touch with every element of the life of the colony. Instead, she is alone. None of her children come near her. And the Little Queen can see that even her attendants stay as far back as they can. Then she realizes—this colony does not revere its queen. It fears her.

For a moment the Little Queen considers abandoning her plan. But she has come too far. This is her only remaining hope. So giving her Queen's Bell the fine chemical adjustments fundamental to her power and position, she casts off her disguise, letting her true scent rise into the hive like a hot bouquet, a shout of autonomy, and she calls to the other queen, mind-to-mind.

Your hive is magnificent, sister.

Instantly this queen stops laying. She swivels her head. And she sees the Little Queen below her.

Her pheromones ring out like pulsing blasts of sound, bouncing off the walls and penetrating all the nooks and crannies of the hive—"We are invaded! Bees guard the entrance! Bees come to me!"

No, asserts the Little Queen, focusing her thoughts on the other queen. I am no invader. I am a single queen. Can you speak to me mind-to-mind?

Workers are spilling into the passage around the Little Queen now, responding to the royal summons and looking for invaders. They see her, and they are afraid. Now that they see that she is a queen, they do not dare approach. They are as terrified of her as they are of their own queen.

No STEAL! screams the new queen at her, mind-to-mind. MY HONEY!

The Little Queen realizes again how far down a different path she has come, if this is the best communication that this queen, the highest, most advanced bee in this colony, can offer mind-to-mind. So she changes tactics, and switches to wingsong and dance. Now all the bees around her can hear the conversation.

"I do not want to steal from you," she sings. "I would never steal another's honey. That is forbidden."

"Attack her!" sings the other queen to her workers, pumping pheromones into the hive from her own Queen's Bell, a frenzied discharge of chemicals designed to whip her bees into a blind rage.

"Sister, I only wish to talk," the Little Queen dances emphatically.

"Talk? You want your honey back. But you cannot have it! It is mine now! Go, my children—destroy her!"

And suddenly everything is clear to the Little Queen. She has fallen in among robber bees.

All the honey around her, every drop in every cell, has been stolen from some other hive. It explains so much; the tremendous variety in the honey stored here, despite a meadow filled with nothing but mountain paintbrush and lupine. The humidity and heat—this hive does not need to cure and process honey; they steal it and store it whole.

Robber bees are not unknown in the annals of bee history, but they are rare. Only a horribly twisted spirit could build her colony this way. It is an atrocity.

The scents coursing through the hive are bringing these bees to the edge of madness. Soon they will overcome their fear of her and attack. She reaches to her own Queen's Bell and creates a field around her which no worker will enter, a ring of pure authority that holds back the building flood of workers.

And she sings to the other queen, "This is abomination!"

"It is life! Look at my colony," says the Robber Queen. "We will grow, three hundred thousand, four hundred thousand. Nothing will stop us. Enough for all to eat. A world of plenty. I take what I need. I provide."

"You debase everything it is to be a queen. Your workers hate you for what you make them do."

The Robber Queen sprints down the comb in a rage, closer and closer to the Little Queen, bringing her pheromones to bear on her workers, drowning out the potency of the Little Queen's protective bubble the way a screaming man might drown out the sound of a beautiful violin.

"Who are you to judge me? You are hardly a bee, you are some monstrosity. And barely old enough to lay larvae. You dare come to my hive and question me? I have hundreds of thousands behind me. I will destroy you!"

The workers press in, those behind pushing against those in front. The Little Queen, exhausted and injured, bruised in body and soul, knows she might be able to hold them off for a few minutes, maybe even for hours, by pumping out a mélange of commands, and projecting her authority, and stinging. Stinging endlessly. Maybe, after horrible struggle, after causing the death of untold numbers of these poor creatures, she might even escape. But for what? To die alone, cold and broken on a rock somewhere, to be eaten by predators because she has no home or refuge? It is sad beyond belief. Perhaps, she thinks suddenly, she *is* a monstrosity. Perhaps there is no place for her.

She has overcome her fear, as the Yellow Queen had said she must. But that was simply not enough. She is defeated.

The Little Queen silences her Queen's Bell. Lifts her protective sphere. And the workers surge forward.

"Crush her! Ball her and crush her," screams the Robber Queen. "She must wear a Death Crown!"

It is over in seconds. There is so much rage. Like a tsunami racing in from all sides they engulf her, and the Little Queen lies still. They lift her and encircle her, six by six, locking the hooks on their legs to build a swarming ball. A Death Crown, from which there can be no escape. They begin to squeeze.

At first the pressure is insignificant. She hardly feels it. But more and more bees layer on, and the force of the ball grows. Soon twenty thousand have joined the killing swarm, and the pressure builds as they adjust their grips and press inward. Still, her keenest sensation is not pain, but a sort of warm satisfaction. This is a Crown, if a Death Crown, and she thought she would never wear one again.

But soon she begins to wonder whether they are strong enough. Her body is different. Far stronger than theirs. Despite herself, she feels her temperature rising, and senses the internal structures automatically realigning to distribute the stresses over the surface of her exoskeleton. Her body is accommodating this swarm as though it is a Crown that she herself has called.

More and more bees, forty thousand, sixty thousand, eighty, mass upon her, and now she feels it. With enough bees, even she can be crushed. She feels herself being wrung from her physical form, pushed down out of herself to enter a different form, a perfect form. She feels a familiar sensation of acceleration.

There is light, coming nearer and nearer. She feels she is in flight, with wind tearing at her wings. Ahead of her a membrane stretches, vibrating, expanding, and the familiar deafening buzz crescendos around her, driving her forward.

She passes a barrier of speed, shock waves surround her, she rides them at supersonic velocity through vortexes of noise and form until— time stutters—and stutters—again—and—

She emerges.

Spread below her is the Plain of Crowns, throbbing with a soft heat. Between her shoulders is the golden thread that disappears, tying her to her body. She is back.

There is no way to know how long she has until her physical form succumbs and she's not floating above this comb, but rather lodged within it, nothing more than a spirit for other queens to visit in the future. The colony crushing her is too large and too driven; there is no doubt that despite her great strength, they will eventually end her life. But she does not resent that. She has made her choice.

Now that she has seen the world outside the Superhive, she finds the magnificence of the Plain of Crowns even more inspiring. She sees more clearly what it represents, and she hovers above it, letting the light and warmth wash over her. It is a privilege that this should be the last thing she sees before she dies. In truth it is a gift. This is the essence of what it means to be a bee. This is the finest creation of her species.

She finds herself drifting over the surface, looking at the upturned faces of the millions of queens below, and wafting toward the leading edge of the Plain, where her own time is.

She can feel, faintly, the pressure of the attacking bees mounting behind her, or above her, somewhere else, in the dark cave above the field of flowers. But it does not hurt. It feels just and perfect. This is her conclusion.

Without moving her wings, her speed over the Plain is increasing. In fact, it seems to her that she is being drawn by some other force. Being summoned. On the horizon she sees the end of the comb, the line representing the most recent generation of queens, and she spies the peculiar jutting formation of celestial wax that represents her own ancestral line. Without any effort on her part, she finds herself flashing toward that outcrop.

Like a speck of dust pushed relentlessly by a draft, she is drawn over the Plain, faster and faster, then down, as if through an opening, out over her own peninsula of comb. Below her flash past the very first Sequestered, and then the successive generations as queens begin to change, to grow, to become more intelligent and self aware. And develop the mind-to-mind.

And then she is hanging above the Yellow Queen, who rises out of her cell to meet her. The Little Queen descends. There is a moment of silence as the two resplendent creatures regard each other.

I HAVE FAILED, says the Little Queen.

YOU ARE HERE, responds the Yellow Queen, SO YOU HAVE NOT FAILED. NOT YET.

I ESCAPED, AND AVOIDED THE GREEN DEATH, says the Little Queen, BUT THEN I COULD NOT BUILD A HIVE. I LOST MY COLONY. I FELL IN WITH ROBBERS. I HAVE WASTED OUR CHANCE, THE CHANCE FOR THE SEQUESTERED TO LIVE.

Down along the golden thread connecting her to her body shoots a sudden pulse. The end is coming quickly.

The Yellow Queen bends close. The mind-to-mind is intimate and gracious, strangely forceful, compelling her attention. No. All here have lost our colonies, in the end, and that is no failure. This Robber Queen is a pariah. She will have no place here when she dies. She has thrown away everything. But for you, hope remains.

Now the Little Queen feels a spasm. Her celestial body twists and bends, as if it will fold back in upon itself. The filament tying her to her earthly body pulls, and narrows farther. She feels herself fading.

How is there hope? she asks. What can I do after I die?

You need not die. Listen. There is a light in the meadow. A bright, golden light.

The Little Queen does understand. It is becoming harder to think, or listen. What meadow? she asks. What light?

The meadow just beyond your earthly body. Outside the robber hive. The Yellow Queen looks upward, and sees the golden thread nearly spent. She bears all her force down on the Little Queen, willing her to listen.

There is still much you do not know about the Plain of Crowns, and the battle we wage. So you must trust me. We see a light. When we close our eyes, we see it. In the meadow. If you go, there is still hope. Do you understand?

The Little Queen struggles through her fog to comprehend. You want me to go back to my body? But I am caught. The Robber Queen has me in a Death Crown.

You have mastered your fear, says the Yellow Queen. Now it is yours. Go now and use it!

And with that, the Little Queen finds herself snapping backward, a thousand miles a second, up and away. The Yellow Queen dwindles below her and the Plain of Crowns disappears and grows dark as she rushes back along her tightening thread.

With a snap like a puzzle piece sliding into a hole, she returns once again to her body. Only now, it is a body on the edge of annihilation. She has only a moment left before the pressure of a hundred thousand bees bearing down simply cracks her open and kills her.

The Yellow Queen sent her back, but what is she to do? A Death Crown cannot be broken. This is how queens have always been killed;

there is no escape. The bees in a Death Crown are enraged beyond reverence or reason. How is she to break free? Once again, even in this last thing, she is afraid she has failed. She is afraid. And she understands.

Her fear. The fatal flaw that broke Crown after Crown when the Sequestered were attempting to escape the Green Death. Fear. The enemy of all other emotions. Including rage.

There is no word in the language of pheromones to incite a hive to unreasoning fear. No statement for that could ever have evolved, because no reasonable queen would ever have used it. Nor are there words in wingsong and dance to create colony-wide panic. But the mind-to-mind—that is a new thing, a flexible language whereby anything at all may be said. The Little Queen digs deep, and brings up fear—the fear she once so tightly controlled in the face of the killing gas. With the last of her strength, she blasts FEAR into the dense crown enveloping her.

Fear. Of everything. Fear of starvation. Fear of thirst. Fear of cold. Fear of death—the hive, the queen, the self. Fear of robbers swarming the comb, stealing the honey, killing the babies. Fear of insidious gas flooding the comb, destroying it all. Fear of darkness, such total and permanent and complete darkness that no light can ever break it.

Fear of failure.

Absolute, overwhelming, life-defining fear.

And because they are already so close to fear, because fear is what drives them, because they feel they have so much to fear, these bees shatter. They fear their own queen, and they fear the things she makes them do. Swiftly, like molten lava cleaves a mighty mountain, the fear seeps out into the Death Crown and it begins to shudder and crack apart. The heat of the Little Queen's fear shears through the ball. Huge shards cleave free, a thousand bees at once, like a glacier calving. Until at last she rests, barely alive, but breathing, on the floor of the hive, while a hundred and fifty thousand bees mass in chaotic terror everywhere around her.

Dragging her injured leg through huge pools of spilled honey, she crawls toward the opening of the hive. The colony has gone crazy— bees are fighting bees, stinging anything that lives. The Little Queen cloaks herself by masking all scent and slowly, hugging the walls, makes her way to the entrance. From there, she leaps. And escapes once more.

But laboring out away from the cliff, on wings so weak they can barely carry her, she wonders—escape to what? How has anything changed? She is alive, though barely. But what can she do? She struggles on, over the meadow, into the wind, above flowers nodding and fragrant, and none of it has changed. She cannot do this alone. She has no more strength to search. There is no light here, no golden light. Whatever the Yellow Queen saw, it is gone. Or it never existed.

The Little Queen begins to spiral down toward the ground, knowing that when she lands, she will not fly again. As she circles down she does a thing bees never do in flight: she surrenders to exhaustion and blocks out the light. Bees do not have eyelids; when they sleep they simply switch off their ocular pathways. She does this now and circles lower, waiting for the end. Blind.

Instantly a golden light appears in her mind. It startles her. Her sight reactivates. She pulls herself out of her dive. A golden light? She searches the meadow, but sees nothing that radiates or glows. She blinds herself again.

And there it is: a steady, golden illumination, coming from the south. She looks. But as soon as she does, she loses her bearings. Was it the north? Or the west? Yes, the west. Then she circles again, uncertain. No. East? Not there. Where did the light come from?

Again she darkens her vision, and the golden light is present. But this time she understands, she will not be able to locate it with her vision active. She must fly within the darkness and let the light guide her.

Bees never fly this way, of course. But the Little Queen has done so many things already that bees simply do not do that this seems a relatively small step into the unknown. And so, blind, she heads across the meadow, toward the golden light.

It grows brighter, if that is possible. It takes on substance, and an outline like a corona. Trusting this force she does not know, she flies closer to it, reaches it, and lands. And opens her eyes.

She finds herself on a rock by a stream, and her first impulse is to drink. She is so thirsty. But then she senses a presence beside her, and she turns.

Lying on its side is a human. She knows this from knowledge passed to her in her natal flights to the Plain of Crowns. Its tremendous eyes are staring wide, its breath stirring her wings.

From the ground, it lifts its massive hand, which it settles beside its face lying open on the rock.

Without knowing what she does, or why, but feeling as though no other path remains for her, she walks slowly forward, and with the last of her strength crawls into the palm of that giant hand. And then her mind darkens, without her volition, as the mind of any creature will do bent so far beyond its natural scope. And the Little Queen sleeps.

Chapter Eleven

For a few long moments Anthony is afraid to move. All he does is lie on the rock and stare at the creature curled in his palm. He doesn't want her to fly off; he wants to watch her. But eventually his cheek begins to hurt where it presses into the stone, so he carefully levers himself to a sitting position, moving the hand with the bee as little as possible.

He's forced to use his injured arm and at one point the pain is too much and he falls back, jostling the queen, but surprisingly she does not move. She seems to be asleep. Once upright, he holds her as close to his face as he can. Her injuries are grave, he sees quickly. She needs critical attention.

The light is now draining from the little valley. Anthony wonders what time it is. He must have slept for hours under that hemlock. His body aches horribly; his head feels like it's being hit over and over with a two-by-four. But his mind is strangely focused. Suddenly he has something in front of him that he clearly needs to do. He needs to get down off this hillside, get home, and save this creature.

First things first, however. He watches her roll back and forth in his hand. She is so light, he can barely feel her. She bounces like a ball of fluff. There's no way he can transport her like this. Even if, somehow, she let him, and didn't fly off, the likelihood of dropping her, or of crushing her, is high.

The explosion in the bathroom has left a piece of his shirt bottom shredded, and even though his right hand is getting weaker by the minute, he is able to rip a piece off. He places the queen in the center, folds the sides together and gathers the pleats. She'll bounce around, but at least he won't accidentally smash her in his fist.

He stands and heads back to the tree line, but once he starts into the woods he sees that going down is going to be a lot harder than coming up. At the best of times, picking his way downward through this steep forest in the quickly thickening dark would be awkward, but with an arm and a leg only half functional, and carrying a delicate payload at the same time, it's almost more than he can manage. At one point he begins to slip, and instead of catching himself with his left hand—the hand holding the pouch—he has to slam full force into a tree trunk, taking the brunt of the blow with his chest. It knocks the wind out of him and he collapses, wheezing. But he manages to hold onto his bag.

By the time he gets through the trees and down the hill, night has come in full. He stops, listening. The band is gone, of course. He hopes against hope to hear the sound of cars, maybe someone picking up their kids from a practice or a study group. But he hears nothing. Spring break has started, and after school programs are finished.

He comes around the shop corner and sees that not a light is shining in any room. The floods illuminate the empty courtyard and the walkways between the buildings, but the school is deserted.

On the benches near the gym he sits, and under a halogen flood light opens his rough pouch to check on the queen. She's awake now, and when exposed she looks up at him. But she doesn't fly off. He wonders if she's even able to fly. He closes the material back around her. He needs to get her warmed up. The temperature is down in the 50's now, which might be another reason she isn't flying anywhere. Bees get sluggish in the cool. An injured bee could easily succumb to nothing but cold.

He lifts the pouch up to his face and holds it lightly against his cheek.

"Don't worry," he whispers. "I won't let anything happen to you." He needs to stand and go, but he's finding it hard to get started. There's something wrong with his eyes. He blinks, and rubs them – and then he sees the headlights. There's a car pulling up to the front of the school. A kid jumps out and heads toward a forgotten sweater hanging on a dark bench. Now Anthony does stand.

PAUL STANDS IN THE EMERGENCY ROOM HALLWAY HOLDING A MASON jar and listening to a man named Dr. Vincent. Occasionally the bee in his mason jar buzzes. He tries to ignore it. Dr. Vincent keeps glancing down.

"I'm surprised they let you in with that," the doctor says. He's not upset. Just puzzled.

"My son can be very persuasive."

"So it's not your bee?"

"I don't like bees."

Dr. Vincent nods. A night shift doctor in the ER has seen it all, Paul figures. Possibly even this.

"Okay. So, Mr. Smith, tell me again how your son got these injuries?"

"We don't really know." The big bee in the jar buzzes. Paul resists an impulse to just shake the thing senseless. "I guess he was hiking behind the school and he fell. Cut himself on a rock, or . . . ?"

Dr. Vincent is shaking his head. "I don't think so." He holds up a small plastic bag, and inside is what appears to Paul to be a dime-sized piece of metal torn off a chrome bumper.

"I removed this from the cut on his arm. I'd say whatever caused the wound was metallic."

Paul nods. Then shrugs. The bee buzzes. What the hell is he supposed to do here? "I'll ask him again. I mean, that's what he told me. Is he okay?"

"He's fine. Mild concussion. Some abrasions. Keep the arm dry for a week. Make an appointment to bring him back to see about the stitches. He'll be out in a minute."

Paul shakes the doctor's hand, awkwardly tucking the mason jar under one arm to do so. Then, as the doctor walks away, he holds the jar up to look at the bee.

"Somehow you are responsible for this," he says. Damn bees. At the end of the hall he sees a red EXIT sign. What he wants to do, more than anything else, is take this bee in this jar out and throw it in the river. Enough with the bees!

He remembers what Mitsy Waterman said—get Anthony focused on something he loves, and it will help get him through this rough patch. It doesn't seem to be helping. It seems to be causing more problems than it's solving. Like tonight, when a parent he didn't even know pulled into the driveway and walked Anthony into the house, limping and covered with blood like he'd been hit by a train—all he'd wanted to do was get this idiot bee into a jar. Then when Paul had basically strong-armed him down to the hospital, Anthony had insisted that the bee come with them. Now here Paul is, standing in a hospital hallway holding a bee in a bottle.

A nurse leads Anthony out. Paul takes a deep breath. Anthony is covered with small bandages, and the dressing on his arm is long and dramatic. Instantly, Anthony reaches for the mason jar and looks inside. It's like he's afraid Paul did something to kill the damn bee while he was getting stitches. Which makes Paul feel a little guilty.

"I wouldn't let him carry that jar," says the nurse, eyeing Anthony. "We gave him a little something for the pain."

"Doubt you'd be able to pry it away from him with the Jaws of Life," Paul tells her. At the mere mention of releasing the jar, Anthony hugs it tight. Paul sees that his eyes are pretty blurry. He reaches out gently to steady his son. *My god,* he thinks, *my kid's on drugs. They had to give him drugs. What is going on here? Am I a terrible father? How did this happen?*

"Okay, well, watch him," the nurse says. "He's good to go." She sees the worry on Paul's face. "Hey, boys are boys. He'll be fine. My kid fell off the roof when he was ten, the next morning he was back to tormenting the cat and throwing rocks at his sister." She ruffles Anthony's hair fondly. "They're just busy little bees, aren't they?"

Anthony falls asleep on the way home. Paul stops at the Hanlens' to get Mat, then when he gets home he carries Mat inside and leaves

Anthony in the car. He tucks Mat in then goes back out for Anthony, but he's not there. The car door is open. Paul immediately turns to the bee yard, where a dark shape is outlined against the fence. It's Anthony, holding the mason jar up toward the bee yard like he's showing off a prize. Jesus, these bees are going to kill us all, he thinks as he goes to grab him.

Anthony wakes up when his father comes into his room. Morning light burns on the wall. He snaps to life with a jolt of pain, like someone just stuck a pin in his lung. The room feels hot, and he is sweaty. Everything aches.

"How do you feel?" asks his dad.

"Terrible." There's something he's supposed to remember.

"No doubt."

Then he remembers. His eyes dart around the room. "Where is she?"

"Who?"

"The queen! The queen, Dad, where is—"

"Your bee," his father says, with undisguised distaste. "It's in the kitchen, on top of the stove, where you put it last night to make sure it stayed warm. Bear was going crazy, I had to put him outside."

Anthony begins throwing on clothes, wincing every few seconds. Everything seems to hurt. It's kind of amazing.

"Take it easy, the doc wants you to rest for a couple days."

"I will."

"Okay. I'm leaving for work," says his dad. "Mat's going to preschool. You going to be okay on your own? I can ask Alice Hanlen to come over . . . "

Anthony shakes his head. His dad watches him pull on pants and push his way into a shirt. Usually when his father says, "I'm leaving," you have about seven seconds to say anything you might need to say, and then he's gone. Today he lingers.

After a minute, he even speaks. In his "casual" voice, he says, "The doc said he pulled some metal out of that cut on your arm."

Fortunately Anthony's head is inside his shirt at the time so his father doesn't see his eyes go wide. By the time his face surfaces his expression is mostly natural.

"What did you say?" he asks.

Still acting like it's no big deal, his dad asks, "You got any idea how metal might have got in that cut on your arm?"

Anthony squints his eyes like he's thinking. He's not that great at lying, and his dad is not very good at being casual, a failure on both their parts due solely to a lack of practice. The difference is, Anthony knows his limits, while his dad has no idea how transparent he is. And the trick to not telling the truth and getting away with it is actually to lie as little as possible.

So he says, "There was metal?"

"Uh huh. Little bits."

"Huh. I know I fell into a tree when I was coming down the hill, and then later I smashed into a rock. Did they find any wood chips? Or rock chips?"

"He didn't say."

"Huh." And then the change of direction. "Did you say you were leaving Mat here?"

"No, he's going to preschool and you're here by yourself. You're still on probation, so stay off the TV and the Internet." His dad is watching as Anthony limps toward the door. He's not even exaggerating for effect; it really hurts. It's supremely convenient.

"Okay, Dad," he rasps.

With a monumental sigh, his father leaves the bedroom, tromps down the stairs, collects Mat, lunch, papers, and keys, and is out the door. Like a rock rolling downhill, inevitable, unstoppable, predictable. *Now that's the Paul Smith I know,* Anthony thinks. He himself takes a lot longer to navigate the stairs, but as soon as he's down, he heads straight for the kitchen.

The mason jar sits on the stove like an offering. Anthony doesn't even remember putting it there. He doesn't remember much from the night before, actually. A lot of driving around really fast, a lot of crying. He remembers refusing to go anywhere if the queen in her jar didn't come too.

He doesn't remember feeding her, but he must have because there is a piece of honeycomb in the bottom of the bottle. At first that is all he can see, the comb, and his stomach drops out through his pockets.

Did she escape? Then he sees a wing behind the comb, and then an antenna—and then she appears. In all her amazing glory. He actually gasps. What is she?

The doctors told him he had a concussion, and it has to be true—it's the only explanation. Otherwise, he would have been up all night trying to figure out what in the world he had found in the woods. She's unbelievable. She's huge, the size of a bumblebee. She's easily as long as the first two knuckles on his pointer finger. And beefy, too. But at the same time, she is entirely streamlined. Like a thoroughbred racehorse. The kind with muscles rippling under every lean inch of their bodies.

And it has to be a trick of the morning light streaming in through the kitchen window but it honestly looks to him as though she glows. Golden light seems to iridesce off of her wings and body. If she isn't glowing, she's by far the shiniest bee—no, the shiniest insect—that he's ever seen. She's like a little golden mirror.

He creeps right up to the edge of the stove and bends down to look at her. He can see his eyes reflected on the convex glass and he looks like a monster. She must be terrified, he thinks.

But she doesn't act terrified. In fact, she acts pretty calm, with just a hint of impatience. Impatience? How does a bee look impatient? Is it the cock of her antennae? The tilt of the wings?

He looks closely at those wings. He definitely remembers at least one of them being injured, more or less irreparably. Yet here she is, buzzing and preening, and there's not a mark on her. And her leg, it was almost broken off; he remembers lying on the rock by the stream and seeing her clutch it up against her abdomen. Yet that same limb seems perfectly fit this morning. He contrasts it with his own leg, which is now beginning to pulse.

"Whatever you ate for breakfast," he tells her, "I want some."

Breakfast. He hasn't eaten anything since breakfast the day before. Never got a chance to eat. And now he's ravenous.

He moves the queen in her jar over to the kitchen table and pours himself a giant bowl of cereal, staring at her while he lobs spoonfuls into his mouth. But he's not actually thinking about this astonishing specimen in the mason jar. Instead, he's thinking about why this is the first time he's eaten since yesterday. He's thinking about the M80 in the boys' bathroom.

He runs through it all in his mind. He remembers Greyson handing him the red paper tube. He remembers putting the dispenser together and lighting the fuse, and seeing the other three boys crowded over by the door. And he remembers the flash. After that, he guesses that he must have passed out.

The queen buzzes. She has the loudest buzz of any bee he's ever heard. The sounds drifting up out of the jar are almost like a song. She moves to the comb and begins to eat honey. And Anthony decides that he doesn't really care about the details of the day before. He's happy to eat, glad to be home, and grateful that all that happened was a cut on his arm and a banged up leg.

"Come on, I'll show you my room," he says, and he picks up the jar. The queen buzzes, clinging to the honeycomb. Anthony carries her carefully to the stairs. But climbing them seems like more than he wants to do—or more than he's capable of. The couch is just as soft as his bed and it's only a few steps away, so that's where he goes instead. Curling into a ball on the spongy cushions, getting drowsier by the second, he wedges the jar against the pillows and drapes his arms around it. Then his eyes close and he sleeps, cradling the mason jar like a stuffed animal.

He wakes several hours later, from a dream that he doesn't remember. The first thing he sees is the golden queen, pushed right up against the edge of the glass only millimeters from his face. She is so close he can make out individual veins and ridges of her yellow, translucent wings. She buzzes, then stops. Buzzes, then stops. Then she backs up, moves forward, and spins. Again and again. It's the way bees communicate with each other, Anthony knows. Usually they are passing on directions to important locations, such as rich flower fields, enemies, or a new swarming site.

How long has she been doing that, he wonders? He yawns and sits up, and the queen stops her dance to watch him.

"I wish I could understand you," he tells her quietly. "You seem like you've got a lot to say."

He stretches. He's actually starting to feel a bit better. The sleep must have helped. He feels lazy and relaxed, but he's left with the sense that he was going to do something when he woke up. What was it? He stands, picks up the jar, and wanders into the kitchen to grab and peel a banana. It's not often that he's alone in the house. He feels sleepy and jumpy at the same time. The light from the window hits the jar in such a way as to cast a shadow of the queen onto the table. She's at it again, buzzing and dancing. Her shadow grows and shrinks as she pirouettes atop the honeycomb. He bites his banana and wonders, *where is her hive?*

That's it, he thinks. *The hive. I was going to check on the hive when I woke up.* Before stepping outside, he fills a bowl with dog food and sets it just inside the door. Then he cracks it and calls, "Bear! Come here, Bear! Are you hungry, boy?"

Bear doesn't appear. With any luck he's down at the pond, digging holes in the Hanlens' lily garden. Anthony steps outside. The air is warm and fragrant. Even far from the bee yard he can smell the sweet bluebells and mountain primrose, a bright scent coloring the breeze.

Suddenly Bear comes rushing from around the corner of the house. He has smelled bee.

"Bear, down!" Anthony yells as the dog rushes him. He throws the door open. "Bear, food! Inside! Are you hungry?" he yells, holding open the door.

Mercifully, Bear decides he would like to eat. Anthony slams the door.

"That's Bear," he tells the queen in her jar. "Be careful of him, he has a thing about bees, And he's totally out of control. Won't sit, lay down, stay. Totally useless."

He holds the jar up, and moves it slowly west to north, showing off the towering Selkirk Mountains, which ring their little corner of the world. "This is where I live," he says. He doesn't know why he's talking to this bee. But it feels perfectly natural. He has a feeling his mother would approve. Then he starts for the shed.

As he gets closer to the bee yard the queen starts getting agitated. She is buzzing, dancing, really sort of going a little crazy. Upside down, sideways, moves he's never seen a bee make. Bright sun flashes off every part of her. Out in the full sunlight she is even more astounding than she looked inside. She actually seems to gather up the sun and bounce it back out of the jar, magnified. It's a trick; Anthony knows she's not actually producing light somehow. But he has to stop and stare. He finds himself simply gaping, amazed, his own hive forgotten. She is so beautiful.

The queen abruptly stops. She's facing the bee yard, frozen on her comb. Her wings are raised, but not beating. He's never seen a bee pose that way.

"What is it?" he asks. But that does feel a little strange—asking a question and expecting an answer? Maybe he was hit harder on the head than he realized. He waits to see what she will do. But she remains frozen, pointed at the bee yard. He starts to wonder if she really does see something over there.

So he begins to walk again, advancing toward the fence, and now he can hear a distinctive buzz. The hive is extremely active. Clearly something new is happening. But he's not prepared for what he sees when he passes through the shed and enters the bee yard.

Bees mass at the entrance to the hive. They make short sorties out into the air, then return—a constant stream. There are so many bees at the entrance it's like a liquid that drips off in bee globs, which then break apart and rise into the air. There's only one thing this behavior could mean. But it doesn't make any sense.

Anthony runs back into the house, forgetting for a moment that he's carrying a bee in a jar and bouncing her violently. Just in time he remembers that Bear is lurking behind the door. He opens it quickly, the dog tumbles out, and Anthony and his specimen slip inside before Bear can turn and pounce.

Anthony heads straight for the phone. Technically he's still not supposed to use it. This feels like it has got to be an exception, though. He dials quickly.

"Henry's Hothouse," says a cheery female voice.

"I need to talk to Bernie," he says.

"Who can I tell him is—"

"It's Anthony Smith. Please hurry!"

He suffers through a moment of mellow music until Bernard's deep voice thunders, "Hey, Little Bee! What's going on? Did your new queen arrive? How'd everything work out?"

"It didn't," Anthony admits. "It was like you said. They killed her."

There's a moment of silence on the phone, then Bernard says, "I'm truly sorry to hear that, Tony. I truly am."

"But that's not why I'm calling. It's . . . is there any reason my hive might be getting ready to pitch a swarm?" Anthony sits up on the kitchen sink so he can get a look out toward the bee yard. Nothing is visible from here. He puts the jar down in front of him on the windowsill.

"Why?"

"I saw it happen in your yard once. The bees started gathering at the entrance. They were all riled up."

"Are they making little test flights out in front of the hive?" Bernard asks. "Gathering at the entrance in a pool of bees?"

"Yeah. But why would they swarm? They're not crowded. You said it yourself, there are probably only fifteen thousand bees in there. That hive could hold eighty thousand."

Bernard takes one of his long, deep rhinoceros breaths though the nose. Anthony can practically see him cupping his chin in his hand, shaking his head.

"Tony, I'm going to say this straight. Your hive has given up. Basically, they are going to fly off somewhere and die. I'm sorry to have to say it so plain. But that's the truth."

"But why?" He can't believe this. It doesn't make sense.

"That hive is basically . . . it's basically insane at this point. All the rules that bees live by have broken down. They don't have a queen, no fresh workers being born, too many drones." Anthony can hear Bernard lean slowly back into his chair. He hears the long, tortured squeak of springs and metal.

"They're going to go. We don't know a lot about bees," says Bernard's sad voice, "nothing really. Why are some colonies extra-clean? Why do some turn robber? We don't know why they do most of the things they do. Or how they know the things they know. But these bees know that there's no future for them now. They're taking matters into their own hands. I know it's hard, Tony. But if they killed that new queen, there's no hope. Just let them go."

"They were my mom's."

"That's just the way the world works sometimes. Do you want to come out to the nursery and talk?"

"No. No, that's . . . no. Bye, Bernie." Anthony hangs up the phone.

The kitchen is silent. No birds, no refrigerator, no barking dogs. No noise. Anthony simply waits, hoping to hear someone say something that will change the way the world works. And then, at the very edge of perception, there comes a sound. It grows louder and louder. A melodious, rhythmic sound, a little like a violin, a little like a flute, if either were being played by the wind sweeping through a meadow. It's coming from the jar on the windowsill.

The queen is facing him. She is buzzing her wings. Anthony has never heard a bee make a sound like this. And when he looks at her the sound changes, becomes shorter, more emphatic. Pulses of sound. Still making this noise, she walks right up to the edge of the glass. She is staring at him.

"I could introduce you to the hive," he tells her. "I could put you right in there. Don't think I haven't thought if it. But that would be sort of like . . . "

Sort of like a death sentence. Wouldn't it?

He takes her off the shelf. She is still buzzing, but it's a softer song now. Less emphatic, more soothing. He holds her up to the light and looks at her. A thought occurs to him.

What if he didn't put her in the shipping cage with the candy plug? She'd be a sitting duck in the cage, no way to defend herself. What if he just set her on the landing board, and let her do what she wanted? If she entered the hive she'd be taking a horrible risk. But maybe it would be one she'd be willing to take. Clearly something happened to her own hive. A queen without a hive is out of balance just as much as a hive without a queen.

He would have to do it at night, when the bees are calmest. After the temperature drops outside and the bees get cozy. Always assuming, he realizes, that he has any bees left tonight. What if they swarm before that? Maybe they've already left.

Jumping like somebody just shot off a starting gun, he races for the door and bolts outside. Bear runs right along after him, excited to be moving in the direction of the bees, destruction on his mind.

"Bear, sit! Stay!" Why does he even try? He slips into the shed quickly, leaving Bear to bark and whine, and heads straight for the hive, hoping against hope that the bees haven't already flown off.

The colony is still there, but barely. Fifty percent of them are in the air, circling like a cyclone, and fifty percent are massed on the landing board. At any second they could all depart; they await only a single, unknown trigger. It is chaos.

Deep in his chest, down behind his shoulder blades, he feels the glow. When he concentrates, it begins to brighten, and the image of a six-sided honey cell floats transparently before his eyes. He's never tried to do anything like this, never tried to convince a colony of swarming insects to stay put. But he can't see why it wouldn't work.

BACK, he says. He pictures all the bees returning to the hive. BACK HOME. And a few of them go. But it's almost like the bees have stopped listening. Mat gets like this sometimes when he is throwing a tantrum, just screaming and crying and there is no way to talk to him.

Anthony focuses on his glow, and stokes it higher. BEES GO HOME, he says. COME ON BEES, CALM DOWN.

And a large contingent of them return inside the hive. But the second he stops concentrating, they come out again. Maybe Bernie is right. Maybe there's nothing to be done. But that doesn't mean Anthony is going to give up. He's just going to need more. It appears that this is going to be an old school fight. Fortunately, he has old school tools.

Inside the shed, beneath a shelf and behind a feed sack, lies an old smoker. This is a tool most beekeepers use regularly, but one Anthony and his mother never employed. He does, however, know how to use it, and he lifts it out now and blows off the dust. It is a copper canister about half the size of a gallon paint can and slightly taller. On one side there's a spout, on the other a bellows. He opens the lid, quickly tears some strips of burlap from the feed bag and packs them loosely into the container, then sets them alight with a barbecue lighter from the drawer. As soon as a small flame has begun, he closes the lid to damp down the fire and create smoke.

He gives an experimental push on the bellows, and a weak puff of white smoke pops out of the spout. A few more minutes of smoldering and it will be ready.

Smoke serves two purposes in controlling bees. First, it blocks one of their two primary forms of communication—the transfer of pheromones from the queen to her children. The thick fumes of a smoky fire overwhelm the more delicate chemical interchange of bee-to-bee, isolating them. Bees isolated from each other become much less active. Of course, they still have their wingsong, but that is a more primitive form of speech and only for use over short distances. Pheromones can propagate throughout an entire hive in a matter of seconds, and travel miles within a hour.

Smoke also drives bees to the combs to begin eating honey. In the wild, smoke means fire, and fire is one of the few things that bees have no way to combat, so they do the next best thing and attempt to use up as much of the stored food as possible in case they have to flee. This distracts them, so a beekeeper can more safely open the hive; it also tends to fill them and make them sluggish.

So Anthony takes his smoker out into the bee yard, wades into the swarm, and starts pumping. For the rest of the afternoon he battles to keep the hive together. He uses the smoker, and he coaxes them with his power. Every time the bees mass to depart, he talks to them, hits them with smoke, sings to them.

HOME, STAY HOME, he chants, hour after hour.

He burns himself on the smoker. Sweat stings his eyes and the cuts on his arms and face. He doesn't stop for food, water, or to rest, and as the afternoon wears on he begins to wonder if he is going to make it. His back aches, his injured leg cramps so that he can barely limp from one side of the hive to the other. His arms feel like they will fall off his body, and it is a monumental task to keep the smoker lifted high enough to do any good.

But more than any of that it is the mental exertion that drains him. The concentration it takes to continually route the bees back with his mind. He's never tried anything like this. He's never used this skill on anything more than a casual basis. It hadn't occurred to him that there might be a real world use for it. But it is exhausting. He feels like he's riding his bike a hundred miles an hour uphill. It's like he has a fever—the heat from the energy is that intense. It makes his hands and lips tremble.

In the end, he manages to keep the bees from swarming. They are not happy about it. They had their minds set on it. But by late afternoon, they have admitted that it will not happen, at least not today, and have retreated sullenly into the supers.

At just about the same time, he sees his father's truck pull into the driveway. It slows and stops, idling as his dad steps out. Anthony can see Mat in the car seat, complaining that he has to stay locked up when all the interesting stuff is happening outside. His father paces deliberately from the truck to stand at the fence. He hitches his pants up, then crosses his arms. He surveys the wreck that has been made of the flower bed during Anthony's battle with the bees.

"Bear get in here again?" he asks.

"No," Anthony answers. He is exhausted. He sits on a bag of fertilizer by the shed. "The hive was going to swarm."

"What's that?" his dad asks. "Swarm?"

"The colony was going to leave forever. I stopped them."

"Oh. You stopped 'em," his dad repeats. He clears his throat. Squints his eyes. Anthony can clearly see there are about three hundred separate things which are occurring to his father to say, none of which, for some reason, he is saying. Finally he just turns and heads back to the truck.

"You're supposed to be resting. Go get washed up for dinner," he calls over his shoulder. Then he starts the truck and continues to the house.

Dinner is tense and silent. The mason jar sitting in the middle of the table dominates the meal. Outside, panting relentlessly, fixated on the idea that there is a bee in the house, Bear can be heard. Occasionally he gives out a plaintive yip.

"Why is that jar here?" Mat asks.

Mat looks to his father and then to his brother. Neither answers. In Anthony's case, it seems like he didn't even hear the question.

"How come there's a jar with a bee at dinner?" Mat tries again. Still no response. Anthony seems completely oblivious, his father just rolls his eyes. Mat pushes his chair out.

"Where you going?" his dad asks.

"I want a bug too."

"Sit down."

"But Anthony has a bug!" Mat points at the jar.

Anthony finally seems to notice that there's a conversation going on. He addresses his brother. "This is different," Anthony says.

"How come?" Mat asks.

"I'm letting her go as soon as it's dark." This is the arrangement he's made with his father. The bee can come to the table, to keep it safe from the dog, then after dinner Anthony will let it go.

"Can I watch?" Mat wonders.

"No," Anthony says.

"Why?"

"You just can't."

"Well, can I help you?"

"No, Mat, stop asking."

"Well—"

"Just eat your food," his dad says. "That bug will be out of the house, and you're going to bed. Now, I don't want to hear anything else about the bug."

The rest of the meal passes in silence, punctuated by Bear's occasional tortured moaning from the yard.

When the meal is over, it is dark, and the time has come. Anthony pushes out from the table and lifts his queen.

"I don't want you hanging around out there," says his dad. "The doctor said rest. Just get rid of it, and come back in. You hear me?" Anthony nods.

"Will you let Bear in the front door while I go out the side?" he asks.

His dad rises from the table, muttering under his breath. Mat watches in disapproval. Bugs happen to be a specialty of his. Just the day before he'd found a pill bug and captured it under a sand pail.

There are so many things he could tell Anthony about bugs, if only someone would let him.

Anthony lifts the jar and stands waiting by the side door, and as soon as he hears Bear come scrambling inside looking for the bee, he steps out into the cool evening. He's nervous. There's no reason in the world for this to work, and he knows it, but still he hopes. It's not impossible. It could work, couldn't it?

As he trudges out to the bee yard, he talks to the queen.

"Now, these bees might seem a bit rough at first," he says. "But it's a good hive. It's always been a good hive." He says it twice. He wants her to understand, since the existing evidence all points to another conclusion.

There is a bit of a breeze pushing the pines around, and the rustling comforts him. It's likely to make the bees even more lethargic. They don't like to fly at night, and a cool evening breeze might be just enough to keep them placid while this new queen enters the supers. After she's inside, assuming she decides to go, all bets are off. At least she won't be trapped inside a shipping box.

The moon is almost full. Anthony decides not to flip on the lights in the bee yard as he goes through the shed. The less interruption to the routine of the hive, the better. There's enough light out to see what needs to be seen.

From the house he hears his father calling, "Anthony, let's go!" His dad's voice echoes faintly off the hills. It sounds lonely. But it means business. He knows he can't linger, or he'll really suffer the consequences.

With just a light tug, the lid of the jar twists open. He kneels down by the landing board and tilts the glass sideways, and slowly, almost regally, the queen strides out, over the lip of the jar, stepping down onto the wooden shelf—and there she stops. Anthony holds his breath. There's no way to know what to expect. Maybe she'll just fly away—she has every right to, as far as he's concerned. There's no way to force her into the hive, and he wouldn't do it even if he could. But he keeps thinking, *A hive needs a queen, and a queen needs a hive.*

She turns around to look into the jar. She looks like she's considering climbing back inside. She samples the air with her antennae. Then she turns to face Anthony. *Buzz, buzz,* she says.

"There's lots of flowers here," Anthony says. "It could be a good life. But I won't kid you. This colony, it's pretty messed up right now."

His father's voice, now with a tinge of anger, bellows again, "Anthony, I'm coming out there to get you if you don't get in here NOW!"

Anthony stands. "Please, Little Queen," he says. "We need your help."

Then with a final buzz, she turns. Quickly she walks under the arch and into the hive.

As Anthony's dad takes the bandages off his arm and cleans the wound, then binds him up again with fresh gauze, Anthony finds himself yawning. His dad sends him to his room as soon as he's done. But after he lies down, Anthony can't sleep. His brain is buzzing at the speed of bee wings. He tosses and turns in the bed like it's made of rocks—there is no way to get comfortable.

In his mind he sees the previous queen, with her attendants, dead in her box, pierced through a hundred times with vicious stingers. She had had no chance. Did he just doom this new queen to the same fate? Just because she is bigger and free to move around doesn't mean she'll be successful. If the colony chooses to swarm and ball her there won't be much she can do—except flee, he supposes. And then he'll be right where he was before.

After a while he sits up in his bed and draws open a drawer in his chest. He lifts out the little shipping box. The stingers are gone. The queen thrown away. And the candy plug is still filling the hole. She didn't even last long enough for the bees to start eating the sweet sugar. The memory won't let him go.

He spends the rest of the night sitting up in bed, holding the box and trying to feel good about what he did.

. . .

He wakes slowly. The smell of pancakes fills the air. It's the one thing his dad cooks better than his mom ever did. His dad's pancakes are things of beauty, brown and crisp on the outside and warm and perfectly soft on the inside. His stomach rumbles even before his mind fully gets going. But then he remembers, and sits straight up—apparently he finally did fall asleep. And now it's late morning. He has to check the hive.

Aching from the battle to stop the swarm the previous day, he stumbles into his clothes. His back is sore, and both arms—the injured and the whole—feel like they might break off at the shoulder. Getting dressed is a bit of a clown act and he's too sore to bend over and put on shoes and socks, but as soon as he's mostly covered, he limps from the room.

"Pancakes," his dad calls as Anthony hobbles into the kitchen.

He doesn't even answer. Barefoot, he labors out past the driveway, then covers the ground between the house and the bee yard at a dead run, warming up, ignoring the pain in his leg. As he gets closer he can see that at least the bees aren't massed around the landing board. There is no cloud of them in the air. That's a good sign. He tears through the shed and out in to the yard, then slowly crosses toward the hive. It's quiet. No angry buzzing, no sign of problems.

But as he moves nearer he realizes that buzzing isn't the only thing missing; there are no bees at all. No bees on the landing board, no bees in the air. And the hive, far from being filled with angry and overwrought bees, is actually completely silent.

"Oh, please," he whispers. Stepping quickly to the super and forgoing the hive tools, he wedges his fingers under the lid and pulls, pulls until his nails bend back, until the top lifts off. Not a sound. He raises one of the racks out of the form. There is not a bee to be seen. Nothing.

The hive swarmed after all. Despite everything. Despite the queen, who probably lies dead somewhere at the bottom of the comb, despite all his work, despite explosions and sickness, it is now finally over.

Chapter Twelve

When she awakes and smells honey, for a moment she fears that she is back in the robber hive. But her actual setting is even stranger than that.

She rests alone within a transparent cave, with a solid top and curving walls. The walls are of the same substance as the disks in the Superhive. There is nothing in this cave but a dripping wedge of honeycomb.

How long has she been sleeping? There is no way to know. Apparently long enough for her entire world to change. Through the transparent walls she sees figures moving, humans. She can tell from her unerring internal clock that it is night, but light floods through the invisible walls from bright orbs beyond her reach. These orbs hang on the walls of some larger cave in which the humans move.

She is in very poor shape now. Her leg and wing are grievously wounded, and the Death Crown cracked her skeleton in several places before she was able to escape. She is weak. She eats the honey in the comb below, and waits for strength to return.

The sounds of the humans filter through to her. They are barking at each other, and waving their arms. There are two, one large and one small. The smaller she recognizes; it is the human she found in the meadow.

Abruptly that human rushes up to her and grabs the transparent cave and holds it. The larger human attempts to take it away but cannot. Their voices boom down on the Little Queen, and she is thrown around the smooth walls as the two of them struggle, until she lands on the honeycomb and grabs hold. Her injured leg aches. What is happening?

Finally the heaving stops. The smaller human still carries her, but now they are moving. They pass out of the larger cave with the glowing orbs, and into the night. Though she is jostled and bounced, she manages to hold her spot on the sticky comb, and sees stars outside, and trees, and a moon.

And then they are inside another small cave and the cave starts to move. She hears a noise like a colony fanning honey, a powerful hum that rises and falls. She rests on the lap of the smaller human, whom she now thinks of as the younger. It lifts her cave to its face, and looks at her.

Then her injuries overcome her, and she sleeps again.

When she wakes she is being held up to the face of the larger human. Outside her cave there is bright light, and white walls, very like the Superhive. The larger human shakes the cave. From the way it shakes and barks at her she understands that it is upset. And she can also see it doing something that means it is unhappy.

Bees have only been interacting with humans for about forty thousand years. This is such a small piece of their one hundred million-year history that it hardly merits attention, except that, more than any other species bees have ever encountered, humans have pushed themselves into bee life. Thus, over those forty thousand years, bees have gained some understanding of the way humans communicate. They do not have wingsong, they do not dance. In fact, it is unclear exactly what they do. But they have faces that form patterns, and these patterns can have meaning. The one she sees now means *unhappy*. The Little Queen limps as far back in her round cage as she can, away from the unhappy human. They are so big and clumsy, these creatures. A disgruntled one could easily hurt or kill a bee.

But then another human appears out of an opening in the wall, this one dressed in white, and the two of them bark at each other. The Little Queen listens. She is sure she can detect patterns in the sounds. They are communicating complex thoughts. There is no accumulated knowledge available on the Plain of Crowns that teaches the meanings associated with these sounds. Could she be the first bee who ever noticed? Or maybe she is, in this as in so many other things, just more perceptive?

Still exhausted, and with her injuries draining her reserves, she sleeps again. When she wakes the third time, she is being carried by the small human back into the cave where the two humans live. The small one places her on top of a warm white surface, then stares at her. In the background the larger one barks. On the face of the small one is a pattern she does not recognize. A pattern a little like *unhappy*, but not entirely the same. Somehow she has the feeling that the human is worried. About her.

"Do not worry, I am fine," she buzzes. Her wingsong echoes in her chamber, and pain flashes down her back. The wing is getting worse. She doubts if the human can hear her, or can understand her if it did hear, but it bobs its head slowly and then turns to follow the larger one out. When they leave, the light dies. And she finds herself wondering, *why did I tell it not to worry about me? I am the one injured. I am the one trapped. I am the one without a colony.*

Since she can do nothing about her colony, and nothing about her imprisonment, she turns to her injuries. Her right foreleg is shattered at the femur, and her right rear wing has been torn at the rotator. She has bathed her leg in honey to prevent infection. But the damage is deep, and the leg is likely lost. Her wing would not be a devastating injury, but she cannot reach it to bathe it in honey. Infection there is likely—in fact, it has already begun. The wound where the wasp bit through her shoulder also shows signs of infection. If she had her attendants, it would be their job to clean where she cannot reach. But now she will have to think of something else.

At her most fundamental level a bee is one of nature's great problem solvers. Right now, the Little Queen's problem is her injuries. She will die of them, from infection alone most likely. Just as the seared worker in the bowl would have died if the wasps had not killed her first.

The Little Queen finds herself thinking about those bees, wondering about the regression she took them through, the metamorphosis from forager to wax bee. Their bodies had actually changed and grown new shapes and sizes, and altered their internal composition in response to the processes she initiated in them. An idea grows in her mind. Something new.

If she could change them, why not herself? What is healing but metamorphosis, the same process her attendants underwent? In both cases there would be transformation. In both cases the body would move from an imperfect or problematic state to an optimal, more desirable form.

If it does not work, she will be no worse off. And if it kills her, so be it. She is dying even now. So cautiously, tentatively, she closes her sight and focuses.

The first thing she realizes is that the glowing golden light from the meadow is near. It piques her curiosity with an amazing magnetic force. But she turns from it. Time for that later.

When she changed the workers, she was changing them from one familiar state to another. But how will she change herself? From mature queen to mature queen? That is not specific enough. She needs a more solid model.

And she thinks, when I visit the Plain of Crowns, I inhabit a body. A perfect body, a perfect version of myself. I will use that as my template. And so she creates it, in her mind.

She draws out the wings and makes them powerful, builds the arms and legs, joint by joint, expands the abdomen, builds out the thorax. She forms a perfect head, a perfect tail, ideal antennae and stinger. She casts her mind back and forth across it as if she were in a hive, creating a flawless honeycomb—testing dimensions, adjusting height, weight, and color. And when she is done, she has it. Her ultimate, ideal form.

Then she awakens her Queen's Bell. Through a hundred million years of evolution this hidden mechanism has evolved into one of the most powerful and delicate tools anywhere on earth, capable of producing complex pheromonic symphonies to regulate and control the life of a colony. In truth, bees and Bell evolved together. Bees evolved a sensitivity to pheromones. More than that they evolved a plasticity, a physical proclivity to respond, so that a queen can make wide-ranging adjustments to her hive with just the release of a few molecules.

Of course, attempting any sort of physical transformation with this tool is a risk. Once a transformation begins, it can spin out of control. The plasticity of a bee's body means it is naturally inclined to respond to change, and change is a double-edged sword if taken too far. Cancer is change, metamorphosis raging out of control.

In her mind she makes builds a channel between the shape of her perfect model and the generative machinery of her Bell. She pours her desire, like fuel, down along this channel, and quickly she feels her Queen's Bell respond. "Make this real," she is saying to a one hundred million-year-old engine of change. And she hopes she can keep the engine under control.

Her temperature quickly skyrockets, because she is both producing pheromones and reacting to them. She is shocked at the pain that fills her. Is this what her attendants willingly submitted to when she healed them? With no knowledge of what was happening it must have been terrifying, this wrenching agony. Even understanding it, she is almost overcome.

But her body is responding. She can feel a looseness in her joints, as though they are filled with honey. It spreads through her physical form quickly, and she falls onto her belly. Her muscles have no strength, her bones have no hardness. She is incapable of movement. She is being remade.

There is a fine line between healing growth and a total, out of control escalation of the body's generative powers. Through the pain and confusion—and, yes, the fear—she bends her mind to rein in the cells which now want to run wild and grow without boundaries; she must contain them within the outlines of her ideal model. She realizes she has begun a thing over which she has very little control, a thing so close to the primal forces of creation that consciousness of any kind, even the advanced consciousness of one of the Sequestered, is poorly equipped to shape it.

Her body begins shaking, torn by conflicting impulses—mortal discipline versus unbridled creation. The heat in her little cave is rising. The process is spinning out of her control. With every second that passes, she moves closer to losing the power to direct this process, and so with her last shining drop of energy, she wills it to stop.

And consciousness exits her body.

When she awakes again, the first thing she sees is the face of the smaller human. Morning light illuminates its great, gray eyes. She moves her body slowly. On shaky legs she stands. She is weak. But she is whole. Her leg, her wing, the cracks though her skeleton, have all been repaired. And now she is ravenous.

Sucking honey from the comb—delicious honey, the most succulent taste she has ever experienced—she watches the human. It raises a stick to its mouth over and over, and she can see it chew. And now, as her thinking clears and her energy returns, she compares the patterns of its face against the things that bees know about humans, and decides that it is male. And young. A boy.

They eat in silence for a time, considering each other. And the Little Queen begins to wonder, just what was this boy human doing in that meadow? Surely not waiting for her. Yet it seems clear that he is the one who has placed her in this cave. He is keeping her. What is his connection to the golden light that guided her?

Then the human barks, stands, and grabs her transparent enclosure. And the two of them are moving. They pass out of the well-lit part of the cave and into a darker section. The human stops for a moment before a long, mounting series of little platforms, seems as though he will begin to climb them, then turns around and lowers himself onto structure like a half hollow log. He sits here for a moment, then settles down on his side. He pulls the Little Queen in her curved enclosure near his face, and studies her. And then his eyes close and he stops moving. And soon the Little Queen's weariness returns. She occludes her optic nerves. And the two of them sleep.

She wakes because the transparent cave is being jostled. The boy is cradling the cave with his arm, and though his eyes are still closed, he is barking, and his face is twisting in the shapes that mean *fear*, and *sadness*, and *worry*. The barking grows louder. The cave rocks dangerously.

She does not know what is happening, but it does not seem as though the human is trying to hurt her. He seems not to know what he is doing at all. And so the Little Queen begins a song of quiet, a song of peace, a song queens use to ease a hive riled by a passing bear, or a sudden noise.

PEACE NOW, she sings. She dances forward, pirouettes, dances back. *PEACE NOW. PEACE NOW. PEACE NOW.*

And soon the heaving stops. And then the boy opens his eyes. She moves up close to the glass. What eyes. Huge. Full. She finds them beautiful.

Then he stands. He creates an opening in the wall of his cave and holds his hands up to his mouth to let out a series of long calls. She has heard this call before, from the other human in the house, the night before and earlier this morning. She vibrates her wings softly, attempting to reproduce it: *BEAR.BEAR.BEAR.*

A dog careens around the corner of the structure and through the opening in the wall, catching sight of her in her cave as it passes and attempting to stop. Bees know dogs, as they know everything else in the physical world. There are Good Dogs, and there are Bad. This dog slides down the passage and the young male human steps outside and quickly closes the opening behind him. The Little Queen recognizes this dog. He is a Bad Dog. He likes to terrorize bees.

Now the boy carries her over an expanse of low grasses toward another small structure. Humans can always be found near structures; it is their preferred dwelling type. This one is green. The smell of flowers grows stronger as they near it. And the smell of bees. Swarming bees. She can tell even before she sees them. The hive they are approaching is preparing to swarm away.

Normally this is an exciting time in the life of a colony. Searching out new vistas, new fields, creating new comb. It appeals to so many parts of the bee psyche: the curiosity, the creativity, the passion for work. But this hive does not smell as though it is excited. It does not smell healthy at all.

The boy has a pattern on his face that the Little Queen recognizes as *happy*, and he holds her up as they near the hive, holds her ahead of him toward the colony as though he is showing it to her. But she sees his expression change quickly when they arrive. *Happy* is replaced by a new pattern: *afraid*.

Does he understand that this hive is not well? Does he somehow care? It does not seem likely, but he is responding to something. He turns with her and runs back to the larger structure, opens the wall and the dog lurches out, sidesteps the dog, sets her on a ledge, and disappears. And she does not see him for the rest of the day.

Faintly she smells smoke as the hours pass. It comes and goes, and makes her nervous, but the fire seems far away or small, and the smell does not get stronger. She spends her time eating. The healing she did with her Queen's Bell depleted her brutally, and she feels she could eat for a year without getting full.

Evening falls, and the larger human returns to the structure. She can hear him. Another small human is with him. This small human appears in front of her and examines her closely. She hears a different sound pattern that she is beginning to recognize, and she transcribes it into wingsong: *BEE.BEE.BEE.*

Finally the boy returns. She can tell he is tired; she recognizes the patterns. Panting. Stooped shoulders. Wetness on his face and body. The boy and the large human bark at each other again—this seems to happen quite frequently—and she hears more familiar sounds: *BEE.BEE.BEE* and *DARK.DARK.DARK.*

All three humans crouch around a large flat surface, lift sticks to their mouths, and chew. Her cave sits in the middle and she observes and listens. *BUG.BUG.BUG*, she hears. Then the boy lifts her and carries her outside.

The smell of smoke clings to him. He must have been near the fire today. His face wears a pattern she does not recognize, but she thinks he might be anxious. He walks quickly and his body radiates extra heat. When they arrive at the hive she is surprised to hear the colony still at home. It seemed very clear when she was here earlier that they were leaving at any moment. The smell of smoke is strong here, almost overwhelming the sweet smell of flowers. Did the fire drive this colony back into the hive?

Most certainly they will swarm tomorrow, when the light comes again.

As they move, the boy holds her cave up hear his face and makes sound patterns. She is recognizing more of them. *HIVE.HIVE.HIVE.*

The boy carries her into the small green structure and closer to the hive, until they are standing right next to it. And then he takes the lid off her cave, bends down, and positions the open end upon the landing board of the swarming colony.

She strides out of the transparent cave. Is he releasing her? Why here? Without thinking, as though he is a bee, she tells him with wing-song, "I have nowhere to go."

The boy whispers back to her, but there are no familiar patterns in the sound. Still, she understands. He is urging her to enter the hive.

She hears the faint sound of the larger human calling in the night, and sees the boy react. She recognizes a pattern in that distant voice, and she plays it with her wings. *ANTHONY. ANTHONY. ANTHONY.* She thinks that might be the sound that identifies him.

More urgently now, he bends close to her. And she hears another familiar pattern in a string of soft, tangled sounds. *QUEEN. QUEEN. QUEEN.* The pattern on his face is *worry*.

He wants her to enter the hive. But why? She supposes it does not matter. She truly does have nowhere else to go. So she sings a final song: "Do not worry," she buzzes, then turns. And quickly she walks under the arch. Outside she hears the boy rise and run back to his cave. Now she is alone. She crawls forward into a nightmare.

It only takes a moment for her to understand what is going on. It is the saddest, most pitiable thing that can happen in all the chronicles of bee existence. This is a colony that has lost its queen, and which failed to raise a new one. It is not, in fact, a colony. It is just a group of bees, slowly dying.

The robber hive was dirty because the bees within it were too distracted by fear to keep abreast of the cleaning, but eventually the trash did get cleared away. This hive is filthy because these bees have stopped caring. No bee has touched this accumulated waste in many months. It is piled an inch deep on the floor of the hive. Dead bees.

Excrement. Wax, propolis, leaves, and dirt. The farther in she goes, the more lurid and dreadful the scene becomes. Unsealed cells with dead larvae within, starved or exposed to the elements. Wandering, directionless workers circling pieces of comb, without the will to stop moving, but unable to eat, drink, or perform useful service. It is an absolute wonder any of them ever managed to summon the ambition to swarm away to die, since they are doing such an adequate job of it right here.

When they see her, the workers stare. It has been so long that they do not recognize a queen when they see one. Many of them—maybe most of them—were born after the old queen died, of eggs she had already laid, so they have never seen a queen. But it's not just the workers. Out of this hive of perhaps twelve thousand bees, there are at least three thousand drones. Three thousand males! In a healthy colony of seventy thousand bees, there should be no more than five hundred males, whose only job, the one, single task they are ever called upon or qualified to perform, is to fertilize a new queen, in the event that one appears. The preponderance of males here tells her all she needs to know about the hive's timeline. For months, many months, this hive has been run by faux queens, who can lay only a few eggs a day, all of them unfertilized, so they hatch out as male.

Strangely, only now does the reality strike her: this hive needs a queen. It is a small colony, an unhealthy, broken hive, beset by melancholy and lost in some strange pain; it would gladly fly into a fire and perish if the bees here could only summon the will to beat their wings. But it is a hive. She trembles, disbelief becoming understanding, becoming joy. It is a hive!

She moves up off the floor onto the comb, looking for the faux queens. COME TO ME! she calls, mind-to-mind. The whole hive hears her, but not a single bee moves.

COME TO ME NOW! she peals, louder and more forcefully than she has ever used the mind-to-mind. Bees twenty miles away could hear that. But the best she gets here is a confused murmur. She moves quickly, from bee to bee.

"Clean yourselves," she says. She pumps the hive full of

pheromones, summoning the hive to work. "Find your jobs," she radiates. "To work!"

But no bee moves. Finally she comes upon a faux. Formerly a worker, she somehow found the means to transfigure herself. Some deep survival instinct produced in her a vestigial Queen's Bell, a barely functional component which made possible her transformation from worker to aberrant egg layer. Some queens would find this repulsive, but to the Little Queen it is commendable. It represents the depth of this hive's will to survive. Deep as that will may have been driven underground now, it once struggled mightily.

"How many are you?" asks the Little Queen. The faux's mind struggles, sluggish and scarcely working. The Little Queen speaks again, more slowly and clearly, mind-to-mind. How many fauxs are there?

"We are fifty," sings the bee before her.

It is shocking. Fifty? Unheard of. The Little Queen would have guessed perhaps five, but been unsurprised if there had been only two. If this faux transformation is, in fact, representative of the hive's will to go on living, she has come upon an exceptional hive indeed.

She could kill this faux. That is what bee history would prescribe. Eliminate the fauxs and assume the role of preeminence. But somehow she knows that with this colony, at this time, killing is not the answer. It could push them all over the edge, with so many of them simply looking for a way or a reason to die. Often fauxs must be killed because they are unwilling to cede control, but this poor specimen can barely muster the energy to talk, let alone resist. Still, if they are not dealt with, they will continue to wander the combs, laying male eggs and upsetting the essential balance.

Come to me, oh you Queens, she calls then, mind-to-mind. All you mighty Queens, you worthy Queens, you saviors of this hive, come!

She begins to dance. And play wingsong. She taps her Bell to release a cloud of alluring sweetness into the hive. And slowly, arduously, as though moving stones with the pressure of her breath alone, she pulls the fifty fauxs from the far corners of the hive, until they are gathered in front of her, tired, beaten, sullen.

You have done your work, good queens, she tells them.

THOUGH YOU WILL NOT BE REMEMBERED ON THE PLAIN OF CROWNS, I WILL REMEMBER YOU. ALWAYS. And then, so swiftly that they cannot protest or defend themselves, she heats her Bell and strikes them with pure, isothermic metamorphosis.

It is frightening to see. She realizes that she has grown adept at this, more so than she had thought, and wonders if she has pushed too hard. The fifty writhe before her. Long ovipositors shrink before her eyes, thoraxes shorten, heads and shoulders realign.

Three of the weakest die, cracking and disintegrating, spilling their vital fluids onto the wax. But the others, panting, mewling, shuddering, regress back to their worker forms and lie trembling before her.

She picks eighteen of the strongest, the ones who are struggling to stand.

"You will be my attendants," she sings, though they are still too weak to perform any duties. And then she moves to address the rest of the hive.

"I am your queen," she sings to them. "And together, we will gather nectar and raise babies and make the finest honey that ever has been made this side of the Plain of Crowns!"

But from the rest of the hive not a sound is heard. One of her new attendants, the very strongest, speaks to her in wingsong.

"You are too late, mother," she splutters, on wings still wet from her transformation.

"It is never too late."

"It is," says the bee. The Queen looks her over. An exceptional worker. Large and powerful, and newly perfect. But so very sad. "We have lost our place. We have lost our path. The hive is lost."

She is so certain, it almost convinces the Little Queen. Almost. "How did you come to this?" she asks.

"There was one who tended us. The golden one. He gave us everything. He made us exceptional. But one day he changed."

The golden one. Could it be? "Why?" she asks.

"We do not know. He became lost, so we became lost. We grew melancholy. Our queen died of loneliness. And the colony did not recover."

The Little Queen casts her mind out through the hive, searching for a spark, a willing mind, a flash of hope, but she finds none.

This cannot be, she thinks. *It will not be.*

LISTEN TO ME, she calls, THOUGH YOU FEEL LOST, YOU ARE PERFECT. THOUGH YOU FEEL RIPPED IN TWO, YOU ARE WHOLE. THIS HIVE WILL RISE AGAIN. I WILL SHOW YOU WHAT YOU ARE!

In her mind, she constructs another perfect form. Measuring, weighing, shifting back and forth across her mental comb, abandoning herself completely to creating, she builds for the hive a perfect model of itself. When it is finished, she makes them look. She forces it into their minds; she links them together to see this beautiful truth. And then, tapping her Queen's Bell, she pours all the desire cresting within her—the desire to be mother to this hive, the desire to be a queen in deed and in spirit—into one single thought.

Once again she says, "Make this so," to her ancient engine of transformation.

It builds in the distance like a storm. It comes closer. A few of the more sensitive begin to look around them. And then, as though a giant wind is working its way through the racks of comb, the bees stagger and fall from their perches, spin and rock and whirl, knock against the walls and crash upon the floor. And when the wind has passed, the job is done.

Outside, the Little Queen can sense the dawn breaking. She calls to her hive, COME! FLY WITH ME!

Fifteen thousand bees rise as one, stream from the hive, and rise into the air.

Through clean air, in bright sun, they twist and tumble past fields of flowers, over woods and through shadows, into light. They fly for hours, cleansing themselves in movement.

Then she leads them back, and willingly they follow. Ahead she sees the green building, and the small white tower which is to be her home. Seated beside it, bent upon himself, she sees the boy.

When they approach, he looks up. She sees the pattern on his face as she flies close. It is *grief*. But when he spies the bees streaming into the hive, it changes. She lands on the board at the entrance to her hive, letting the colony stream in behind her while she watches him. There is much work to be done before she can begin laying, and these bees will need her complete attention in order to recover from their ordeal and become autonomous, self-motivated workers. Still, she remains on the board until the last of them is inside. Because she senses that this boy is an important part of her hive. An essential part. He is . . . almost bee-like. He is, she thinks, the golden one.

She attempts to reach him, mind-to-mind. DO YOU HEAR? she whispers, looking up. DO YOU HEAR ME? But there is no answer. He is not so bee-like that he can understand her speech. But perhaps she can learn his, she thinks. In time. With practice. She will learn to talk to him.

She steps out onto his proffered palm, and feels herself lifted upward toward his face.

Water flows from his eyes. "Thank you," he whispers. It is a pattern she recognizes.

ANTHONY. ANTHONY. ANTHONY, she sings with her wings. Then she lifts up from his hand, and enters the hive to begin the job before her.

Chapter Thirteen

Spring break. The birds sing a little sweeter, the flowers smell a little richer, and sunlight feels warmer and more nurturing. For a thirteen-year-old boy, every moment of a day like this is a golden coin flipping through the air and falling perfectly into your pocket, one after another, in an endless succession of sublime, magical adventures.

Unless, for some reason, you're not allowed on the Internet. "Dad, please," Anthony begs. "Hasn't it been long enough?"

It's breakfast, and his dad is chomping through his one piece of toast and slurping down his cup of coffee. He doesn't seem inclined to budge on this issue. Mat sits in his booster chair watching the interplay. He may not know it, but he's stocking away strategy for his own future spring break tests of will. Hot cereal slips down his cheek as he looks back and forth from one to the other. He knows how it's going to end, but he's still fascinated.

"Internet's a privilege," says his dad, finishing off his toast. "You need to demonstrate you're mature."

"I know, but it's—"

"What's the point, anyway? You're just gonna play games and e-mail your friends. Go outside."

"I need to e-mail Bernie. There's stuff I need for the bees. This is really important."

His dad shakes his head, but to Mathew's surprise he doesn't immediately issue another denial. *Hmm*, thinks Mat. *Bees. Is that the secret? All you have to do is talk about bees?*

Anthony waits while his dad finishes. It's a very delicate moment, things could swing either way. Then his dad wipes his mouth with a napkin.

"Okay. Bee stuff only. No phone calls, unless it's bee stuff. I'm serious." He stands. Mathew spills cereal in his lap. He has just witnessed a miracle.

"Down, Bear," Paul pushes the dog away with his foot, "Goddamn dog!" He lifts Mat from the chair, grabs his papers, and heads for the door.

"Down, Bear!" Mat squeaks. Bear somehow hears "Up, Bear," a command no one in their right mind would ever teach him, and Paul and Mat just manage to get out the door without being crushed against the wall.

The house is empty. Anthony slams down the rest of his breakfast and runs out to check the bees. First things first. He's still not convinced that any of this is going to last. With the way his life has been going, it could just be a setup for another disaster. But when he gets to the bee yard, the hive is happily humming, and workers have already cleared out huge piles of refuse that's piled around the base of the hive. From all that he can see, some sort of normalcy is returning to the colony. It's too early to crack the supers and see what's going on inside; the bees need a chance to get adjusted.

But touching the hive-mind will not distract them. If he asks nothing of them, only watches, they will not even notice. It is easy now, the way it used to be, for him to access his gift. He pulls the hexagon up and nudges a thought through it, out toward the hive. It almost blinds him.

There is a hive-mind there. One like he has never seen before. Brilliant and hot and massive. What is going on? This colony is going from one extreme to the other, from no hive-mind at all to an astonishingly powerful hive-mind. It must be reacting to its near-death experience, celebrating, producing extra energy as it gets back on track, although that is really no explanation for the mind he touches. And it seems to be getting stronger and bigger, even as he watches.

He runs back into the house and heads straight for the computer. The pictures he took of the Little Queen in her jar are better than he could have expected. First he sends one in an e-mail to Bernard.

Hey Bernie, what kind of bee is this? She's my new queen! She seems like she's bringing the hive back. Do you know?

He fires it off. Then he starts prowling online, looking at images and comparing them to his queen. He goes to all his usual sites, but of course he's seen all the pictures there already. So he starts posting to forums, and including images: Found this queen, does anybody know what kind she is?

After a while Bernard writes him back.

Hey Tony, never seen anything like that before. But if she's got your hive hummin, that's all I need to know! Good job, Little Bee.

Anthony's day is spent going back and forth from the computer to the bee yard. The bees are in a great mood; they circle him when he appears, and they start following him back to the house. Soon he realizes that there are at least two bees in his room with him at all times. They are contentedly poised on the windowsill, testing the air with their antennae and occasionally buzzing to each other. He opens the window and pushes out the screen, but the bees stay put.

By the time his dad returns, he has posted at least fifty pictures, all over the Internet, everywhere from mom-and-pop honey suppliers to university research forums. His main concern is that this special queen will require some kind of special care. Does she have good cold tolerance? Are her hives slow to brood, or fast? Will they need extra food in the form of sugar supplements to get them to their peak health? But no one, anywhere, has any idea.

"Anthony, dinner," his dad calls. He looks at the clock. It's early for dinner, but that suits him. He'll be able to spend the rest of the night searching for information about his queen.

The vibe seems a little weird when they all sit down to eat. His dad is slightly jovial. Something is obviously going on, but all Anthony wants to do is chew and leave. Not tonight, though.

His dad drops the bombshell about halfway through the meal. Mat is picking through his peas looking for an excuse not to eat them, and Anthony is wolfing down his fish sticks to hasten his escape, when his dad clears his throat.

Uh-oh. Mat and Anthony look accusingly at each other—*what did you do?* The throat clear is a very bad sign.

"After dinner tonight," Dad says, "I want you to go put on some clean clothes." Throat clear. Pause. Chew. "We're going to a party."

The boys stare. There's nothing in their experience to compare this to. What does he mean? He could just as well have said, *After dinner we are going to float to Mars on elephant-shaped hot air balloons.*

"What's a party?" Mat asks.

"What?" Chew, swallow. "You know. A party. It's a party."

"Is it my birthday?"

"It's nobody's birthday."

Mat and Anthony glance at each other again, like nurses in an asylum when a particularly dangerous crazy man starts acting up. *You go get the Thorazine, I'll call security.*

"Do I have to go?" asks Anthony. "There's—"

"Yes, yes, you have to go!" says his father, just barely stopping himself from slamming down his beer bottle. He shakes his head and looks around the kitchen for someone to commiserate with. He rolls his eyes. "It's . . . you know. It'll be *fun*. It's a *party*."

"Will there be cake?" Mat wants to know.

"Yeah, Matty, I think there will be. Now eat your peas, and go put on a shirt." All Mat needs to hear is the word "cake" and his entire outlook changes. You could lure Mat into a pit of rabid weasels if you threw a handful of chocolate cake in first. Anthony's not quite so gullible.

Clearly there is something going on. But what? He doesn't actually suspect that he and his brother are being sold off to a work camp, or put up for adoption, but what could it be? Is this some strange way to get Mat to go to the dentist? Some nighttime dentist? All Anthony wants is to stare at the computer and try to figure out his bees. Now there's going to be a party?

Things get even more bizarre after they are all dressed. They are standing in the entryway and Anthony's dad looks at them, then pushes aside the winter coats hanging on the coat rack to reveal a mirror that Anthony had forgotten was even there. His dad checks himself in the mirror.

Then he takes a comb from the little shelf under the mirror and says, "Okay, guys, let's comb our hair."

It's like the apocalypse is coming. Anthony and Mat obediently comb their hair.

Mat is past caring about the danger because of the promise of cake, but Anthony's suspicions are growing by the second.

Once on the road, Mat asks his usual hundred questions a minute from the back seat, "What's ferocious mean?" "How do they make tires?" "Did you ever see a wolf fight a bear?" And Anthony stares out the window wishing he were at home. Every now and then his father reaches down to try to tune the radio, but Anthony can see that he's actually looking over at the passenger seat. Does this all have something to do with me, he wonders?

"Where is this party?" he finally asks.

"The Keys," his dad answers casually.

That's the expensive section of River Bend, set on the water where it backflows into a series of manmade channels. Rich people with boats live there. His father has built a few houses in the Keys, but the family has never gone visiting there, not even when his mother was alive and they actually used to go visiting. As far as Anthony knows, they have no friends in that part of town.

"Whose house?" he asks.

"It's, just, you don't know her," his dad tells him vaguely. "I think you're going to have fun. There will be some other kids."

Oh, great. The perfect way to start spring break, trapped in a house with clumps of adults and force-friended to a bunch of kids who don't want to be there either. *There's always my concussion,* he thinks. *If things get too horrible I can just complain about dizziness and go sit in a closet.*

Dusk is setting in as they pull up to large gabled house on a cul-de-sac. Anthony recognizes it.

"Hey, Dad, this is one of yours," he says. His dad nods.

"Yeah, we built it for the Collinses, but they sold it a year ago to . . .

" He trails off, then pretends to adjust the radio. Then he turns off the car.

"Okay, let's go," he says, turning to Mat. "Now, Mat, I want you on your best behavior, okay?" Mat nods. If you looked straight into his eyes you could see though them into his brain, where visions of cake float against a field of magic clouds.

"And Anthony. This will be fun. Maybe you'll meet some people. Okay?" Anthony is very tempted not to give his father the satisfaction of a nod, or even an acknowledgment, but something about the way he is looking, tight-lipped and nervous, makes Anthony's head bob. Just once. But it's enough for his dad.

They can hear music when they reach the front door, but not anything Anthony is interested in. Stuff his dad would like.

A lady greets them. She smiles.

"Hi, Paul. Come on in," she says. Mathew instantly hugs her.

Oh my god, Anthony thinks, looking at his brother clinging to the legs of a total stranger, *it's pathetic. Offer him cake and he turns into a Care Bear. What an embarrassment.*

"Hi, Mathew," she says, smiling down at Anthony's brother. How did she know Mat's name?

"Anthony, this is Miss Jensen," says his dad with studied formality.

"Call me Cindy," she tells Anthony. She has very beautiful blue eyes. And he has to admit she's got a pretty good smile.

But obviously someone needs to show her that not all the Smith kids can be purchased with the promise of baked goods. So he gives her the barest shrug/nod and glances out at the lawn.

"Anthony, can you say 'hi'?" growls his dad. It's clear he won't take no for an answer. But it's a matter of family honor as far as Anthony is concerned; someone needs to balance out Mat's crazed congeniality— he's still at it, hugging her knees and smiling like a lunatic—with some sensible reserve.

"Maybe we can chat later," Cindy Jensen says, looking at him. None of it seems to have phased her. "Why don't you all come in?"

"And have some cake?" Mathew asks.

"I'll show you where the cake table is," she says. He takes her hand and they walk into the house together.

No pride, Anthony says to himself. *No pride at all.*

The first thing he does is separate himself from his family. No one has asked him to watch his brother, which is a once-in-a-lifetime stroke of luck, and he wants to get away before that oversight is corrected. So he heads for the back of the house.

The main thing he notices is how clean the place is. There is white furniture everywhere. You couldn't let Mat loose in here for thirty seconds or he'd wreck the place. There are a few other kids, but they seem to be sticking close to their parents. He passes a table with sandwiches and grabs several. The adults are all dressed up, and he recognizes a few of them from his dad's business. They don't seem to be eating. What a lame party.

At the back of the house are large sliding glass doors leading out onto a deck, and with the feeling that he's escaping a prison, he steps outside and closes the doors behind him. He takes a deep breath, and raises the sandwich to his mouth.

He actually remembers when his dad built this house. It was before Mat was born. Before his mom died. He can recall playing among the studs before the drywall went up, and he remembers this deck. The day it was finished he'd spent the entire afternoon running around the edges, before the railing went up, daring himself to fall off. It has a rounded rim that sweeps out toward the river. He'd caught a frog down there that summer.

He steps off the deck and wanders down toward the water, eating cheese sandwiches in huge bites and thinking about how much has changed since those days. *Life is change*, Mr. Charles is fond of telling his class.

But everyone knows that change sucks. Doesn't it?

"Hi," says a voice behind him. He turns. He sees her painted Vans before he sees the rest of her. It's Mary. "I saw a frog down there."

You don't go sneaking up behind people eating sandwiches and say hi, and start talking about frogs, Anthony thinks, *because their mouth is going to be full when they turn around and they're going to look like an idiot.* He swallows, too quickly, and cheese sticks to the sides of his throat, refusing to budge. He tries to cough. But the cheese is in there like a plug. He tries to take a breath and realizes that he's in trouble.

He pushes on his stomach, and looks around for something to drink. He's starting to panic. It's the most helpless feeling in the world —he can't breathe in, he can't breathe out, and he can't make a sound. He grabs his throat, and little spasms start going through him as he attempts to suck in air.

"Are you okay?" Mary asks.

Anthony shakes his head. Now he's pounding on his stomach, but that's not helping at all. He's feeling dizzy.

"Are you choking? Hey!" says Mary. She runs down the stairs from the deck. "Do you need help?" Anthony just stares at her, wild-eyed, not knowing what to do. He realizes he's going to die. He falls to his knees, his spasms grow more violent by the second.

Then he feels Mary grabbing him from behind and wrapping her arms around him and Pulling! Pulling! Pulling! The cheese flies from his mouth. He collapses onto his knees, sucking air in heaves, like a dying fish. His eyes are watering, and disgusting mucus pours from his nose and mouth, long gobs of thick slime. He falls forward onto his hands and lets it drain. The mucus actually makes it hard to breathe, there's so much of it, and his body is so out of control sucking air. But finally his heaving subsides, and he sits back on the grass.

He notices that Mary is gone, and looks around just as she comes down off the porch with a towel to squat beside him on the lawn.

"Here, I got you this. It's from the bathroom, but they won't miss it." He takes it, and wipes his face.

"Don't tell my dad," Anthony croaks.

"Why would I tell your dad?" she asks.

He shrugs. All he knows is that parents often get involved when there's a situation like this, after the fact, when it just makes matters worse. *You could have died*, people say, and then they hurry off to summon your parents. Who are furious at you for almost dying. At least he will be spared that.

They wait there beside the river in silence while his mucus drains and his breathing returns to normal. They can just barely hear the mellow music from inside the house, and Anthony periodically blows his nose into Cindy Jensen's fluffy, light blue hand towel. After a bit he starts feeling like himself again. Enough so he can feel embarrassed beyond belief.

Mary speaks just then. "I almost choked one time on a hot dog," she says. "We were at a party like this, and I was in someone's Jacuzzi. I was, like, ten. And it got caught in my throat, I probably wasn't even supposed to be eating it in the water, and finally someone figured out what was going on and they turned me over and pounded on my back, and the hotdog flew out into the water."

"Wow," Anthony says. "Gross."

"Yeah. And then I threw up into the Jacuzzi."

"Oh, my god," he says. She is laughing. "Is that true?"

She nods. "Yeah. And you know what the worst thing was?"

"Wait, did someone go get your *parents*?"

"Yes! After I already survived! It's so stupid, my god!" They laugh for a long time, and then finally they stop, and just lie on the grass, looking up at the stars. Anthony feels comfortable. Surprisingly, totally, comfortable.

"After that, I vowed to learn CPR," Mary says finally. "I had a class two years ago."

"Is that what you did on me?"

"Yeah." Her voice takes on a speculative tone. "I always wondered if it would really work."

"You must have got an A in that class."

"I mostly get As. I can't really help it. It's kind of an OCD thing." She turns her head to look at him. "You know, I wanted to apologize for when I apologized the other day."

"What?"

"Your bees. I'm so sorry to hear about your queen. That really sucks."

He sits up. This whole thing with the party had gotten him completely sidetracked; it's been hours since he even thought about the bees. But now he does. And he smiles.

"It turns out my hive is going to be fine," he says.

"Really? I'm so glad." She really sounds glad. He's surprised. Most people think of bees as pests. "So what happened?" she asks. "Did you requeen?"

He thinks for a minute before he answers. "I kind of did. How come you know so much about bees?"

"I had a hive," she says. "Carniolans." He waits for her to continue. He ends up waiting a while. The frogs in the water fill in the silence with croaking.

"What happened to it?" he finally asks.

"Colony Collapse Disorder. Sorry. Did I do the thing? I forget to talk. I think I think too much."

Anthony shrugs. To prove he doesn't care he waits a long time before he answers.

"I know someone else whose hives were hit. He lost three supers."

"I researched it after that. It's really awful. Just about every plant on the planet needs bees to pollinate it. What if they all just died? We wouldn't be able to grow food. Everything would die."

This sobering thought silences them for a while. Over the river they hear and then see an owl as it emerges from the trees, circles, and dives. They hear a faint cry as it lifts its dinner into the air and carries it back to its nest. The world is indeed a frightening place. But life goes on.

"So are you new in River Bend?" he asks.

"No. I used to live here. My parents got 'separated.'" She makes air quotes with her fingers. "And I went to Florida with my mom. We were there for two years. Then my parents got back together. Can you believe it?"

"After two years?"

"Yeah. That never happens, right? So we came back to live with my dad. That's him in there."

Anthony looks. The party has picked up a lot of steam since he left. Now people are eating, and there's a lot of laughing and moving around. He recognizes the man she points to.

"That's Sherriff Bailer," he says. "Your dad is Sherriff Bailer." Stating the obvious. He changes the subject so the smile twitching at the corners of her mouth won't turn into a laugh at his expense. "So you're going to start a new hive?" he asks.

"I really miss it. My mom never loved them. So my dad . . . it's complicated." She points through the glass doors into the party, changing the subject herself. "That's *your* dad, right?"

Anthony looks. His father is standing in a circle of people, laughing. Then he's talking, and everyone listens, and then they laugh. It's a very weird sight, like seeing a deer drive a car past your house. Unnatural.

"Yeah, that's him."

"So what's the deal with him and Cindy Jensen?" Mary asks, lying back down on the ground. He looks at her.

"What do you mean?"

"Are they a thing?"

"A thing?"

"Yeah. My parents have known her for a long time. She's cool."

"They're not a thing. He doesn't even know her."

"Oh, I beg to differ. They were going at it pretty hot."

"Hot?" What is she talking about?

"I saw them in the hall when I got your towel."

"No, believe me." He shakes his head emphatically. "We don't know her." Just then he sees Cindy inside, carrying a tray. And he notices Mat at her side, with his hand around her leg, sucking on his thumb. Just trailing around after her like a puppy. It's kind of starting to make him mad. And Mary insisting that his dad knows Cindy Jensen makes him mad too. And why is his dad in there laughing? What does he have to laugh about? What exactly is going on here?

"Well, I think you're about to meet her, then," she says. "I mean, they were pretty intense."

"I don't care what you think you saw, okay? He doesn't know her!"

Mary stares. She doesn't say anything, but you can tell it's an effort. The easy camaraderie of a moment before has completely vanished.

And then a tiny shape lands on his shoulder. Mary's eyes light up. "Hey, don't move," she says. "It's a bee." Anthony looks down out of the corner of his eye. A worker sits on his shirt, quietly buzzing her wings.

"Hey, bee bee bee," he whispers. He reaches for her.

"Don't scare her," Mary says. But Anthony holds out his hand and the bee steps off his shirt onto his palm.

"That's the friendliest bee I ever saw," Mary comments.

He examines her. "Wonder what's she's doing out at night?"

"That looks like an Italian Russian," she says, bending close. "They're supposed to winter over better than pure Italians."

"It's true. Mine are Italian Russians," he tells her. He holds his palm up so the light from the party falls on the worker, and speaks to her softly. "You shouldn't be out here in the dark. Where's your hive?"

She's doing a little dance on his hand, circling, then stopping to face him, then circling, then stopping to face him. Mary watches, looking back and forth from the bee to Anthony. Then, with a final wag of her tail, the worker jumps off his hand, circles his head a few times, and buzzes away into the night. They gaze out at her as she disappears.

"That's kind of weird," says Mary after a moment.

"I guess. Hey, are you hungry? Want to get a sandwich?"

"Only if you cut it into really tiny pieces first," says Mary. "And I better be there when you eat."

"Very funny." They start to move back inside, but then he stops.

"Hey," he says. He feels awkward and out of his element, but also compelled. "Thanks."

She seems surprised. "What for?"

"You know, for . . . basically saving my life."

Mary shakes her head. But she thinks about it for a minute. "I didn't. But that would make a great greeting card category," she says.

"Thanks For Basically Saving my Life?" he asks.

"Yeah. From Dad, Grandma, Sister, or Friend. Then every year on this day you could get me a card. Forever."

"I'm serious. No one ever saved my life before, so thanks." Wow, he thinks, that sounded idiotic.

"I didn't save your stupid life."

"You did. In the last month I've been blown up, burned,and choked. No one else really helped me."

"You would have been fine. Let's go inside."

The two of them head in from the deck and he sees his father coming through the living room of white furniture, carrying Mat in his arms. His dad motions toward the front door. "Let's go home," he says.

Really? Anthony thinks. Has that much time gone by? He realizes that a lot of the adults have already left. Mary's parents and his dad are among the last.

They all gather their things and leave in a final clump of guests. Cindy Jensen introduces Anthony's dad to Mary's parents and then, bending down a little, she shakes Anthony's hand.

"I'd hoped we'd get a chance to talk," she says. "But maybe next time. Would that be okay?"

Conscious of his dad watching, Anthony nods. Cindy smiles her pretty smile, then turns and hands his dad Mat's coat. *What is it with this lady?* he thinks. *She needs to go get some kids of her own.* The adults begin saying their good-byes.

"I really loved how that bee just crawled on your hand," Mary says quietly to him as they wait. "And then just stayed there, dancing."

"Hey. You get A's. I get Bees." She laughs. It may be the best joke he's ever told. The adults don't notice. Then he has an idea. It's a bold idea. It's far outside his usual comfort zone. But for some reason he says, "Do you want to come see the hive? I mean, it's just getting back on its feet. But you could see the new queen, she's amazing, she's . . . " Anthony trails off. He feels a sudden strange hesitance taking about his queen. "You should just come see her," he finishes. "If you want to."

"I'd love it," Mary says.

ON THE RIDE HOME, ANTHONY'S DAD IS DOING THE THING AGAIN where he pretends to look at the radio, but actually he's looking at Anthony. Anthony is feeling an emotion he hasn't felt for a while. He wonders if it shows. He's not going to jinx it by giving it a name. But, for the first time in a long time, he feels okay.

"So what did you think of the party?" his dad asks, trying hard not to seem like it really matters what Anthony thought.

"It was okay," Anthony says. In a battle of casual versus evasive, Anthony will always beat his father.

"Did you like the people?"

"They were okay," he shrugs.

Anthony's cell phone chimes. He pulls it out. His father sighs and holds out his hand.

"You know the agreement. I see the incoming texts, you get to keep the phone." Anthony passes it to him reluctantly. His dad glances down and frowns.

"What does this mean?" He hands it back. It's from Mary. ok ur rite, I totally saved ur life! you owe me a card.

"That's just this girl," Anthony tells him. Then he yawns before his father can follow up, and says, "I think my concussion is making me tired."

Neither of them says anything else on the way home, each lost in thought and thankful for the darkness of the cab. In the back seat, Mathew sleeps the warm, deep slumber of the deeply contented and cake-fed.

When they arrive at the house, his dad carries Mat to bed and Anthony streaks upstairs to the computer.

And there it is, or rather, there they are—a group of e-mails sent through one of the bee forums. There are three of them, all sent in the last two hours, all from a poster named VespaKeeper. The first one reads,

Dear BeeBoy13,

hello! That is a beautiful specimen and I think I can get you some information about it. Would you please let me know where you live, so I may send you extensive documentation?

VespaKeeper

The next one, half an hour later, says,

Hello BeeBoy13, I have been thinking about your bee and have realized that there might be some danger to you. If you will send me your address I will immediately forward you important safety information.

VespaKeeper

And the final one, sent just a few minutes ago, reads,

BeeBoy13, I have not heard back from you in regard to your extremely dangerous queen. It is vital that you forward me your address in order to receive information that could save your life and the lives of those around you. Whatever you do, do not let her breed!

VespaKeeper

It's not exactly what he'd been hoping for.

If he's ever been certain of anything, it is that the Little Queen poses no risk to him. Or those around him. But why would this Vespa-Keeper insist that she does? And give out his address to a stranger online—is this person kidding?

He climbs into bed, now worried and sleepless, wishing he had not been so diligent in sifting out every single online forum and posing his questions. He is afraid he has stirred up a nest of something—something better left unstirred.

Finally he falls asleep, but not before he sees, on the twin bedposts to the left and right of his headboard, the two bees that seem to have taken up residence in his room.

They settle down on their little round perches, and watch.

Chapter Fourteen

T he next days pass for the Little Queen in a brilliant blur of industry. Once pulled back from the path of destruction down which they had been headed, she finds her new bees to be exemplary. They are dynamic, intelligent, and responsive. No match for bees hatched from her own eggs, of course, for the Sequestered, altered by generations of terrible trial, are almost a different breed—but these are the very best honeybees that natural selection ever produced. The previous queen, whoever she had been, was an exceptional bee.

As a first order of business she sets the colony to cleaning. The refuse she climbed over when she first entered the hive is pushed out the entrance. The wax combs are repaired. The cracks are sealed. By the end of the first day, the true perfection of form which is her new home reveals itself through the debris, and she is amazed. This honey comb is as near to flawless as anything bees have ever produced, each six-sided chamber aligning perfectly with the next, down to the nanometer. The form and dimension are so immaculate that she finds herself mesmerized. It is another example of the unusually advanced character of this hive. It is so perfect that not even the Sequestered ever produced anything like it.

Soon she begins to lay. Stored in her ovipositor are hundreds of thousands of eggs, fertilized by drones present when she first hatched from her cell. These eggs will last as long as she herself lives. Now, slowly traversing the face of this amazing comb, depositing an egg in each rejuvenated cell, she begins the sacred task of expanding the colony.

A normal queen will lay anywhere from one to two thousand eggs a day. Each of these eggs is instantly attended by a worker, who feeds it, positions it, and then caps the cell in which it rests with a layer of wax so the egg can begin gestating. But the Little Queen is capable of laying many more eggs a day than a normal queen. She's not even certain of the number. Five thousand? Ten? At the end of her first day of laying she has deposited six thousand new eggs in the comb, all of which will hatch as glorious bees in the line of the Sequestered—and she feels that she has not come close to her potential. But she cannot afford to lay any faster, because she barely has enough workers to attend to the eggs she is producing.

There are so many jobs to perform in a hive. Attending to eggs. Cleaning. Foraging for nectar. Creating honey with nectar returned to the hive. Her bees are stretched very thin, and she must be careful not to overwork them. Until her first brood hatches and the hive begins to grow, she is limited.

So she lays, and pauses, and lays, and pauses. This gives her a chance to survey her surroundings. She has scouts out everywhere and she receives constant reports. Both in person and through mind-to-mind, these scouts paint her a picture of the world outside the hive. Her new bees are not adept at mind-to-mind over long distances. She receives images from them, but cannot communicate back unless they are within a few hundred yards of the comb. So several times a day she leaves the hive, while her workers catch up with the eggs she has laid. With attendants in tow, she scouts her new kingdom. Queens—more than any other bee in a colony—are curious creatures.

THROUGH ONE OF HER SCOUTS SHE BECOMES AWARE OF THE approach of BEAR. He is digging a hole in the meadow, practicing in case he needs to bury anything. And so, as she has done for the last three days, she gathers a cloud of her adopted daughters behind her, and leaves the hive to meet him. She has chosen Bear as the tool she will use to teach herself to speak.

He hears her coming. Three days ago, when this first happened, he ran at her and her coterie, barking and snapping. By yesterday all he could do was stand in confusion, whining. And today, she sees him preparing to run away. But bees are faster than dogs.

Swift as a diving hawk, the Little Queen and the bees she has at her sides strike down from the sky and form a globe around Bear's head. This thing she is trying would have been so easy with her own daughters, but it is still doable with common bees; this learning to shape air with wingsong.

A human makes sound by shaping its throat muscles, which vibrate as breath rushes past. But bees have no such muscles. However, as she learned in the tunnel beating back the Green Death, bees have other ways to control the shape and flow of air. A group of bees working together can do miraculous things with air, as long as they have someone to guide them and make them work as one.

The Little Queen suffuses herself out through the minds and bodies of the cloud encircling Bear's head. He is shaking. He knows he cannot run. He knows he cannot hide. He knows what is about to happen. It is the deepest humiliation for a dog such as Bear. But there is nothing he can do.

The wings of seven hundred strong bees now begin to tune themselves to one frequency and to beat together at one speed. The Little Queen makes her adjustments, a little slower here, a little faster here. And then STOP. For a millisecond. And GO STOP GO, all across the surface of the globe, shaping and vibrating the air within the globe. A long, slow hum begins, then becomes a high-pitched keen, then drops and rises and modulates back and forth for a minutes while BEAR rolls his eyes and pants. PULSE. SLOW. PULSE. PULSE. And then it forms. A word.

SIT.

Bear whines. The Little Queen sends a bee down to land on Bear's rump. Stinger poised.

SIT.

And Bear sits. He is not happy. He is slobbering and his eyes are wild. He has been stung many, many times in the past. But it is one thing to be stung by a bee while in the destructive throes of a mad fury. It is another to contemplate the single, painful potential of one thinly barbed pointer waiting to strike. It's just easier to *SIT*.

The Little Queen is satisfied. She has been practicing this sound with her bees. It is a simple sound. A single sound. Now she tries another. It takes several minutes to form. Her bees are growing tired. But she pushes them, just a little. They are strong. And then it comes: *DOWN.*

Bear eyes the cloud of bees. But there is no escape. He watches two bees swing down out of the sphere and poise their stingers, one behind each front knee, and he flops his legs forward and stretches upon the ground. *DOWN.*

Enough. The Little Queen lifts her globe away and sends most of her workers back to the hive. Bear, howling, dashes off.

She has assigned two workers to guard the boy, Anthony. She considers him part of her colony, in some way that she cannot yet explain. And though her bees shadow him everywhere, and through them she sees and hears everything he does, she still feels compelled to be near him whenever she can. It brings her calm, and strength, and seems to heighten her sense of purpose. So every tour of her environment begins with a visit to the structure where he lives, to what she has learned is called his ROOM.

There is a hole that in the side of his structure, a WINDOW, and flying through this she finds herself in his ROOM. He is sitting at his DESK, tapping his fingers on a machine with many small squares, and does not see her. When he is barking she likes to sit and listen, because she can decipher patterns even more quickly in person than through her watchers, and she has been trying to teach herself his song. She feels she might be able to reproduce it, if only she hears it enough. But right now he is silent, and so, drawn by her curiosity, she flies past him to explore the rest of his structure.

There are two levels, and each of the three humans who live here, ANTHONY, MAT, and DAD, has his own room. On the bottom level are the KITCHEN with the TABLE and the TV, and the room where BEAR, the GODDAMN DOG, stays when he is inside. In the kitchen there is a machine that fascinates her. Sounds emanate from a grill on its surface. Melody rolls across her, and she has been spending quite a bit of time listening. One tune in particular she likes, with the repeating pattern BLUE EYES CRYING IN THE RAIN.

Today there is something new in the kitchen. One of the windows facing the bee yard has a whirling new machine in it. The Little Queen has begun to understand that humans have an innate ability to find these machines, she does not know where in nature, and then use them. Machines fascinate the Little Queen. Machines perform tasks; they are the very embodiment of productivity, and if there is one thing a bee is drawn to, it is productivity.

She flies closer to this one. It is noisy. It fits snuggly into the window, and has a mesmerizing perfect mesh on the side facing the kitchen. Within that is a haziness, as though something is passing again and again, very quickly. As she gets nearer, she begins to feel a draft, and then very swiftly she is pulled toward the machine.

"Back," she tells her attendants. But her leading scout is already too close, trapped in the vortex. She fights, but she is drawn slowly closer.

"BACK!" she says again, driving her bees backwards and to the side, out of the draft. She watches helplessly as her scout is drawn into the machine and then crushed by whatever mechanism is creating the vortex.

It is a dangerous place, this world of Anthony's. There is another window open near the vortex machine, and she leads her attendants out, then circles back to examine the machine from the other side. A powerful wind buffets her, disbursing smells from inside the structure far out over the land. A hive could cure a thousand combs of honey with a machine like this. If it did not kill all the workers first.

Even when she is flying, studying Anthony or laying eggs, the Little Queen is monitoring impressions from the foragers and scouts on the periphery of her kingdom. As she turns from the vortex machine to head back to the hive, a sight comes to her that causes her momentarily to falter in flight. A wasp. Not the kind of wasps bees have fought and lived beside for hundreds of millions of years. No, what she sees through her scouts' eyes is one of the massive black Death Wasps that attacked her in the bowl.

She watches as this wasp approaches her bee. The bee does nothing, assuming that the wasp will pass her by without even noticing. But the Little Queen suspects that this will not happen.

Fly! she speaks, mind-to-mind, as loud as she can. But this scout is beyond its hearing range, and it simply watches, innocent, expecting things to go as they have since the beginning of bee history. The first hint that something is wrong comes when the wasp lands on the branch where she sits.

FLY! FLY! calls the Little Queen. Now she is racing for her hive. Perhaps she can get in range before the situation reaches what she knows will be its inevitable climax.

The wasp steps carefully closer, and finally the bee begins to back away, confused. But now it is too late. Fast as a lightning strike, the wasp pins the bee to the branch with a huge claw, then bends close. Opens its mouth. And licks the worker on the back.

The Little Queen understands what is happening. The wasp is hunting—for her, she believes beyond any doubt--and is looking for any smell or sign of her on the body of this worker. Smell that is, most certainly, there to be found.

The wasp suddenly releases the bee and backs away, waiting. After a single moment of orientation, the worker takes to the air, flying back to the hive.

NO! shouts the Little Queen. TURN AROUND!

The worker is leading the wasp straight back to the colony. And once they are located, she fears that they are lost.

TURN! she screams, mind-to-mind. Is she still too far? She is flying like the wind now, outpacing her attendants the way a robin might outpace a drove of moths, yet still her worker does not hear her. She races past the hive, flashing out over the fields to head the fleeing bee off. And finally her message reaches it.

TURN BACK! FLY TO THE RIVER! DO NOT RETURN TO THE HIVE! she casts forth from her mind. And the worker turns. Dutifully, despite all instincts telling her to seek the safety of the enclosing hive, she turns and heads away. And the wasp follows.

The Little Queen slows. She finds that she is trembling, and not from the speed of her flight. These wasps are killers, and they are stalking her. She feels an emptiness. She has no idea how to confront this threat. Move the colony? Place all the foragers on the perimeter as guards? There is only one place to turn—she must visit the Plain of Crowns. She hopes her new colony is ready.

Her attendants rejoin her as she reaches the hive. "Too fast," they reproach her. "You fly too fast." She leads them inside and takes stock of the combs. She has just over four thousand workers here, likely not enough to form an effective Crown. The rest are out foraging beyond the range of summons. But then she stops, and counts again. No, she realizes. There are more than four thousand. There is a subset of the colony usually overlooked: the drones. If she counts the drones, she has closer to eight thousand, which would give her the bare minimum needed for a Crown. Drones never participate in a Crown. Drones never participate in any useful daily activity in the hive.

But they are bees. The colony supports and houses them. Perhaps they only need to be asked.

I WILL WEAR MY CROWN, she calls, urgently. Her attendants spring to action. They lift her and ring her. These bees are so much smaller than her own children that she wonders if there will be enough, even with the drones. A certain critical pressure and temperature must be achieved in order to transverse the membrane between this world and the Plain. But if they fail, it will not be for lack of determination. They rise eagerly to do her bidding.

First her attendants, and then layer upon layer of workers, hook themselves together and strain to surround her. A queen is literally as well as figuratively deeply in touch with her colony in this moment. She can plumb the most profound depths of the hive's heart. What the Little Queen sees here is nothing short of joy. Joy to have a place. Joy to have a queen. And as much as those and more, it is joy for Anthony. This is why she has begun to consider him a part of the hive—because these bees love him. The malaise that affected them stems from him, and now that Anthony is once again visiting them, and wearing the pattern that means *happy*, the hive is at peace.

And so they squeeze, with all the power that happiness can command. But it is not enough. The Little Queen is too solid, too strong, and the structures in her body have grown even denser as she has moved toward maturity and strengthened herself exothermically. Despite their passion, these workers alone will not be enough. She will need the drones.

A drone is called upon to do only a single thing in his life: meet a new queen in the air on her one mating flight and fertilize her eggs. In so doing, he is ripped in two to fall from the air and perish before his body strikes the ground. Many seasons can pass where no new queen is born to take a mating flight, and drones born in those seasons do nothing. Each season a new set of two hundred or four hundred is born, to linger lazily by the landing board, and drink honey from the cells, and do their business without ever cleaning up. Drones are unused to the demands of a queen. But they are big, bigger than workers. And the Little Queen needs them. Every second that passes, the wasps could be closing in.

Drones, Crown your Queen, she commands. And they stop their idle strolling, or wake from their naps. And look at each other. Has someone spoken to them?

Drones! To the Crown! Your Queen calls you! There is confusion in their ranks, but such is the power of the Little Queen's summons that they begin to climb the walls, all thirty-five hundred of them, so many more than any hive would ever typically carry. Surprising even themselves, but moving steadily once they have begun, the drones add their weight to the Crown. Their large, indolent limbs link round, and for the first time in their lives, they feel the pleasure of work.

Now the pressure mounts. The Little Queen feels her body conforming, feels the heat rising. Down, down her mind is pushed, as the drones exhibit an unsuspected strength and determination. *What a wasted resource,* thinks the Little Queen, even as she feels herself enter a second body and senses the phantom wind buffeting her wings. *There must be other ways to use this strength. My drones are mighty indeed.*

And then she is through, and a peal of thunder fades behind her. She hangs over the Plain of Crowns. Below her the uncountable rows of queens gaze upward, still and unblinking. Waiting.

This time the Little Queen finds that she has appeared very near the border with the Now. She can see the comb of the Sequestered and in a moment she is flying over the queens in those cells, until below she sees the Yellow Queen, rising up to meet her. She lands.

Each time we see you, daughter, you grow more magnificent, says the Yellow Queen. She seems to bow before the Little Queen. You are coming into your power. The Little Queen wastes no time on talk about herself.

My colony is threatened, she says. There are wasps, new wasps that hunt me. Large wasps, who hunt for more than food. And they have the mind-to-mind. When she speaks the word "wasp," the Yellow Queen's wings flash, and she tenses her stinger. But she says nothing while the Little Queen continues.

With my own daughters, she continues, large and powerful, I was able to defeat a small group of these wasps, but just barely, and all were lost. My new hive is strong in purpose, but small in number. And they are not the Sequestered. I fear that if we are discovered before my own eggs hatch out, these black wasps will destroy us. I cannot run from them; clearly they will find me. I do not know what to do.

The Yellow Queen regards her, then looks to the sky above, as though checking for clouds, or consulting the wind.

The time is coming, she says slowly, very soon, when bees everywhere will be thrown into a deadly struggle for existence. You cannot run. You cannot reason. You can only resist, and hope.

Resist how? pleads the Little Queen. The wasps may know where I am, they are so close. My bees are glorious, but they are only common bees. And these wasps—she shudders when she thinks of them—these wasps will destroy them. And then my eggs.

Then you must make certain that your eggs hatch before the wasps come.

THE WASPS COULD COME AT ANY MOMENT! She feels as though she is falling deeper and deeper into a hole from which no one can lift her. *There is no help to be found here*, she thinks. *I ask too much. I ask the impossible.*

YOU HAVE ALREADY DONE THE IMPOSSIBLE, says the Yellow Queen. No thoughts go unremarked on the Plain of Crowns, the Little Queen realizes.

YOU HAVE CHANGED FORAGERS TO WAX BEES. YOU HAVE CHANGED FAUX QUEENS TO WORKERS. AND YOU HAVE CHANGED YOUR OWN BODY, HEALED WOUNDS THAT OTHERWISE WOULD HAVE KILLED YOU. THIS IS WITHIN YOUR POWER.

WHAT IS?

YOU HAVE MANY THOUSAND CELLS FULL OF EGGS. MAKE THEM HATCH. ACCELERATE THEM.

The Little Queen tries to imagine such a thing. She can see how it would be similar in some ways to morphing a wax bee or a faux. But to perform this feat on even a few eggs would take all her energy. I DO NOT HAVE STRENGTH FOR THAT, she says.

LOOK AROUND YOU AT THIS PLACE, says the Yellow Queen, gesturing. WHAT DO YOU THINK THIS PLAIN IS CREATED FROM? NOT TRUE BEESWAX, BUT PURE ENERGY. THIS IS THE ENERGY THAT INFUSES AND SUPPORTS ALL BEE LIFE. WITH THIS ENERGY, ALL THINGS ARE POSSIBLE. USE THIS.

HOW CAN I USE IT? The Little Queen struggles to understand. IT IS HERE. AND I AM THERE.

THERE IS SO MUCH MORE TO THIS THAN YOU KNOW. THERE IS NO TIME TO EXPLAIN IT ALL, EVEN THE PARTS THAT WE UNDERSTAND OURSELVES. BUT THERE IS A SOURCE, A SOURCE OF ENERGY FROM THIS PLAIN, AND YOU CAN USE—

Suddenly the Little Queen jerks upward off the surface of the Plain. What is going on? When she sends her mind back to her Crown, she understands. Her drones are weakening. Strong, but unused to work, they have very little stamina. And now they are falling dead from the crown, spending the last of their life force in the service of their queen. As they fall, the Crown fails.

In thrusts and heaves, she rises back up away from the Plain, away from the Yellow Queen. WHAT IS THE SOURCE? HOW CAN I—

But the Yellow Queen has no chance to speak before the Little Queen is ripped backward through the membrane between the worlds, into her own hive, where the Crown is splitting apart in chaos. Drones fall dead to the floor of the hive, and her confused workers release each other and collapse in sheets. It will be many days before these bees are ready to Crown her again. It takes so much out of a hive.

She has no idea how to proceed. Around her, rack after rack of honeycomb cells sit filled with the fruits of her prodigious capacity to lay, more than twenty five thousand in all. Eggs so full of potential, but so vulnerable. To accelerate their development, all of them at once, as the Yellow Queen suggests, would require unimaginable energy. More than a living body could possibly provide. There is not honey enough in the world to fuel a transformation like that.

The last time she felt this lost, she was spiraling down to the meadow outside the Robber Queen's hive, her eyes closed, certain that after she landed, she would never fly. Has it come to that? The black forces of death surrounding her, hemming her in?

She occludes her eyes. And in the dark she sees it.

The strange, golden ball. The mesmerizing glow. The ball of light that guided her off that meadow. So familiar. So warm. So like—her eyes flash with sight again. Yes! So like the Plain of Crowns! Is this golden light somehow coming from the Plain of Crowns?

To investigate she will have to get closer, but that will mean flying with her eyes off, which she is hesitant to do at the best of times and which seems a particularly bad idea with the death wasps on the hunt. But if the light truly is from the Plain, perhaps there is another way to approach it.

In her mind she pictures her perfect form, the body she inhabits when she visits the Plain. And when this is clear to her, she sends it questing through the dark void, toward the light. As she draws closer she feels heat, and smells the intoxicating scent of a hundred thousand blossoms. How can it be that light should carry scent? It pulses like a heartbeat. She is closer than she has ever been before. She sees that it is not, in fact, a glowing ball of light. Deep within the ball she spies the breach through which the light pours: a cell. Six-sided and perfect.

She feels energy infusing her, beating on her, an unremitting wave of power. She flies closer, and the energy becomes dense. It pushes her, forces her backward, but she struggles against it. The heat grows more intense, as does the noise, and the overwhelming scent of nectar. Until at last she hovers, barely able to keep her position, over the center of the cell. She reaches down with a delicate forefoot. And touches it.

When she draws her foot back there is a thread, a slender elastic thread like a swirl of honey clinging to her foot; through this thread courses power. She backs away, and the thread stretches. Faster and faster, all the way back through the darkness to her own body lying on the floor of her hive, until her perfect form settles into her real form. With her eyes still off, watching this throbbing tendril of energy stretching back through space, she wonders: *Do I dare?*

But the answer is obvious before she asks. She must.

She stirs her Queen's Bell to life. The thread seamlessly appends to it, as though they were made to go together. Along this new channel, from the place where pure bee energy begins and ends, she begins to channel power.

Chapter Fifteen

Anthony is awakened in the morning by the sound of Bear barking outside. This has happened every morning for the last three days, and he can't quite figure out what is going on. He scrambles from bed and looks out his window.

Yes, Bear is at it again. He is in the field, halfway between the house and the bee yard, by himself, standing in one place, barking and whining. Three days ago he seemed to be going crazy, running in circles and biting the air. Yesterday the running and biting had stopped, and he just stood in one place barking. And today, something very odd is happening.

Bear seems to be listening. He cocks his head, and whines, and barks. But the barks are different from any sound he's ever made before. Then suddenly he sits. Almost against his will, it seems. And then slowly, whining and shuffling his feet, he lies down.

What in the world? Anthony throws on some clothes and runs downstairs. "Bear barking!" Mat calls though his oatmeal as Anthony lopes through the kitchen. "He's funny!"

Out the back door Anthony sprints, until he sees Bear in the field. And then he stops. From here he can see what was not visible from the window: Anthony could swear that Bear's head is ringed with a cloud of bees. Or rather, not a cloud, but a sphere. A perfectly round ball of bees. Before he can come any closer, the bees disperse, and Bear lets out a plaintive howl and runs off. Was Anthony imagining it, or did Bear seem to be ashamed of himself?

Anthony heads back to the house. His father is setting the fan up in the kitchen window.

"Starting to get hot," he says. He switches it on to hear the satisfying whir, then turns to face his son. "See, bought this twenty years ago, good as the day it came off the shelf. She'll pull some hot air out of this kitchen. So what's on your plate today?"

"You know, you said my friend could come over," Anthony reminds him, certain that his father hasn't forgotten but is in fact trying to slide a conversational wedge into Anthony's private life.

"I said . . . oh." His dad nods. Now it's all coming back, uh-huh. "Yeah, the girl from the party. Well, she seems nice." He takes a drink of coffee and watches Anthony, the picture of guileless disinterest.

The thing his dad most wants to do—talk about Anthony's friends —is the thing Anthony is least interested in doing.

"Going up to my room now."

"OK. Well. You have a good time with your friend." His dad lifts his bag, throwing in his invoices. "Come on, Mat, let's get going."

Upstairs, Anthony sits at his desk and checks the windowsill. There they are, his bodyguards, as he has begun to call the two bees who seem always to be with him in his room. He opens the window so they can get back to the hive if they want, but they decline, and settle instead on the ledge.

What he wants to do is check his e-mail. After those first three messages from VespaKeeper asking about the Little Queen, he didn't receive anything else for three days. And then last night, just before he went to bed, came another message to his most private address, BeeBoy13. Anthony has quite a few e-mail addresses, but this one he uses only on the bee forums. He pulls the e-mail up again and reads it. The message says:

The government is offering up to $10,000-worth of free honeybee safety and hive replacement services to beekeepers in the Selkirk

Valley/River Bend region. Please select the location below which is nearest to your hives to determine eligibility.

This is followed by a link to something called the South Idaho Agriculture Agency, but the link is no good. Below it are three satellite images. One of them is an image of the eastern side of River Bend, one of them is in Selkirk Valley, two towns to the west. But the third is an image of the Hanlens' farm, one section over from Anthony's house. Only a few hundred yards from his hives.

The Hanlens do not have bees. And Anthony does not give out this e-mail address except on very respectable forums, so he gets basically no spam. What is going on here? Is this e-mail related to the earlier messages from VespaKeeper? He doesn't know whether to lie about his location, or ignore the message. And before he can make up his mind, he hears the ring of a bell in the front yard. Looking out his window, he sees Mary riding up on her bike.

"If my dog runs over, don't worry, he's friendly," Anthony shouts out the window. "I'll be right down." He runs out to meet her.

Bear is nowhere to be seen, which surprises Anthony. Bear never misses a chance to knock a guest over. Mary gets off her bike without the usual canine wrestling match. She's wearing slightly blue riding goggles, a yellow hat, striped leggings under shorts, and the ever-present hand-colored Vans. On her back she wears a book bag stuffed so full the straps are pulling her shoulders back. The entire look could be considered marginally odd.

Anthony has been feeling queasy about this visit ever since they'd set it up the day before. He doesn't really know anything about Mary. And he's really bad with people he doesn't know. It's a feedback loop that doubles down on his insecurity every time it passes go. But her eager greeting dispels his doubts.

"Hey," she yells, smiling and out of breath, "I rode over as fast as I could. I thought you might need somebody to save your life!"

"Ha, Ha." Anthony fake laughs, but the grin that follows is very real.

"Let's see your bees," she says.

He leads her toward the bee yard. She marvels at the flowers as they approach, and lauds the high sturdy fence. But before she will even enter the shed, let alone exit out into the bee yard, she insists on stopping, opening her backpack, and donning her bee suit.

Anthony watches. The fact that she could compress the entire thing into the book bag is amazing enough, but the really amazing thing is the outfit itself. He can't remember seeing a suit as elaborate as hers. It's all white, with zippers, pockets, layers, and Velcro. The black veil, which drapes over her head and hangs suspended about six inches in front of her face, seals along all edges like a space suit. It is impressive. And, as far as Anthony is concerned, ridiculous. But he says nothing.

"Okay," comes her slightly muffled voice from somewhere inside the outfit. Her gloved hands make a last adjustment to the seal around her boots. She looks at him.

"Where's yours?" she asks.

"I think it's in the basement," he tells her. "Come on."

It's not easy for her to navigate in her outfit, but Anthony guides her through the darkened shed. She moves ponderously. Every few steps she looks like she's going to lose her balance, like a top spinning down or a toy robot running out of batteries, but then she rights herself. When they reach the outer door, she stops.

"Seriously, where's your bee suit?" she says.

"I never really wear a suit," he says. "But it's cool if you want to." He steps behind her and guides her through the door. "We're almost there."

Once out among the flowers, Mary looks like an alien, but in the bright sun she regains some of her mobility and balance. She moves around the periphery of the fenced yard, checking out the flowers.

"Your honey must taste amazing," she tells him quietly. Anthony watches. She's actually doing everything right. Speaking softly. Moving slowly, letting the bees get used to her before approaching the hive. She might look a little like the Michelin Tire Man, but she's comfortable around bees.

"I just let the bees eat. I don't really harvest honey," he says.

She rejoins him and together they approach the hive. There aren't many bees around today, which is a bit of a surprise to Anthony. They had been really active since the new queen took over.

But bees definitely have their own rhythms. They know what they're doing.

Mary sees it before he does, and points to the landing board. "Hey," she says. "Those bees don't look great."

She's right. One after another bees are wandering out to the landing board and falling over the edge, to lie still and lifeless on the ground. He bends down and picks one up.

"It's okay," he says after a moment. "It's a drone. I've been expecting this."

"Why?" Mary sounds worried.

He picks up bee after bee, all males. "This hive had almost four thousand drones by the time the new queen got installed. Because of the fauxs. And bees are pretty hardcore. They must be cleaning house. You can't have all these drones sitting around drinking honey and not doing any work. They're expelling them." It's a little odd the way it's happening, he thinks, with half-alive drones coursing from the hive and falling off the landing board. But what else could it be?

"I've heard of faux queens. This is amazing. I feel like I'm watching a nature show." Anthony can't see Mary's face through the dark netting of her bee veil, but the excitement in her voice makes him smile. She's heard of faux queens? He's never had anyone to share bees with other than his mom. This is new, but he could get used to it quickly.

And that's when the dizziness strikes him. Sudden and total, he feels himself tilting to the side and falling. It's as if the world has gone into fast motion, as if gravity has accelerated and his body can't keep up. He can't even put out his arm to protect himself, but fortunately he falls into a bed of flowers. He feels a weird hollowness inside, like someone is stretching him out, unspooling his innards.

"Hey, you okay?" Mary asks him. He tries to sit up. Something is going on inside him. It's not easy to talk.

"I see lights," he manages. And it's true. Superimposed on his field of vision is a small golden glow. It pulses, and if he shifts his eyes it follows. It's growing.

"Can you walk?" Mary asks. He tries, but the best he can manage is a slow crawl. "Could be sun stroke. Let's get you into the shade." Groping unsteadily, with Mary's assistance he makes his way back to the shadows in the shed and leans up against the wheelbarrow. And then the light show really kicks in.

The glow begins to solidify. A form takes shape, a tiny form, a million miles away. A familiar form, that grows larger and larger: a cell. A six-sided honeybee cell. Only this time, he did not summon it himself. This time, it is thrusting up from within him, entirely on its own.

It's outlined in gold, throwing out slow plumes of light that remind him of fiery eruptions lifting away from the surface of the sun and falling back. Around the edges of the cell, points of light crackle and race. Slowly but surely, it expands to cover his entire field of vision. Blinding him. Much bigger, thicker, and more encompassing than it has ever been before.

"What's going on?" says Mary. She's taken off her bee helmet and now crouches in front of him. He voice is worried. Strange house, strange boy, strange behavior. But she's keeping it together. "Describe it to me."

So he does. The best he can. She listens for a bit, then she starts to nod.

"No pain, right? But these lights keep getting bigger and bigger?" He nods. There may be no pain, but the sensation of being stretched out in a long, thin line is growing. "I think maybe it's an anaphylactic migraine. A migraine with an aura, but without pain."

"I never. Heard of that," he says. In fact, though there isn't any pain as such, it is becoming very difficult to talk. Just concentrating with this crazy production flashing in front of his eyes is difficult. And if the feeling of being elongated gets any more intense, he is going to scream. It's like his insides are being stretched while his body stays the same shape.

"My cousin has it. Up to thirty percent of the population may have undiagnosed migraine-related disorders," she tells him. "It will start to fade in a little bit."

But it's not starting to fade. In fact, he realizes, as of that moment, he officially can't see a thing. *I'm blind*, he thinks, *except for this huge, throbbing, golden hexagon floating in front of me.*

Then his body stiffens.

"What's going on?" Mary says.

Now he can neither see nor talk. The sensation of being stretched, which had been confined to his gut, bursts out to affect the rest of his body. He feels like a plank, suspended in the air, his feet a thousand miles from his head.

That's when the energy starts to flow.

From his feet up through the hexagon and out the top of his head, it's like he's become a fire hose. Some immense, ancient energy is surging up within him, unstoppable as the tide, and the entirety of that force is being funneled through the tiny cell of honeycomb throbbing in his mind. And then going out his head. Out and up. A fountain of wild force spraying into the ether.

Distantly he can feel his body trembling. And he can sense, somehow, Mary reaching for her cell phone.

"Don't. Call. Stop." It's all he can manage. But she pauses. The rush of energy builds—he feels like it will blow the top of this head off—he feels the walls of the hexagon in his mind straining as though they will burst—he feels his back arching—his mouth opens—

Then it's over.

His body stops trembling. His vision clears, except for a tiny pinprick down in the corner of his field of vision. The sensation of being stretched relents. He takes a deep breath and sits up.

"Oh. My. God. What the hell is going on? Are you okay?" Mary asks.

"I can't believe you were going to *call*. Who were you calling? I thought we were on the same page about that kind of stuff," he complains. His voice is raspy, like he's been yelling at Mat for an hour. And he feels loose and light—but it's not a bad feeling.

"Choking I can handle," she says. "I took a class. I don't know anything about epilepsy."

"I thought I had a migraine."

"I don't know what you have. You seem to have a lot of stuff." She watches him. "How do you feel now?"

"I feel pretty good, actually. Hey," He cocks his head to the side like Bear trying to decide if he's heard someone calling him to dinner, "do you hear that?"

It's not an actual sound, but he can't think of how else to describe it. It's a rustling. Or a roaring. It might be totally silent. Or it might be really loud.

"Uh, no. Hear what?" says Mary. She's watching him closely. He can tell she's starting to have serious doubts about him. Apparently she has her limits.

"Come on," he tells her, standing and hurrying back to the yard. "It's the bees." She rushes out after him, barely remembering to put on her veil. Anthony feels, as much as hears, the sound. Slowly building. A rumble. It's coming from the hive. He approaches slowly. There must be three thousand dead drones littering the ground below the hive now, but there is no activity in the bee yard. There are no bees in the air. The hive itself, though, seems to Anthony to be beating like a drum.

"You don't hear that?" he whispers.

"You're freaking me out a little, weirdo," she says. "I think something is wrong with . . . "

But her voice trails off. A procession of bees begins to rise from the hive. They are huge bees. Shiny, golden bees. Anthony recognizes them instantly—these are the Little Queen's brood. They have to be; they are unlike anything he's ever seen before—except for her. But how is that possible? She's been laying for six days, and it takes twenty one days for an egg to go from larva to young bee. But there's no denying the evidence. The air is quickly filling with thousands and thousands of tiny, flickering demi mirrors. The host produces a roar as loud as a lawnmower.

"Look at the color," says Mary, her voice rising to be heard above the sound. "Are those your bees?"

"I told you this new Queen was different," he shouts. They watch as rank after rank rises into the air, then begins to flit in circles, up and down, back and forth. For all the world like they are playing.

"They just hatched," he says. "This is their—"

"It's their play flights!" she says, excited. "Just out of the eggs! But why are there so many at once?" Anthony and Mary stand dumbfounded. A colony hatches two thousand bees on a really, really good day. This is ten times that, and all of them came out of their cells at the same moment.

A spark among the dancing flickers catches Anthony's eye. It flashes up out of the hive to loop high above the massive, darting cloud, and it hovers there. Then it tilts and dives. Right at Anthony.

"Anthony, look out!" Mary cries, pointing and ducking despite her thick bee suit. But Anthony holds out his hand, and the Little Queen lands on his palm. He holds her up near his face.

"Wow," he says to her, looking back and forth from her tiny form to the multitude behind her. "Just . . . wow. Nice work."

Mary slowly peeks from his side. "Is that her?"

"Mary, meet the Little Queen. Little Queen, this is Mary. Inside this suit. Somewhere." The Little Queen does a dance on Anthony's palm and stares directly at Mary.

"It's like she knows what you're saying," Mary says. "She's absolutely fantastic. But what is she? I've never seen a bee like that."

The Little Queen turns back to Anthony, and she begins to dance, buzzing her wings. There is clearly a pattern to what she is doing. She repeats it over and over.

"Is she trying to tell you something?" Mary asks.

Anthony feels his stomach rumble. It's been hours since he's eaten, and since then he's had his first migraine, his first epileptic seizure, and he's witnessed an episode of beekeeping thaumaturgy. It might be time to get lunch.

But the Little Queen is insistent. Almost angry. And then he realizes: these bees are hungry. There can't be much honey gathered in the hive yet. Considering the few days the Little Queen has had to get things back on track, he'd be surprised if there were any honey at all. These young bees need food.

"Hey, come with me," Anthony says to Mary. He lofts the Little Queen into the air. "Be right back," he tells her.

He takes Mary into the larder and grabs two jars of his mother's prime honey. Usually he's extremely careful about using this. It's almost a religious occasion when he opens a new one. But that's just about what this amounts to, he thinks. He grabs a couple of cookie sheets from the bottom drawer in the kitchen and dashes back out to the yard with Mary. They each take a honey jar and a cookie sheet and make two separate feeding pools, which are quickly surrounded by thousands and thousands of hungry bees.

After that Mary just sits quietly, draped in white cloth and netting, watching. Anthony, however, moves through the cloud in wonder. A cyclone of bees follows him everywhere. The Little Queen rides on his shoulder occasionally, and when she does, a sphere of bees—not a chaotic swarm, but a clear, decisive sphere, like what he saw around Bear—forms around his head, and again he thinks he hears a song. Is it something from his dad's radio? It seems to come to him from out of the sphere around his head.

He feels a connection to these bees unlike anything he has ever experienced. The hexagon flares in the corner of his eye, and he has only to begin to think an instruction for the colony to respond. He holds out his hands and bees pile up in his fists. He tosses them up and they remain in their clusters and fly off in groups, like balloons ascending into the sky. He waves his arms, and bees swirl before him in response. It's like he's conducting pieces of magic fluff in a video game. He lifts a handful of bees, cups his other palm around it, holds it out in front of him, and opens his hands – a tight ball of bees hovers there, like he has created a levitating basketball in space. He points his finger at it, and it moves around, directed by the power of his gesture. He holds both hands out in front of him, imagines a square, and the bees form a square. Pictures a triangle, and there is a hovering triangle. He pictures Mary's face and it appears, a golden portrait of hovering bees.

"These bees . . . are . . . magic," says Mary, eyes wide. After a pause she adds, "Or you are."

If fighting to keep the hive from swarming had been a struggle, this is the opposite. It's so easy, it's almost as if he's not doing it at all. The glow inside him seems to surge up of its own accord in response to his faintest wish. It's like he's been driving an old truck with a manual stick shift, and someone has given him a sports car with automatic transmission. Everything happens so quickly and effortlessly.

Finally the young bees begin retreating to the hive, and Anthony and Mary retreat back into the house to get themselves some food. They make sandwiches, which they take to Anthony's room.

"You kind of have '*a way with bees*,' don't you?" Mary says. She's careful to let him know that she is making the most understated observation in the ENTIRE WORLD with the judicious use of air quotes.

And only then does he realize—he's done it again. It felt so natural hanging around with Mary out there, in his own bee yard, with his newly reborn hive, that he hadn't even thought about hiding his power from her. He looks at her. How much does he really trust her? Completely, he decides.

"I've always been able to get bees to do things. The truth is, I can talk to bees."

Mary stares. But after a moment she nods. It's is hard to argue with what she has just seen. She points at the bee sitting on Anthony's window sill. "What is she thinking?"

But he shakes his head. "No, I can't do single bees. There's, like, a hive-mind. The whole hive together forms a personality. I talk to that." He pauses. "Only these bees feel different. It feels more like I'm talking to one bee." The image of the Little Queen flashing down out of the air and buzzing until he gets food for the hive comes to him.

"And not only that. There's a thing inside me. A kind of a shape. And when I touch the bees, it gets in my eye. It kind of . . . " He trails off. He sounds crazy even to himself. What must Mary be thinking, listening to this?

But she does not look like she thinks he's crazy. Her face is flushed. She is really looking him over. It's actually making him kind of uncomfortable. "You can talk to bees. You really can. And these are some amazing bees. Where'd you get this Queen again?"

"I just *found* her," he says. "But look at this." He shows her the e-mails, both from VespaKeeper and from the supposed government agency. He points to the satellite pictures. "I think somebody's after her. This is the Hanlens' section, right next to us. And have you ever even heard of this South Idaho Agriculture Agency?"

Mary shakes her head. "Google it." So he does, and they find nothing.

"What do you think I should do? Ignore them? Tell them I live in Selkirk Valley?"

"I don't think it matters. If they've narrowed it down to three choices, it won't take them long to check them all."

They study the e-mails for a moment in silence, chewing their sandwiches. Mary points, and speaks with a mock vampire accent. "'Vatever you do, don't let her breed.' Hah! I guess that's pretty much out the window. This VespaKeeper guy sounds weird."

Weird is one of Mary's favorite words, Anthony is coming to realize. Maybe that's why she likes him. Because all this stuff actually is really weird.

"What does he mean, 'danger to me or the people around me?'" Anthony wonders out loud. "The Little Queen's no threat. Not at all. Not in a thousand years."

"Maybe the danger isn't from her," Mary says. "Maybe it's from VespaKeeper. Or whoever sent these satellite pictures."

"Do you think anyone would try to hurt her?" he asks.

"I don't know. People hurt people all the time. Why not hurt a bug? Who would really care except for us?"

Abruptly, what had been a bright, amazing day turns somber for them both. Anthony sees that Mary is as deeply invested in the Little Queen as he is. Which makes him feel oddly comforted. *Two is just better than one*, he thinks. But it also makes him feel a little guilty. If the first thing you do after making a best friend is put her in danger, does that say anything in particular about you?

Chapter Sixteen

For the first time in many weeks, the Little Queen feels secure. Her hive is filling. She has twenty-three thousand bees of the Sequestered, and another eleven thousand of the original bees, more than she has ever had at her disposal before. Each of the Sequestered is as productive as ten normal bees, or, as she has come to think of them, the Forerunners. The Forerunners in this hive are exceptional in their own way, but they are still no match for the Sequestered in strength, endurance, or intelligence. Much of the unusual effectiveness of these Forerunners is due to the fact that they have been kept and watched by Anthony, which is an advantage now shared by the Sequestered. It is Anthony himself who is the primary reason for the Little Queen's newfound feeling of security.

He is the source of the power she plied to accelerate the development of her eggs, to hatch in seven days what should have taken three times as long. Somehow this human boy Anthony carries a piece of the Plain of Crowns within him, or a pathway to the Plain. To have such a resource at the disposal of an earthly colony is safety unlike anything bees have ever known. She feels that, with herself at the head of the Sequestered, and Anthony at her side, there is no challenge she will not be able to meet.

She flies through what Anthony calls the BEE YARD, and watches her colony at work. She can envision a time in the not too distant future when she outgrows this one hive structure. Normally that would mean a swarm, and new queens fighting for dominion over a new hive. But the Little Queen has a different plan.

There are three other empty white hive structures in the same bee yard as the one she occupies now. She lands at the entrance to one of them and crawls inside. It is laid out with the same precise and perfect dimensions as her present hive. She feels confident that she could expand here, and then to the other two, creating a colony of unparalleled strength and size. It's not a thing that bees ever do. But there has never been any bee like the Little Queen.

It is at this moment that she receives a communication from one of the Sequestered scouting near the borders of her kingdom. MOTHER, THERE ARE WASPS.

She tunes into this bee's position and sees a dark, heavy flier cruising near the tree line, twenty feet from her scout. A Death Wasp.

DO NOT MOVE, she commands. Together the two of them watch as the Death Wasp swings closer to the trees, ranges out over the meadow, then returns. And heads directly toward her scout. Three more wasps break from the cover of the forest and converge toward the same hidden nook.

They are hunters, and they have located the scout. They will recognize the Little Queen's smell. And they will come for her if this bee flies to the hive. If they use the same strategy they previously employed, they will wait until the scout flees, then follow her.

But now the Little Queen has something that the wasps have never seen. Could not suspect. She has twenty-three thousand of the Sequestered at her back.

RETURN TO THE HIVE! she calls to her worker. It is time to end this, once and for all.

The hiding bee bursts from her foliage and dashes across the meadow, and all four wasps turn as one and follow. The level of coordination these creatures display still amazes the Little Queen and sends chills through her body. They are three times the size and ten times the strength of ordinary wasps, and much, much smarter. There are other large predatory fliers that bees live with and around, but these wasps possess the mind-to-mind, and synchronize themselves when they hunt. It is a horror that must be snuffed out.

Too FAST, she tells her worker, who has begun to outdistance the wasps. They are larger and stronger, but the Sequestered are faster. Not that the wasps are trying to catch the fleeing scout; they are following and letting her lead the pack back to the hive. Where the Queen is ready.

Suddenly from other positions around the meadow, other scouts and foragers begin reporting.

WASPS, MOTHER.

DEATH WASPS BY THE FALLEN PINE.

WASPS NEAR THE SPRING.

Quickly she cycles through these impressions, and realizes that there must be more than one hunting pack ranging the forest. Somehow all of them have been alerted. *More evidence of mind-to-mind,* she growls.

ALL BEES TO THE HIVE! she broadcasts. And like a single organism, the fifteen thousand Sequestered not already at work in the hive rise from flowers, or turn from following scent trails, and speed back. Back to their Queen.

The reports keep coming in. Wasps by the broken stump. Wasps near the garage. Wasps passing the house. She begins to realize that she is not dealing with a few hunting packs. Or even a single nest. This is something different. This is an invasion.

She counts greater than a thousand of the dark beasts, and more appearing every moment, all speeding directly to the hive. She has made a mistake. Her feeling of security has led her astray. She estimates it will take four of the Sequestered—versus sixty of the Forerunners—to kill one of these Death Wasps. She still has the force necessary, but even if this invading force is turned, she will not be able to kill every single wasp. A few hunting packs she could have destroyed. But there will be no way to ambush and surround all these insects. Some will escape, and betray the hive's position to whatever it is that controls them.

They keep coming. Fourteen hundred now, like a thin black mist converging from all quarters of the meadow. The first of her foragers are returning, diving into the hive, prepared to die defending their home. And arrayed against them—the Little Queen shudders, she can hardly believe it, it has happened so quickly—at least two thousand wasps, dark, powerful and full of hatred, with black mandibles snapping in flight, inbound and only moments away.

The sacrifice is too high. Perhaps half her bees dead, and more wasps will come. There must be a different way. These wasps want her. Let them catch her.

She bursts from the hive entrance just as the first of the hunters arrives at the landing board. And from her Bell she peels a royal scent, a scent that says, "I AM HERE!"

And then she flees.

The wasps follow. Every single one of them. Trailing scent behind her, she leads them on a wild chase, now slowing, now speeding, and they track her like the tail of a giant horse, each following the path of the wasp in front. She leads them up, high above the meadow, and they follow. She can fly for hours, perhaps days, and stay in front of this horde. But then what? They have her scent. They will not let her go.

Unless they lose that scent, she thinks. Quickly she heads downward and streaks for the trees. When she enters the wood, she begins a long and torturous route, woven deep, deep into the forest. She flies for an hour, through bushes, down streambeds, past dead animals, and up hillsides.

And then she becomes invisible. Just as she did in the robber hive, she masks her scent completely, flies forward a hundred feet, then hides in the bowl of a tree.

The wasps falter forward, then double back. At first they are confused. Consummate hunters, the idea of losing a trail is abhorrent to them, but it has happened. Their rage grows. She watches to see which way they will search. Again, they prove more cunning than ordinary wasps. In the absence of an identifiable target, they turn and double back to the target they know: back toward the hive.

They will have to be killed, she sees. While they live, while any of them lives, there can be no safety for the hive. If there is a battle, she is confident that her bees will emerge the victors, but at a terrible cost, and even then more wasps will come if just one escapes to spread the word. If only she could decoy them. If only she had a machine, like the humans, to bear her scent and lead them endlessly in circles.

A machine. She freezes for just a moment as the thought strikes her. Yes, that's it. A machine to spread her scent. It is a terrible gamble, but if it works, it will end them. Every single wasp.

There is not much time. The company of wasps has risen above the trees, eschewing the zigzag path she flew to get them lost, and is speeding back to the hive. The carnage will be terrible once that battle begins. She flies as fast as she can, the other way. Toward the kitchen.

Through her guards she can see the wasps arrive at the landing board. The entrance is some protection; since these animals are so much bigger than typical wasps, only a few can enter at once. But as soon as they are in, they begin wreaking terrible slaughter. The Forerunners are the ones who suffer most. They have absolutely no chance in the face of these monsters; they are pinched in half three at a time, as though they are made of leaves.

DIE. QUEEN. DIE, she hears. Wasps that talk. It still amazes her.

She reaches the kitchen and darts in through the open window. The FAN is on. This will not be easy, or safe, but she must not falter. She lands six feet from the vortex of air being pulled through the whirring machine. And clinging carefully to any tiny irregularity that presents itself on the granite counter, she edges herself toward the vortex. Slowly closer. Until she feels as if her wings will be peeled from her back, and her legs tremble with effort of holding on. And at last, in position, directly below the mesh, she taps her Bell, releasing her royal scent: "I AM HERE! I AM HERE! I AM HERE!" she shouts with pheromones. These molecules of scent are stripped off her body and cast out of the house by the fan.

They are propelled out past the lawn, past the driveway, and into the bee yard. It takes only a single molecule to snap these wasps to attention, to set these hunting beasts on her trail. And when it happens, two thousand six hundred and four rage-blind wasps bent on her death drop what they are doing, rise like a deadly shadow, and follow the trail back the way it came.

The Little Queen is weakening. The vacuum sucking her scent into the fan wants to do the same to her. But she can see the wasps approaching. If she can hold out another minute, she may escape entirely. Quickly the wasps reach the WINDOW, and begin to mass outside, fighting into the wind. They cannot approach. They are stuck.

Not so smart after all, thinks the Little Queen. But she anticipated this. These wasps have the mind-to-mind. Let them see what a double-edged sword it can be, without the intelligence to wield it well.

INSIDE, she broadcasts to them. She includes a picture. THROUGH THE OPENING. INSIDE. I AM WAITING. KILL ME.

They churn in confusion, but only for a moment. To the left of the fan they see the other open window, and stream through.

HERE, she says. KILL ME. IF YOU CAN. They see her as they enter the kitchen, clinging to the counter in front of the fan, and without another thought in their minds they dive toward her, stingers dripping and jaws open to rend. And then the first of them crosses in front of the fan.

And disappears. The others do not even notice, they are so bent on her destruction, and as they pass into the vortex, they vanish. *Ffftp. Ffftp. Ffftp.* In they course, tens, hundreds, a thousand, two thousand, through the window and into the kitchen following their trail, to see her taunting from her precarious redoubt.

HERE. COME TO KILL ME. KILL ME! The slaughter is unbelievable and merciless.

She fears the black torrent will never end. The spinning blades of the fan grow dark as wasp blood coats them, but the creatures keep coming, diving in a stream toward her, only to be sucked into the fan and annihilated. The sound, * fftp* becomes a constant, a groan, a scream, until she fears the fan will break.

And then, at last, there are no more. Slowly, with trembling legs, she backs out of the sucking wind. Once, she slips and is almost drawn to her own death, she is so tired. She backs far, far away from the wind before she takes flight, not trusting the strength of her wings to battle even the smallest breeze. She loops around the inside of the kitchen and passes back out the open window. But a grim truth has occurred to her.

This has become, if it had not been already, a fight that will involve Anthony. It will put him in peril. And she wants, as much as anything in her life, to protect this human boy. He is as important to her as her hive. He is her hive.

Chapter Seventeen

Sherriff Bailer rolls his squad car to a stop, and turns to look at Anthony and Mary. "Big day for you kids tomorrow," he says. "I bet you can't wait to get back to school." Anthony and Mary nod. Clearly he is mocking them, though he hides it well. The end of spring break looms like a cliff they are about to be pushed over.

"I'll see you in the library after third period," Mary says as Anthony hops out. He shuts the door and waves, and the squad car slides away through the warm afternoon shadows. The visit had been as much Sherriff Bailer's idea as the kids', Anthony feels. He had felt scrutinized. Not exactly like a criminal, but definitely like a suspect. The Bailers had a nice place. There were horses. They had a gun range out in back and a swimming pool. But none of it was interesting to Anthony, though he had enjoyed hanging out with Mary. He'd wanted to spend as much time as he could on this last, precious free day, with the bees. And now he is home. The Smith Family ranchero, once again. Spring break never felt so short.

A few strides down the driveway, and he hears the wingsong of two large bees, bearing in, each to a shoulder, then feels the infinitesimal pressure of insects landing.

"Okay, ladies, let's go home," he says to his bodyguards.

As he passes the shed, a swarm of bees races out to greet him. Instinctively he scans for Bear, but the Lab must be out eating a neighbor's garbage. He'll be horribly disappointed to miss this opportunity.

"Beehave, bee hive," he yells at the bees, who swoop upward. He spins his arms above his head and a tornado of bees forms, stretching thirty feet into the air. Then he remembers, and quickly disperses them with a wave of his hand. He scans the road, the woods, the air, and sees no sign of anyone watching. He has to learn not to get carried away.

He and Mary discussed it all day without coming to any decisions. Without more information there's nothing they can do but wait and watch. And keep a low profile.

Still no Bear as he gets closer to the house. But it seems like there's a shape of some kind on the ground in front of the kitchen. A long, thin hole. He runs toward it. No, he sees, it's a not a hole, it's flat. He looks upward. Nothing in the sky to cast a shadow.

And then he reaches the black smear. He sees that it's composed of thousands of dead insects. Not bees. Wasps? They are crushed, so it's hard to tell. And if they were wasps, they were huge, beyond anything that usually lives around River Bend. What is the world happened here?

The splatter on the ground is shaped like a funnel, and the pointy end starts several feet in front the kitchen wall. Just below the fan in the kitchen window. Which, he sees as he raises his eyes, looks as if it's been dipped in tar. The two bodyguards on his shoulders are buzzing a low, satisfied song. Like a growl. They are deeply satisfied with the mess.

He comes into the kitchen and sees nothing out of place. The only difference is the fan, noisier in its spinning, and coated with black. He unplugs it and lifts it down. His dad will want to see it.

Bear comes bounding in the door then. The bees on his shoulders buzz.

Anthony lets fly with a preemptive, "Stop, Bear!" and is astonished to see Bear stop. He stares at the dog. Is it a trick of some kind? Or is the dog sick? Bear licks his slobbery chops like he's waiting. Waiting for what? Anthony is at a loss. What is supposed to happen after your dog obeys you? This is something that's never come up before.

Anthony says, "Sit, Bear."

And Bear sits. It's a miracle.

"Down, Bear," Anthony tells him. And down Bear goes. Anthony drops slowly into a kitchen chair, watching Bear lie on the floor without moving. Waiting for instructions. Finally he remembers to say, "Good dog." And Bear twitches his head to the side. It's not a phrase he's familiar with.

What is going on here? Wasps sprayed dead on the lawn, a dog that suddenly does what you tell him to do—is the world ending?

The phone rings and Anthony jumps, startled. Then he hurries to answer. This is the emergency phone, which basically never rings. He has a cell, and his dad has a cell. The sheriff calls on this line when there's a fire. Is that what's going on? Is a fire turning all the animals crazy?

"Hello?" he says. And he's surprised to hear Mrs. Hanlen's voice on the other end. "Oh, Anthony. Is your father home?" She sounds a little rushed. Unlike her.

"No, he should be back with Mat anytime. Can I give him a message?"

She pauses. At last she says, "No, it's probably nothing. It's just . . . some men came to the house today. Asking about bees in the area."

Anthony's face goes cold. "What about bees?"

"They didn't say. I didn't like 'em, I'll tell you that. Black shiny sedan. Dark windows. So I ran 'em off. But I was thinking of you. You have bees. Your mom's." Mrs. Hanlen would never in a million years pry into someone's business. But Anthony can hear that she's worried about him.

"Did they say anything else?" he asks.

"Nope. Like I said, I ran 'em off quick. But I got their license. So I thought I'd give it to you folks. You can keep an eye out." He grabs a pen from the fridge. "Idaho plates. 769BW44."

"Thanks a lot, Mrs. Hanlen," he tells her sincerely. "We'll keep an eye out."

"You be careful, okay? And say hi to Matty for me. Bye bye."

As Anthony hangs up the phone, his dad's truck pulls up. And for some reason he can't quite explain, he stuffs the paper with the number into his jeans pocket.

Mat barrels into the house.

"At preschool today I played Iron Man," he says as soon as he sees Anthony. "And I got a time out for throwing sand on Jackson's hair, and then I drew a bird, and why is Bear lying on the floor?"

"I think he's sick," Anthony tells Mat.

"Get out, Bear," Mat says, and Bear springs up and leaves. Mat laughs. Seeing Bear do what you ask is like seeing a piece of bread make itself into a peanut butter sandwich. Mat disappears after him.

Anthony's dad comes into the kitchen and lays a few papers on the counter, along with Mat's lunch box and his briefcase. He sees the fan.

"What the hell? What'd you do here?"

"I didn't do anything," Anthony says, "A bunch of bugs or wasps or something flew into it."

"Just what we need around here, more bugs. Go get ready for dinner." Anthony starts to leave. "I've got a few things to talk to you boys about tonight," his dad says with his back turned at the sink. "So, you know. Be ready. Just listen is all."

Oh great, more talking.

Later, at the table eating microwaved meatloaf and carrots, Anthony watches Mat play with his new toy.

"Look, Dad. Bear, sit!" says Mat, and Bear, compelled by his new obligation to mind, pants and sits. Mat howls with laughter. "Look, Dad. Bear, lie down!" Bear lies down. More laughter. "Dad, look – Bear, stand up!" Bear stands, Mat laughs.

"Okay Mat, that's—"

"Bear, sit!" Bear sits. "Bear—"

Abruptly Paul rises from the table, crosses to the kitchen door, and throws it open.

"Bear, out!" he commands. Bear slinks outside as fast as he can go.

Paul sits back down at the table. A moment passes, a quiet, typical moment where the only sounds are silverware on plates and Mat chewing with his mouth open. Then Anthony's dad clears his throat. Anthony and Mat freeze.

"So, I've been thinking," their dad says. Then demonstrates the idea by not saying anything else for a while. Mat and Anthony slowly return to their dinner.

"Cindy Jensen and I have been seeing each other, and I think you are going to really like her," he finally continues. Or starts an entirely new conversation. Or becomes a completely new person and pretends to be their dad and eats carrots.

"What are you, what?" Anthony asks. But his mouth is suddenly dry.

"Cindy Jensen. You met her at the party."

"What about her?"

"Well, when grownups, when people have feelings for each other," his dad begins. But he stops again. He rubs his eyes, leaving a tiny speck of gravy on his cheek. "Cindy will be around more, that's all."

"Around what?" Anthony asks.

"Us. Around. She's going to be a part of our life."

Anthony stares. He isn't hearing this. His dad can't possibly be saying what it seems like he's saying. Then Anthony sees what must be going on.

"Oh. You're doing some work on her house," he says. "I thought I saw some boards on the deck that were—"

"No. I'm not working on her house. She's going to be a part of our lives. I care about her. She's a good person, you're going to like her. We're going to meet her tomorrow for dinner." And somebody kicks the meatloaf out of Anthony's stomach.

"Is this like a playdate, Dad?" Mat wants to know.

"Yeah, Mat, sort of. For grownups and families."

"Cool. Can Cindy be our new mom?"

"Shut up!" Anthony finds that he is standing at the edge of the table, brandishing his fork. Mat stares, slack-jawed. "Shut up, Mat! What are you talking about? We don't need a new mom!"

"She's not a new mom, she's—" Paul tries to say.

"Is she moving in?" Anthony demands. His father looks away. "She's . . . we'll have to see, we'll take it—"

"No! No! How could you do this?" Anthony is crying. "This is wrong!"

"Tony, sit down now, let's—"

"I will never sit down! I hate Cindy Jensen! Am I the only one in this family who still cares about Mom?" And he dashes from the table, out the kitchen door and into the night.

Chapter Eighteen

The air outside is cooler than in the kitchen, but Anthony still feels hot. He slams the door and runs without knowing where he's going. And two tiny shapes keep pace with him, flying above either shoulder.

He blinks past his tears as he runs, stumbling but refusing to stop. For a moment he thinks about going to the bee yard, but that's the first place his dad will look, and he wants to hide. He wants to disappear. Or rather, he wants everything else to disappear. So he heads for the trees.

When he was little, Mat's age, he had a fort deep in the woods made of fallen limbs propped against a boulder, pine needles piled on top for a roof. The fort is long gone, but the boulder is still there. Half-blinded by tears, separated from it for many years, he still finds it in the middle of the night and slumps down beneath it.

His mom found this place once. When he was seven. He'd done something he felt was within his rights, gotten into trouble, announced he was going to run away, and retreated to his fort. For hours he'd crouched there, watching ants crawl through the pine needles and getting hungrier and less comfortable, until his mom crunched up through the trees. She'd squatted down at the door, and without speaking spread out a blanket. It was the only time he can remember that the two of them ever had a picnic alone. It's a memory he hasn't revisited in many years. It causes him to double over with painful tears now.

He actually, literally can't believe that his father would do this. Cindy Jensen? Cindy Jensen can't plant a flower to save her life— Anthony saw her yard. And she has stupid white furniture and curly hair and a thousand other things that make her unfit. There is just no comparison to his mom. It's unfair—to him, to Mat, and to the memory of the person they all loved.

Or the person he thought they all loved. Now he wonders. How much could you love a person if it's this easy to just throw them out of your life? For Anthony, his mom is a figure who can never be replaced. For his dad, apparently, replacing her is just a matter finding someone wearing the right shade of lipstick.

The rock at his back is cold and hard, but everything else in his life seems made of papier-mâché. These huge holes being torn in his existence can't be repaired, he knows. These are holes he's going to have to live with. They will define the shape of his life from this day forward. And however much he wants to, he knows he can't go back. He can't even run away. There is no one left to stop him.

His bodyguards alight on his hand to sample the tears that have dripped there, then lift upward to hover in front of his face.

"Nobody cares," he tells them, barely able to get the words out. "She's dead. Who's going to look out for her? She's gone." Both of the bees begin a slow circle around his head. He continues to cry, until he notices that their buzzing has grown louder. He looks up to find he is ringed with bees.

Hanging directly in front of him is the Little Queen.

"You shouldn't be out at night," he tells her. He wipes his face with his shirt. There is a sphere of bees encircling his head, a clear, symmetrical globe, buzzing softly and hanging in perfect position.

"Seriously," he says. "Go back. You need to rest. The honey flow is starting."

The sphere grows tighter, then looser, and the tone of the bees' buzzing wings rises and drops. It's actually kind of comforting. As if they are singing to him.

In fact, the more he listens, the more he thinks he hears a melody. Something from the radio. Willie Nelson? Something his dad listens to. And then that melody shifts, and he hears something different. Long, drawn-out tones. Like backward recordings of speech.

He looks at the Little Queen, wings beating softly right before his eyes. She's been hanging there for a while, watching without turning away. He can feel the breeze of her strong wings on his wet cheeks.

And then he hears it, an eerie, protracted *aaahhh*, which turns into a word. Spoken by the wings of bees.

ANTHONY, he hears.

He wants to talk. But he is afraid he's dreaming. He is afraid he will wake up. *ANTHONY*, he hears again.

The sound comes from everywhere around his head. It's an unearthly resonance, elongated like someone talking underwater, but very easy to understand.

ANTHONY. CAN. YOU. HEAR. ME?

It is the Little Queen. She buzzes up to touch his forehead, as though poking him to get his attention.

"I can. Hear you. You're talking?"

I. AM. LEARNING.

"That's impossible."

NOTHING IS. IMPOSSIBLE.

He tries to figure out what is going on. It seems that the wings of the bees around his head are being coordinated in some way to make sounds. Short words are very comprehensible. Longer words get mushy toward the last syllables.

"But how?"

I. PRACTICED. ON. THE GODDAMN. DOG. AND. WILLIE NELSON.

Somehow that breaks him up. Hearing the Little Queen floating in the air, against all reason, against all the ways things are supposed to happen in the world, and repeat his dad's cursing. It's just too much. Anthony begins to laugh. It goes on a long time.

ANTHONY.

He sits up, but he's still convulsing. It's not really laughter, he knows. It's a combination of disbelief, fear, hope, and sadness. Plus this talking bee did just call Bear a goddamn dog. He's grinning and crying and barely in control.

YOU. ARE CRAZY?

This stops him. "What?"

YOUR FACE PATTERN. ARE YOU. INSANE?

"No. What? I'm, I mean, maybe I am. I don't know." He takes a breath. He stares at her. "You're really talking."

MY SCOUTS. SAW. YOU CRYING.

"Yeah."

WHY?

"It'd be hard to explain."

WHAT IS. CINDY JENSEN?

He's having a hard time keeping up with the conversation. This conversation with this bee. He shakes his head.

"How do you know Cindy Jensen?"

I HEARD DAD. THROUGH. MY SCOUTS. IS IT. AN ENEMY?

Oh, god. What is going on here? What is this bee asking him? How do you explain something like this to a bee? Is Cindy Jensen an enemy? No. And yes. What is he supposed to say? He does the best he can.

"Cindy Jensen is not my mother."

The Little Queen floats in front of him for a long time. Anthony can hear wind in the trees, and crickets coming out. From the stream on the other side of the property comes the croaking of frogs. Finally the Little Queen speaks again.

WHO IS YOUR. MOTHER?

"My mother is dead."

YOU HAVE LOST. YOUR QUEEN.

"Yes."

ANTHONY.

"Yes?"

I WILL BE YOUR QUEEN.

And then he is crying again, all over again, titanic sobs that come in waves. He tries to stop. He wants to talk. But there's nothing he can do. There's a cord inside him that has been pulled, and something is pouring out. He's afraid the Little Queen will leave, or grow frightened. Or even insulted. But she waits. Finally it's over, and he can speak again.

"Thank you. Really and truly. But I don't think it works like that."

YES. IT DOES. WORK.

"Not for people."

FOR EVERYTHING. A QUEEN PROTECTS. HER COLONY. YOU ARE MINE. I WILL PROTECT. YOU.

Anthony's phone rings. And such are the priorities of middle school life that even here, in the midst of the most amazing conversation he has ever had—arguably the most astonishing conversation any human has ever had—he checks to see who is calling.

Mary.

"Hello?" he says, flipping the speakerphone on.

"Hey, Anthony. What's up?"

He eyes the circle of bees around him, the night beyond, the Little Queen buzzing directly in front of his face.

"Um . . . different stuff," he says.

"Like what?" her voice asks.

"Sort of, um, talking to the Little Queen."

MARY. HELLO, says the Little Queen.

There is a long pause. "What. Was that?"

"That was her," he says.

"Who?" Mary asks.

"The Little Queen."

He holds the speakerphone up toward the bees. "I'm in the woods. There's, like, a ball of bees around my head. She's making them talk."

"Okay, weirdo. That's too weird."

MARY. I AM. HERE. ANTHONY. IS CRYING.

"Hey," he protests, "I am not."

YOU. WERE.

"Wait a minute," Mary says. He can imagine the look on her face. She's squinting. She is pulling on her hair. One of her eyebrows is arching like Spock. "Are you for real serious?"

"Go ahead. Ask her something," he says.

He can almost hear her brain clicking. Then from the speaker phone, her voice, "Little Queen, where did you come from?"

I ESCAPED. FROM THE SUPERHIVE.

"What's the Superhive?" Mary asks.

THE PLACE. I ESCAPED FROM.

Anthony laughs.

"What was it like?" Mary asks.

FILLED. WITH HORRIBLE. DEATH. GREEN DEATH. DEATH GAS.

And then Anthony is not laughing. All three of them are silent. Until Mary, realization in her voice, breaks the silence.

"Anthony, that's it! Don't you see? She escaped. Now someone wants her back."

YES. THERE IS DANGER. DEATH WASPS. CAME TODAY.

"Yes!" Anthony says. "I saw wasps. What happened?"

HUNTER WASPS. EVIL. CREATURES. THEY WANT. ME DEAD. MORE WILL COME.

Mary's voice from the phone cracks, and softly she says "Anthony. You know what the scientific name for wasp is? Vespa. Anthony. VespaKeeper."

Anthony feels a chill. The night feels colder all of a sudden. He puts his hand in his pocket—and feels the note with the license number from Mrs. Hanlen. He pulls it out. The puzzle pieces are starting to pile up, although he feels like he's wearing mittens and a blindfold trying to snap them together.

"My neighbor called," he tells Mary, holding the paper up as if she can see it. "Some men showed up at her door. Asking about bees. She got their license number."

MY SCOUTS SAW. THEM.

"Did you recognize them?" he asks the Little Queen.

THERE WERE NO. HUMANS. IN THE SUPERHIVE. ONLY BEES. AND GAS.

"Anthony," Mary says, "e-mail me that license plate."

From the woods to his right comes a loud *CRACK*, a branch being snapped by a foot. He freezes.

"Shhh," he says.

IT IS A. DEER, says the Little Queen. *MY SENTRIES. SAW HER. APPROACHING.*

The night has become oppressive and dangerous-feeling to him. He wants to get back inside. He speaks to the Little Queen. "You have to move the colony."

MOVE. WHERE?

"Anywhere. Anywhere but those supers. You have to do it now. They know where you are. Move tonight."

The Little Queen takes a moment to answer. *ANTHONY. TO MOVE A. COLONY AT NIGHT. WILL BE HARD. IS IT IMPORTANT?*

"Very, very important."

THEN I MUST. BEGIN NOW.

And the ring of bees rises and disperses into the darkness, leaving behind only his bodyguards.

"Is she gone?" Mary asks.

"Yeah. I need to get back inside. Lock your doors tonight. We don't know what we're dealing with yet." He hangs up. The walk back to the house is the longest of his life. He has never been as happy to have company as he is to have his two bee companions with him on that walk.

In bed, with the covers pulled high, Anthony finds it hard to sleep. Not because of mysterious e-mails. Not because of the threat of men in dark sedans or of wasps visiting in the night. But because of something the Little Queen said.

"I will be your Queen," she told him. He's not sure what that could really mean. It seems impossible, impractical, and, under the present circumstances, probably dangerous. But nothing else anyone has said to him for four years has made him feel like that one sentence has. Safe. Loved. It's a feeling he'd do anything to keep.

HE WAKES ONCE DURING THE NIGHT, THINKING HE'S HEARD A NOISE. He looks out the window into the dark. There is no moon, but he can see the outlines of the shed and the bee yard. Nothing is moving. He stays at the window for thirty minutes, staring until his eyes water, but as far as he can tell, no creatures of any kind stir in the meadow. He hopes the Little Queen was able to get the colony moved. He goes back to bed when he can no longer keep himself awake, and in his dreams he sees the golden hexagon, pulsing in space. It is not a restful night.

ON THE WAY TO THE BUS STOP THE NEXT MORNING, ANTHONY notices that the shed door is hanging open. He dashes over. The lock is missing. He enters the shed. Nothing looks disturbed.

Out in the bee yard everything looks the same. But the lid of the hive has been left open, just the slightest crack. Something he would never do in a million years. He runs back into the shed and grabs the pryer, then lifts the lid completely off the hive.

It's empty. Not a bee to be found. But something dull gray lies on the floor below the racks. He can only get at it if he pulls all the racks out. He removes the racks to find a small metal cylinder without markings, smooth on all sides except where a nozzle protrudes.

DROP IT, comes a whisper. He realizes that a thin sphere of bees is ringing his head. *THAT IS DEATH GAS.*

He drops it like it's a rotting corpse. *THEY ARE WATCHING*, says the whisper. And the bees disperse.

Someone tried to kill the bees last night. And they're still here, watching the hive.

When he climbs onto the bus, he is shivering.

Chapter Nineteen

T he school is abuzz. Blood has been found in a school bathroom, so the rumor runs, though no official word has come down and the bathroom in question is taped off. Some sort of explosion, say those in the know, which collapsed the roof of the lavatory. A boy's hand was blown off and found in a nearby dumpster, is a popular addendum. Some insist it was an entire leg.

The only sport played with any passion at River Bend Middle is 8th grade boys' basketball, and many—particularly the 8th grade boys' basketball team—are certain whatever happened in the bathroom must have been due to an attack by rival Ketchum Falls Intermediate. But Ketchum Falls is 50 miles away, and few can seriously picture a team of 8th graders getting rides from their parents to go wreck a distant bathroom. Still, the basketball team vows never to forget. The loss of any room, even a bathroom, is a loss of school pride.

Of course, River Bend Middle itself is home to any number of ready suspects, boys who now walk the halls with a puffed up glow. "Hey, what are you looking at?" they say. And, "BOOM!" they yell into the girls' bathrooms, safe in the knowledge that they had nothing to do with the incident.

The real culprits keep their heads down, and watch, and wait. Two sets of culprits, waiting for two distinctly different things. One set smirks but stays silent, ready to step quietly back into the shadows and disappear if an investigation turns their way. The other culprit finds his peanut butter sandwich sticking to the roof of his mouth, refusing to be swallowed, as he ponders much larger problems than toilet roll holders.

Mary texts Anthony as he sits in the lunch room trying to eat. Come to the lib rite now!

He throws his phone is his pocket, abandons his sandwich, and hurries out into the tense halls. He had texted her about the poison gas canister during first period. She texted back that she was working on something important.

In the library, she leads him past the computer stations, toward the back of the room. She talks softly as they go. "I've been thinking. Maybe we should tell my dad about the gas. He could send a car out there."

"To do what?"

"Patrol. Don't you think we should?"

"I don't know what to think!"

"Shh. In here. Let me show you something."

She takes him into the office, sits him down in front of a computer, and types an access code.

"Ever heard of LexisNexis?" she asks. He shakes his head. "It's a research tool. They use it at colleges." She types a few more passwords as pages appear. And then she is inside her account. Welcome, Mary, it says across the top.

"Librarians use it too," she says. "I asked my dad to run that license plate. I told him a friend thought some guys had been following her. I got an address. After that it was pretty simple. Look."

She shows him a screen with the heading, Lightning and Angels. He scans it. "Just tell me," he says. "I didn't get much sleep last night."

"This is a private laboratory doing government contract research. It's right here in Idaho, not far from River Bend. Lightning and Angels. The car is registered here. What kind of work do you think they do?"

"Weather?"

"No. Agricultural research. Guess what they mainly study? Colony Collapse Disorder."

Anthony's head is fuzzy, but even he can see the connection. "They study bees?"

"Yes." She clicks several links; pages of graphs and statistics flash past.

"These reports are really complex. And a lot of it is redacted, you know, blacked out. But it seems like they are sequencing the honeybee genome."

He rubs his temples. "Genetic engineering?"

"Plus some kind of breeding program. And here's the guy in charge of it all. Kristapor Davidson." Anthony studies the picture. Black hair, smile. Normal and boring looking man in a suit.

"So this is the guy who wants the Little Queen back?"

"Or wants her killed."

Suddenly there is a loud pounding on the window. Greyson, Alex, and Sandy stand outside.

"Great, the goons," Mary says.

"I'll take care of them," he tells her. "Stay here."

He leaves the office and closes the door carefully behind him. Greyson steps forward. Sandy and Alex hang back. Greyson produces a magnetic smile.

"You are now the explosives king! Sandy and Alex thought you were dead."

"I'm not," Anthony says.

Greyson waits for him to continue. Then, "Come on, Badass." Greyson pats his pack. "I've got another one. Let's go blow a mailbox."

"I'm done."

Greyson stops smiling.

"Done?"

"No more. Count me out."

Greyson's eyes get a flat look. Like something inside is retreating to make room for something else. He studies Anthony for a moment.

"You didn't e-mail over vacation," he observes.

"I'm not supposed to e-mail or text. According to my dad."

"Huh," Greyson nods, looking through the window at Mary. "Saw you check your phone during lunch."

"I'm not *supposed* to text," Anthony says. "Doesn't mean I don't."

"Just has to be the right person," Greyson says.

Sandy and Alex are watching this exchange with open mouths. It appears to them that Greyson is not in total control. But they are not sure.

Anthony waits.

Greyson shrugs. "Well, we're leaving campus. Get your bag."

"I'm staying here," Anthony says. Then he turns to go back into the office.

"I think you should come with us," says Greyson. He steps close. There is a purr to his voice now, a tone of smooth menace. "I really think it would be a good idea."

"I have bigger problems than what you think," Anthony tells him. He reaches for the doorknob. Greyson gestures, and Sandy grabs Anthony. Anthony pulls free. Sandy tries again and Anthony pushes him back. Sandy stumbles, then looks at Greyson, at a complete loss.

"Just leave me alone, Greyson," Anthony says.

Behind them, Mr. Amber, the librarian, appears. He is stacking books, oblivious to the confrontation, but near enough to shut it down.

"You're not thinking about telling anyone where that bomb came from, are you?" asks Greyson, quietly.

"No."

"I know Mrs. Waterman called the cops. Talking to them would be a very, very bad idea."

"I told you. I'm not saying anything."

Greyson tilts his head to one side. Then to the other. Watching Anthony. It's like he's triangulating on Anthony's face, really getting the range. Then he nods once and leads the other two boys off. At the exit to the library he turns. He points a finger at Anthony like a gun, and pulls the trigger. His dead eyes do not blink. Anthony waits until they are gone. Then he returns to the office.

Mary and Anthony spend the rest of lunch researching anything to do with Lightning and Angels, or Kristapor Davidson, or genetically engineered bees. But the pickings are slim. All they figure out is that for a guy in charge of an operation as large as Lightning and Angels seems to be, Kristapor Davidson has a very limited track record. He seems to have gone to school at Michigan State in the 80s, where he got a bachelor's degree in marketing. But after that he dropped out of the academic and job scene completely for fifteen years before suddenly reappearing and starting this company.

As they are leaving, Mary says out loud the thought that has been on both their minds for an hour.

"She's genetically altered, isn't she?"

He nods. "Look at her. There's never been a bee on earth like that."

"What do you think they were trying to do?"

"Who knows? They're researching Colony Collapse Disorder. Did they make her immune?"

"Maybe you can ask her."

It's a good idea. He decides to do it as soon as he gets home. Unless there are people watching the property. But how would he even know? With these thoughts spinning through his head, he and Mary part ways and head to their classes, planning to meet again after school.

During English, while the rest of the students are reading *The Outsiders*, Anthony makes his way forward and puts a paper on Mr. Charles's desk. The teacher looks at it, then looks at Anthony, nods without speaking, and goes back to his book. It has been accepted, Anthony sees. He hopes it's enough to pass.

Making his way back to his own desk, he sees that Greyson, Sandy, and Alex's seats are empty. They must have cut school after the library, to go deface precious art or throw rocks at baby rabbits. They do like throwing rocks.

As he is sitting back down the door opens, and Mrs. Tobbler, the school secretary, puts her head in. "Anthony, you're needed in the office," she says. Everyone in the class looks up.

He leaves his books and bag behind, and joins Mrs. Tobbler in the hallway.

The overpowering scent of roses assaults him. Mrs. Tobbler's signature scent. It's almost staggeringly powerful. Fortunately it's not with him long. Mrs. Tobbler is hurrying down a side hall.

"You go on ahead, hon," she says. "I have to use the ladies'."

"What's going on in the office—" he asks, but she is through the door and halfway to the stall before he finishes. So he starts the long walk to the office.

On his left are door after door, and behind each a classroom. As he walks he imagines kids bent over books, and kids talking behind the teacher's back, and kids waiting to get home and play Xbox. He even imagines a few with problems, big problems, like a dad who just lost his job, or a mom in prison. But he can't imagine another kid anywhere in the world with his problems. *Is it just me*, he thinks, *or does it really seem like I'm always the one with the crappiest stuff going on? Everybody thinks that about their life. But with me it's actually true.*

Along the hallway across from the classrooms are windows that look outside, through a grassy courtyard and into the trees. He's on the other side of the school from where he disappeared up the hill and found the Little Queen. This wood looks out over the city of River Bend, and down at the Priest River itself, snaking through the dark trees and canyons like one of Mathew's drawings of a snake. Long, random, and thin.

He hears a thunk on the window. Then another, and sees that as he walks he's being paced outside the window by bees—his bees, the new breed, the Little Queen's daughters. It had been difficult to convince his bodyguards to stay outside this morning. They had met him when he stepped off the bus and headed for the school doors. Bees in school would just have created more problems, so he insisted they remain behind. Now, apparently the Little Queen has sent a thousand more.

They are trying to get in the window.

"What are you doing here?" he whispers at them. "Go away." The school is many miles from his house. Had they flown the whole distance? How fast are these bees?

When they see him look, they cover the window, darkening it. He waves them off, but they don't move. He trots farther down the hall, and they follow. And then they find an open window, and pour into the hallway.

"Get out," he hisses. "You can't be in here."

They quickly form a halo around his head. And from somewhere—

he can't tell where, it could be anywhere, miles away or just around the corner—the Little Queen speaks to him.

ANTHONY. DANGER. DON'T GO TO. THE OFFICE.

He freezes. "What do you mean?"

MEN. WHO WANT TO. HURT YOU. WAIT THERE.

"What men? Who are they?"

BAD MEN. RUN. FOLLOW MY SCOUTS.

Some of the bees break from the halo and head back the way he came, toward Mr. Charles's class, and he follows, confused and growing frightened. The rest of the insects keep a loose swarm around his head, while a few trail behind, the rear guard. Before they get all the way back to the classroom, they take a side passage that leads to the gym.

Ahead is an exit. The scouts bob impatiently, waiting for him to arrive. "You know this school pretty well," he says.

MY BEES. FEEL COMFORTABLE IN. THIS HIVE.

He opens the door. She stops him. *WAIT. FOR THE SCOUTS.* Ten of the bees slip out in a clump, then separate like fighter planes at an air show, shooting off in different directions.

SAFE. GO.

He steps out onto the courtyard.

GO TOWARD THE. TREES, says the Little Queen. *WE WILL —WAIT!*

From the forest across the courtyard he sees a shape erupt, a flying shape, black and fast.

WASPS. THAT MEANS MEN—

And at almost the same moment a side door near the office opens and two black-suited men in sunglasses step out. "Hey!" one of them yells.

ANTHONY RUN! shrills the Little Queen. From a separate section of the wood he sees another shape burst—a large yellow group, flying at three times the speed of the wasps. Another body of bees! She has kept some in reserve.

*MY BEES WILL. DELAY. THE WASPS. AND MEN. BUT THERE ARE MORE. BE CAREFUL. **RUN!***

And then the bees ringing his head dive down and away, flashing toward the two suited men. Behind him he sees the bee swarm overtake the wasps in flight, and a giant cloud of black and gold spins through the air. He can hear the battle from where he stands, like two leaf blowers swinging back and forth. Nearer to him the bees reach the suited men, who grasp their belts, trying to pull canisters free. They are being stung—and begin to scream. Apparently being stung by the Little Queen's scouts is far, far worse than being stung by an ordinary bee.

Anthony takes off running toward the parking lot. The sky is darkening. The first shower of the summer is packing the sky overhead with blue-black clouds. He thinks, *maybe if I can find a teacher or a parent leaving I can get a ride, or hide down there among the cars . . .* He doesn't have a clear plan.

He scrambles around the back of the gym, to stay out of sight of the office. Above the tennis courts, there's a steep hillside of loose rock and dirt, which he jumps out onto like a cliff diver, sliding down feet-first in a storm of dust. Halfway to the bottom he twists his ankle. Then he limps across the tennis courts, and finds himself at the edge of the parking lot.

There are fewer cars here than he'd expected. There's really no place to hide. On the far side of the lot is a dense thicket of trees, and just below that is the entrance leading to the long, winding road down to town. He limps for the trees, running as fast as he can.

Halfway across, he hears a car start. Behind him a dark sedan roars to life. It is several rows over, but very few cars separate them. Anthony can't run any faster, but at the speed he's going he doesn't think he's going to make it to the trees.

Then he sees another car. And he recognizes the driver—it's Ms. London, the music teacher.

"Hey, wait," he calls. She is driving toward the entrance, probably finished for the day. He waves his arms and screams.

"Hey, MS. LONDON! WAIT!" She hears him and stops her car.

"Anthony? You're filthy! What are you doing out of school?"

The sedan behind him is picking up speed three rows over. Anthony runs around to the passenger side of Ms. London's car and pulls on the handle.

"Quick, let me in!"

"Anthony Smith, you tell me what is going on this instant. Right. Now."

He reaches in through the open window and unlocks the door himself. "Drive!" he yells as he climbs in.

"What is going on?"

"My dad. He's, he's, in the hospital!" Anthony looks over his shoulder. The sedan is passing them down another row, heading for the entrance, to seal it off.

It starts to rain. Single giant drops, like gumdrops plummeting from the sky, two or three a second.

"Go FAST!" he screams. "We have to go!"

Ms. London, bewildered, puts her foot to the floor. The black sedan reaches the end of the row it is on, and, tires squealing, it turns the corner. They are not going to make it, Anthony realizes. The sedan is going to block the entrance.

In the dense woods near the lot entry, three pairs of eyes watch events unfolding in the parking lot. They are malevolent eyes, surprised eyes. They have been watching Anthony since he entered the parking lot. They watch the cars converge on each other. They measure the distances, and the angles. And most of all, they mark the view of Anthony in his seat, seen through his open window. Target of opportunity.

When Ms. London's car passes close, there is a mad scramble in the dirt among the trees, and then those three watchers rise. Three right arms cock backward, three fists clutching payloads, and three arms flash forward.

In the car Anthony realizes that Ms. London still has not seen the sedan. Or perhaps she thinks it is going to stop. He starts to point— and then the first stone, a sharp, angry rock, smallest of the three and spinning erratically, reaches the car. It strikes the rear passenger window, smashing into it and cracking it. Ms London turns, startled.

Then the second stone, larger, lumpish, arching, and heavy, lands on the hood of the car— *CRASH!*

"What is going—" Ms. London says.

And that's when the third stone, polished smooth, symmetrical and perfect—a stone which many would call beautiful, but a stone with a deep and terrible flaw—finds its mark. The accurate stone.

This stone passes through the open window. Enters the car.

And crushes Anthony's temple. Then drops into his lap.

Blood courses from the wound. He slumps forward, unconscious.

"Anthony! Anthony, are you—" yells Ms. London, who does not see that the sedan that had raced ahead for the entrance has skidded to stop, blocking her path. The men in the sedan would not in their wildest imaginings predict that a teacher with a student in her car would attempt to crash their barricade. But they see her coming on. Without slowing. It must be a bluff. IT'S GOT TO BE A—

The sound of the impact is tremendous. It's heard in the school. It is heard in the town. And it's heard by three stunned but ecstatic stone throwers as they flee through the woods, seeking shelter from the storm that is now bursting forth in great violence.

Chapter Twenty

For three days the rain, a constant, drenching Idaho downpour, has kept the Little Queen trapped. While bees can technically fly in the rain for short distances, they seldom do—without eyelids, there is no way to keep the water from blinding them, and their primary navigation tool, smell, is wholly useless. So the Little Queen has waited.

She was able to send bees from the school to follow the ambulance bearing Anthony to the hospital, and so has been able to keep a close watch on the outside of that building. Any of the bees that she tried to insert into the hospital itself were quickly tracked down and killed, if they were able to find a way in at all. Insects are very unwelcome in that environment.

The thing the Little Queen wants more than any anything else is to see Anthony. When she shuts off her vision, she sees the light from the cell within him. She has watched it grow dimmer and dimmer since they carried him into the big white building. Anthony is fading.

The larger human, DAD, spends all his time at the hospital. And the smaller human, MAT, sometimes comes home with MRS. HANLEN, to eat and sleep, but is often with DAD. This evening the Little Queen plans to try a desperate scheme in order to get herself nearer to Anthony. She is watching even now, ready to put the first pieces of the plan into action.

She has moved some of her colony in short wet jumps out of the forest where they hid when they fled the hive, to under the eaves of Anthony's house. Now she waits with these bees, watching Mrs. Hanlen's parked car in the driveway. The pattern has been that Mrs. Hanlen and Mat arrive home, enter the house, spend an hour or so here while Mat eats and puts different clothing onto his body. Then they drive off. Her scouts subsequently see the car arrive at the hospital. So if the pattern holds true, Mrs. Hanlen should be stepping out of the kitchen door at any moment with Mat.

The door opens. The humans appear. Mrs. Hanlen opens her umbrella, an ingenious thing humans have that keeps the rain off their heads. And then she and the boy run out to the car. Mrs. Hanlen opens the back door for Mat.

The Little Queen drops from the eaves and dives for the car. Timing here is everything. Mrs. Hanlen and Mat are blocking the door and looking into the car. The Little Queen has arranged a distraction, but it needs to come—there! Around the corner of the house, barking, bouncing, and wearing a thin halo of bees, comes the GODDAMN DOG.

The halo breaks away as soon as Bear approaches the car, leaving him to execute his part of the plan seemingly on his own.

Which he does perfectly. Shaking mud and slinging water, he bounds up to the open door and attempts to climb in.

"No, Bear, down!" says Mat.

"Oh, Bear! Oh, no, no—" Mrs. Hanlen attempts to pull Bear out of the car, and for a moment the Little Queen fears he will do his job too well and actually get inside. But then Mat and Mrs. Hanlen manage to pull him, yipping and lunging, back toward the house. Leaving the door to the car open for a few seconds.

In a dense teardrop shape the bees drop through the door, soaking wet, and shoot up under the front seat.

"Silent now," she tells them. They cluster tightly and cease their buzzing. A moment later Mat is back in the car, strapped into his seat, and the car is moving. The bees cling to the underside of the seat through bumps and turns and several episodes of wild acceleration. Mat loves the ride, but any conscientious adult might think twice about entrusting their child to the transportation stylings of Mrs. Alice Hanlen if they had the benefit of the Little Queen's view. Still, after half an hour, they arrive at the hospital. Mrs. Hanlen pulls into the parking structure, takes Mathew from the car seat, then closes the door and locks it.

Now, beneath the seat, the Little Queen settles in to wait. She has her scouts deployed around the hospital, and she knows the comings and goings. She is aware of a pack of black sedans, parked at specific locations, occasionally replaced by other black sedans, and she has seen the men inside these cars. She knows that the parking lot is under surveillance. She will need help to make it inside the hospital.

The rain continues, an unyielding downpour. The Little Queen watches cars come and go within the parking structure and along the road leading to the dropoff bay in front of the hospital. Then finally, approaching from the south, she sights the automobile she has been waiting for: a yellow BUICK. Just as it has done for the last three days, the Buick pulls up to the hospital entrance, disgorges its passenger, and pulls away. Her scouts at the entrance are ready. They dive down through the rain toward the scurrying umbrella.

Mary usually loves the rain, but for the last three days it has been her worst enemy. Dark days and stormy nights. It feels like she's creating the weather with her own inner life, instead of living through some long, slow storm.

She's visited Anthony after school every afternoon since he was admitted, begging her mother to drop her off on her way to work so that her father can pick her up two hours later. Her mom is busy, but reluctantly makes time, and her dad has other things on his mind all the time anyway, so he barely notices her grief. She feels as though she's the only one who cares—other than Mr. Smith and Cindy Jensen, of course, who are practically living in Anthony's room.

She waves to her mom as the yellow car pulls away from the hospital entrance and then, umbrella open, hurries down the walkway to get out of the rain. But before she reaches the door she hears a familiar sound. Zipping down through the rain and under the edge of her umbrella come two bees. They buzz unhappily and settle on the metal struts over her head. She stops.

These are the Little Queen's bees, huge and bright, though now soaked and slightly bedraggled.

"What do you need, bees?" she asks. She has to admit she feels ridiculous talking to them.

They buzz, and move around to the back of the umbrella, behind her head. She spins the umbrella so that they are facing her again, but just as quickly they move back behind her. So this time she turns herself. Now she is facing away from the hospital. The bees take up stations near the rim of the canopy, clinging precariously, and facing outward. They buzz and dance. Stop. Buzz and dance. Stop.

"Are you trying to tell me something?" she asks.

They turn, and buzz near her face, then turn again and crawl out toward the edge of the umbrella and stop, facing forward. Away from the hospital.

"Is this like a nectar location dance?" she asks. "You're trying to tell me where to go?" So she begins to walk slowly forward, in the direction of the bees at the edge of her umbrella. This takes her across the looping driveway in front of the hospital. When she reaches the sidewalk on the other side, the bees shift around the rim ninety degrees, so they cling to the struts to her right. They buzz loudly. She turns to face that direction, twisting the umbrella handle as she does so to keep the bees in the same position. Now facing down the sidewalk with the bees directly ahead of her, she begins to walk.

It's like a bee compass, she thinks. But where is it leading me? Left past the flag pole, then left into the parking structure. Right, and right again, up the stairs and then out onto third floor covered parking. She finally comes to a worn-looking red Camry. The bees under her umbrella fly over to it and land on the ledge by the rear window. She follows, and peers inside.

There's a car seat, and a few pieces of paper, but nothing out of the ordinary.

Until she looks through the car at the door opposite her, where a clump of bees clings to the door handle, heaving up the lock. The door pops open. The bees back off. Mary goes around to the other side and looks in.

"Hello?" she says. "Little Queen?" She only sees a few bees. She pokes her head farther into the car.

"I'm Mary," she says to the bees. "We spoke on the phone?"

From beneath the front passenger seat rises a mass. Most of these bees settle on the rear seat. Mary hesitantly gets in and shuts the door, and a small flight of insects rises to form a sphere around her head. She tries not to slink down in her seat. It is definitely freaky, seeing the way these bees move. Perfectly coordinated, almost like a machine. At the same time, it's one of the most beautiful things she has ever witnessed.

And then, floating in front of her, the Little Queen herself appears. *MARY*, says a voice from everywhere around her. It's different from when she heard it on the phone. Much more human and melodious. Beautiful even.

"Hi," she manages after a few seconds.

ANTHONY IS DYING.

Tears spring to Mary's eyes. "No," she says. "The doctors say it's too soon to tell. He's in a coma."

HIS LIGHT IS. FADING. I SEE THIS. WHEN I TURN OFF. MY EYES.

Mary shakes her head, and the Little Queen bobs right and left to try to stay within her line of vision. "He can't die."

WE. HIS COLONY. MUST DO WHAT. WE CAN.

"What do you mean?"

IF I CAN REACH HIM. I WILL TRY. TO HELP HIM.

"Well, go! Go now!"

THE HUNTING MEN. AND WASPS. ARE NEAR. I WILL NEED YOU.

A few moments later, the nurses on duty see the little girl who has been visiting the boy in 310 enter from the rain. She gives them her wan smile. They give her their delicate finger waves. Such a sweet, sad slip of a thing. The whole episode is such a tragedy.

Gingerly, seeming to struggle slightly with an unanticipated weight, the girl collapses her umbrella still holding it above her head. This seems a little odd. But people do odd things at the hospital. Only when it is folded does she slowly lower it with a bump to the floor and lay her jacket over its top.

She strolls carefully toward the elevator. She sees the man in the lobby, reading a newspaper with a duffel bag at his feet. He's not trying to hide. And he's clearly watching everyone as they come in and out. She tries to walk normally, but the bees in her umbrella weigh fifteen pounds, and she's afraid to bump it against her leg or on someone passing by for fear the bees will be crushed. But at last the elevator arrives, and she steps in.

The Little Queen has brought twelve thousand of the Sequestered with her to the hospital. She hopes it will be enough. She would have brought more, but was compelled to leave some at the house to protect Anthony's family. Once again she finds herself with too few bees and too many objectives. But she has made her best guesses, and now the plan is in motion. It is too late to change.

Time is running out. Since she arrived in the parking structure, she has checked Anthony's glowing cell continually, and the light it emits, or the light that pours through it, is fading by the minute.

Mary carries the umbrella down hallways and around corners, then at last she stops. The Little Queen feels the umbrella tilt as it is leaned up in a corner. Now she waits again, while Mary, Mrs. Hanlen, Mat, and Dad talk. Dad's voice is haggard and thin.

Mary is attempting to be cheery.

At one point Mrs. Hanlen steps outside to speak to a doctor. The Little Queen can just hear the conversation.

"Is he better today?" Mrs. Hanlen asks.

"He's comatose. There is no change to his injuries. His paralysis will be complete, I'm afraid. If he wakes up." Mrs. Hanlen stifles a sob.

As soon as she can, Mary excuses herself. She tells Dad that she will see him tomorrow and exits, but she leaves behind her umbrella. It is not too much longer before Mat and Mrs. Hanlen leave also. And then the room is silent. The Little Queen sends a scout crawling up to peer above the rim of the umbrella, and she can see Dad staring at a book.

Anthony lies in a bed. Dad sits at the foot of that bed, and he is very tired. Soon he nods. Then startles awake. Blinks. His long legs cross and uncross. He repositions the book on his lap, bends his head down toward it . . . and is asleep. And the bees swarm out.

Anthony is wrapped in bandages. His eyes are closed. Tubes enter his body through his arms and through his mouth. His skin is the white-yellow color of old honeycomb. And his breathing barely moves the sheet on his chest.

There are machines everywhere in the room, beeping, whooshing, clicking, and humming. But the Little Queen has long ago overcome her fear of the machines humans use. She only has eyes for Anthony. She lands on his forehead, then crawls up to rest atop his head. She sets guards at the entrance to the room.

And from her position on his scalp she says, I WILL WEAR MY CROWN. Instantly all twelve thousand of her bees surge up and begin to Crown the Little Queen.

She shapes this Crown with herself on the peak of Anthony's head, and rings his skull with bees. She includes him in the Crown. And when all the Sequestered are layered, hooked together and tight, she bids them squeeze.

WITH ALL YOUR POWER, MY CHILDREN, WITH ALL YOUR HEART, CROWN YOUR QUEEN!

They pull together, shift, and adjust position, and slowly, powerfully, they clutch the Little Queen and Anthony together in the Crown.

The Little Queen lets go with her mind, letting the heat and pressure of the Crown separate her perfect form from her earthly body, and she sinks downward.

In that energetic space where her own non-physical body exists, she feels another form. It is Anthony. Just as she had expected, just as she had hoped, humans also have a perfect form. And now she feels herself settle into him. She and Anthony, Crowned together, closer to each other than ever two creatures have been before. Close enough, she hopes, to save him.

She can sense clearly that Anthony's physical body is brutally injured. There is inflammation everywhere, broken bones in his spine and his face. Nerves have been severed in his neck and his mind has retreated somewhere she cannot see. These are all things which she could set right—if he were a bee. But the pattern of human physiology is fundamentally different from that of bees. If she is to have any chance at all, she needs to learn his system quickly.

So she stings him. With her fading connection to her physical body she positions her stinger above his scalp and plunges her needle into him. And then she pumps her poison into his blood. As much as she can make.

Just as human doctors inject radioactive isotopes into the blood to mark the shape of tumors, the position of vessels, the density of organs and bones, so now the Little Queen uses her venom to trace the shape of Anthony's network of tissue, bone, nerve, and organ, and display it in sharp relief.

It takes only twenty seconds for blood to circulate through a human vascular system. It is a marvel of fluid dynamics; it leaves the Little Queen breathless and amazed. Sixty thousand miles of vessels, arteries, veins, and capillaries, and blood takes a mere twenty seconds to circulate through it all. When complete, the Little Queen is ringed round with a glowing map of his system, down to the cellular level, her venom pulsing in the darkness. She can clearly see where his injuries lie, and what must be done to fix them. But it is Anthony who will have to do the work.

Her entire plan now rests on a guess she has made, a theory she has come to believe with nothing but her intuition to guide her. She stills her emotions. Focuses. And using the mind-to-mind, she calls out, ANTHONY, I AM HERE.

THE RN ON DUTY AT THE 3RD FLOOR NURSES' STATION IS DRINKING tea and waiting for her shift to change. Her replacement is late, and since this is the third time it's happened this month, she plans to submit a formal complaint. *No way I should have to pick up the pieces of somebody else's inability to—*

The blood pressure monitor in Room 310 flashes a warning. At the same time, the EKG screen displays anomalous readings across the board. The nurse pushes away from her chair, and summons the floor nurses.

. . .

Anthony, wake up. Can you hear me? She calls him in the darkness. She knows he must be present, somewhere.

This is her gamble. That Anthony, attached as he is to the Plain of Crowns, will be able to hear her with the mind-to-mind. That he is infused with golden energy at some level deep enough that this most private bee language is one he will be able to speak, if she whispers it from this intimate platform, the interior of his mind.

Anthony. Awake! She can feel harmonically that she is correct, that her words are not disappearing into a vacuum but are striking a receptive vessel. Somewhere. Yet he does not answer.

The light from the golden cell has now dimmed almost entirely. It seems to her that there can only be a very few moments left before it will go out. She steps upon the side of the cell, easy now with no energy pushing her back, and crawls around it, passing six perfect creases. What, in fact, is damming the light? Is it an obstruction she can clear?

Her footsteps on the surface of the wax-colored hexagon create echoes within it. One end, to her right, is sealed into an invisible membrane—the membrane she crosses when she enters the Plain of Crowns. But the other side, the front, where the light comes out, she can reach. She inches over the rim, feeling carefully with her forelegs.

And then she understands. Very little light can come through because the cell is capped. Just as honey cells are capped after they have been filled with honey, or while larvae pupate, or to seal away a diseased worker, so this cell has been capped, and only the faintest glow can come through.

He is here. She is certain. Hiding? Waiting? She does not know.

Anthony, she calls. She strikes the cap, and it reverberates. But it can only be broken from within.

Through the translucent casing she sees a form stir. It shifts, as though turning in bed. And his voice speaks.

I'm asleep.

Anthony. You are dying. You must help me.

I want to die.

Now she senses, rising from the cell like the odor of decay, the same overwhelming despondency she confronted in the bees when she first entered her new hive, filled with fauxs. It is hopelessness. Self-hatred. Loss of will. This is what nearly killed the hive. This has been hiding within Anthony, and he imposed it on those bees without knowing he was doing it. How long, she wonders, has he wanted to kill himself?

NO MORE DEATH, she tells him.

I'M SLEEPING, says his voice. So young. So very small. IT'S MY FAULT. GO AWAY.

I WILL NOT GO.

A moment passes. A beat. She feels time slipping away from them. ANTHONY. LISTEN TO ME. I AM YOUR QUEEN. LISTEN.

The shadow shifts closer to the membrane. A dark form presses it as though looking out.

MOTHER? he says.

ANTHONY, COME OUT.

MOM? ARE YOU HERE?

She pauses but a fleeting second. YES. I AM YOURS. AND YOU ARE MINE.

MOM, I'M SO SORRY! The anguish rings like a bell.

SORRY FOR WHAT?

FOR LETTING YOU GO. I SHOULD HAVE SAVED YOU. I SHOULD HAVE TRIED HARDER. I'M SO BAD. I'M SUCH A BAD SON. IS THAT WHY YOU LEFT?

His sadness is overpowering, thick and bitter like sap from a dying tree. Whatever the injuries to his physical body, she sees, it is grief that kills him now.

The Little Queen bends near to the cell and whispers, LITTLE BEE. I LEFT BECAUSE DEATH TOOK ME. AND DID NOT TAKE YOU. THE ONLY LESSON DEATH TEACHES IS THAT THE COLONY GOES ON.

I WISH I COULD HAVE TOLD YOU HOW SORRY I AM. FOR ALL THE BAD STUFF I DID. MAYBE YOU WOULDN'T HAVE DIED.

TELL ME NOW.

It begins slowly, but the words come faster and faster.

I WISH I HAD SAID IT. I'M SO SORRY. And there is a glimmer of life in this tiny, quiet, tormented voice.

I DON'T KNOW WHY I'M SO BAD. I'M SORRY I STOLE FIVE DOLLARS FROM YOUR PURSE. I'M SORRY I TOLD YOU I DIDN'T LIKE YOUR PICTURE. I'M SORRY YOU HURT YOUR BACK BECAUSE OF ME AND ALWAYS HAD YOUR PAIN. I'M SORRY I WASN'T BETTER AT MATH. I'M SORRY I YELLED AT YOU WHEN WE WERE CAMPING. I'M SORRY I WASN'T BETTER, MOM. I'M SORRY I DIDN'T TELL YOU HOW MUCH I LOVED YOU BECAUSE I LOVED YOU SO MUCH AND I MISS YOU. SO MUCH. I MISS YOU. I MISS YOU SO MUCH..

AND I FORGIVE YOU, she says. FOR ALL OF IT. AND I LOVE YOU. WILL YOU HELP ME NOW, AND DO THIS ONE THING FOR ME?

WHAT?

COME OUT OF THIS CELL.

Anthony has been dreaming, and now he awakes. Where is he? Somewhere small. And a voice, a voice from his dream, is calling him.

Where is this place? Behind him stretches a long tunnel, and at the end of that, a golden light. And before him, there is a wall. Hard. Cold. Smooth.

Clearly he should move toward the light. He is drawn that way. But something keeps him near the wall. The voice from his dream.

ANTHONY, COME OUT, it says. From beyond the stone.

Back, through solid rock? When there's such comfort to be had, such warmth, the other way?

ANTHONY, YOUR TIME IS ALMOST UP. COME BACK. I AM YOUR QUEEN, AND I CALL YOU!

His Queen? The Little Queen?

WHERE ARE YOU? he asks.

COME OUT OF THE CELL. COME TO ME THROUGH THE BARRIER. YOU BUILT IT. YOU CAN BREAK IT.

Somehow the Little Queen is here with him. She wants him to go through this wall. He pushes on it. There is more give than he expected. He presses hard—the cold film stretches and grows warm. Hot even.

But then beside him a form coalesces. He recognizes it instantly. This form, menacing, black and powerful, is the dark companion to his gift, the one he drew up that day on the ledge. The monster that tilted him forward, off the ledge. That pushed him close, nearer the bomb.

And this force now reaches out with a globular, horrible appendage, and pulls his hand from the wall.

BREAK THIS CAP AND EMERGE, he hears the Little Queen say. He is so confused. This isn't a dream? He was dreaming. He just woke up from a dream. But then—a moment of panic—why is he trapped in this place? Again he tries to push against the wall, but now the monster wedges itself between him and the wall, blocking out the light.

What is this thing? He stumbles back a step, panic setting in. Where did this thing come from?

Now it bears him back up the tunnel, toward the light, and his panic grows. His strength is failing. Malevolent black soot eyes sap his will and freeze him. He has only enough energy left to force out one final thought.

I'M AFRAID!

And he hears her voice. So like his mother's.

THE SEQUESTERED LEARNED IN OUR PRISON THAT YOU CANNOT CONTROL THE WITHOUT. BUT THE WITHIN—THAT IS YOURS AND YOURS ALONE. A CREATURE MASTERS HER FEAR WHEN SHE ADMITS THAT WHAT SHE FEARS IS HER.

And now he sees, this creature has his face.

He reaches out, and the creature does not stop him. He touches its chest. And it freezes. *It's me*, he sees. *This is the thing my mother was afraid of. It's inside me. It's not a thing I can ever escape. It's not a thing I can run from. It has to be owned.*

It has to be absorbed. He pushes forward then, into it, through it. Black mist bursts in the air around him, and he breathes it in. All of it. And then he steps ahead, toward the wall. The avatar of grief is within him now. He understands that it has always been there, but now at last he can feel it directly, absent numbness and denial, his pain and sorrow. He will have to address it. Like a wound, he will have to find its scope, experience it completely, and draw it closed. But at this moment there is no time. So he pushes it down, away, into a safe, empty place inside himself. Then he turns to confront his immediate problem.

Pressing both his hands deeply into the suddenly elastic wall, he rends downward. His fingers grab and claw. *Out*, he thinks, *I want out of here. Out OUT!*

A few fingers split the membrane and he tears it. Sheets of film come down in his hands. It is no thicker than paper, than a gum bubble. It is not there at all.

COME OUT, says the Little Queen. I WILL GUIDE YOU FORWARD.

He feels tremendous faith in her power, as though nothing bad could ever happen to him while she watched. So he does what she asks. He emerges through the opening.

And then it seems he is floating in space, and around him a vast glowing network—lights projected on screens, or glowing ribbons hanging from a ceiling?—whirls and beats. Alive. And he realizes it is himself that he sees.

LISTEN NOW. The voice comes from all around him, like when she speaks from the sphere of bees. But this tone and pitch is perfect. He recognizes this voice. It is his mother's.

YOU ARE IN A HOSPITAL. YOU ARE DYING. I HAVE COME TO HELP YOU. I CAN SHOW YOU HOW TO HEAL YOURSELF. ARE YOU READY?

WHAT'S WRONG WITH ME?

MANY SMALL THINGS. BUT THIS, a section of the glowing network draws his eye, WHERE BLOOD POURS INTO YOUR BRAIN THROUGH A BROKEN VESSEL, AND THIS, another section glows, WHERE THERE ARE BROKEN BONES IN YOUR SPINE, THIS IS WHAT MUST BE FIXED QUICKLY. THE REST WILL HEAL ON ITS OWN.

HOW CAN YOU FIX IT?

I CANNOT. YOU MUST.

THAT'S IMPOSSIBLE.

NOTHING IS IMPOSSIBLE. I HAVE DONE SUCH THINGS. I USE CHEMISTRY FUELED BY ENERGY—MY TOOLS. YOU MUST USE ENERGY ALONE. LOOK, ANTHONY. ENERGY. THAT IS YOUR TOOL.

Anthony turns to look behind him. The small compartment where he had been trapped is now a glowing cauldron. It is almost impossible to look at. WHAT'S THIS LIGHT? he asks.

THIS LIGHT IS INSIDE YOU. THIS POWER IS REAL. IT COMES FROM THE PLAIN OF CROWNS. YOU CAN SHAPE IT.

HOW?

How do you a change a chaotic flight of bees into a ball? A horse? A triangle or a square? How do you control bees? Remember? You imagine, and it happens. You must imagine a new form for these injuries. Use the light coming through this portal. This is your birthright, Anthony. I believe that everything that has happened has happened to bring you *here.*

He stares into the tunnel. He can feel this power the Little Queen wants him to use. It's like a wind that pushes something inside him, but doesn't touch his skin. As if there is a sail, broad and taut, within his breast, catching the momentum of the light and converting it to power. Power he can use.

He understands what the Little Queen is saying. The experience of shaping bees in the air is something he could reproduce here. He could shape this energy.

What shape should I create? he asks.

That, I can show you, she says. Look to the venom. It will guide us.

In the waiting room on the third floor, a suited man reading a magazine looks up. A nurse rushes past him, heading down a hall that has been the suited man's particular study for three days. A moment later, two more nurses follow, trailing a cart with pulmonary resuscitation equipment.

The man stands. This probably does not concern him. But a closer inspection will not hurt. He starts down the hall.

Paul wakes from his sleep. For the last three days he's spent every second here, watching Anthony slowly slip away, feeling his own life slip away as well. Nothing has ever been this excruciating. Not watching his own father die. Not the lingering death that Laura suffered. Nothing could ever compare to this.

His book has slipped to the floor. He can't even remember what he's reading. He leans down to pick it up, and as he straightens, and wakes more fully, he notices a difference in the room. A new sound, a hum. Or buzz. Or less than that, a rustle. Where in the room is it coming from? The bed.

He can't at first comprehend what he is seeing when he looks at Anthony. Did they put a new blanket on the boy while he was sleeping? Or is it something to help him breathe? Paul stands and steps closer. And when he sees what is really covering Anthony's face—engulfing his entire head—he screams.

The approaching nurses hear the screaming as they run the halls. At the far end of the corridor they see Paul stumble backward out of the room, look frantically right and left. When he sees the nurses, he begins to yell. "Bees! There are bees in here! They're on my son!"

These nurses have heard everything. This does not phase them. Whatever they find in that room, they have been trained to deal with. Or so they think. They prep their tools as they run.

Following behind them, the suited man also hears the screaming. But when he hears Paul's words, his reaction is different. He immediately stops, reaches into his breast pocket and pulls out what looks like a glasses case.

He opens it. And like a corps of tiny hunting helicopters, a hundred black-winged shadows rise. They begin to circle, the way any predator circles: concentric, expanding rings, casting to pick up a trail.

The man makes a quick call, speaks a few words, and sprints down the hall after the nurses. The shadows follow, then pass him, like hunters whose hounds have treed their prey.

Paul screams, then leaps back into the room. He sees his son begin to convulse. Short, sharp jerks, as though electric currents are repeatedly cracking across his nervous system. Those small hands clench; the thin back arches. Anthony's mouth opens through the mask of bees, but no sound comes out.

Paul dives for the bed and begins swiping at the bees. They cover Anthony's entire head, and they are impossible to get off. They seem bound to each other, it's like they're not separate insects at all but a single shell. Claw as he might, he cannot dislodge even one.

. . .

DOWN IN THE MAIN LOBBY OF THE HOSPITAL, THE OTHER SUITED watcher hangs up the call his companion just placed to him. There is a hospital-wide warning singing from the loudspeakers now, and no one is watching him. From the duffel bag on the floor he takes a large black plastic box, and slides a catch free. The top lifts off. A huge cloud of black-winged beasts bursts free. Without a second's orientation the swarm rises to the ceiling, a flat fan moving above the line of sight of the nurses who scurry in all directions. It launches itself in the direction of the stairwell.

The suited man reaches into the bag again and withdraws a dull grey metal canister. Clutching this like a hand grenade, he follows the swarm.

THE LITTLE QUEEN WATCHES IT ALL THROUGH THE EYES OF HER scouts. She sees the suited man release his few wasps, sees the nurses, sees Dad screaming and clawing. She feels confident that her Crown can withstand the pulling and scraping of a few human fingers. Her bees are strong, and short of death, nothing will break the bonds that bind them to each other.

But death is a possibility, with the wasps coming on. ANTHONY, WE ARE ALMOST OUT OF TIME, she says.

She turns her attention back to him. It is taking longer than she had expected. The light from the Plain is less powerful than she had thought, or his injuries are more extensive. But she marvels at his talent. He is brilliant at what he does. He wields his power as though it is what human boys have always done. Instead of throwing, or running, or leaping, it is biomorphic engineering.

Anthony uses the light from the Plain of Crowns like a white hot sculpting tool, playing it across his injuries, exciting the cells to reform and realign them. Human cells do not have the native tendency to change state that bees' do, and Anthony must rely on the Little Queen's venom to initiate the transformative spark. It is a painstaking process. She can see it is causing him extraordinary anguish. Stimulating her venom this way must feel like drawing sandpaper over his innermost nerve pathways. Dead cell groups drop off the network, new cells form, bones shift across neurons. Fluids drip in shining rivulets through tissue as he works.

HURRY, she says.

I'M TRYING, MOTHER, LITTLE QUEEN, he pants. She can feel his body convulse with the effort. His young, young body. *Why are we all so young when we are tested?* she wonders.

She sees the wasps arrive first, before the nurses, and before the suited man. She is expecting an immediate attack, but that does not occur. Instead, the wasps take a position above the bed, spread out on the ceiling. There are fewer than one hundred of them. What are they doing?

Then the nurses turn the corner—and stop. The lead nurse calls to one of the others, "Call animal control! Get me—"

And then the suited man enters the room at a run.

"Everybody out!" he yells as he launches a gray canister at the bed.

Things are moving too fast for Paul, but one thing he knows—regardless of what anybody says, he's not leaving this room. He stands by Anthony and continues to rake at the insects on the boy's head. What is keeping these things stuck together?

A purple gas begins to billow through the air. It's coming from the foot of Anthony's bed. Is something leaking? This goddamn hospital is run by Keystone Cops! Where are the professionals, where are—

With a sharp gasp, Paul finds himself unable to breathe. It's the gas. He falls to his knees. The nurses all fall also, and try to creep for the door. But Paul claws himself back up to Anthony's bed, and grabs his legs. With his last strength Paul thinks, *I've got to get Anthony out of here.* But then the gas overwhelms him, and he slumps across the sheets.

THE LITTLE QUEEN CAN SEE WHAT IS HAPPENING. BEES ON THE outer layer of her Crown are falling away, slowly revealing her position. But she is surprised. They are not dead, just unconscious. She backs her scouts out of the room, and tells them AVOID THE GAS! Now she understands. The wasps spread on the ceiling are not affected the way every other living thing in the room is. They are immune to the gas.

They hold their position, waiting. And there is only one thing they could be waiting for.

Layer after layer, her Crown peels away, closer and closer to revealing her. ANTHONY, I HAVE BEEN FOUND, she tells him. I WILL BE TAKEN. YOU MUST— But that is all she is able to say. The Crown breaks apart, and the gas reaches her.

Anthony feels the Little Queen's presence disappear inside him. He feels the effects of the gas taking hold of him as well, and his mind begins to blur around the edges. From his unique position within his own body he observes this cloud of drowsiness as it sweeps across his senses, like a tsunami flooding quickly over the borders of awareness. He watches section after section of his body shutting down. He can actually see nerve impulses being interrupted. He sees the protein involved, sees how a chemical from the gas interrupts its activity.

And he thinks, *I wonder if I can stop that?*

The venom in his veins is an engine, the light from the hexagon its fuel. He imagines one small change to his body, a minor adjustment to a certain molecular bond, a far less monumental change than those he has already wrought to his bones and vascular system. This change propagates throughout his body in a chain reaction, a game of molecular dominoes, chemically changing the way impulses are passed through his nervous system.

And instantly the effects of the gas are gone.

Anthony opens his eyes. And sits up.

Chapter Twenty-One

Anthony rips the breathing tube out of his mouth. Gas fills the room, and on the floor are three sleeping nurses. His father clings to his bed, insensible. Everywhere there are unconscious bees. But he doesn't see the Little Queen.

He looks up—the wasps on the ceiling are gone. They waited until she was exposed by the gas, and then they took her.

He pulls the tubes from his arms and leaps from bed. He has a horrible headache, but what else is new? It seems like he's had headaches for the last two months, with explosions and crashes and god knows what. He steps from the room. He does not even take a second to wonder that he can walk at all.

Orderlies rush down the hall. Alarms sound everywhere. Where have they taken the Queen?

A bee buzzes him—a scout that escaped the gas. It leads him back down the hall away from the orderlies. He follows, passing a stairwell where the sound of someone running up stairs booms. His scout takes him around a corner and stops. They wait. A wave of dizziness overwhelms him, and he almost faints. Deep within him, extraordinary processes continue to transform and realign his physiognomy. It will take some time for this fire of transformation to burn itself out.

He hears the door to the stairwell burst open, and a rustling roar like a waterfall, coupled with running footsteps, issues forth and moves away toward his room. He peers around the corner. Wasps, at least a thousand. And a suited man, wearing a breathing mask, disappears into his room. He wants to go back. It's obvious to him what those wasps will do. Twelve thousand helpless bees lie on the floor, ripe for slaughter. But he can't fight wasps by himself. He has to find the Little Queen.

The scout leads him down three flights of stairs. By the time they reach the bottom, he's completely out of breath. He kneels down, his stomach lurches, he throws up. There is blood in his vomit, but he heaves himself to his feet and stumbles out into the lobby. The greeting station is staffed by a single nurse, and she is on the phone. She doesn't see him as he limp-runs out the front doors.

It is raining outside. His scout has taken him as far as she can go. *Now what do I do?* he wonders—when a black sedan bursts from the parking structure, crashes the gate, and almost slides onto the lawn while taking the turn that bends into the access road. It speeds around the loop, going for the main road.

Anthony heaves his legs into motion and points his body toward the forest. He knows these woods well; he played here as a 9-year-old boy many afternoons while his mother was in the hospital and his father was conferring with doctors. He knows there's a chance he can beat this sedan to the road. And he has to beat it, because he feels very sure what its cargo must be.

Rain blinds him as he runs. Dimly he feels his feet sliced by broken sticks and rocks. The pain in his stomach doubles every ten steps, but he runs on. Branches whip him, and his hospital gown is shredded. He slides through a feeder creek and over the top of a berm, and finally down onto the road.

He waits there, bent double, heaving in gasps and fighting to stay on his feet. The rain streams down his face like someone's spraying him with a hose. It gets in his mouth and in his ears. He can't see, or hear, so he steps farther out onto the pavement. Ahead, he sees headlights. He stands in the middle of the road and holds up his hand. Stop.

Little Queen, he thinks as loud as he can. Are you there?

. . .

SHE WAKES SLOWLY. SHE IS PINNED IN A BOX, THIN WOOD ON FOUR sides, mesh on the top. The box is gripped in a human's hand.

LITTLE QUEEN, ARE YOU THERE? she hears. It is Anthony.

YOU LIVE, she says. I AM HAPPY.

WHERE ARE YOU?

IN A TINY MESH BOX.

A SHIPPING CAGE. ESCAPE.

I CAN'T MOVE.

Seconds pass, and she hears nothing. She tries to spread her wings, to wield her stinger, but the walls around her press tight. And then, Anthony's thoughts return.

OKAY. THEN WE'RE GOING TO BURN YOU OUT.

And she feels a massive jolt of energy strike her. He is feeding her the full force of the Plain of Crowns, channeled through the cell in his breast. He is transforming her. He is heating her up.

How is this possible? she wonders. *Can my body withstand this? How has he learned so much so quickly?*

But there is no space for thought or planning, her temperature rises so quickly. It is all she can do to keep from passing out again. The thin wood around her bursts into flame—and the hand gripping her flings her forward.

She bounces on the dash as her box falls apart. Rain hisses on the hot remains. Rain. There is a space where the window has not closed. Space where she can escape.

ANTHONY, she calls. But hears nothing. Through the windshield she sees him, lying face down on the road. This burst has taken everything he had left. He is motionless.

The driver and the passengers are focused on her. They do not see Anthony on the road, through the rain. There are only seconds until he is run over. And only one thing she can think to do.

She rises off the dash, fills her stinger with poison, and pierces the neck of the man driving the car. He screams and spins the wheel, sliding the sedan sideways down the road, and slaps his neck.

To crush her.

. . .

WHEN ANTHONY COMES TO, HE FINDS HIMSELF LYING ON THE pavement, in the rain. Across from him, propped up in a ditch, the rear wheels of the black sedan spin idly. On the ground on the driver's side a man has pulled himself from the car and lies in the rain. He's moaning and writhing. Anthony pushes himself to his hands and knees and crawls near.

LITTLE QUEEN, he says, but no answer comes.

The man in the rain, barely coherent, has blood on his face, his nose is broken, and his front teeth are missing. But he's holding his neck, as though his main wound is there. And then he passes out and his hand falls away. And Anthony sees the Little Queen. Or what remains of her.

She's still alive, but her body has been crushed and broken into two pieces, smeared apart across the strike she delivered. This is a thing which cannot be mended. Reforming a bone a millimeter farther off a nerve pathway, or knitting soft tissue where a blood vessel has ruptured, these are monumental achievements. Rejoining two severed sections of a crushed body is far beyond that. Beyond either of them.

Still her legs move. He lifts her off the body of the driver and shields her away from the rain. He is crying.

YOU CAN'T DIE, he says. WHAT WILL I DO?

QUEENS DIE, ANTHONY.

I NEED YOU.

She is almost gone. Anthony's mind is blank, but for the thought, *Can this really be happening again?*

She speaks softly. He has to hold her an inch from his skull to hear her, she is so weak.

I HAVE ENJOYED KNOWING YOU. ANTHONY. ENJOYED MY LIFE. BUT THE HIVE GOES ON. EACH GENERATION A TINY BIT BETTER THAN THE LAST. THE HIVE IS EVERYTHING. YOU ARE THE HIVE NOW, ANTHONY.

I CAN'T, ALONE. NOT ALONE.

YOU WILL NOT BE ALONE. I HAVE LEFT YOU. A GIFT. NEXT TIME YOU RUN AWAY. YOU WILL FIND IT.

He can feel her spirit rise. Her tiny arms stop swimming. She lies still.

DON'T LEAVE!

Not again! Please! Please. He sends plea after plea out into the rain. But no answer comes back.

Chapter Twenty-Two

Anthony is in the hospital for another two weeks. He's told a thousand times by a hundred different people what a miracle it is that he's alive. The fact that he is not only living but bears no sign of the traumatic injuries that brought him to the hospital in the first place is something so far beyond the experience of any of the doctors that they hardly mention it. They just look at him, compare x-rays, and mutter. Impossible, but undeniable. As soon as the doctors will allow it, the sheriff and a succession of law enforcement officials take his statement. It's exhausting and depressing. The only thing that brings him any happiness is regular visits from Mary.

He tells Mary everything that happened, of course, and he tells the people taking his statements almost nothing. Talking bees? Intelligent wasps? Healing power? He and Mary know they'll be considered absolutely crazy if they tell the real story. So all they say is, "Some men were trying to catch Anthony's bees. And everything spiraled out of control." But the rest of the story hangs over both of them like a cloud.

Once, while his father is visiting, Cindy Jensen appears in the doorway with flowers. Anthony has no idea what to say, or how to act. He can't speak to her. When he sees her all he thinks about are the mother figures that she is not, and never can be. After ten minutes she turns to leave, beaten back by his silent wall.

But the Little Queen's words come back to him. *The hive goes on.* And as Cindy is passing out the door, he finds a voice.

"Thanks for being around for my dad. My dad and Mat. Thanks for helping me take care of them."

The smile she gives him is vivid. Honest. She will never be either of the mothers he has lost, he thinks. Time will tell what she might become.

The only other visitor of note he has is Bernard, who appears in the doorway one afternoon while his father is away. He has a basket of flowers, and a jar of honey.

"Little Bee," Bernard says, eyes wide. "Oh, Little Bee."

He bends over the bed and gives Anthony the most delicate embrace a man of his size possibly could.

Anthony tells him the story, the only person aside from Mary who hears all the pieces. Bernard listens, and his eyes grow graver and graver. By the time Anthony is done, Bernard's face is pale.

"She asked me to keep you safe," Bernard says, his voice a stricken whisper.

"There was nothing you could have done. And it's over, Bernie. I'm fine."

He doesn't feel fine. He feels empty. But that is the peculiar responsibility of the hospitalized, to make their visitors feel comfortable. "You visited her, didn't you, Bernie? When she was here? The last few weeks?"

"Of course."

He wonders if he looks like his mom did, thin and white and bruised. It is a painful thought. But he finds that he can endure this pain. The pain he cannot endure is the pain of not knowing.

"Bernie, she told me that touching the bees killed her."

"I know."

"But how could that be? Do you know? Please, Bernie, if you know anything, please tell me. None of it makes any sense."

Bernard settles deeper into his chair, and turns to Anthony. "This was your mother's place, to tell you this. But now, I guess, I'm all there is." Anthony leans forward, eager. Then for a moment it seems as if Bernard will change his mind. He reaches for the jar of honey he brought to Anthony, and turns it in his hands, where it looks small as a wine cork.

Finally he goes on. "Anthony, your mother was a Keeper. Do you know what that is?"

"A beekeeper?"

"Not just a beekeeper, though she was that too. But a Keeper."

"No. I don't know what that is."

"There were Keepers in ancient Egypt. In Africa. In Europe. Twenty thousand years ago, thirty thousand years, there have always been Keepers, as long as humans have existed. A Keeper is a human who speaks for the bees." Anthony listens. It is too much, for a moment, for him to register. Bernard can tell.

"This is a strange way to tell you this," Bernard acknowledges, "and not a great place, I guess. But there you go."

"So," Anthony thinks, working it through, "does that mean you're one too? A Keepers?"

"I am. I speak for the bees. I guide, guard, and gather."

"But how did she become one? Who made her a Keeper?"

"The Overspirit of the Bees. The Golden She. A person is born a Keeper. You were born a Keeper, Anthony."

While on the one hand it is utterly preposterous, it also sounds absolutely obvious. Plain, simple, and true.

"Why didn't she tell me?"

"She was afraid. I'm sure she would have, eventually," Bernard says. "She was the best of us. And she saw things that we did not see, not until it was too late. Colony Collapse. An ancient imbalance, returning to the world. She thought she could solve these problems. We told her not to. Anthony, she went places with her Mate Hive that no one has gone before."

"Mate Hive?"

"Every Keeper has a Mate Hive, a colony they bond with for life. And your mother used her bond to try to change her bees. Bees are so malleable. You know this. The queen has pheromones, the bodies of her bees grow and change. Your mother thought she could create a colony that would not be susceptible to the things that were coming. She used the power she had, she went deep, deep with her Mate Hive, and she planted change within that colony. New growth." He shakes his head, remembering. "Her bees were fine. But the growth she planted spread to her—she shared it, she had too. The problem is, human cells are not as malleable as bee's. In humans, growth new just spins out of control. Uncontrolled growth, Anthony. In her cells."

It takes a moment for Anthony to realize what Bernard is saying. "My mom got cancer from what they did with the bees. From changing them."

"She knew it might happen. She accepted the consequences." Anthony knows his face must be changing, because Bernard is rushing to finish. "She took this risk because she thought it had to be taken. She was the best of us. Her mastery was, well, there are only a very few who see as deep. And none, in my book, who see as far, though you might hear a different story from *them*."

Bernard pauses a moment, rehashing some internal dialogue. After a moment he seems to remember where he is. He continues.

"Until you came into the world, that is. You, Anthony. The world has never seen a Keeper like you. She was afraid your gifts would take you far from her. Maybe... kill you."

It is true. He can feel it. The Keepers. The cancer. The Mate Hive.

But an image has been forming in his mind as Bernard has been speaking. The reason his expression is growing cold is not because of his mother's sacrifice, or his own peril. It is because a picture of dark wings and black jaws has come to him. He turns to Bernard.

"Bernie. Are there other creatures with Keepers?"

Bernard nods. But he does not seem to want to divulge more.

"Can wasps have Keepers?"

Bernard nods again, slowly. The two of them sit in silence after that. The thought of Death Wasps roaming the land at the hand of some dark master is enough to make Anthony wish Bernard had never come to visit.

．　．　．

EVENTUALLY THE DAY COMES WHEN ANTHONY IS ALLOWED TO return home. They wheel him to the front of the hospital. The sky is high and blue, and the sun is warm. Mary is there. From a bag she lifts a pair of hand-colored Vans decorated with a bee motif. He thanks her and puts them on. His dad pulls the truck around. Anthony says goodbye to Mary and climbs in, and the truck begins a slow journey home. The slowest trip he's ever taken with his father. Like they're going to a funeral.

"Dad, I'm fine. Speed up," he says.

"The doctors said to take it easy," he father tells him. "So no bumps." *Maybe we should just buy a car with shock absorbers,* Anthony thinks.

The day after he gets home, Mary comes to visit. It's late afternoon, and she rides over after school. His father is at work, and Anthony won't be going back to school himself for another week. The doctors are insisting on a schedule, probably because it's the only thing about the situation they can control.

She knocks on the door. He lets her in quickly and they retreat to his room. They have talked in the hospital, but this is different. Finally, this is private.

"Have you gotten any more e-mails?" is the first thing that Mary asks. Anthony flops down on his bed.

"No. There's no reason I would." He leans back and looks at the ceiling. "They got all the bees. They're through with me."

"My dad keeps asking me questions." Mary sits beside him. "He's suspicious. I would be too."

She sighs, and runs her fingers over the windowsill where Anthony's bodyguards used to wait, morning, noon and night. Mary's eyes drift to the window again. She sighs.

"So they're all gone?" she asks. She gestures outside, around the property. Everywhere. "All the bees?"

"The wasps came and got them. Just like they did at the hospital. I found dead bees under the eaves. All around the bee yard."

"I wish I could have gotten to know her better."

Join the club, Anthony thinks. He's starting to feel bitter again.

Only now it's worse, because he notices. A month ago he was mostly just numb. Now every stray thought is painful.

"You know, it's kind of weird," she says after a moment.

"What? Every single thing that's happened?"

"No. Dead bees in the bee yard. I thought the Little Queen moved the hive. I thought those supers were empty."

It is true. He hadn't thought of it. Why would there be bees in the yard? There was nothing out there, no hive to defend. Bees would not willingly engage in a battle with no precious ground to defend.

Unless...

"A sacrifice," he whispers.

"What?"

"A diversion. To make it look complete."

Mary watches him. His face is lighting now, as understanding comes.

"She told me she left a gift," he says, almost to himself. But Mary hears.

"I remember. What did that mean, *'don't run away again'*?"

"No. *'Next time you run away,'*" he corrects. "*'Next time you run away, you'll find it.'* He tries to think back. That night when the Little Queen first spoke to him in the fort, how much did he tell her about it? He can't remember whether the story of running away and only getting as far as the fort came up, of being relieved and happy when his mom came out with a picnic. Could it have?

He stands. "You want to come for a walk with me?"

The two of them step out the kitchen door, and Anthony is about to turn and head into the woods, but then he stops. He scans the trees. He looks into the sky. He peers out at the road.

"I'm going to take the long way," he says. "I don't know why. Just in case."

"The long way where?" she asks.

He just walks.

Mary follows him, and he strolls with what seems to her forced casualness through the meadow, following the line of trees. He dawdles. He picks up rocks. He points out birds to her. Slowly he makes his way farther from the house, and only when he is almost to the fence between their land and the Hanlens' does he step into the trees.

"What are we doing?" asks Mary. But Anthony holds his finger to his lips.

It is dark beneath the branches, and damp from the rain. Moss hangs in streamers, weighing down the trees, and drops fall from the canopy of green above them to roll down the backs of their necks. Anthony leads them deeper into the wood, and it gets cooler. Slippery wet dead logs make walking treacherous. But still Anthony leads them deeper.

Finally he turns at a right angle and takes them across, back toward his house but now deep in the forest, walking parallel to the tree line. It is slow going. The woods seem to want to keep them out. But whenever they come to a spot that seems impassible, Anthony finds a way through it.

And then he stops. They both hear the same thing. Something large buzzes over them through the wet trees. They look up, into the damp, dark branches. And they spot it—a flash of color. Golden color.

The breath catches in Mary's throat. "Anthony, it's them."

He nods. They push on into the dark vegetation, and begin to see sentinels sitting in the branches, silently watching them pass. Little golden sentinels.

"Where are we going?" she whispers. It is such a strange feeling, the dark, dripping woods, the canopy hanging down, and bees watching everywhere, that she finds herself whispering without knowing why.

"The fort," he whispers back. And then he stops her. And points. Ahead is a large rock, a finger of stone thrust up from some realm deep in the earth, as though to take the temperature of the world above. And within a bowl just at eye level on this rock, there is a swarm of bees.

Mary hangs back, but Anthony moves forward, like a sleepwalker. Closer, and closer, and soon bees are clustered on his shoulders and piling up on his head. He gestures and they spring up from his body and form a shape, framing the bowl: a hovering, hexagonal cell.

There's honeycomb attached to the rock. These bees have been busy. There are very few of them, but they are strong. They are protecting a precious gift.

"Mary, come here," he whispers, waving her close. A group of bees sweeps around behind her and urges her in. These are Anthony's bees. They do his bidding, even when he is looking elsewhere.

She steps closer, carefully, slowly. She feels nervous, as if she's breaking into someone's house. But Anthony takes her hand when she is beside him and pulls her close. And she sees the eggs.

The bees are attending a shard of comb no more than sixty cells wide and forty cells tall. Small by any measure, but impressive indeed if they built it from scratch, in the rain, in only a few days.

"Look there," Anthony says, awe in his voice. He points to a row of cells, and she sees a particularly dense cluster of bees topping one cell.

"What is it?" she asks.

MOVE ASIDE, he says to the bees. Quickly they step away from their position, and Mary sees what they are focused on: an egg.

A queen's egg. Throughout his body he feels the Little Queen's venom, bound into his very blood by helixes of bright chemistry and purest energy, pulse. Pulse like fire.

"Every generation is just a little better," Anthony says, unable to take his eyes from the comb. "That's what she said. I wonder what this one will be like."

Chapter Twenty-Three

When life leaves the Little Queen's mangled body, held in Anthony's trembling hands, she falls upward. She rises out of her twisted form. Darkness surrounds her, and she ascends.

Days pass, and still she rises. It is pure motion, without context, without marker. But at last she sees a shape. A familiar form, a hexagon. It is the cell in Anthony's breast, showering her with golden radiance. She is traveling there.

More time passes, a week, a month. Is time real here? Are moments truly passing? The closer she comes to the cell, the more slowly time passes. It takes her a year to travel a foot. Ten years to cover an inch. But the moment arrives when she is close enough to reach her foreleg through the breach.

Violently and abruptly she is sucked upward, like a fish torn from a stream with a hook in its mouth. And for a time she knows no more.

She awakens in a world of soft light and pressure. It is the inside of a honey cell; she has been here before, when she first emerged from her egg. Now, as then, her cell is capped, and so she begins to chew through the soft wax above her. After a time she emerges, damp and trembling, to find herself looking up from a cell on the Plain of Crowns.

All around her are queens of the Plain. Her own cell is far out on the peninsula of the Sequestered. The adjoining cells stretch backward, away from her, each with a queen, and beyond that more, repeated and repeated. And each and every one of these queens gazes upward. Just as she finds herself doing. Transfixed by what she sees.

It never occurred to her that the queens on the Plain might be looking at something from their vantage in the comb. She had assumed they were simply waiting. To be visited. Endlessly waiting. But now she sees that there was more to their lives than simple suspension. These queens, looking to the heavens for so many millions of years, are observing a goddess.

The Golden One. The She. An immense, flawless Queen, floating motionless, lit like the sun, gazing down upon them, magnificent. The Little Queen knows without being told that the Golden One is the source of all that is perfect: the perfect honey, the perfect comb, the perfect song. The Golden She is the mold from which the spirits of all earthly bees are forged.

And this magnificent entity is under attack.

Beginning far away to the east, and tapering as it nears, boils a horrible, billowing headland of cloud and darkness, and astride this, directly above the Plain of Crowns, looms the celestial figure of a Wasp. Immense as the She, this Wasp, dark as pitch and tar. And its claws have the Golden She about the throat.

The scale is huge beyond imagining. The two entities crest against each other, ancient and massive as galaxies colliding in the sky. There is no visible movement. No way for the Little Queen to tell how long ago this began, or where, or how. Yet the terrible truth is clear; the the Golden One is being decapitated by a vast black Wasp, while a hundred million generations of frozen queens gaze upward, powerless to intercede.

About the Author

From Kevin: The Little Queen was originally intended to be part of a series. It still could be, if people want it, because I loved writing LQ's adventures :) There's an unpublished Epilogue which introduces elements planned for a second book, and anyone interested in reading that can sign up at kevinhincker.com, and LQ's daughters will email it to you.

Kevin Hincker lives and writes in Los Angeles. You can connect on social media, by messaging on Goodreads or Facebook. He's likely to respond, especially if you want to talk about books! You can also email him after joining the list on his website.

Remember, the best way to get more books in a series that may or may not stop at one book is to review the one book that does exist, which you can do after clicking this link: https://www.amazon.com/review/create-review/?ie=UTF8&channel=glance-detail&asin=B00UKTLZ3C, or searching for The Little Queen on Amazon.

facebook.com/theLQ

goodreads.com/khincker

Also by Kevin Hincker

The Einstein Object

Printed in the USA
CPSIA information can be obtained
at www.ICGtesting.com
LVHW011943010624
781991LV00008B/740